Second Edition published June 2021
Published by Indies United Publishing House, LLC
Cover art designed by Damonza

Hardcover: 978-1-64456-301-4
Paperback: 978-1-64456-302-1
Mobi: 978-1-64456-303-8
ePub: 978-1-64456-304-5
AudioBook: 978-1-64456-305-2

Library of Congress Control Number: 2021937261

INDIES UNITED PUBLISHING HOUSE, LLC
P.O. BOX 3071
QUINCY, IL 62305-3071
www.indiesunited.net

WARNING: This book will offend you.
Or, it will remind you.
Possibly both.

To the other walking wounded.

Thanks, Jayne!

# FRANK VAUGHN, KILLED BY HIS MOM

## D. KRAUSS

INDIES UNITED PUBLISHING HOUSE, LLC

# CHAPTER 1

Butch sat on the porch watching the girls skip rope:

"Frank Vaughn, killed by his mom
Lying in bed alooone,
She picked up a bat
And gave him a whack
And broke his head to the booone
One, two, three, four, five, six, seven..."
...and so on.

Cindy reached the twenties before snagging a toe, but Frank's mom couldn't have hit him that many times. A lot, but not that many.

Immortalized in skip rhyme. Amazing. It had been what, only a week? Frank was still on TV. Pat Jarrod, the Channel 7 news anchor, was all grim last night while narrating the film of Frank's dad escorting Frank's mom, very pretty in a silk dress and beehive hairdo, into the Lawton Court House. Mr. Vaughn was wearing his class-A uniform and dark glasses and looked like the President of Vietnam, and his wife looked like Mrs. President of Vietnam.

"They're Filipino," dad said.

Could've been a state visit, except no one was happy.

Butch was surprised when Frank's dad helped Mrs. Frank up the courthouse stairs. Odd. He should be really mad at her, but there he was, being nice. The girls weren't being nice; they were making fun of Frank, which wasn't right. It wasn't Frank's fault.

1

Cindy was in again and the others—Lynn and Debbie, Carla from down the street, Maria and Joseph (who might as well be a girl), and some random passersby—were doing their best to trip her up while staying on the Frank call. You'd think they'd get tired of it, go on to "Spank" or "Battleship," but no. Butch should go over and tell them to stop, but that would invoke the deadly kid "Ewww!" response and its follow-up, "Go away, you big baby, we'll do what we want!" and even Cindy would join in because this was the herd, although she'd be gentle. He'd be humiliated and might get his suit, the same one he wore to Frank's funeral, dirty, which meant a beating and not going to Dale's graduation. Best to stay here.

Graduation. Sure making a big deal. All of them dressed up, even Art with some put-together shirt and skinny tie that wasn't a suit at all, something Butch, with great delight, repeatedly pointed out. Cindy had on a flowered dress with a yellow silk belt and Mom had brushed her red-blonde hair until it was full and fluffy and floated like a cloud, as it did now inside the rope... twenty-four, twenty-five, twenty-six. She wouldn't get dirty.

Never did. Even when they had mud ball fights and slid head first, screaming and laughing, down the crap hills piled up by the bulldozer guys building apartments near the ball fields, only Butch came back with twenty or thirty layers of dirt hiding his identity. She was untouched. She was perfect.

She was beautiful.

Butch watched her, and his heart soared and knew he was lucky to be her brother... okay, adopted brother. All the boys wanted to cut the string on her finger but she wouldn't let them, and all the girls wanted to play with her, just her, but she played with them all, no favorites, her laughter ringing up and down the hallways of B.C. Swinney Elementary.

Because of Cindy, the bullies more or less left Butch alone and the other kids tolerated his goofiness. In any other family, that'd be enough. But she favored him, him, over the smart, handsome boys who pursued her on the playground and the sophisticated girls who called her on the phone. Butch was her sole companion when she ran through the alley and over the crap hills. They rolled down the slopes together until they were so dizzy that earth and sky blurred and then they lay on their backs and made things out of clouds and said their secrets and never,

ever, told on each other. She didn't call him stupid or spaz or any of the other names everyone including dad did; she covered for him, made him look better than he was. She'd somehow disentangle him if he went over there and screamed at the girls for making fun of Frank. Without her, he'd be dead.

Just like Frank.

Tommy walked up the mile-high steps onto the porch and scooted Cha Cha, who lay next to Butch, out of the way. The dog smiled good-naturedly as Tommy sat down and handed Butch a *Journey Into Mystery*, "To Kill a Thunder God"! Good cover with the Destroyer on it and Butch flipped to "The Crimson Hand," one of the *Tales of Asgard*. He'd already read it, but he liked to re-read things he liked, and the Norse myths fascinated him. Tommy had *X-Men* #12, "The Origin of Professor X"! and Butch glanced over. His copy was in the house. He and Tommy had bought probably the last two left at Carl's Drug Store, thank God, before someone else got them. Good issue, but he wasn't sure which origin story, Professor X's or Juggernaut's, was the more compelling. Juggernaut was magic, not a mutant. That made him hard to defeat.

Tommy caught his glance and shook the X-Men at him. "You wanna read this one?"

Yes, but Asgard first so Butch finger-waved him away, already back on the *Hand*. Tommy grunted and turned to the page showing Juggernaut at Professor X's feet, helmet off, surprised by a Professor X-guided Angel attack. Butch momentarily abandoned Asgard for Juggernaut's terrified face. There's always a weakness. Just had to find it.

"Why you all dressed up?" Tommy asked.

"Dale's graduation."

"Oh." Tommy nodded and looked at the girls. Tommy was in sixth grade now but, next year, on to middle school. Next week Butch turned ten, double-digits at last, teenagery mere scattered months beyond, a birthday of grand implications heralded with cupcakes and ice cream and singing and presents and maybe, please God, that longed-for GI Joe. Butch looked forward to it with all the twittery anticipation of a Christmas morning. But their mutual promotions might have a dangerous effect on their friendship.

Tommy lived right next door, very convenient for a best

3

friend, and there were hardly two hours straight in the day that Butch wasn't at Tommy's or the other way around. They played army, with Tommy the Americans and Butch the Germans, or Civil War, with Tommy the North and Butch the Rebs, or Marvel, with Tommy as Dr. Strange or Reed Richards and Butch as Dormammu or Doctor Doom. Occasionally, Chuckie from two doors down joined them when he wasn't in trouble, or Dale (funny that he had Butch's sister's name) from across the street when he was visiting his aunt. But those were interludes Butch really didn't like because, invariably, Chuckie or Dale teased Butch about something stupid he did or said and Tommy let them continue until Butch cried and went home.

The best times were right now, side by side, reading Marvel. Tommy got him started a few years ago, dragged Butch and his weekly quarter off to Carl's. "Don't buy baseball cards, jerko, lookee here!"

Tommy had spun the magazine rack to a slot containing *Fantastic Four* #1 with that big green thing coming out of the street.

Wow.

Butch liked Batman, and Sergeant Rock and the tank haunted by the ghost of General Stuart in *GI Combat*, but this! He bought the *FF* and a *Two-Gun Kid* and still had one cent left over for bubblegum with a Luis Tiant and Tug McGraw inside to trade later.

So who's the jerko, jerko?

They had raced to Tommy's back porch and Tommy read the comics aloud because Butch couldn't read yet. First grade was still months away, and he hadn't gone to kindergarten like Cindy and Art. If it hadn't been for those comic books and *Green Eggs and Ham*, Butch wouldn't have had a clue what a letter was, much less whole words, when he walked into Miss MacDonald's first-grade class that fall.

Now, look at him. He read as well as Tommy, maybe better. Butch had read *The Adventures of Tom Sawyer* five times already, loving each pass-through. Miss Hale, the most beautiful second-grade teacher in the world, had read it to them during story time. Enthralled, Butch had pestered her to do so again, and she asked, "Would you like to read it for yourself?"

Would he!

"Maybe a little advanced, Butch, but if you think you can do it..."

He sure did think he could do it. Hadn't he blasted through the *SRA*s, didn't he swap *Happy Hollisters* with the third graders and wasn't he a Marvel True Believer? She lent him her copy and he finished it in a week, and Miss Hale was so astonished she gave it to him when school ended. He could read anything now, couldn't he?

Call me a bookworm, dad, I don't care.

But all that was in jeopardy. If there was one group of kids with which middle schoolers had no truck, it was elementaries... like Butch. Butch would ascend to the middle grades when Tommy was already in ninth, one year away from high school, and ninth graders had even less truck with seventh graders. Their friendship was aging out. It was more than likely that this summer was the very last time that he and Tommy could, or would, remain the best of friends.

That prospect gave Butch the chills, and he glanced apprehensively at his very best friend in the entire universe and, oh my God, look at this, Tommy was still on the girls. Butch frowned. Tommy had the narrowed eyes that dad got whenever he looked at bent-over girls or girls walking by in their bathing suits. Butch always looked away feeling guilty, even though he didn't understand why. Dad, though, stayed on them; smiled, too.

Wait. Wrong word—'leered,' yeah, that's it. An ugly word. But appropriate.

Tommy's gaze was on Lynn, who had taken over one end of the rope, and Butch got mad. Lynn, although closer to Tommy's age, was his, dang it! And nobody else's narrowed-eye target. "Hey!"

Startled, Tommy looked at him. "What?"

Butch pointed at the *X-Men*. "You done?"

"Yeah. I thought you had it."

"I do, but it's in the house. Trade."

Tommy made an exasperated sound and swapped the books. Butch smiled secretly.

"You heard what's going to happen with Reed Richards and the Invisible Girl?" Tommy asked.

"What?"

"They're getting married."

5

"Really?" Intrigued, Butch said, "How do you know?"

"The Annual."

Butch considered. "What if they have a kid?"

They looked at each other. "*Whooaaaa!*" erupted simultaneously and they laughed and slapped backs and crowed as Cha Cha, ever ready to share enthusiasm, sat and barked along, as the two, well, three of them, speculated what powers the kid would have: the ability to stretch an invisible hand or force field across an entire city, or maybe something entirely different. Would the kid be classified a mutant, which meant attending Professor X's school, or an accident, like Spiderman, and remain with FF, which would then become F5? They had a very stimulating discussion.

"Time to go!" mom called from behind them.

They both jumped as the rope skipping dissolved and Cindy made her goodbyes and Cha Cha fled to the kitchen. Mom looked down at the boys with suspicion, then smiled and said, "Hello, Tommy."

"Hello, Mrs. Deats," Tommy said, ever polite to adults.

"How's your mother?"

"Fine, ma'am." Tommy's mother, willowy and pale, disappeared for hours into bedrooms. Something sinister about that. She seemed frail, and Butch held his breath around her, afraid he'd give her a cold or something. He'd never seen her sick nor had Tommy ever said she was, but mortality hovered about her and Tommy looked grim whenever the conversation turned in her direction.

"Well, tell her I was asking, will you?" Mom smiled again, and it was warm until she caught sight of the comic books and her brows furrowed. "For the life of me, boys, I don't see the attraction."

Butch held his breath, suddenly fearful of confiscation, but Tommy, good with adults, said, "I know, ma'am. They seem stupid, but we really like them." He gestured at Butch. "Butchie learned to read with them."

Mom scrutinized Butch; she shared dad's sentiment that he spent far too much time with his nose stuck in books and comics. "Yes, well, I suppose, but I think you learn bad words from them."

"Oh, no, ma'am," Tommy was solemn. "They wouldn't let us buy them if that was so."

Mom looked ready to debate that but Cindy flounced up, all whirling skirt and hair, and gave Butch and Tommy a dazzling smile that melted them both. Sure enough, she wasn't even sweaty, although Mom fussed and pulled at things as she breezed by.

Mom turned to Butch. "We have to go," insistent. He stood and socked Tommy in the shoulder while hissing, "Don't call me 'Butchie!'"

Tommy grinned and mouthed it as Butch stomped through the door, looking down to avoid a stumble. To his horror, he saw a dirty spot on his trousers. Jeez! He hadn't even moved!

Mom stopped him halfway in the foyer, Cindy long gone, and he was dead. Dead. He could already feel the tears rising to greet the inevitable slap and banishment to the bedroom and missing the graduation—which wasn't a bad prospect—and Thursday night television, which was.

Why does this stuff keep happening?

Mom knelt down. "Are you all right?" she asked softly.

He blinked back the tears he had placed for immediate aid and dispersal and stared at her, confused. "What?"

"Are you going to be okay?" she fussed with his collar, adjusted the lines of things, and pointedly ignored the dirty spot.

Again, what? What's this?

Butch got a little scared. "I... yes, I guess. Mom?"

She stared back, dark eyes and short dark hair and puffy cheeks, endearing in a mom, all pulled into worry lines. She pulled him into a hard, lung-shattering hug. "You know I love you, don't you?"

Shocked, Butch dropped into a defensive spasm that ended up as an unintentional hug back. Breath caught in his squeezed chest and turned quickly into a held-in sob because mom was always in pain, such pain, and it wasn't fair, and he had to make it right because no one else would. "Yes, mom, I know." The sob escaped.

She squeezed him tighter. "I'm sorry I've treated you so badly these past few weeks. I didn't mean to."

Past few weeks? part of his brain chided. How 'bout past few months? Past few years?

"S'kay, mom." More sobs and the tears he'd reserved for the dirty pants switched allegiance, a couple springing loose and making a break for it down his cheek.

She pushed him out to arms' length. "You think ..." she stopped and frowned and looked to her left.

Butch clutched at her arms.

What do I think, mom? That you don't love me the way you love your real children? That you only tolerate the Foundling out of Christian charity but deep down you wish I weren't here? Are you going to tell me that's not true? Then show me!

"Your dad's there," she muttered and straightened his collar as though she'd been doing that all along and surreptitiously wiped his tears before Butch looked over her shoulder to see dad, in his dress uniform, half hidden in the door, face shadowed and roiling. The Watcher from the Dark, terrible and deadly.

Icy fear shot through Butch's heart because dad knew, knew, he'd been crying, and dad hated that. "You wanna cry? I'll give you something to cry about!" and the whistle of belt or whip made good the promise.

"Are we going or what?" dad said from around the perpetual cigarette in his mouth.

Mom nodded and said nothing because there was a good chance her voice was choked with the past moments and dad'd hear it and pounce anyway. Butch risked a look. Dad glowered at them but turned for the kitchen and the dangerous moment passed.

Mom squeezed his arm conspiratorially and stood up, straightening her skirt so Butch could use it as a shield to get into the hallway. "Wash your face," mom called after him, sounding more like her old self in that.

Butch felt conflicted. Survived another moment. But lost one, too.

# CHAPTER 2

Butch went to Lawton High School once to see Dale in *Rebel Without a Cause*. She played a Gang Girl who made chicken noises at the guy playing James Dean, then pretended to watch the drag race happening off stage. The sound effects guy made the crash sound, and she flung herself into the arms of some Gang Guy and acted scared. Butch was impressed. He'd seen the movie on TV so knew the story and wasn't confused by the bare stage, which was a classroom of folding chairs lined against the walls for the audience. Theater in the Round, Dale called it, and Butch thought it worked well. He'd waved at her when she exited, but she ignored him.

Actors.

That had been in a side part of the school accessed from a back parking lot and wasn't really much. The front, though... wow. It was *big*. Butch goggled at the sweeping granite steps and wide portico and columns, and then they entered the foyer... wow. It was *bigger!* White tile stretched in more directions than a compass, cascading down more hallways than Butch thought possible, all of them lined with millions of lockers that dwindled into the distance like one of those trick pictures. Gigantic trophy cases stood all over the place filled with gold statues of football and baseball players and guys with their arms raised like they were saying something, team portraits marked with dates going back fifty years arrayed behind, the athletes grinning and mouthing at the camera. Flags and banners and portraits everywhere.

9

Beat Swinney all to heck.

"Watch where you're going!" Dale yelled at him.

Startled, Butch looked at her and then down at a red-and-black emblem painted on the floor, a depiction of some strange, snarling creature holding up a threatening paw, or what he guessed was a paw. The eyes were big and the mouth squared and bewhiskered and he immediately thought of a Chinese dragon dog he'd seen in a book once.

Fascinating.

A circle of Latin words surrounded the creature. Butch recognized Latin now. He'd asked Mrs. Moore, the fourth-grade teacher about a Latin phrase, *Sic Semper Tyrannis*, in a *We Were There* book about Gettysburg.

"It's the language of Rome," she said, "It means, 'Thus to all tyrants.'"

Fascinating.

His foot hovered over the creature's face and he knew, based on Dale's reaction and the aghast stares of nearby high-schoolers, not to put it down. Instead, Butch pushed hard and made a rather spectacular leap over the image, landing spider-legged on the other side, sure he'd ripped his pants, but without laying even a toe on the beast. Not bad.

"Stop fooling around," dad said, lighting a cigarette.

Humph. Such an acrobatic move was worthy of praise, not judgment, and he fell in beside Dale, feeling somewhat peeved. "What is that thing?" he asked.

"The school mascot," she answered absently, intent on other people.

"What is it?"

"A wolverine."

"A what?"

"A wolverine." Annoyed, she stretched her neck and gave a big wave to someone.

Butch glanced back. It certainly didn't look like a wolverine, more like a ferret-monster or maybe a vicious skunk. "Why can't you step on it?"

She gave him her you-ask-too-many-questions face. "Because it's bad luck."

Butch considered that as they stopped at an intersection of hallways, a people knot in a pool of bodies skittering here and there. Made sense. Shouldn't insult mascots by stepping on their images, especially ones that looked like dragons. Might make them mad.

Dale's face brightened. "Hi!" she said.

Mike, already in his graduation gown, stood there smiling. "Hi," he replied and then smooshed Butch's hair. "Hey, sport."

Butch evaded the continued hair attack and grinned. He liked Mike, who called him 'sport' and 'surfer' and other hilarious things and talked to Butch about music and explained album liner notes. He always wanted to know what Butch was reading and encouraged him to read more, unlike everyone else. He hoped Dale married him. "You bothering your sister?" Mike asked.

"Always," Dale snorted and Butch almost rolled his eyes backwards as she pushed Mike toward the rest.

Mom smiled at him, Cindy smiled even more, Art picked at his sleeve, and dad frowned. He didn't like Mike. He didn't like any of Dale's friends, of course, but Mike less so because he was slight and pale and wore big goggly black glasses and had real thin hair and dad said he wasn't a man. Or maybe more because Mike had driven Dale and a few others to see the Kingston Trio in Oklahoma City a few months ago and a truck hit them and Dale's nose got smashed, and she had to have an operation and now had a scar.

Or maybe dad didn't like anyone kissing Dale, although he really shouldn't worry. Mike barely touched her, something Butch knew because he spied on them a lot. Mike touched Butch more than he did Dale. Made sense—roughhousing was fun; kissing was icky. Except if he got to kiss Lynn.

Mike, always easy, laughed with Mom and Dale while keeping a wary eye on dad who had taken his usual belligerent pose. "Full scholarship," dad said to him through a forced smile, "That's really good. Too bad no one else got one." He looked pointedly at Dale, who frowned. Prey and predator eyed each other, one sensing escape, the other determined to prevent it.

"San Francisco State isn't half as expensive as Berkeley," Dale said, like she'd said every day for months now. "My grant takes care of most of it and I've got a job waiting." Exasperating because, Jeez, how many times did she have to explain this? Even Butch got it.

C'mon, dad! What's the big deal?

11

"'Waitin', all right. In the school cafeteria," dad sneered, "Hope they let you keep the scraps."

"It'll be enough," Dale's eyes were deadly and Butch shifted out of range. She looked that way before she pounded him. Dad's look, twice as deadly, and the one he usually got right before he initiated the half-murder he called a whipping, answered hers. He'd whip Dale right here if pushed enough.

Dale, are you crazy?

"You should stay here," dad said.

"Why? You're not!"

What?

Instantly puzzled, Butch looked at Dale as if she'd spoken a foreign language, and then turned to the others. Mom looked helpless, Cindy as puzzled as he was, and Art... clueless. As usual. Did this mean dad was going away on orders like during that Cuban missile thing?

He was about to ask, but dad had gone seventeen shades of purple and lightning spewed out of his ears and oh, God, no. Dale had somehow lit dad's fuse. And when the dad grenade exploded, there would be a bloody, awful mess, right here on top of the wolverine.

Mike grabbed Dale's elbow and pulled her out of combat stance. "Let's go!"

Good thing, because dad was just moments away from a massive Frank Vaughning.

Mike levered an arm into Dale's back and hustled her along the hallway as she fought him. "Tell me to stay?" she raged, "*He's* the one abandoning Mom!" but Mike soothed and shushed and got her quickly into the crowd.

What??

Butch spun in place, admiring Mike's quick thinking and escape while completely dumbfounded by the things Dale said. "What's she talking about?" he asked Mom and dad in mid-spin.

Dad ignored him, eyes zeroed with the intensity of a Cyclops eye-blast on the retreating Mike and Dale, a look chilling Butch to the core. The dad-storm roiled and groaned and looked for outlet and Butch took another prudent step out of reach, careful to avoid the wolverine. Several people stopped and stared, but the presence of strangers was no deterrent and Butch held his breath, wondering how this would end. A frightened and frozen tableau stood arrayed about the insane-eyed dad, who remained locked on target as Mike disappeared around a corner with the still struggling Dale. "Come on," he snarled, throwing his cigarette into an ashcan, then wheeled and moved into the crowd as it funneled down a hallway.

The rest of them looked at each other and gave a collective sigh of relief. Crisis averted. Butch looked at Mom expectantly, but all she did was frown at him and then slip behind dad. He and Cindy exchanged "who knows?" shrugs and fell in line, Art, unfortunately, still with them.

# CHAPTER 3

The crowd tightened into a caterpillar moving in fits and starts. Butch had a hard time keeping up and half-feared getting lost, so he made a real effort to keep Mom in sight, shoving past people who told him how rude he was. Sorry, but he wasn't getting left behind, wandering the halls of this gigantic school forever, kids laughing at him by day and the wolverine chasing him at night. The crowd packed into a set of double doors then widened out so quickly that Butch stumbled through, losing his balance.

"Stop fooling around," dad snapped from the side of some bleachers, the others already there and staring at Butch.

Jeez, wasn't my fault.

He looked down at the floor to avoid seeing the serves-him-right look in the eyes of adults filing past. Dad stepped up the bleachers and they trooped obediently behind, Butch taking extra care because falling would be final proof of his fooling around tendencies and dad would kill him right here, to the cheers of onlookers. They finally selected a row and squeezed in without further Butch mishap.

Whew.

And *wow*.

They were up so high! The floor was like a mile away and the people milling around down there, parents and dressed-up little kids mingled with green-gowned high-schoolers, were so tiny Butch couldn't recognize features.

Just how far have we climbed?

He wondered if they would, at some point, need oxygen.

14

Breathing through those big rubber masks, like the one on dad's flight helmet ... that'd be great.

He followed the bank of lights that stretched three miles across the ceiling to an endless set of ten-story bleachers on the opposite side peopled with the same well-dressed faceless creatures as on the floor. Man, this place was even bigger than dad's hanger on Ft. Sill, which was really just a giant metal tent open at either end, the helicopters arranged neatly down the sides. Sitting up here was like being on Mt. Scott, without the wind or cold. Butch suddenly felt afraid. He didn't want to fall.

He stole a glance at the others for reassurance. Art was absorbed in his belt buckle. Cindy stared around with wide, interested eyes and glanced at him and smiled and Butch wished Art wasn't between them so they could talk about how wonderful and scary this all was. Mom and dad sat frozen, cigarettes dangling, their face lines flowing down down down as they stared without movement at the hubbub below. They didn't look scared at all—they looked mad. And sad. At least Mom looked sad; dad never looked anything else *but* mad. Butch inwardly shuddered. He hoped it wasn't because of him.

Music started and Butch tried to locate it. Everyone stood up and blocked his view, so he stood with them and craned and swiveled and peeped to snatch a glimpse here and there between the wall of people. Green gowns marched through the double doors and into rows of folding chairs. The people in the stands watched, faces solemn but proud. Butch understood that: getting out of school forever was pretty important.

But, then, didn't you have to go to college or join the Army or something? Not much of an improvement.

The music ended and everyone sat and, five minutes later, Butch had lost all interest. Some green gown on the platform talked into a crappy microphone, echoes blurring the words.

Booooring.

Butch squirmed and Mom's ten-foot-long finger poked him hard in the ribs. Settle down! He glowered at her while Art smirked and he felt like cracking the little freak, but that would get him killed. Dad sat stone-faced, ignoring the transgression. Butch turned back to the sea of necks in front of him.

He wished he had a comic book. Maybe *Magnus, Robot Slayer*. Leeja Crane, wow, so gorgeous, like the Inhuman,

Medusa, but not quite as beautiful. Magnus was perfect as her boyfriend. But how did he slice through robots with just his hands? Granted, he used that karate stuff the old guy taught him but, still, nobody can cut through metal without superpowers and Magnus didn't have any. Right? Butch wasn't sure. Magnus just might be really tough.

That's what he needed, Magnus arms. Slice through the people in front of him like so many robots and escape, leaving metallic heads and torsos twitching on the floor. Only they wouldn't be metallic; they'd be human and bloody and mangled. Butch felt a bit queasy.

Frank Vaughn had been all mangled and bloody and twisted. It was so bad, the paper only showed a black-and-white front-page photo of a body under a speckled sheet, two skinny, lifeless arms out and next to his sides. The coffin was closed and Howie said that's because Frank had no face.

No face.

The whole team had gone to the funeral. All of them had on white shirts and black pants, but Butch also wore his black jacket because Mom insisted. Coach Sasser asked, in the same exasperated voice he used every time he showed Butch how to swing the bat, if he'd forgotten they were all wearing white shirts only. Butch didn't remember anybody saying that. There was no place to put the jacket, so he had to wear it. The team stood in a line in front of the coffin and a photographer from the paper probably thought it was a good picture and snapped it and there he was for all of Lawton to see, the only one wearing a jacket.

Great. Another inadvertent foul-up which made him look, once again, like a spaz.

Because of the jacket, everybody at the funeral asked if Frank and he were good friends and how did Butch feel. Carlton, that big bully jerk, sneered that Butch wasn't Frank's friend at all and a lousy baseball player to boot and shouldn't have been on the team with Frank, who was a good player. Butch almost cried as he walked home after being dropped off at Swinney. It hurt because it was true.

He *was* a lousy baseball player, probably the worst one in America. He was so bad that he didn't want to leave the bench and he prayed no pop-ups came his way when the rules forced the coach to put him in right field. And he always struck out. Well, not always, sometimes he'd get on base when the pitcher hit him in the back or when he was pinch-running for Skipper, the kid with the polio braces who squeaked like a rusty car when he swung the bat, but who was a great hitter. Then, oh no, Coach gave a steal sign. No way Butch'd make it, but off he went, and the defender had time to take a nap before Butch got there for the inevitable tag-out. He hated the contemptuous look in the other team's eyes, which was worse than his own team's because at least the other team thought he might be good; that is, until he did something stupid. His team already knew he would do something stupid.

He should quit. But dad always told people Butch played baseball, so he stayed. Dad didn't really have anything else to say about him.

The only time Butch actually played alongside Frank was the last practice before Frank's mom killed him, when both of them were shagging throw-backs to Coach. He knew Frank, of course. Everyone did. Frank was the nicest kid in school, always polite, funny, ran with the popular crowd but wasn't a jerk like them. Said "hi" to Butch in school when no one else did, let him bat first at practice, waved to him when he showed up. This time, he let Butch get most of the throws, even though Butch missed the majority and had to run them down. Frank was patient, encouraging, tossing a couple of easy ones his way.

That'd been nice.

Three days later, Frank was dead. Just like that.

Butch peered around a fat guy sitting in front of him to see what was going on, but another green gown made another unintelligible speech, so he sat back. A wave of sadness washed over him.

Just like that, Frank.

Butch was at Swinney when he heard. It was the same day school let out for the summer. Butch had skipped all the way home, singing "School's out, school's out, teacher let the monkeys out," every step yes sir behind every other kid he approached, the girls making that *twa* sound because he was so annoying, but he didn't care, didn't care. They were out! out! out! for three whole months. Mom was taking one of her do-not-wake-me naps, so he'd gone back to play on the equipment since Tommy wasn't around and schoolyards were different in the summer, more relaxed. It had suddenly clouded up, like the sky was preparing for the news.

As he came around the corner, he ran into Howie and Dave standing round-eyed on the sidewalk beside the Music Room. "Didja hear what happened?"

"No, what?"

"Frank Vaughn's dead!"

Utter shock. "Huh?"

"Yeah! His mom beat him to death with a baseball bat."

"What!"

"Yeah! He forgot his report card."

Butch gawped, slack-jawed.

How absolutely trivial. Jeez, all she had to do was swat his behind and send him back to retrieve it. The office was still open, so what's the big deal? And how absolutely unlike Frank to make such a goof-up.

Report cards were the whole reason for school. Butch never forgot a report card because he got extra quarters for "As" and he'd anticipated the 75c that Reading and Spelling and Writing earned him this time, which meant six more comic books and three more sets of baseball cards. No "Fs", like Cindy, a grade that could subtract quarters to the point of no allowance. And if Frank, every parent's favorite child, was beaten to death for such an insignificant spazz-out, what were Butch's chances?

Butch had been scared ever since. And sad.

"Frank," he whispered, surprised to hear tears in his voice. Was he that upset about a kid he hardly knew?

Yeah, 'cause it was all so blasted unfair. There was Frank, a sheet over his head, and Frank's mom, beehived hair and looking beautiful on TV. So unfair.

Butch shook himself. Seemed pretty stupid to get this upset about a kid who was now a skip rhyme and worm food and had no face and whose mom was gettin' the death penalty, at least that's what dad said. Maybe it was just too warm up here, and the suit scratched, and he was bored completely out of his mind and Mom poked him and that's why he felt bad.

"Thanks a lot," Frank said.

Butch went from too warm to ice cold as Frank, sitting on the riser in front of him, turned around with a hurt expression. Real hurt. His caved-in nose gave him a convex look, and his jaw hung at a weird angle. Butch didn't know how he could speak, but ghosts could do anything. "Bwa?" was all Butch could muster.

"Relax," Frank said, "not here to kill you. Been enough of that already." Said ruefully.

"What? How?" was a little bit better, but still not sparkling conversation.

Frank shrugged. "We can come when called. You called. No one else seems to care."

"About… you getting killed?"

"Yeah. Everyone's acting all freaky and upset but they don't call for me. Still, worm food?"

"You heard that?"

Frank smiled a very crooked smile which, given his misaligned jaw, must have taken quite an effort and pointed at the gym floor. "So what's going on here?"

"My sister's graduating from high school."

"Cindy?"

Butch's eyes popped. "You know Cindy?"

"Well, sure. I'm dead, not stupid." And he gave Butch a sneer, made all the more frightening by his eye falling out. "Sorry," he said, popping it back in.

Butch shuddered, but still managed a snort. "Not Cindy, Dale. Cindy's our age. How could she be graduating?"

"Oh. Right. Didn't realize. Time's a little… different now." Frank explained. Which was no explanation at all.

Butch leaned forward. "So, what's it like?"

"Cold," Frank said. "Lonely." A pause. "You'll see."

Butch immediately panicked and Frank cracked up. Laughing, that is, not face-wise. "Gotcha!" he said.

"Very funny." Butch groused. "So you'll show up every time I call you?"

"When it's unfair."

Butch reached a consoling hand but hesitated to actually touch Frank. Dead boy cooties. "I know, I'm sorry. I don't mean to be."

"Oh, not unfair to me." Frank shook his head, which resulted in a couple of teeth flying out. "Unfair to you."

"Huh?"

"What's about to happen to you."

Something sharp and hard poked Butch in the side and he jumped. Mom's finger. "Wake up!" she mouthed at him. Disoriented and terrified, Butch looked wildly around but Frank wasn't there anymore; some man and woman in matching tweed outfits (hers was a skirt) stood in Frank's place, applauding. Everyone was standing and applauding, except Butch. Bewildered, he jumped to his feet and craned his neck but no broken Frank face anywhere, only Cindy, who grinned at him and made snoring noises. Okay, so, he fell asleep and missed all the speeches and all the green gowns marching up the stage and getting their diplomas and throwing their caps in the air and now it was over.

There is benefit in nightmare.

# CHAPTER 4

Dale didn't pile into the car with them for the trip back home and Butch couldn't care less. She was too old, too remote from his interests, their relationship best summarized by her constant, irritated scream of "Buuuutch!" Besides, she was on her way to California, maybe tonight. He'd miss her music, though: Pete Seeger and his little boxes, the Limelighters and their Madeira, my dear, and Peter Paul and Mary with their *Puff the Magic Dragon*, which he liked better than the Irish Rovers' version. But, in the scheme of things, no great loss, especially since it was Thursday night and that means…

*Jonny Quest*, the greatest television show ever.

Butch wriggled with excitement and pleasure, causing Art to scream, "He's touching me!" at Mom.

Shut up, twerp, because *ooooh boy!* Jonny and Hadji and Bandit and Dr. Quest, what a genius, and Race, what a tough guy, and all their adventures. Can't wait, can't wait!

By the time they pulled into the driveway, Butch fairly vibrated off his seat and flew out of the car before it came to a complete halt, getting a "Hey!" from dad.

Sorry, gotta go because it's almost time, almost!

Butch flew through the door and skidded to a halt on the throw rug inches from the TV and pulled the knob and watched impatiently as the bright lines flew around and spread out and expanded and slowly, slo-o-owly formed a picture.

C'mon c'mon!

Moments later, Cindy and Art skidded into position beside

21

him, both sharing his urgency. All three jockeyed for position; Cindy and Butch teamed up to deny Art any space. Had to be careful or the little brat would start squalling and Mom, because Art was her little baby-aby favorite, would intervene and allocate Art far more floor space than his status allowed, so Cindy and Butch worked covertly to edge Art out...

"Turn off the television," dad said.

"What!" Butch whirled, well, tried to whirl, actually crabbed. Lying on the floor didn't allow much whirling. "But, dad!" Butch, aghast, wailed, "*Jonny Quest* is coming on!"

Cindy and Art echoed his cry in volume and intensity. At any other time there'd be an exchange of shoulder punches for simultaneous utterance, but this was a crisis. Cha Cha, sprawled in the doorway connecting the living room with the kitchen, raised a concerned head. All of their focus was on dad sitting in His Chair, an overstuffed brown monstrosity which had a lever on the side allowing it to tip dangerously back.

Lots of fun, but don't get caught playing with it or God help you.

Dad was still wearing his suit, hadn't bothered to change, just lay there with an unreadable expression on his face. Butch couldn't tell if he was tired or mad or both. Or had gone suddenly nuts because...

C'mon, dad, Thursday night television! Thursday! Night! Television!

Butch looked at Cindy, who swiveled between Butch and dad, open-mouthed, stricken, hair falling to one side, and drew strength.

"Da-a-a-a-ad!" in his best pleading tone because he could not miss *Jonny*, no way, no how! Art chimed in, too, earning a second shoulder slug that Butch would pay later but not too hard because Art at least sensed enough of the looming tragedy to disregard personal safety.

Dad let out an almost imperceptible sigh, but Butch saw it and hope blossomed. Dad looked up at his trophy, a giant deer head hung on the wall, third biggest buck ever shot in the US or something like that. Time and the universe stopped, but, after a moment dad said, "All right."

Butch whooshed a great big sigh of relief, then turned to Cindy, who smiled encouragement, then to Art, who still looked

FRANK VAUGHN, KILLED BY HIS MOM

aggrieved because he hadn't caught on yet.

Shut up! Shut up! Shut up! Don't say anything stupid, you little twerp. Butch gave him the snake eye.

Mom, sporting the same unreadable expression as dad, sat on the couch catty-corner to dad's chair and Butch half-feared she would take up dad's now abandoned decision to shut the damn idiot box off because she believed they all watched too much television anyway. But she didn't. She just stared at the deer head.

Bears are now calm. Do not poke.

Butch twisted back to the screen as Jonny's opening credits started and unconsciously broke into a floor-bound rhumba in time to the music and... a re-run: the *Double Danger* episode, the one where Race got duplicated.

Not that great, not like *Turok*, but it was still *Jonny* so go with it.

A half-hour and four hundred commercials later, the closing credits rolled and Butch lay back, satisfied, and grinned at Art. Cha Cha came over and lay between them, a world restored to order.

...distant whistling sound in the upper atmosphere...

"Turn off the TV."

Oh no, oh no no no. For God's sake, dad, *Flintstones* and *Bewitched* are up next!

Butch felt a little guilty using "God" like that because it was disrespectful but this was an emergency and invoking divinity seemed appropriate. Maybe it was okay as long as he didn't say it out loud.

Good question for Sunday School.

He wailed again, joined by Art and Cindy. Too bad Dale wasn't here to add voice because she loved *Bewitched* better than the cartoons, which were too babyish for her, eewww-uuwww, Miss Too-Big-for-her-Britches, so Butch heightened his volume to cover her loss. Dad relented again, Mom stared off, and they got through Fred as Super Stone. "Bey-he-he-HA-ha!" Butch and Art bellowed at each other and Cindy giggled and dad said nothing. Mom said nothing.

Odd. By now, she should have said something: stop scuffing the floor; it's too noisy in here; go do your homework...

...but there isn't any homework, nope, nope, NOPE! School's OUT!

He surreptitiously hummed the School's Out song and wondered why Mom had taken no notice of their limbs sprawled too close to a TV exposing them to the same kind of radiation that killed everyone when the Russkies dropped the Bomb so run under the porch while brushing off particles like that stick boy in the duck-and-cover commercial.

Speaking of commercials... Hubert!

Glee split Butch's face as Hubert barked and Granny said, "How did you get in here?" and then Hubert, "Madam, how do you do?" with those sudsy eyebrows and Granny on the phone, "Operator there's a man in the bathtub, operator, a man..." and Hubert, "Granny, it's me." Mr. Bubble. Bub Bub Bubble. Butch laughed like he always laughed every time Hubert suds'd up because it was just as funny the 500th time as the first.

And then they were through *Bewitched* and Samantha's nose had gotten Darrin (Derwood) in trouble with Larry so she and Endora had to come up with the new advertising campaign and it all worked out. It always did, of course; the fun was in how.

...altitude reached, triggering mechanism engages...

"Turn it off. Now." Dad's dangerous voice and Butch didn't hesitate, reached up and pushed the button and the picture imploded down to that whirling little white dot, desperately struggling against its ultimate demise, colors playing around the edges and trying to flare but no, no, little white dot of TV world, die. Butch wondered where it went.

He turned. Thunderclouds rode dad's brow and the black light of insanity flared in his eyes and fear struck Butch from heart to stomach.

What'd I do, what'd I do?

He furiously inventoried behavior of the past week—bought those reviled comic books, rode around the block way after dark chasing bats instead of coming home and helping around the house (whatever that meant), walked through the forbidden sewer pipes with a gaggle of other kids to the park... quite a list. Any one of them could be the cause of his death

Like Frank, the baseball bat coming down down down.

"Your mom and I are getting a divorce."

*Ka-blooie.* Complete and total annihilation.

A strange balance of sudden relief and absolute horror seized Butch—dad was not going to roar down on him like the Furies wielding a belt, cutting hard and deep across legs and back and butt to punish another one of Butch's myriad sins, but... what he just said! He gasped, in chorus with Cindy and Art. Mom said nothing.

"You have to choose who you're going with."

Then the blast wave overwhelmed him and he burst into tears. Cindy did, too, as did Art, but from the sheer panic induced by everyone else crying, not because he understood. Their faces were instantly transformed into those tragic masks printed on the SRA covers.

Dad pushed the leg extension down and levered up and Butch's tone changed from misery to fear because this was it, the belt was coming off and dad would lay into them because they were crying. Crying indicated strong opposition and dad never allowed opposition, strong or otherwise, to anything he said or did. Ever. He usually expressed his outrage by whipping everybody within arm's reach half to death. The resulting shrieks of pain made him angrier and he stroked harder until the leather sang on skin because he was always right, always. About everything. Subsequently, they had learned not to express any opposition of any kind to anything.

This, though. This was too much. And Butch couldn't stop crying, got louder, even. So he braced.

But dad did not, with the deftness of long practice, unleash the belt. Instead, he wordlessly strode out of the living room and down the hallway and into his bedroom. Butch stayed in fear tone because dad might retrieve the Mexican whip, his favorite weapon when in uber-fury (uber was a neat word from *X-Men*). But he didn't come back.

Cindy somehow had made her way to the couch and she and Mom hugged, rocking back and forth in mutual tears because Mom had started crying, too, but Butch wasn't sure why. Dad's words included Mom in the decision so it couldn't be shock. Sharing Cindy's misery, he guessed. And Art's, as her eyes swept past Butch and fixed on the little twerp. Of course.

Butch stood, chest heaving to catch the off-rhythms crying required. Cindy peered at him from between Mom's arms with her 'help me' face.

No, Cindy, not this time. You have all the help you need.

Art, still bewildered, looked at him with his usual 'what's

going on?' face but Butch didn't want to explain. He didn't want to be with these people or in this room one second longer. Let's get out of here. He wheeled about and headed for the bedroom.

On reflection, probably not the brightest of moves because the kids' bedroom was opposite Mom and dad's and Butch was in mortal danger. Both bedroom doors had slats that angled down and were neat for reconn'ing the hallway before stepping out, but that cut both ways. Dad could be staring at Butch right now, timing his movements to catch him flat-footed, the first object of whip rampage. Butch's breath caught in terror but dad's room was dark and silent and the danger passed when Butch hastily skipped across the threshold and closed the door.

He sat on the floor with his back to the toy box, an old black trunk underneath the window that overlooked Tommy's house. Art's and Butch's beds were on the left, black headboards against the blue wall, separated from each other by a black chest maybe fifteen, thirty feet tall. Butch could barely reach its top drawer; Mom had to get seldom-used clothes, like his funeral shirt, out for him. Cindy's bed was against the right wall and window, set at right angles to the boys' beds.

This arrangement made for an interesting set of blanket-shrouded canyons and culs de sac perfect for little green Army men to ambush unsuspecting Nazi platoons stumbling foolishly to their deaths on rainy days when playing outside was impossible. But at night, when Cindy and Art were asleep and Butch wasn't, those same canyons became the haunts of ghosts and wee beasties (a neat phrase from the SRAs—hey, that rhymes!). Hiding in the shrouds where the dark folded, they grinned at him while waiting for him to fall asleep so they could scurry up the blankets and bury razor-sharp teeth into his neck, red eyes glowing with lustful satisfaction. To stay alive he forced wakefulness, desperately trying to stop his shivering and whimpers because that called them, and they would pop out of the canyons and dance their evil little dances and do unspeakable things until he screamed, waking himself at daybreak, puzzled he'd survived the night while Cindy and Art razzed him and Mom dismissed it as mere nightmare.

The beasties weren't due for hours, but Butch would welcome them now. They'd be a mercy, draining his blood and leaving him withered and empty, to be found around bedtime by uncaring Mom. She'd scream and dad would run in and they'd both fall to their knees and hug each other in agony, "Our son! Our son!"

That'd show 'em.

He sobbed.

What's going on? Why a divorce? Okay, yeah, they fought all the time and dad hit Mom all the time because she made him so angry. Well, stop doing that.

She knew how dad was; she'd warned them enough—don't make your dad mad and we'll be all right. Couldn't avoid it all the time, because there were so many things that made dad mad but he gave signs when riled, like a dog with its hair up, and Butch had enough experience to read them and knock off whatever he was doing. She knew those signs, too, yet here we are so she must have done something that didn't trigger a warning.

What? Dinner?

Maybe it wasn't good enough, although, whatever they had, meatloaf (which Butch loved) or squirrel (which dad brought back from hunting and wasn't half bad, once Butch got over the initial revulsion) or squash (which Butch hated, threw up once eating it) seemed sufficient.

Maybe Mom slept too much. She was always napping when Butch came home from school, the house dark and threatening, and he stayed outside until she woke. Once, he had to pee really bad but was so terrified of disturbing her that he'd walked into Tommy's house and sat on the couch and waited for someone to notice and let him use the bathroom. Tommy's Mom had been incensed and threw him out and later told Mom, who beat him, despite his explanation.

Maybe dad didn't like her naps, either.

But that shouldn't be an issue now that school was over because Mom couldn't sleep with them running in and out grabbing Kool-Aid or sneaking mouthfuls of Redi-Whip and making hasty peanut-butter-and-sugar sandwiches, Mom snapping, "Get out!" when she caught them.

Not it.

The kitchen table sessions, then. Mom sitting there with Mrs. Wayne (Lynn, Debbie, Mary and Rose Ann's mother), both of them dark and brooding and glaring at Butch whenever he made the mistake of tripping in to get a glass of water or steal food. One time, Mom had beaten Butch right in front of Mrs. Wayne because he'd said "piss and moan" to Art, who was pissing and moaning about something. The little twerp ran crying to Mom and she made Butch stand there while she hit him and hit him and hit; Mrs. Wayne had looked on approvingly. Butch, hurt and humiliated, had gone right out and socked Art, who ran crying all the way back to Mom, big baby tattletale, so Butch hid out with Tommy until dad got home. Something else was going on by then and they forgot his attack on the Favored One.

Something about that session had been odd. There'd been a heaviness between Mom and Mrs. Wayne, dark and festering, like a turd in the bed sheets. Butch's crime had interrupted their discussion and he was sure the beating was more about that than what he'd said, especially since it was one of Mom's favorite phrases. Parents got mad and lashed out whenever kids bothered them, but her overreaction was like Butch busting into the bathroom while she was tinkling.

Tinkle and turd, Jeez, was everything about the toilet?

Butch shook his head miserably. There's no way to figure this out. It was something Adult, which defied analysis, and their foggy, baffling world gave only rare hints of meaning. On *Playhouse Theater* or *Alfred Hitchcock*, the man, black-haired and suited, the woman, blonde and dressed in white, a darkness tightening their faces with regret and lost chances, something they had done or not done sometime before, maybe shown during the play or referred to in dialogue, he couldn't tell because he didn't understand. Something to do with love and relationships and marriage and family and normal things that, somehow, did not become normal and the man and woman were now broken.

On the radio, the songs. Well, dad's songs, at least, that country stuff Butch hated because it sounded way too much like Texas and Pawpaw and Butch didn't really like Pawpaw, who was mean in the same accents. Dad's songs were doleful, about wimmin' and whiskey and cheatin' hearts, and dad's singers sounded like they hated reading as much as dad did. "Git yer nose ouddat book, boy! G'wout and pull weeds!"

Jeez.

Not the good songs. Someone's boyfriend's back and someone's gonna get a beatin'. Butch understood that—you don't mess with another man's girl. Rhonda helping someone get someone else outta their heart, yeah, got that, too, but he liked the beat more than the words, good for bouncing his head off the back of a couch while blasting Kay-oh-Em-AAAA!!! Oklahoma City! Elvis cried in the chapel and there were leaders of packs; all made sense. Not like the hard songs, the Yardbirds screaming for your love or Johnny Rivers claiming seventh sonship. Those had something wicked underneath that made him uneasy.

Wickedness.

The same thing that stirred witches and flying monkeys stirred hard songs and TV plays, but in a different manner: with a leer, like the one on dad's face when he stared at bent-over girls. Narrowed eyes, too. Narrowed eyes were prevalent on TV and in the movies, but were never acknowledged. Only adults seemed to know what they meant.

There was some connection between narrowed eyes and a lot of the world's frenzy. Frank's mom, no doubt, had narrowed eyes when she reached for the bat. Dale had flipped out after seeing the frenzied movie *Hush Hush Sweet Charlotte*, came home nervous and unable to sleep. Dad had played tricks on her, hiding a carved coconut skull in her bed. Dale screamed and Butch found that so hilarious he snuck into her room, quietly opened the door and dangled the skull just inside until she screamed again and called him names. Maybe it wasn't the skull that scared her but the frenzy that led to decapitation, a frenzy signaled by narrowed eyes. There was little chance Dale'd get her head cut off, but there was a great chance she'd have her eyes narrowed.

So, the divorce came from narrowed eyes? No way.

Hitting and screaming and narrowed eyes had defined existence ever since Butch could remember. Just the way things were. It wasn't right, he knew that, and he had often wondered why God allowed his adoption by this particularly mean and crazy family. He'd be better off with his real Mom in Germany or with a poorer family, as long as they didn't yell and beat. Tommy's family, yeah, although Tommy's Dad occasionally whaled him. But that was prompted by something legitimate, Tommy not doing the lawn or sassing. Normal stuff.

So, not the narrowed eyes, per se, but the mysterious force behind them, the Wickedness, something he didn't understand and never would because no one talked about it. Too many things weren't talked about. Mom sometimes wouldn't let him play with Tommy, even though it was a perfectly nice day and he would be out of her hair. He asked why but she looked at him with her mad face and he stomped off to the bedroom and pulled out books and cried because Mom was being mean for no reason, no reason at all. Or dad wouldn't come home for a few days and Butch asked why and Mom would just snap, "Shut up!" Or Lynn said she couldn't play with him and went into the house while her mom slammed the door and he stood on the sidewalk blinking. Then, a few days later, they'd be playing like nothing happened and he never found out why the change.

Given the propensity for keeping secrets around here, he seriously doubted he'd ever find out why a divorce. It would carry to the grave. A hundred years from now, he'd stand beside dad's deathbed, the old man already a skeleton. Butch would fall to his knees, tearful, imploring, "Please, dad, why did you and Mom divorce? Why?" Dad's empty eye sockets would open and a bony hand would grasp Butch's arm and he would say, "Son! Forgive me!" and then the death rattle.

Fine. Okay. Great. So, dad said choose.

Choose.

Butch got up and stared at the trunk a moment, wondering if an impromptu fight between Army men was the best course right now, then headed back toward the living room, pointedly ignoring dad's door. If he came roaring out right now swinging the German sword, the one he took off a dead Nazi, it'd just be overkill. He'd already cut them in half.

Mom and Cindy were still on the couch, still hugging, an occasional sob punctuating their conversation, which was nothing more than several consoling words strung together. Art was still on the floor, still blinking.

"Well?" Butch asked.

They all looked at him, the storm off horizon now but its aftereffects in their eyes. Cindy regarded him evenly and said, "I'm going with Mom. So's Dale." Which was silly. Wasn't she going to California?

"I'm going with Mom, too." Art.

"I'm going with dad," Butch announced.

Spontaneously. And insanely.

This had the same ground-zero blast effect as the divorce announcement, the three of them gaping like he'd completely lost his mind. Which he had.

Take it back, you idiot. Choose Mom.

She was violent but only in relation to dad. When dad was deployed to Florida during the Cuban Crisis or was at Ft. Eustis for three months of school, Mom had been vibrant and alive and actually fun. After the divorce came through, she'd be fun again.

But Butch couldn't leave dad feeling like no one loved him.

Cindy looked stricken. He stared at her, equally stricken. Who would he talk to now, make secret plans with, play Ken to her Barbie, plot Art's daily torment? He'd miss her. He loved her so. Mom and Art registered nothing, like they expected it. Someone had to sacrifice, and it was incumbent on the oldest son to step up.

Especially since he wasn't one of them.

Okay.

Butch headed to dad's room. It was dark and noiseless, and he half-feared dad was in there dead. Maybe he'd plunged the German sword through his heart, the golden lion on the hilt snarling while drinking the blood oozing from the wound. Or he'd used the whip to hang himself from the ceiling light and was spinning slowly in the wet breeze of the swamp cooler, whip handle slapping his popped-out tongue and eyes with each turn. Butch shuddered, steeled, and entered.

Dad was on the bed, facing away, quiet. He looked small and Butch flashed on *The Incredible Shrinking Man*, which had scared Butch silly until its astonishing and noble ending, the man contemplating an infinity of smallness he would forever roam.

Finding advantage in tragedy, how do you do that?

Couldn't, in this case, because dad's tragedy was self-made and he'd shrunk from sadness, not radioactivity. Butch, though, could help him regain size.

"I'm going with you," he said.

Dad said nothing, didn't even move. Maybe he was dead. No, Butch detected barely perceptible breathing—he was alive but paralyzed, unable to respond. A self-made coma.

"Pack," dad's graveyard voice whispered from the dark. "We're leaving tomorrow morning."

This could have been the killing blow, but you can't kill what's already dead. Except vampires. Butch stood a minute then went back to his bedroom, crawled between the sheets and lay there, fully awake, packing be durned.

31

The die was cast. He'd made his bed and was now lying in it. There were no 'tag tag no-take-backs.' This was his spilled milk over which he could not cry. Butch would be getting in a car early tomorrow morning with dad. No buffer, no protection. And they'd leave. Just leave. Into black lands of great terror and danger. Butch might never come back, and he would turn ten, then eleven, then thirty, alone. He looked at the blanket canyons where the wee beasties huddled and whispered.

"You guys aren't that scary anymore," he whispered back.

# CHAPTER 5

Sunrise, barely.

Butch struggled with the giant brown suitcase containing half his clothes and all his comics, none of which, by God, he was leaving behind for Art to mess up. Bleary-eyed and goofy, he'd hastily packed it after dad screamed at him to get up and get moving while Cindy asked stupid questions and said he better write. So he had to get a notebook and ask Mom for their address, and she got upset and went into the kitchen and Cindy began crying and dad had screamed for everyone to shut up. Butch didn't cry. It was all too weird for crying.

Still was. Dad smoked next to the back of the Rambler as Butch levered the suitcase through the wagon's gate. Thanks for the help, father of mine. The suitcase settled on three or four cases of C and K rations.

"What're those for?" Butch asked.

"We gotta eat something out there, don't we?"

Butch stared at them. Dad had maybe a thousand WW2-era cases stacked inside the storm shelter. Old, but still good. They ate them all the time, especially when the big storms roared down on Lawton, and the sirens wailed and lightning strobed as they ran, screaming, in their nightclothes across the yard to the colossal iron shelter door that dad held open while angrily waving them inside. The door crashed shut and they somehow scrambled down the steep, concrete steps without falling. Dad lit a kerosene lamp, fumes mixing with the horrible musty reek of underground cement, the light throwing shadows under the cots where wee

33

beasties including trolls and slugs and other subterranean horrors lived, and Butch knew, just knew, he would be eaten. But dad turned the radio on and Mom opened C-Rations and they listened to the weather while eating cold ham stew and beans and those really good round chocolate bars wrapped in aluminum. The cans even had cigarettes and matches, which dad took away, but he let them have the P38s, even though Butch still couldn't open a can with one.

After a while, it got downright pleasant. Sometimes he was disappointed when the all-clear sounded.

"We're eating those?"

"I thought you liked 'em."

"I do." But, hey, road trip, dad: McDonald's; the Colonel; the Drumstick down on Cash Boulevard with their super excellent hamburgers. C'mon!

"Then stop complaining. Not made of money, y'know."

Butch pressed his lips together. Great.

Mom and Cindy and Art stood beside the car, tallest to shortest like grim parade watchers. Butch regarded them suspiciously. This can't be real. Must be a joke Mom and dad were playing on them, or a lesson about taking things for granted. You love this house? You love this neighborhood and the kids and school and Oklahoma and winter blizzards and grasshoppers and dust storms, do you? Do you? How'd you feel if you lost it all? Lost Mom, your sisters, your brother... hmm, well, maybe not Art so much, but everyone else? Then, appreciate it!

He went cold inside. Please, God, let it be a lesson, let Mom and dad go "surprise!" and laugh and slap each other on the back because what a hilarious joke, no matter how many years it had taken off Butch's life, haha. I get it, good one, let me just fish the suitcase out and bump it back up the steps and into the bedroom and we'll all have breakfast and a good chuckle and I am not, absolutely not, going anywhere.

"We gotta go," dad grunted. "Say goodbye."

That startled him into full wakefulness and he panicked, staring at Cindy. She looked equally panicked.

What the heck? This was really happening? Really?

"Goodbye, I'll miss you," Cindy whispered and stooped and hugged him and stepped back and he was speechless because that was it.

Done. Over. Finished.

Tongue-tied, immobile, all he could do was look at her. She was neutral, no tears, no words, a strange light in her eyes. Art just frowned, baffled, as usual.

Mom pulled Butch in, her boobies smothering his vision and hearing, and he wriggled a bit to get away from them. She released him, a hurt look in her eyes.

No, Mom, it's not what you think. But how could he speak of boobies in front of everyone? He dropped his eyes in helpless shame.

"Be a good boy," she said and stepped back in line with Cindy and fished for a cigarette.

Mom, no, the beast is stealing me, rescue me.

He leaned forward in expectation, but she was rooted, frozen. Dad stood with his cigarette, looking off, not rooted, vibrating with his constant impatience, something always stirring beneath his surfaces. Look at him over there, so eager to be gone, drag the boy child off to lands unknown.

This was really happening.

This was really happening.

No lesson here: only dad taking him away.

Scream, Butch. Rip your suitcase out of the window and fling it into the street for later retrieval and run, hard and fast, behind the house and across the fence and down the alley and into the culvert and straight for the park where no one could follow and no one could find you except Tommy later, and you'll be safe.

But then dad would be alone, traveling with tearful eyes because his own son did not love him. No one loved him.

So unfair.

"I will," he said solemnly, looking at Mom while holding down the gigantic choking baseball that somehow got into his throat. He opened the heavy passenger door and slid in, pushing and pulling into position. Dad slammed the gate and got in opposite, wordless. He started the Rambler and the radio came on, hazy, crazy days of summer. Oh no. Butch wasn't getting a summer.

Help me.

They pulled away. There was no help.

He pressed against the window, watching them recede. Art was looking at Mom who was looking back at Art and, no doubt,

Mom would sweep him up for comfort because she always did, but never, ever the Adopted One.

Then explain yesterday, smart aleck.

I can't, I can't, I don't know what's going on.

Cindy stared after them. He didn't need to see her face because the grief was written in her stance and his heart snapped in half. They passed Tommy's house and Butch freaked because he hadn't told his best and only friend in the world that he was going... no time, no time... and Tommy would wake and look for him but he'd be gone, gone. The halves of his heart fragmented. He didn't know insides could hurt so much.

The curve took them out of view and they were at the Ft. Sill road now but dad turned right, away from the gate. Butch whirled in panic and found Carl's, sanctuary and repository of all things *Marvel*, and then a trick of the road blocked even that.

"Settle down," dad snarled and Butch froze then dropped hard and small into the seat. Dad had a twenty-foot wingspan and could reach anywhere in the car without taking his eyes off the road, raking faces with sulfur claws and leaving maggots to burrow gleefully into the skin and eat through to the brains while you screamed and screamed.

But he had to take one last look, just one, and he canted about, slow and careful.

Yes. There. Mt. Scott. Already receding.

Goodbye.

# CHAPTER 6

Butch stared out the window. Gulf stations loomed then evaporated, as did billboards advertising Sherer's and Howard Johnson's and the really tough Marlboro Man. A Burma Shave came up...

*Use This Cream*
*A Day Or Two*
*Then Don't Call Her*
*She'll Call You*
*Burma Shave*

...and Butch smiled. Good one. He hoped there'd be more. There weren't. Butch scanned ahead, leaning forward eagerly as a sign approached, hoping it was the little Coppertone girl and her exposed butt. Disturbing and wrong, but exciting...

Winstons. Nuts.

Country music played on the radio and Butch inwardly groaned. Sometime in the next hundred miles, they'd pull over for gas and Butch would fall out, crumpled and dried.

"What happened?" the horrified attendant would yell, scooping up Butch's parchment-like body, tongue lolling and eyes like raisins.

"Oh no!" dad would scream, slapping hands to head, "I killed him with country! Oh why, oh why didn't I tune in KOMA?"

Butch chuckled.

"What's funny?" dad asked.

Startled, Butch glanced at him. "Nothin'," he muttered, then hunched into his seat. Dad glared then turned back to the road, puffing hard on a Raleigh.

Whew.

"I fell in to a burnin' ring of fire," Johnny Cash sang and Butch hummed along. Good song, almost rock, so what was it doing on a country station? Maybe Cash didn't want to be a rock and roller, even though he sounded like one. Why not? Rock and rollers were madcap – Butch liked that word – while country singers were just mad.

Butch peered at dad covertly. Is that why he liked country? Couldn't tell, since dad gravitated to a lot of bumpkin stuff like "Blue Moon of Kentucky" and "Back in the Saddle Again" and "Walkin' the Floor Over You." You got the money, honey, I got the time... Dad sang that at the top of his voice, over and over. Or, "Goooooooodniiiiiight, Irene, goodnight!" in the hallway as they got ready for bed.

Jeez.

Dad always burst into one chorus or another of really stupid songs at absolutely the dumbest moments, like right in the middle of TV or while an actually good song was playing on the radio. "Mrs. Brown You've Got a Lovely Daughter" and dad's suddenly bellowing "Yer cheeeeeetin' haaaaart" while Butch and Cindy screamed "Dad!" because it was the Hermits, for God's sake! They never actually said 'God's sake' because that was suicidal, but they would try to reason with him:

"Dad! It's the Hermits! We can't hear!"

"What? Hermits? What are you listening to crabs for?"

"They're not crabs! They're English! Gawd!"

"English crabs? I didn't know English crabs sang!... will tell on yeeeeeeew... YOUR CHEATIN' HAAAAAAAAAAART..."

Oh, man.

Or worse, he'd yodel. Yodel! YoDe-LAYD-eHoo-Delayde hoooo-DEEEE-LAAAY-DEE-HEEEE-DELAY-DEEEE-HOOOOO... Gawd that was sooooo embarrassing. And dangerous. It signaled a mood swing, dad feeling combative and he'd reach out, teeth bared, dark light glowing his eyes, and twist a finger deep and hard into Butch's ribs while Butch yelled "Quit it!" and tried to get away. Dad'd twist harder and laugh, saying, "What? That doesn't hurt!" but oh yes it did and Butch'd struggle and dad'd get mad and start slapping and there Butch was, in the middle of a beating.

Look at him sitting there, face like stone. I am not safe.
I want to go home.

Home. "The Green Green Grass of Home." That was a good
country song, very sad, about a guy facing the electric chair. Who
sang that? Not Johnny Cash.

It's good to touch the green, green grass of home. Yeah. Like
the grass in the backyard, tarantulas running around throwing up
their front legs as Cha Cha pounced and battered them all over the
place, barking delightedly while Butch laughed and laughed.

On the back porch this morning, Cha Cha, black-and-white
head cocked, had a big smile on his face, tail wagging. What a
good dog. They'd had him since last summer when he'd nosed
under the fence and wiggled and crawled and whined so
pathetically that Cindy and Butch insisted on keeping him and
Mom got mad and dad pretended to be but said okay as long as the
dog slept outside. Cha Cha loved to grab hold of people and start
doing the cha-cha on their leg, hence the name. He tried to do that
this morning while Butch hugged him goodbye, one last dance for
old time's sake, but Butch pushed him off.

And now, poof, Cha Cha was gone, like his house and sister
and best friend and school and baseball team. Which was sort of
an upside. And, poof, he'd never see Jonny Quest again. Butch's
heart fell fifty stories and his breath caught.

Don't cry, don't, you'll get killed. Quick, on to something
else, another country song, yeah. Let's see…

Counting flowers on the wall, that don't bother me at all.
Good song, especially when the guy with the deep voice sang…
"Captain Kaahngaroo."

"What?" dad asked.

"Nothin'," Butch muttered again and sank lower.

Patsy Cline came on and dad hummed along. Crazy for
crying, crazy for trying… okay, fine, just please don't sing along.
Thank God there's no yodeling prompt in this song.

Patsy Cline and Hank Williams were dad's favorites, and
Butch gave him credit because he liked them, too. "Kaw Liga"
was the best Hank Williams song. Or was that George Jones?
Although, "I can't help it if I'm still in love with you," was a
contender. Dad recorded all his Patsy and Hank albums onto tapes
using his big German reel-to-reel tape deck, the microphone hung
in front of the Grundig's speakers while he played the albums on

the turntable and threatened dismemberment to anyone who made a peep within five square miles. He threw a shoe at Butch once when he'd raced in to grab soldiers for a big neighborhood war in Tommy's backyard. "Goddamit! How many times have I told you to shut up when I'm doing this?" and Butch tried to say he didn't know but dad got madder and ripped the needle across the record, probably scratching it, and Butch barely escaped with his life. Didn't get the soldiers, either.

He shuddered. Got caught in the sudden explosion.

Dad's rages were of two types: the aforementioned sudden explosion, bloody and overwhelming; or the overheating reactor, cooking and bubbling until critical mass. Couldn't do anything about the first, but the second could be diffused if recognized in time. Wouldn't necessarily stop the chain reaction but it could be delayed and, hopefully, explode on someone else. Dad was exhibiting reactor signs now. He'd been silent ever since they left about seven hours ago (or what felt like seven hours), his jaw tight and his eyes, sunken to begin with, had almost disappeared into the caverns of his eye sockets, so probably thinking about something that pissed him off.

'Piss,' the word that always got Butch into trouble. Criticality approached. Need cooling rods.

Roger Miller crooned "King of the Road," appropriate, and, also, opportunity. Butch liked Roger Miller. "Dang Me" and "Chug-a-Lug" always tickled him. The guy wasn't serious, like Bob Dylan or Gene Pitney, but he wrote good songs. And was a neutral topic.

"Dad?" Butch asked.

"What?"

"What's 'King of the Road' about?

"A hobo."

"Oh. I thought it was about a thief."

"Why'd you think that?"

"Because. The locks."

"You mean, 'Each lock that ain't locked when no one's aroooound... traaaailers for sale or rent...'"

Oh no, dad had picked up that part, enthusiastically supplementing Roger's nasal tone. Butch supposed, in the interest of survival, he could tolerate it.

What the heck, join him.

"No home, no car, no pets, I ain't got no cigarettes!" Butch trebled and, waddya know, they were singing together, dad intent on his driving and Butch intent on dad to see if the cooling rods worked, engineer's kids and rooms to let and, yes, each lock that wasn't locked. It didn't dawn on Butch until it was over and they both chuckled as a commercial for farm insurance took over that it was a lonely song. No home, no car, no pets.

That's me. I got the car, but little else.

Maybe dad realized the same thing, too, because they both lapsed into silence. Dad seemed awash in sadness, a gray thing on his heart like clouds that obscured the sun. But why? Dad had gotten away from Mom and the house and the Army and the stupid girls and stupid Art and all the things he hated, so he should be laughing and teasing and making Butch uncomfortable and wary because, when dad was having a good time, it could so easily turn into something else. But he wasn't. He just sat there, dark and brooding.

Odd.

Maybe because Butch was with him? Hmm. If dad hated them all, then Butch's decision to tag along was a serious error. Instead of making a clean getaway, dad was now stuck with Adopto-Boy and not free until he resolved this little problem. Dad's eyes sought a wooded trail or side road leading into the plains where he could turn off and, minutes later, be out of view of any witnesses or police and then...

Resolve this little problem.

Butch's eyes widened in terror. He peered ahead and saw a hundred, a thousand roads careening into Oklahoma scrub where he could be murdered and buried and forgotten, forever. Frank's mom had murdered him over a stupid report card. How much a better incentive was complete freedom? Dad was demon-plagued while beehived Mrs. Vaughn was beautiful, and if beautiful and beehived Mrs. Vaughn so easily murdered her son...

Butch swore the car drifted toward each marked and unmarked road that came up, as if gleefully asking dad, "This one?" or "How 'bout that one?" or the next one, any of them, perfect for strangling the little boy and throwing him to the ants. Let's try this one! Butch gathered breath to scream.

Wait.

You moron, you're forgetting something. Dad said "Choose,"

indicating he wanted someone to go with him, so dad was actually pleased with Butch, the one person in this whole world he could count on, not like those losers who stayed behind. Butch's scream dissolved into a stifled breath of relief. He wasn't going to end up like Frank Vaughn, a no-face shape under a bloody sheet, a pop-eyed ghost on a bleacher. At least not yet, especially with more distraction.

"Dad?"

"Yeah?"

"What are those numbers on the signs?"

"What signs?"

Butch pointed at a white marker that loomed and blurred and was gone, Doppler effect for the eyes. It had two sets of numbers, one framed in a shield, the other by itself. "Those."

"You don't know?" dad's undertone was one of ridicule and Butch's cheeks burned. Yeah, he knew they were route numbers but why were there two? That's the part he didn't get. "No," was all he said.

Dad smiled, the pleasure of humiliating others, and Butch consoled himself with the successful distraction of it. "Those numbers tell me what road we're on."

"So what road are we on?"

"What did the numbers say?"

"I don't know."

"What, you can't read numbers?" ridicule tone again.

"I can read numbers. I can read a lot of things."

"Bookworm," dad snorted derisively and Butch ground his teeth. Dad loved that word, using it at every given opportunity, like those times when he dragged Butch, so absorbed in something he was reading that he simply did not hear Mom call him for dinner, out of the bedroom. Or when Butch sat on the porch turning the pages of a Happy Hollister so fast—c'mon, c'mon, what's the reveal?—and dad, slap to the back of the head, "Bookworm! Finish the yard!" Art and Dale had taken it up and even Cindy from time to time.

What's the big deal? Why did everyone hate his reading?

"I'm not a bookworm." Sullen.

"Yes, you are," dad said with finality. "So, what road are we on?"

Butch blinked. Dad still wanted to do this? Okay. He leaned

forward, intent on the road and yes! There! A road sign! Go for it. "281?"

"That's right. This is Highway 281, which goes north to south. You can go to Chicago or San Antonio either way. You know where those are?"

Butch gave him a contemptuous look. Please. Butch knew all the state capitals and the times table to ten, even though he didn't really like doing the times tables, so what do you think? "Illinois and Texas." Butch was smug.

Dad's eyebrows went up. "So, you do know. I'll be damned. All right, smart boy, where's Trenton?"

"New Jersey. It's the capital."

"You know the capitals?"

"All of them."

"Let's hear it."

Butch took a big breath, "Montgomery Alabama, Phoenix Arizona, Little Rock Arkansas..." alphabetically, the way he had memorized them.

"Little Rock ain't the capital of Arkansas."

Huh? "Yes, it is."

"No, it ain't."

"Dad, it is, too."

"No, it ain't. Fayetteville is."

"Dad, it's Little Rock."

"Son, I'm tellin' you, it's not. It's Fayetteville."

Now Butch was mad. "Dad, it is too Little Rock." He'd gone through all the states with Mrs. Ward and could see in his mind, right now, the big Rand McNally pull-down map in the front of the classroom. So neat to grab the big hook on the bottom and it — schloomp — rolled up, so get the stick and hook it back down, but don't let the teacher catch you and there was pink colored Arkansas with a big black star next to Little Rock.

"It's Fayetteville." Dad groused. "What are they teaching you in that school?"

That's it. "It's LITTLE ROCK!" Butch shouted and leaned forward to get the emphasis right and screwed his eyes shut with the effort. There!

Uh-oh.

You just yelled at dad.

You idiot. You fool.

Going to die over the capital of Arkansas. There was something absurd about that, but then dying over a report card was just as absurd, wasn't it? He steeled himself for the coming blow.

Silence. It grew into a moment much longer than dad's fists usually accommodated, so Butch looked over. Dad glowered out the windshield, cigarette cocked at a mad angle. "All right!" he muttered, "It's Little Rock. Still think it's Fayetteville, though."

Butch's mouth dropped open. What? Had dad just... deferred to him? Think that's the right word. Must be a trick and Butch scrutinized dad's hands on the wheel but no, they were loose and dad looked calm, no storm clouds on the brow.

Well, all right.

Keep it going, Butchie old boy. "So why are there two numbers on the sign?"

"Huh? Oh. One's for the state, the other's for the county."

"The county?"

"You know what a county is?"

"Yep!" Another opportunity to shine. "We're in Comanche County."

"Not anymore. We're in Cotton County now."

"What?" Butch looked out the side window. It was the same scrub and flatness, punctuated by sudden woods and rivers, they'd passed ever since Lawton, so when did they exit Comanche? He sat back, feeling home dwindle.

Dad didn't notice. "There's only so many roads going through one area and the state and the county share them, so they put their different numbers on the signs. Here." Dad waved something under his nose: a map. "Find where we are," dad ordered.

'Harbor, Open 24 Hours' was printed on the front in script, which Butch wasn't that good at reading, but this was clear enough. He clumsily got the map apart and quickly located Lawton, his heart warming — home. The towns of Geronimo and Cache little dots on the outside and Mt. Scott marked and Ft. Sill. Hmm, Mt Scott looked far away on the map, yet he could see it clearly from the front yard. He looked for the front yard but Lawton was just a blob and he couldn't find Lincoln Avenue. Cache Road, yes and there, 281.

"Did you find it?"

"I think so."

"Good. We're about ten miles from Randlett. Find where we

are on the map."

Randlett, Randlett... Butch traced the yellow line marked '281' but it changed above Ft. Sill into two different roads. Really confusing. The 281 line went to Anadarko (neat name) and its offshoot, 277, swayed to the right toward Chickasha.

Hey look, there's Lake Ellsworth!

Dad had taken Butch and Art and Tommy camping there once, on some island smack in the middle of it. Butch had seen his first scorpion there. He'd been standing by the fire, and the scorpion emerged from the dark, coming right at him, mean look on its face and tail and claws up, ready to strike.

"Dad," he'd asked, watching its approach, "is that a scorpion?"

"Sure is," dad said and walked over and stepped on it. No more scorpion. Butch hardly slept that night. No one did, all of them cold and cramped and huddled together, uncomfortable in the bottom of the boat while swatting at a zillion mosquitoes. Scorpions, though, scary, evil looking scorpions, could be crushed underfoot. Reassuring.

"Well?"

He was past Anadarko and still no Randlett. The 281 split into something else at a town called Watonga, which looked like it was seven or eight hundred miles away from Lawton, at least on the map. Had they gone seven or eight hundred miles?

Dad's calloused finger suddenly stabbed right next to his own, startling him. "You're going the wrong way. We're going south. On a map, that's toward the bottom." The finger withdrew.

South? A warning bell rang in Butch's mind. He picked up 281 at the bottom of Lawton and traced it down the map to where it merged into both a bigger line and a red one, '281' and '277' printed inside a shield superimposed on the lines, and there were numbers inside circles on other roads and it was just too hard to figure out...

And then it wasn't. "I found it!" he said, tapping the map with his finger.

Dad looked over. "Yep!" He sounded pleased. "You did." He pointed a little above the dot marked 'Randlett.' "That's about where we are now."

Butch stared at the place where dad's finger had been. How neat to see where you are on a map. He looked at Lawton and measured the distance with his finger—a knuckle and a half away. He held his hand up to the windshield to see if it matched with the road, but no. The pull-down Rand McNally had a scale-of-miles to figure out distance and so did this map, in a square part called 'Legend.' What legend did they mean, Pecos Bill? Persephone? Why wasn't it called a 'Key,' like on the Rand McNally?

He measured his finger against the scale and then checked the distance to Lawton. Twenty, no, forty miles away. Forty miles? That's it? That's not far, not like the Rockies or Chicago or Antarctica, which were millions of miles away. Forty miles was actually walking distance. He stared hard at the pavement whizzing by. Pop the door, roll out, stand up, dust off and head back. Should take, what, an hour or so? Maybe longer—it usually took him fifteen minutes to reach Swinney from the house, which certainly wasn't forty miles; probably ten, so figure two hours, three. Doable.

He looked at the pavement again.

Hmm. Moving pretty fast. Better wait till we stop. Gonna have to gas up in Randlett, right? Maybe dad will look around and say, "Good enough, we're living here." I can walk to Lawton from time to time, visit everyone. Gee, if I had my bike, I could go every day!

Neat.

He sat back in a much better mood and grinned at the map. Just forty miles away, right there on the Red River across from Texas...

Texas.

Butch paled. The warning bell turned into a full-blown Chinese gong. "Dad?"

"What?"

"Where we going?"

"Pawpaw's."

Butch stopped breathing. He looked at the map and yes, the road crossed into Texas at Burkburnett and then on toward Wichita Falls where they always stopped for gas and food when they visited Pawpaw's.

In Big Salt.

Oh no.

# CHAPTER 7

They entered Big Salt from the tractor-store side, passed the Salt House—"Only house mada salt in aaaaall the US a A!" — and turned onto the main street. Butch hunkered down. He didn't want to be seen.

"Ain't thatya cousins?" dad asked.

Butch peeped at a bunch of kids in a distant field playing baseball. No doubt two or three cousins were mixed in there. Great. If dad stopped, Butch would have to get out and run across and join in and there he'd be, in a group of kids he didn't know being asked to play and proving, within seconds, he couldn't. He'd embarrass his cousins. Again.

Dad craned his neck but wasn't sure, so they kept going.

Whew.

They crossed the triple set of tracks, which was the only neat thing in town. Well, wait, the movie theater was neat and so was the drug store with its ice creams and candies, but the tracks were the best. How many times had Butch and his cousins salted the tracks with pennies and then paralleled a train, waved at the engineer who blasted the horn and waved back while the brakeman on the caboose steps threw Tootsie Rolls to them? Too many to count. They pried the pennies off the track for later flinging at each other like tiny discuses and readied for the next train. Asleep in Mawmaw's living room, blasted awake by the midnight trains roaring by, horns wailing, their lights whipped through the windows and ran across the walls fast and scary while Butch huddled under the blankets and shivered with delight.

Factor in the trains, Big Salt's not so bad.

Butch relaxed a bit and slid up. Admittedly, he'd had some pretty good times here. The cousins were actually fun, especially Rob, who was hilarious, and Belinda, blonde and willowy like Cindy and always game.

Yeah, not so bad.

But then they turned on the dirt road past the tracks and Mawmaw's house loomed and who was he kidding?

Dad slipped the Rambler up to the ramshackle fence and turned it off, the engine running on. Butch stared at the house. It was The Addam's Family and Munster Mansion combined, a sun-blistered hulk that reached up between giant chinaberry trees, girded by weather-beaten gray-and-brown clapboard, the surface scaled and dripping with lichens. It was single story but had walls so high it looked like two, crowned with a gangrenous, steeply gabled tin roof. The windows were dead eyes, peeling and warped; they looked at you hungrily. Things brooded inside. A plank porch ran around the entire house, the only worthwhile feature. Butch had a merry time racing around it at night, throwing chinaberries at his cousins.

Until the ogre, the monster inside, shuffled out and roared and grabbed kids and threw them into the brambles.

Pawpaw.

Dad sat quietly, his cigarette ash dangerously close to dropping. He looked mad. Butch wondered at that. Dad liked this place, judging by all the times he dragged them down here, the car jammed with suitcases and fussing kids playing "I Spy" and throwing things at each other while dad yelled for them to shut up and Mom shriveled in the front seat. He always postured here, stood in the yard like he was happy or proud while Butch and Cindy and Rob and Belinda screamed and laughed and ran one direction then stopped short and ran the other, silent and afraid because Pawpaw would suddenly appear.

"Cain't you keep them damn kids quiet?" Pawpaw snarled as Death Eye, a milk-solid white cue ball stuck in his head, gleamed and ran with strange fluids as it spun in rage. Don't get caught in Death Eye's gaze. On prompt, dad whipped off his belt and lashed as they fled. Maybe he was doing them a favor when he urged them away from Death Eye, but it never felt like it. It felt like joy, dad showing Pawpaw he, too, measured up as cruel and murderous and a crusher of families.

Chip off the old block.

Butch knew what that meant—Tommy's father said it when Tommy did something worthy. Tommy's mom said it, too, if the deed wasn't so worthy. Butch silently thanked God for his adoption: He'd never be a chip from this block.

Dad suddenly turned an upset face full on Butch. "You gonna sit there all day?"

Startled, Butch spazzed; his hand turned into a club as he reached for the door handle.

C'mon, get out!

Too late.

With an oath, dad moved straight through him, raked horn-like fingers across his stomach and crushed Butch's hand as he wrenched the door handle open. Butch yelped. Dad pushed hard with his elbow and Butch fell out and landed on a knee.

"Can't even open a damn simple door," dad muttered as he popped his own and yanked himself straight up as he leveraged an arm on top of the Rambler. Butch watched through the front seat for any menacing movement in his direction. But dad was focused on the house, confronting it.

Momentarily safe, Butch crouched near the tire, inventoried hurts, and decided the hand was worse than knee or stomach. He looked it over. It felt like his fingers hung on by little threads but he saw no blood or horribly angled bones. Dang; without clear evidence, he'd only get the "You big baby, shake it off!" response from any nearby adult.

"Y'all rite?"

Butch looked up. Mawmaw waited on the porch, hands on hip, schoolteacher glasses pointed at him, washed-out gray hair falling around her ears and her wrinkled and weary face. Kindness gleamed out of her dark, dark Choctaw eyes. She was full-blooded —or no, no, that's not right—she's half and Pawpaw was half, or something like that, which meant dad was half-Indian, or, no, wait, more than that, some odd percentage. Butch didn't grasp fractions and, anyway, had never got a straight story from anyone on exactly how much Indian blood of what tribe flowed through Deats' veins. Which meant not through his, one of the drawbacks of being adopted. At least he was German.

"He's fine," dad answered for Butch as he strode through the half-off rusty gate and up the dangerous steps. He kissed Mawmaw on the cheek and slapped her on the back before slamming through the screen door. Butch saw endurance in her eyes. She bore a lot, he knew.

"Well, c'mere, boy." She waved him in. "So I can look atcha." Butch shuffled up and Mawmaw pulled him in tight. The ever-present reek of chewing tobacco and cooking grease wafted from her gingham and Butch squirmed his nose away. He didn't like that smell, even if he liked Mawmaw.

She put him at arm's length. "You all right?" she asked again, but not about his ejection from the car, he knew. "Yes," he said and she nodded and pressed him again and he endured the reek by taking small breaths. "Lord, Lord," she whispered, "the trouble of it all."

Butch liked her tones of sorrow and reassurance. Odd how she mixed the two, but practice makes perfect, and Butch felt calmer. She was an ally.

"Well, c'mon in, I've got food." She pushed him toward the half-open door. Ugh, lunch at Mawmaw's: pinto and string beans and squirrel and cornbread, which was about the only thing on the list Butch could readily stomach.

Please have a lot of cornbread.

The screen door slapped them, and Butch stumbled over a rag rug carelessly tossed on the landing. Old yellow wallpaper drooped from the ceiling, drifting through layered spiderwebs where Daddy Long Legs massed and watched hungrily. Daddy Long Legs were all right, but not in packs. The floors were buckled and gray and Butch watched his step, afraid he would fall through. An old, yellow, unbalanced couch pressed against the far wall, flanking one side of the kitchen doorway, while Butch's favorite rocking chair, a green-upholstered wooden monstrosity, flanked the other. He yearned to rush over, plop down and get it going because it had great action and he could swing and sway while watching the little yellow square-box Philco, or read Mawmaw's True Romance magazines, his heart pounding strangely as frightened, scantily clad women who sat on beds stared helplessly at him, as if he were the menacing brute boyfriend. But Mawmaw ushered him past, darn it.

They stepped down to the kitchen. Dirty brown water roiled in a pot on the old gas stove. Pinto beans. 'Ugh' affirmed. A giant bowl of steaming greens waited on the mile-long metal kitchen table that stretched from the middle of the room to the smeary front windows blocked by stained paper pull-down shades. And a bowl of corn-on-the-cobs next to a lifesaving platter of cornbread...

...and, oh look! Sandwich meat! Whew.

Dad, already seated, looked down at the tabletop and frowned. He hadn't filled his plate yet, a bit unusual. Mawmaw had food cooking day and night and the first thing done on a visit was stuff your face. An empty plate insulted her and Butch had no intention of doing that.

So why was dad?

"Sit, you sit," she said, pushing Butch at a chair. He slid in opposite dad, wary, unable to read him, and he edged slightly out of slap range. Mawmaw lingered over the pot, muttering a few things that indicated the pintos weren't ready.

Good.

She went over to the washing machine, one of those old-fashioned wringer types. Butch watched as she poked around inside the open tub and pulled something out. She put an end of the something between the two rolls and ran the handle around and it pulled through, water sluicing back into the tub. She snapped the something, a dishtowel, and hung it from a small wire suspended above the machine.

Fascinating.

"Eat your lunch," dad snarled.

Startled, Butch hastily pulled the corncob bowl over and put two on his plate. Fill up on edible things before the pintos arrived; that way he could wave off more than a spoonful.

"What you being such a hog for?" dad growled and Butch's face burned. He looked at the cobs guiltily and moved to replace one.

"Oh, let the boy alone, Owen." Mawmaw appeared next to the table with pintos and Butch watched in horror as she spooned way too many on his plate. "I got plenty of corn. We're having a good crop."

Butch stared as the brown mush enveloped his cobs. He was grateful for her intervention but, oh man. How was he going to extricate the cobs? He felt sick, and also felt dad's growing attention. Had to do something. He carefully picked up a cob, letting as much pinto as possible drip off before buttering it. Maybe he could smother the taste.

The back screen door slammed and Butch glimpsed a whirl of brown and plaid and jeans that resolved itself into a panting Rob, framed in the Passage of Death. "Hey!" he screamed, waving frantically at Butch. Rob screamed everything.

"Boy!" Mawmaw said disapprovingly and dad looked over, equally disapproving, but Butch's hopes soared. Rob vibrated, half here and half already gone, beckoning, desperate to be off.

Go for it.

Butch slipped off the chair and was already around the table before dad yelled, "Hey!" but Mawmaw, bless her, said, "Just let them go," pardon from the governor. Butch cleared the three downward steps into the Passage of Death, catching Rob's blur against the distant sunlit screen door, the only Safe Way Out. This was Pawpaw's bedroom and the dust and tobacco smell assailed Butch, forcing a sneeze. Pawpaw's murderous iron bed was on the left and he glanced at it fearfully, but Pawpaw wasn't lying there, Death Eye leaking toward the ceiling, the old man and his Eye brooding and dangerous and ready to grab any kid who got a little too close. An open chest of drawers and about two thousand cardboard boxes holding all manner of mildewy clothes stood scattered and chaotic on the right side of the room. The Passage bisected the bed-and-boxes gauntlet. Things could grab you from either side, so Butch ran.

He launched directly from the stepless doorway onto the grass and stood uncertain, dazzled. The sun gathered on the tin roof of the gray, gapped, and weather-beaten shed to his right and threw beams at him like Cyclops but of heat, not force, and he gasped. An old rusted tractor, the kind they used in the thirties, sat in knee-high weeds under an overhang of the shed, the one-hinged door beside it half open, the entrance shadowed, lifeless. Butch stared, holding his breath. Inside, among the dust and dimness, were rows of rusty cans overflowing with nails and screws, interspersed with equally rusty jars of Mawmaw's cannings, all haphazard on roughened wooden shelves overlooking roughened wooden tables, inexpertly made. A haven of wasps and heat and snakes. And Death Eye.

"C'mon!" he heard in the distance and triangulated on Rob's blur fading toward Big Salt. "Wait up!" he yelled and was through the overgrown gate, past the garden where shoulder-high corn stood neatly in three rows. He saw Rob hit the paved road and cut up toward town.

Butch beelined straight across the dirt road and up the berm, panted his way through the scrub and leaped across the ditch, landing hard and caving the side a bit. He scrambled to the first set of tracks and took a quick glance for a moving train but there was only an abandoned freight car sitting dangerously to the right so he picked up speed and cleared the bed to parallel Rob, who zipped past the crossing gate at the second tracks. Butch hit those about the same time and had a few feet on Rob when they both reached the big tracks, where Butch slowed to make sure there were no trains.

A couple of overall'd workers in straw hats looked up from digging something down near the tin-sided depot. "Git off thar, you stupid kid!" they yelled and Butch pushed harder, looking back to see if they pursued.

Nope.

He stumbled over the last rail, which actually helped him slide down the berm, and busted through the weeds, picking up a good collection of burrs on the way. "Got any money?" Rob yelled at him from the corner of the dark-brown railroad building a block away. In one motion, Butch wiped the sweat off his brow and patted his pocket, confirming dimes and nickels and pennies. "Yup!" he called. Rob bolted toward the drug store and Butch slowed to a walk, taking a breath and getting there about a minute later.

Now that was fun. Big Salt's not so bad, is it? Grinning, Butch pushed inside.

Rob already had RC Colas and Debbie Cakes and Bazooka Joes lined up on the counter and was racing back for more. "I don't think I got that much," Butch said, worried they'd be arrested. Rob patted his own pocket and Butch heard coins jingling.

Okay.

"Well, boys!" The big storeowner was behind the counter. "Now ain't this a fine day to be running around? 'Course it is, 'course it is." He swept a meaty hand at the loot near the cash register. "Now y'all just get what you need." He swept the same meaty hand at Butch, urging him on, a big smile on his balloon-head face wobbling over a wonderfully constructed beer gut. Butch, still grinning, ran down the aisle to the freezer. Rob was buried halfway inside.

"Don't we have enough?" Butch asked.

"I want a Push-Up." Rob's muffled voice came from deep inside the smoking, ice-covered interior.

A Push-Up! Yeah!

"Let me get it." Butch pulled Rob, squalling, out of the way, but, c'mon, I've got at least a foot's reach on you. He shoved into Antarctica, pushing around Fudge Bars and Eskimo Pies but pausing at the ice cream bars because he liked the chocolate dip more than the vanilla it covered.

"Push-Ups!" Rob insisted.

All right, all right.

Butch located two and Rob yanked them out of his hand and was already bouncing around the register when Butch finally got out of the freezer.

They were three cents short and Rob's face fell into pre-prepared cry lines. Rob could cry on command, quite the talent, but it wasn't going to help them here. Butch shook his head and started calculating what to put back. Probably didn't need the Bazooka Joes but that still left them a penny short, so something big had to go, a soda or a Debbie Cake. Not the Push-Ups. Vital.

The storeowner hovered, face reflecting Rob's grief. Suddenly the meaty hand was back, waving a magical pass over the loot as he swept it all into a bag. "Boys," he said, "get me next time, h'yeah?"

Rob looked at him in astonishment and, with no further prompt, grabbed the bag and was out the door with a, "Thanks, Mr. Randall!" trailing.

"Thanks," Butch echoed up the stomach to the balloon head, "Really, thanks a lot. We'll pay you back."

Meaty hand never stopped waving. "I know you will, son. I know your dad. Now you better go catch that little heathen before he eats it all hisself," said with another magic pass at the door. Balloon head all puffed and smiling and happy that boys spent their little cash and boy-moments with him, and Butch gave him an appreciative smile as he stepped out, sweeping the street and picking up Rob's shirttail flying around the corner near the tracks.

"No, you don't!" he called, bolting after him.

# CHAPTER 8

He caught up at the main tracks and they balanced on the rails, checking for trains, evading a couple of pickup trucks at the next crossing and, suddenly out of town among the cottonwoods and chokecherries that grew on either side of the berm. Rob handed him a Push-Up and Butch pulled off the cover, licking the orange cream that stuck to the underside and then holding it, not sure what to do. Suzy Spotless said every litter bit hurt, and Butch agreed. Take a look at all the crap and papers and cans lying along the tracks, for example. Butch folded the sticky cover and put it in his pocket. Rob dropped his on the cross tie, but Butch didn't say anything.

The sun was a lava sledgehammer wielded by some malicious fire spirit, hard and hot on their heads and shoulders, wham wham wham! The air wavered as it rose, shimmering the view and making the distant track slide to the right then left, a bridge to somewhere else. They could walk right out of this world and into one filled with fairies and witches and the gods of Greece, lost forever, prey to unspeakable things. He glanced back to make sure the town was still there.

"Watch for snakes," Rob said and Butch returned to this world in a hurry. He scrutinized the track and berm. You couldn't be too careful.

The ice cream slid down his throat—Freezehead!—and he gasped, opening his mouth to relieve the sudden pain. Rob giggled because it was happening to him, too, and they tried to outdo each other with cries of pain and dramatic clutchings at their temples until the ice cream was gone and their stomachs were cool and separate from the hot air smothering them.

Rob handed him an RC Cola and a P-38 but Butch, still baffled, wordlessly handed everything back and watched as Rob snipped off the cap in about a half second. He was embarrassed, but Rob just grinned and took a giant swig. "Payment," Rob said and Butch snorted, but it was a fair exchange. He took his own swig.

Peanuts. We should have gotten peanuts to pour into the sodas.

Dang.

"So your parents are splittin' up?" Rob suddenly asked after tipping back half his own bottle.

Butch stared at him. "How'd you know that?"

Rob shrugged, "Everyone does. It's all they been talkin' 'bout. So why they gettin' divorced?"

Great. The hundreds of uncles and aunts and cousins who populated this town were now discussing dad and Mom. Butch wondered how many times he would have to answer this question. Like he could. "Dunno. Guess something happened."

"Like what?"

"Dunno."

"Your dad have a girlfriend?"

"Huh?" That caught him off guard. "Well, yeah. Mom."

Rob laughed, "No, stupid. I don't mean your mom, I mean another girl. Besides your mom."

The concept so astonished Butch he forgot to reply with the required, "No, you're stupid," which meant Rob was ahead. "Well, no!" he snorted, using the boy-are-you-stupid voice, which put them even.

"You sure? That's why they all get divorced." Rob, suddenly fascinated by something glowing in the sunlight on the side of the track, raced ahead, careful not to slosh his RC. Turned out to be a bottle cap, which he kicked.

"What are you talking about?" Butch asked as he caught up.

"That's what happened to Carl's parents last year, 'member? Uncle Stone ended up marrying the girl and then divorced her six months later. Now he wants to marry Carl's mom again, but she's got this rodeo guy for a boyfriend. You know they had a fistfight?"

"No."

"Yeah. Uncle Stone got a big black eye out of it."

Butch blinked. Wow.

Rob scuffed at something buried by a crosstie. "They all divorce and marry each other," he said quietly.

True. Each time Butch came here, the blood uncles and aunts had new partners, often making interchanges among themselves. It was impossible to keep track of who was married to whom. There were always a couple of new faces and new stories, such as Uncle Stone and the buckaroo. One summer, all the aunts sat around Mawmaw's table talking in hushed and urgent tones about a recently dead aunt who was, they asserted, poisoned by her new doctor-husband over some kind of insurance policy and "nobody did nothin' 'bout it!" They were outraged and Butch felt their frustration, but when you switch out spouses annually, you're bound to pick up a creep or two.

But that's just them. Dad and Mom had been together as long as Butch could remember, so those customs didn't apply. "He doesn't have a girlfriend."

"Then why they gettin' divorced?"

Back to that, and Butch didn't have an answer. "I don't know. I guess..." He felt suddenly helpless.

"What?"

"I guess they're just tired of each other."

Rob snorted, "That ain't no reason."

"Why not?"

"All of 'em are tired of each other. My mom and dad are tired of each other, but they ain't gettin' divorced."

"How do you know?"

"C'mon! I know. That's stupid."

"You're stupid."

"No, you are."

And they were off. There was no way Butch was going to be stupid, so he kept it up and they were in round five, growing more and more irritated with each other, when Rob suddenly stopped. Butch almost whooped in triumph, but Rob hadn't quit; instead, he stared down the track. Butch followed his gaze and saw a blurry figure in the distance. Rob squinted then broke into a broad smile. "Hey!" he yelled, rivaling any train whistle, waving a frantic arm as he pounded down the track.

"Who is it?" Butch called

"Belinda!" Rob gleefully called back and accelerated.

Butch's heart fluttered a bit. He peered at the blur, which had stopped and waved and then trotted up to meet them, moving like water in the heat. He made her out now, thin and tall and tomboyish in her dungarees and plaid shirt, long blonde hair flowing behind, squished freckly face, big smile. His heart fluttered a bit more.

"Well, hey!" Her voice was a bell. She made two words out of 'hey' like everyone down here, but, from her, it was a song. "When'd you get here?"

"Uh, I think... dunno, maybe an hour ago?" Butch looked away, embarrassed he sounded so stupid.

Rob must have won.

"Watcha doin'?" Rob asked her as he fished around in the sack to give her a Bazooka Joe while he polished off the rest of the RC, everything in one motion, then flinging the bottle over the berm, end over crystal-flashing end.

"Jus' walkin'," she said casually and took the Joe, popping the gum elegantly in her mouth. She read the little comic strip and chuckled and passed it around. Mort was late for class because he obeyed the traffic sign: Slow School Zone. Corny. Butch chuckled, too. The fortune read "Avoid evil companions. You will find it hard to get out."

Hmm.

"You all right?" Belinda asked him as they all three turned back to town.

"Yeah. I guess you know, too, huh?"

"Um-hm." She nodded.

"Told him everyone knew." Rob danced on the crossties, jumping from one to the next.

Butch made a dismissive lip smack then glanced at Belinda. She did not sweat — she glowed. Butch suddenly felt sticky and malodorous and moved a bit away so she wouldn't catch a whiff of his BO. The comic advertised a birthstone pendant for 150 wrappers. He wondered how it would look around her neck.

"So you gonna live here now?" she asked.

Butch's eyebrows rose. Live here? He hadn't considered that. Was that dad's intent? "I don't know."

"It'd be nice. You know a lot of people already."

"Yeah, but..."

Belinda, the people here scare me to death. They're rough and country and given to things I'm bad at, like fighting and tackle football and marathon baseball games and hunting and fishing, too, although I like fishing. I'd look stupid and spastic over and over and get beaten up and laughed at and dad would be shamed and slap me around. I'd be alone, an outcast, not blood, which explains why I can't run as fast or hit as hard or join as easily in the cruelties they preferred.

Worse, they knew things he didn't, narrowed-eye stuff, the knowledge of it putting an edge to their laughter and a deeper meaning in their sneers. And they knew he didn't know and howled their ridicule in country tones while pointing fingers at his furrowed brow and absolutely would not tell him what was going on. It made him feel lesser.

How could he explain that?

"It's awright." Her hand went to his shoulder, and he was stunned by its soft, caring feel. He blinked at her.

Could she read his mind?

"Hey!" Rob, always at full volume. "Everyone's here!"

They had reached the crossing guards and could see Mawmaw's house clearly. Hundreds of pickups, with an aberrant sedan or two, were squeezed together out front and jutted halfway in the road with no order or reason, enfilading the Rambler.

Rob bolted, dodged a tractor negotiating the tracks and getting a fist-shaking from the guy driving. "C'mon!" he yelled over his shoulder, a blur aiming for Mawmaw's. There was something contagious about a race and Butch and Belinda looked at each other and were off, similarly evading cars and yells, leaping tracks and scrambling over berms and ditches, gasping laughs at each other, drunk with the joy of it. She pulled ahead, coltish legs stretching and he didn't care, just didn't care about the heat and the rough ground and the sweat and losing because it was good, so very good.

They pounded up the porch, she a good stride ahead and anyone watching would razz him about losing to a girl but no one was out here, Rob's entry still evident by the bouncing screen door. Belinda paused, her chest heaving and her cheeks rose-red, and she looked at him and smiled, but it wasn't one of "ha, I beat you!" It was a different smile altogether. She held his eyes for a moment too long and something thrilled in him, something he couldn't define. She opened the door and slipped inside. It took him a few moments to follow.

# CHAPTER 9

Relatives by the score filled the kitchen, their cigarette smoke fogging the room. Mawmaw fussed at Uncle Anchor, who, apparently, had just smacked Rob over the way he'd flown in, setting up a three-way squalling match with Rob outdoing them all. Belinda stood near the icebox, watching and frowning, staying out of reach.

Dad sat in the same place as lunch, clutching a big glass of Mawmaw's syrupy sweet ice tea, his cigarette at attack angle. Uncles and aunts arrayed about him in a perfect mix of boy girl, boy girl, all their eyes hooded and dark, glared at him. Storm clouds hovered, dad its vortex. Butch took a step back.

Mawmaw tugged at Rob, now flat-out crying. He tore away and flew down the Passage of Death. Microseconds later, the screen door slammed and Uncle Anchor yelled, "Boy! I'm gonna skin you for that when we get home!" He would. All the uncles and aunts delighted in skinning their offspring.

"You're just makin' things worse," Mawmaw said but the expression on her face wasn't about Anchor and Rob, it was about the table war.

"Stay out of it, Maw," Anchor growled, his face dark and stormy, like dad's.

Mawmaw peered down the Passage. Watching after Rob, Butch supposed. He looked at Belinda, who had pushed her hair back and studied something in the sink. She'd run away, too.

Anchor and Uncle Stone sat directly across from dad, staring at him, both flanking Aunt Garnett, who stared in another direction. The others took lines of sight away from dad, their faces piercing and murderous. Everything said before Butch came in hung in the air, a cryptogram of bloody and violent words dissolving in the smoke. It took him a moment to decipher: the relatives were mad about the divorce.

Which was surprising. Butch thought they'd slap dad on the back and say you're better off now, Owen, stay here and we'll have a good ole time. Don't worry 'bout Adopto-Boy over there, he'll be fine, just fine. Why, we might even toughen him up a bit, make him more of a Deats. Butch saw their faces elongate and their tiny eyes get even tinier while serrated teeth, too much for their mouths, gleamed and spilled out of their cheeks and lips. He gasped.

Big mistake.

All the angled eyes suddenly had a focus: his chest. Aim points. Butch almost fell over from the force of their malevolence. Belinda looked at him fearfully.

"Whadyu doan in hyeah, boy?" Aunt Garnett, her face turned down so fiercely that Butch thought it would turn inside out.

"You kids shouldn't be in this kitchen a'tall," Aunt Crystal—younger, but as acidic as the elders—chimed in, "You shouldn't be hyeah t'all."

General grumbling erupted around the table and Butch swore their faces really did elongate. He stepped back but miscalculated and went smack against the jamb. Trapped. The pack leaned forward, licking their chops.

"Leave the boy alone," dad said quietly but with a sense of menace underneath it so threatening that it startled everyone, especially Butch. The pack returned to him, except for Stone and Anchor who had never moved off dad to begin with, the challenge in their eyes deepening. Dad accepted and his own rage threw a deeper challenge back and the heat rose, and Butch knew they were going at each other across the table any second.

"Stop it!" Mawmaw's voice cut like a whip through the thickening, ugly thing. "Now you all just stop it right now!"

She was a tiny tornado, no longer frail and helpless. "Butch, Belinda." Mawmaw looked at them both. "You go outside right now. Right now." She waved them toward the Passage.

Mawmaw's words threw the mob into some confusion, presenting opportunity. Belinda tilted her head to the door and slipped around Mawmaw, who stood as their shield. Butch slid after, keeping as much distance from the table as he could. The aunts looked at him with want, a terrible want: tear the child apart and drink its blood in honor of their unholy master. The uncles resumed their murderous dad watch.

Butch ran.

Using speed to thwart Passage Dwellers, he hit the screen door as hard as Rob, flying into the yard. Three aunts and uncles roared out another promise of skinning and he looked back nervously to see if they pursued.

No. Whew.

Belinda stood there, stricken, pale. Butch walked up to her. "What was that about?" he asked.

"You," she breathed.

Like a baseball bat across the face. "Huh?"

She shook her head. "They was arguin' about you, said Uncle Owen shouldna brought you, shoulda left you." She looked down at him, a light in her eyes, concern, or maybe... fear? "Said it was all your fault."

"Whaaaatt?" he rocked back, another bat blow. "My fault? How is this my fault?"

"I don't know."

"But..." Pearl Harbored. Juggernaut smashing down the Professor's wall. "I didn't do anything!"

He could imagine how he looked, mouth wide open, teary, protest on his face. And how she actually looked—unsure.

"I didn't do anything!" he repeated, beset by that very familiar, very present sense of injustice, of a world that turned on him for reasons he could not fathom. People laughing at him inexplicably, like one summer, the boy at the lake who mocked Butch's walk, or Leslie and Harry getting up from the ground to de-pants him while the girls on the playground sneered and catcalled as he fled. What? Why?

"I didn't do anything," a whisper now, the misery shutting off his voice.

Belinda's mouth was set in the Deats' line of disapproval. She blinked slowly, considering. "It's okay," she said, finally, "They're always fussing about something." And she placed that compassionate hand on his shoulder again, priest touching the leper. Butch could have showered it with kisses but she'd punch him in the mouth, so he silently reveled in the disturbance of her touch.

"Let's go find Rob," she said, turning that laying-on-of-hands into a friendly pat, a diminishing Butch suddenly didn't like, and walked toward the big shed.

Butch followed, unsure. The aunts and uncles had made him something unholy, take out your crosses and throw them at the vampire. Belinda was listening to them, but at least she had not staked his heart and burned his coffin; perhaps willing, instead, to leave her garden window open at midnight. For a moment, he enjoyed a thrilling image of Belinda lying in her bed, filmy negligee silvered by moonlight, her head turned, freckled neck exposed, vulnerable. His stomach twisted.

They both stood in front of the weeded-over tractor, trying to see into the murk beyond. Sometimes Rob would burrow in there. Butch hesitated. Creepy-crawlies infested the place and he didn't much feel like encountering one, except maybe a grasshopper—they were neat. They spat tobacco juice when grabbed. Or, tie a string to a leg and they would hop like crazy until the leg came off.

Might be worth a look.

But there was no disturbance in the weeds betraying passage, so Rob had gone somewhere else. Belinda frowned and swept a glance past the shed to the big silver propane tank planted against the garden's back fence. It looked like a submarine and became a prop for games of U-Boat or Prince Namor or anything else water related until a passing adult yelled, "Git off'n thar, you'll blow the place up!" something that had never happened the bazillion times or more they'd jumped on it. Rob wasn't on top, so Butch peered down the dirt road running past the ramshackle two-story house next door. Quicksand lay that way and Butch wondered if Rob had blindly stumbled into it, screaming for help as he was sucked down like a safari porter in a Tarzan movie. He shuddered and looked around for a rope or branch or something to pull Rob out.

A couple of black kids carrying cane poles walked up the dirt road, staring at Belinda and him. Butch waved tentatively. The kids looked at each other then back at him, frowned, fixed on the road and kept walking. Butch was disappointed. He wanted to tell them he didn't think black people were dirty and stupid, like dad said. But maybe they'd had experience with Pawpaw.

Last summer, he sat with Pawpaw watching the Democrat convention on television. Four or five black men and women stood in the front row dressed in prisoner stripes and held signs promoting Johnson. Johnson might even have been speaking, he wasn't sure. Butch didn't understand why they were dressed that way, thought it was odd they'd let prisoners into the audience. "I'm for Johnson, too," he said, proudly, to Pawpaw.

"All the jungle bunnies are for Johnson," Pawpaw spat bitterly. "Is that what you are?" Butch slunk out of the room and avoided Pawpaw the rest of the day. He didn't want to be called that.

He wished he could tell the black kids he wasn't like Pawpaw.

Belinda didn't even see them but pushed through the half-hinged shed door and slipped inside. Butch followed. Had to be careful in here. Mawmaw's squashes and jellies and chow chows were precariously jammed together on the wooden shelves.

Ugh.

Mom and dad put up cans, too, mostly jelly, taking grapes from the vines that covered the backyard arbor. Dad was always yelling and hitting while they boiled the grapes and drew off the skins and poured the jelly. Butch wondered why they even bothered. No one ate the jelly; it was too watery and sour, and all watery food was yucky and dangerous. He stared at a jar of yellow sludge, Mawmaw's corn mush.

Poison.

The shed "L-d" to the right and Belinda stepped around, Butch dogging, and almost knocked her over when she stopped short. She glared him off. "Sorry," he mumbled, not sorry at all because of the unexpected contact with her butt, quite thrilling, but wrong, very wrong. He stepped back and saw Rob sitting on the floor against another shelf of cannings, the dusty sunlight from a fly-flecked window highlighting his red face, streamy eyes, and shed-grimed clothes.

"Go 'way," he muttered, hiding his face.

Butch felt sympathy. Dangerous to let someone in this family see you cry. "I'll-give-you-something-to-cry-about!" then wham! slap, or even a whipping.

Jeez.

Belinda slid down the wall, sitting next to Rob. She reached out to hold him.

"Stop it! Whadya doin'?" Rob shouted and pushed her, which Butch thought was crazy. He'd let Belinda put her arms around him.

Belinda fell to the side, trying to regain balance, and Butch leaned forward to help. His fingers brushed a jar and it wobbled and he watched in helpless terror as it spun and fell. Puloink! It broke wetly and the smell of chutney, sharp and sweet, filled the air as the gunk spread across the floor.

"Dang it!" Belinda muttered and swiped at the sauce that had splashed across her shirt.

"Now look what you done!" Rob threw a hand at the mess, the tears still in his voice.

"Me?" Butch pointed an accusatory finger at Rob. "You made me!"

Blame him, Belinda. He pushed you.

"I didn't make you! You're just stupid!" Rob was now full-on angry.

"Am not!" and he made a useless hand motion at Belinda to help her blot the sauce. She waved him away irritably and pulled out the tail of her shirt, spat on it and rubbed at the stains.

Butch saw her stomach. He gulped.

"Well, lookee, lookee here," someone chortled from behind.

Butch whirled.

Oh no.

Cousin Carl. And Cousin Ricky.

# CHAPTER 10

Carl stood at the turn, arms crossed. Ricky's pig head bobbed up and down at Carl's shoulder, grinning evilly.

Carl was all Deats, especially in the small slits for eyes, but with a more open face accentuated by a tan and smoother features than usually found in the species. Handsome, Bobby-Rydell handsome, his smile melted hearts for three counties around. But it was a viper's smile and trouble hovered about him, whispers of ruined girls and stolen trucks, nights in jail. Rawboned and furious, his arms corded and strong, Carl gave Butch Indian burns and Wet Willies as Pigface Ricky held him down, chortling and snorting. Carl was a mean, stupid bully.

And he had them all trapped.

"Why, Ricky," Carl spoke over his shoulder to Pigface, "I believe we've got some kids playing where they ain't s'posed to."

"Why, I 'spect you're right!" Pigface laughed in his high whiny voice, drawing out the syllables longer than normal. According to Rob, Pigface was retarded.

"And what's this?" Carl knelt down and picked at some broken glass near his feet. "Oh, I don't believe it, Ricky, these dumb kids done broke Mawmaw's prize chutney jar. Ain't she gonna be upset?"

"She shore is, she shore is!" Pigface's head bobbed up and down with enthusiasm, his fat body perfectly framing Carl's more dangerous one.

Carl stood up, holding one of the pieces of glass. "Now," he sounded calm, but Butch could hear the joy in his voice, "which one of you twerps did this?" He bounced the piece of glass like a knife.

Butch was in Carl's reach with no place to run. He looked around helplessly. Rob squatted, narrow and angry. He hated Carl and Pigface more than Butch did, having to deal with them every day while Butch only had these intermittent episodes. So what better way to deflect the coming fury than by telling on Butch? He would certainly tattle on Rob if the situation were reversed. Maybe he could diffuse the blame by telling them about the push. Butch took in a breath to prepare, but Rob said nothing.

Belinda sat quietly, her shirt still out, the chutney stain an accusation. All she had to do was point a finger and then Carl would drive the piece of glass deep into Butch's eye, pull out his brain, and eat it. But she also said nothing, calmly looked at Carl. With her stomach still showing.

Butch couldn't help staring.

Carl stared, too, and so did Pigface. It looked funny, the three of them standing there mesmerized by Belinda's navel. But it wasn't funny, it was wrong, and a wave of guilt ran through Butch and he shuffled and looked away. Belinda glanced at him, a tiny smile on her face and something odd in her eyes.

Carl stirred with a danger that made Butch step back, alarmed. But Carl was fixed solely on Belinda, the glass shard still active in his hand. A different purpose worked his face, a strange softness around his eyes that made Butch blink. Not the murder of a few moments ago but still something violent. Pigface hovered, an evil grin splitting his cheeks almost in half, eyes throwing off black sparks.

Belinda didn't move, didn't cover up, left herself open. A charge kindled the air, the moment before thunder breaks. Butch stared at her, wondering what had changed.

"I think you boys better leave," Carl said, low and husky. The sniggering thing that smelled of bathrooms, of alleys, of shacks at midnight was in here now, Pigface's leer painted with it. This was bad, very bad and Butch was suddenly afraid, knowing that if he ran, like he so desperately wanted to, there would be tragedy, and, if he didn't, Carl would eat his brains. He didn't know what to do.

"No," Rob said quietly.

Everyone turned toward him, all surprised except Belinda, who almost looked uninterested, regarding Rob with a mild gaze.

"Whadju say?" Carl glared, the menace back in his voice, shoulders returning to belligerence and assault.

Rob stood, fists tight, a wild light in his eyes, confrontational and ready for war. "I said 'no.' You leave!" he snarled.

Butch gasped. Rob had crazed fits of temper that came on like a storm, usually at the quietest moments like when they were walking down the tracks or pulling chinaberries off the trees. This looked like one of those.

"Boy, you crazy?" Carl stood as tall as possible, face red, fists tighter than Rob's and the cords on his forearms rippling. But he held back. He'd seen Rob's frenzy before and was wary.

"I said 'Leave!'" Rob suddenly screamed and swept a big jar of green beans off the shelf and cocked it back, velocity and murderous intent clear to all. Butch flattened against the shelves to lessen any effects of bad aim while Carl instinctively threw up protective arms. Pigface gaped, reactions too slow, so would get the brunt of a 60 mph jar.

"Stop it," Belinda said.

Everyone froze and looked at her. A beam of light had fallen on her face. Butch caught his breath because she looked so beautiful, a girl who would never be beautiful except in moments like this, calm, luminous.

"It's okay," she said to Rob, soothing the angered beast. "Put it back. Go ahead, put it back," and she waved a hand at the shelf.

Rob hesitated, the war in him seeking expression, but her voice healed and he looked at the jar and looked at her and then, slowly, returned it. The frenzy dissipated, heat waves came off his head, and Rob visibly slumped, pulled into himself, beaten.

"Go on now," Belinda urged, "Go on. You two go on. I'll be all right." Soft, a gentle stroke of the cheek, and Carl started, electrified. Butch flinched, expecting Carl's calloused hand to wrap around his neck, but the big jerk stepped toward Belinda, instead, a dog wriggling by the dinner table.

"Yeah, she'll be all right," he grinned but his tone otherwise, and even Butch was stirred enough to push off the shelves, without knocking anything over, thank God, and turn toward him, fists clenched. Rob's hand grasped the jar again and Carl's look darkened, ready.

"No," Belinda said, defusing them again, "It'll be okay. Ain't no need to start something. You two go outside and I'll find you," and she nodded toward the L, pushing them with her eyes. Butch looked at Rob, who turned the jar in his hand, undecided, tight and angry, and fixed on Belinda. She nodded again and he returned the jar and stamped past Carl, shoving him a bit as he did, and disappeared around the L.

They all focused on Butch: Carl still dark, Pigface confused but predatory, and Belinda, well, hard to say. There was an urge on her face and it wasn't for him.

Because he didn't measure up.

Like at baseball practice, after flubbing so many balls no one threw to him anymore, or when the kids on the playground ran away from him, or Tommy said he was a baby and went over to Chuckie's alone. What was going on between Belinda and Carl was ugly and wrong and thrilling and, definitely, not for him.

And from Belinda's expression, not something new.

Without looking at her, he slipped past Carl, who couldn't resist a shoulder knock, and Pigface, who elbowed him toward the shed door. Butch caught his balance and looked back.

Pigface stood in the L, profile to Butch, watching something. Butch wanted to cry out; instead, he slipped through the half-off door.

# CHAPTER 11

Rob stood right there, face tight, big rocks clenched in both hands. "We're gettin' Belinda out."

"What?" Butch goggled at him. "Are you crazy? We'll get killed!" Carl and Pigface would gut them both and tie their innards to the rafters.

"I don't care! I hate those two, hate 'em!" Rob's face corkscrewed in rage.

Butch was aghast. So, he had to yell "Banzai!" and crash his Zero into the deck of the Enterprise because Rob was mad? That's no reason! It's not like Belinda wanted rescuing, anyway, so why die?

Because enlightenment awaited.

The Wicked Thing.

A tremor went through him. Yes. The Wicked Thing. Run inside and all will be revealed. Carl and Pigface would beat them to a pulp with the rocks, of course so, consider... is it worth it? Consider other things: he'd cross a line, be forever altered, Agon stepping into the Terrigen Mist. Everything'd be different. He'd understand all the bad jokes and obscene movements and the urge to see girls naked. He'd read the Wicked Thing's spoor. Stand at the L, grasp the Cytorrak crystal. The power, but, oh, the madness.

Yes, worth it.

"Well?" Rob, vibrating and ready. He stared at Butch, who swallowed, steeled, and nodded, a gesture of a courage he didn't have. Rob grinned, combat on his brow, handed over a rock and pawed at the canted shed door. Butch's stomach frenzied. The

71

irreversible moment upon him…

"H'yeah!" the voice smashed into their spines with all the force of Black Bolt's cry. Rob actually bounced off the door, dropping his rock. Butch did, too, and turned.

Pawpaw.

He stood about fifteen feet away, all belligerence, all murder. Short; Butch saw the top of his head, that is, the top of the ever-present frayed yellow straw hat, wisps trailing into his face. He wore the ever-present overalls, too, and the striped chambray railroad shirt. Pawpaw had never worn anything different in the entire time Butch had known him, even during his and Mawmaw's Golden wedding anniversary bash down at the lake. Pawpaw was dark, sunburned, Indian blood obvious, his features squashed and fallen, nose blurring into mouth. Three days of gray stubble outlined his chin and lips, the only visual aide for marking them. A few bottom teeth grimly held on.

All that was a mere frame for Death Eye sitting in the left socket, a remnant of some 1940s' railroad accident. It was a wholly separate being, moving under its own power. It drilled into souls and sucked them out, damned forever. Butch shuddered as it flowed over him, evaluating.

"How many times I told you boys stay outta dat shed?" Old man's treble. A silly voice, actually, to go with such a terrifying figure, and if Butch were anyone else, he'd laugh. Others had laughed at Pawpaw and discovered how quick and strong he was.

"Belinda's in there," Rob blurted. He wasn't tattling. He wanted help.

"What she doin' in there?"

"Carl and Pig… I mean Ricky, got her trapped."

Butch looked at Pawpaw expectantly. He'd fix this, maybe for the wrong reasons, but all the same.

"They do, do they?" and then Pawpaw did something Butch found astonishing.

He smiled.

Pawpaw moved, placing both of them in range of his steel-vised hands, a very dangerous place to be. "She'll be awright," he said, smiling even broader while Death Eye spun and gleamed toward the shed door, feeding off the evil. "Do her some good."

"But…" Rob spluttered and Butch was speechless. Do her some good? There was no good Carl and Pigface could do for anyone. Wasn't Pawpaw going to storm inside, throwing kids and jars around in his standard maniacal rage?

Pawpaw's face got uglier, if that was possible. "Ain't no 'butt' but yours, which I'm gonna tan into next week you sass me s'more, boy!"

Rob stared, mouth open, more astonished than chastened. As was Butch. "But Belinda's in there!" he protested, the unfairness loosening his tongue.

"That ain't for you, that ain't for either a ya. You boys git, and you don't say nothin'. Y'heah me?" Death Eye spun and dripped and gibbered, about to eat them.

"But you just can't leave her in there!" Butch wasn't being brave, just logical. Pawpaw had no other course but to march in there, knock Carl and Pigface's heads together, and pull Belinda out. After that, if he wanted to tan all their hides, okay, but he couldn't abandon her. It wasn't allowed, wasn't the way grownups handled these things.

"Boy, what I tell you?"

"But you can't, Pawpaw!" Dang it! Pick up a board and whale them all around the house and call Mawmaw as his witness and proclaim loudly what bad kids they were so aunts and uncles could join in secondary punishment.

But don't walk away.

"Boy," in a voice low and dangerous and Butch froze. Death Eye had found a victim.

Pawpaw pointed a talon at Rob, who stared at Butch like he was crazy. "Go home. You Pappy wants to tan you anyway, so go. He's waitin'. And you." He turned full onto Butch, the meanness a river in him. "Go crawl under my bed right now."

"What?" That was, without a doubt, the most bizarre order Butch had ever been given.

"You heard me, now git!" and he pointed back at the house. Butch looked at Rob, baffled, but Rob just shook his head and trudged off, giving Pawpaw a wide berth. Pawpaw watched him go, turning Death Eye back to Butch, "Wad I tell you? Now go, you go. Better be under there when I check!"

Butch looked at the house, still baffled. Whack! Pawpaw's iron hand clipped him on the shoulder, pitching him sideways. Butch stumbled into a run straight for the Passage of Death, and looked back fearfully.

Don't let him catch you; he goes nuts, worse than dad.

Pawpaw was reaching for the shed door.

Oh, good! He was going to save Belinda after all. Sacrificed yourself for the team, Bucky.

Butch almost smiled when he stepped inside but lost that urge immediately. Dusty sunlight scribbled pencil lines across the room. Silence. Everyone must have left. Even Mawmaw seemed to have gone, or maybe napping in her back bedroom. He glanced left and right down the Passage, but nothing moved.

Whew.

He looked at the murderous iron behemoth barely restrained by the torn spread thrown carelessly across it, then bent down and peered underneath. He could make out some ratty cardboard boxes and rolling dust bunnies the size of dogs under there. The railing was rusty and pocked and he ran his hand over it, feeling the sharp points.

No way he's crawling under there.

Butch sat back. This was crazy, just crazy. He'd get all dirty and what if Pawpaw came in and lay down for a nap? He'd be crushed.

But if Pawpaw came in for a nap and he wasn't under there, then he'd be worse than crushed. Eviscerated, chopped up, and served in a stew.

With a slight sob, Butch lay down and started pushing underneath the rail. It scoured his lower back as he wormed his way under the big iron springs toward the middle. He stopped, gasping. It was tighter under here than he'd thought and he was having a hard time breathing.

Died of dust asphyxiation, ma'am.

He could see Mom, hand placed dramatically over her heart, face stricken, as she got the news. Adopto-boy had been drowned in dust, his body thrown, forlorn and cold, into a lonely grave. Oh, why hadn't she treated him better? Why hadn't she treated dad better so there was no divorce, no going off to Death Eye's lair, no dust murder? Why couldn't she be nicer?

Why couldn't all of them?

Jeez.

Not right, just not right. Every dang one of the people in this criminal enterprise called the Deats' family should get away from each other. Well, moron, wasn't that happening? Dad's gone off to find someone who won't make him feel so mean and now Mom can find someone nicer. Mom's new husband will buy Cindy and Art toys and take them to movies and make sure they get new clothes for school and let their friends come over and Mom will bake cookies and have parties and play games and let them stay up late. Cindy and Art will have fun and be safe and won't cry themselves to sleep anymore.

Dad will marry some lady who'll give him better kids, not doofuses who can't play sports or don't understand which tool he means when he yells for it. They won't spend their time buried in books or playing alone in dark rooms but will go hunting and fishing, demand to go, in fact. Dad will shine and smile and his better kids will flock around yelling "Daddy! Daddy!" whenever he comes home from work. They'll make things for him and show him their homework and get his beer and take off his boots, tell him how they stood up to bullies and how popular they are and other parents will call and say how much they like his new kids.

And there's Butch, standing in a doorway looking in, the Dark Child, the Adopted One, out of place, out of synch. They'll frown and look at each other. Perhaps he'd be happier with his mom? So back to Oklahoma and Art and Cindy—well, Cindy—will be happy, but New Father will frown at the Dark One's sportslessness and goofballedness and while New Father enjoys the quirks of Cindy and Art, this Dark Child is nothing but an embarrassment. And Mom doesn't want to lose her new husband, does she?

They'd send him back to the orphanage.

A stab of fear lanced Butch's heart. This was his constant terror. He didn't remember an orphanage, probably because he'd never been in one. Mom and dad had picked him straight up from his German mother, but that didn't exclude the possibility. It wouldn't be like one of those workhouses where they serve only gruel, he knew that, but he'd be alone. Completely alone. Monitored by an indifferent staff full of discipline, he'd sleep in a row of beds with several other sad and lonely orphans. The bigger kids would treat him roughly and his one or two pathetic friends would cough out their tubercular lives, unloved. He'd stand at large windows staring at bleak landscapes, cold and empty.

Or worse, his real mother would come for him. He'd imagined that scenario a million times. There'd be a knock on the door and Mom would open it and—sinister swell of violins—Real Mom. Butch had seen pictures of her when dad set up the Bell and Howell and went through several carousels of slides he had taken over the years, some even from WWII. Dad was a camera fanatic and always taking photos with the Canon he got in Japan before he went to Korea. He'd even had a portrait studio in the basement of Pop-Pop's house when Mom and dad were living with her parents right after the war. Butch wondered why he stopped doing that.

There were two slides of Real Mom—one holding baby Butch while standing next to Mom, the other, alone in a garden. Butch had studied those slides intently. Well, for the few seconds dad allowed before advancing to the next one. He'd tried to find them in the carousels once, but dad caught him and smacked him hard for touching his stuff.

Mom and Real Mom looked almost exactly alike. Maybe it was the way women dressed back then, vests and blouses and permed hair falling down in waves. Real Mom wore glasses, though, something Butch thought odd. She was Mom's housemaid when they were all stationed in Germany and couldn't keep her baby because she was German and had no money and no family and nowhere to go so Mom said she would take him. Dad had no sons and Butch would fill that role and Mom had said he was so beautiful when he was born that "We loved you the first moment we saw you."

What changed?

Art, of course, born one year and five months after him. Mom went crazy; spoiled Art, gave him everything and made Art fat and asthmatic and pushed the Foundling away. It may be true that Mom once thought him beautiful, but Butch didn't remember that. He only remembered the pushing away.

So there's Real Mom on the porch, hair in the same perm, wearing the same glasses and she wants Butch back. Mom says no, but Real Mom has some kind of court order, and policemen stand behind her looking grim and say the Foundling must go. Butch looks at Real Mom but she is a stranger; she tries to hug and talk to him but he cannot feel or hear anything and there he is at the top of the airplane gangway looking back in horror at Mom standing at the bottom, hand on her heart, face stricken because she does love her Foundling, after all, and Butch doesn't want to go to Germany and be a Nazi. So, he leaps off the stairs and breaks at the bottom. Dying, he looks up, and there's Mom, tears in her eyes.

He sobbed.

"Boy?" a surprised voice spoke from above the mattress, "Is that you?"

Dad.

Butch gasped. Man, he'd been so wrapped up in tragedy and daydreams he hadn't heard dad come in.

"What in the hell are you doing under there?" Dad's brown, beat-up, paint-speckled shoes were right opposite. Butch held his breath. But what are you going to do, pretend you're not here?

"Nothing," he said.

"What th... get your stupid ass out from under there!" dad yelled.

Died of strangulation, ma'am.

Butch didn't move. "Well?" The anger rose in dad's voice. He'd lift the bed and stomp him to death, so, fate sealed, Butch wriggled out, scouring his back again. Dad stepped back enough to give him room and then snatched Butch up by the back of the neck, shaking him once. "What were you doing under there?" he demanded again, murder in his voice.

Butch cringed and folded up for least exposure to the coming blows. "Pawpaw told me to get under there."

"What?"

"He told me to."

"Why?" and dad shook him again. "What'd you do?"

"Nothing!"

Dad's grip tightened and the frenzy glowed in his eyes as he pressed his face into Butch's, almost burning him with the Raleigh tip. "Boy! What'd you do? Were you playing on the propane tank again?"

"Nooo!" Butch gasped because dad's fingers were about to break through his skin any moment and lock around his spine, "We weren't doing anything! We wanted him to go save Belinda and he got mad at us and told me to get under the bed!"

"What?"

"Belinda! Carl and Ricky had her trapped in the shed and they were... they were being mean. They threw us out. We told Pawpaw, but he told me to get under the bed."

There.

Dad straightened, the frenzy dying although his fingers didn't relax. He looked down the Passage of Death to the yard as his face worked through a baffling mix of revulsion and pleasure. "Oh," he said, "Oh."

Butch couldn't tell if dad intended to blast out of the Passage with the Furies at his heels and provide backup for Pawpaw or start chuckling like Dishonest John.

Dad did neither. Just stood there. Butch moved cautiously against his hand and dad let it fall. Safe, for the moment. Butch looked down at himself. Filthy.

"You're a mess," dad confirmed and started brushing the dust off, a series of glancing blows only separated from a beating by trajectory. Butch endured it, knowing dad intended aid, although his help was often as deadly as his rages.

Dad gave up after a few moments and let out an exasperated breath. "Go take a bath. Change clothes."

"A bath?" Chills ran up Butch's spine. Mawmaw's bathroom, dark and cobwebbed with a floor that had broken through in a couple of places, was more terrifying than the Passage. There was a huge clawfoot tub listing in the middle, its pipes rusty and malevolent. Unspeakable things lived underneath it waiting for a kid to climb into the lukewarm water before rising and tearing out a throat with their devil teeth, the toilet stained and smelly and equally dangerous. The place scared him so much he usually waited until they were at some uncle's house before using the bathroom, even though most had outhouses. Just as scary, but at least he could bolt if something climbed out.

"Yes, a bath," dad said irritably, "And then go to bed."

"But," Butch spluttered, "it's not even dark yet!"

"I know, but we're getting up real early. We're leaving."

"Huh?"

"We're leaving. As soon as it gets light. Maybe even sooner."

"But..." A million questions and a million fears crashed headlong, bumpers buckling and metal screeching and bodies dying in craven agony against shattered windshields. But dad had already moved down the Passage and couldn't... or wouldn't... hear Butch's plaintive, "Dad, what's going on? Why were all the aunts and uncles discussing me and why does Pawpaw let bad things happen to Belinda and when are we going home? Are we

ever going home?"
Where are we going, dad?
The questions fell to the floor.
Butch took in a quiet breath. Go brave the bathroom. It's not half as scary as this.

# CHAPTER 12

They drove straight at the rising sun. Butch watched it change from rose to yellow, benign to stabbing. Already sleepy from the early start, he drifted off, Mawmaw's brick-hard eggs-and-bacon with grits and cornbread, lots of cornbread, acting like Sominex. No talk at breakfast, just her sorrowed silence and Pawpaw's snoring from the Passage. A train went by while they ate, hooting once or twice in the pre-dawn dark. Lonely sound…

He jerked awake to a train horn bearing down on him but no, dad was blowing the car horn at some idiot. Dazzled, he squinted. The sun was higher and off to the right, so they were no longer going east. North? Back to Lawton? Butch held his breath. This needed confirmation. He eyed dad, who was in Combat Driving Mode—hunched at the wheel, lip-clenched cigarette poised like a missile. Don't poke the bear.

Butch recalled Tommy's patient effort to teach him directions: "Put your right hand to the rising sun, okay? No, dummy, your right hand. The other one. Okay, now, look straight ahead. That's north. So what's behind you?"

"The alley?"

"Ah, geezewoo, of course it's the alley. What direction is it?"

"Huh?"

"South. That's south. Got it?"

Butch smiled. Good ole Tommy.

Okay, do it. Butch pointed his right hand at the sun.

"What are you doing?" dad asked.

Butch flinched, raising a shoulder for protection, but dad was just curious. "Getting directions."

"What?"

"Getting directions. You know, like a compass."

"A compass?" Dad looked over. "You mean, figuring out north?"

"Yes."

"How're you going to do that?" Amused tone.

Butch reacquired his sun point, turned, and placed his left hand in line with his eyes which grazed the outside of dad's shoulder. "That's north," he announced proudly.

"Very good," dad said and Butch glowed. Second time he was right about something. "So which way are we going?"

Silly question.

"North." Butch was on a roll.

"Not quite," dad replied.

Huh? Butch stared at dad and then back at his pointed hand. What do you mean? He was facing straight ahead from where he'd shot the sun, and that's what Tommy said to do, so...

"Yes, we are."

"No, not quite." A stir of irritation in dad's voice.

"Yes, we are," Butch insisted. Dang it all, you just said I was right!

"You going to tell me about directions?" Dad was definitely irritated now and glared at Butch. Butch glared back. This was a point of honor.

"It is too north," Butch stated, flatly. He wasn't going to argue. It was settled.

"Well, yeah, that's north," dad's spear hand followed Butch's left one.

"So I'm right," he said, smugly, and folded his arms across his chest.

"You're not right. We're not going north, we're going sort of north, and if you were trying to go north this way, you'd get lost, boy." Dad stabbed the cigarette down at the seat, his eyes flaming. "You'd get lost and you'd starve to death or bears would eat you, just 'cause you think you know everything."

Butch felt a stirring of unease. He didn't want bears to eat him, so reevaluate. Dad was a grownup and a helicopter pilot and had to find his way across the country while flying. He'd know tricks Tommy didn't.

81

"What do you mean 'sort of north'?" Butch asked.

"We're going northeast."

Wait. What? "Northeast?"

"Yeah, north by east," and dad sniffed like that settled it. Butch conceived a series of angles—go straight north for some distance then turn east, then straight north then east. Etch-a-Sketch driving.

"That's silly," he said.

"What?" Dad's brow crinkled.

"Driving like that."

Dad was baffled. "What are you talking about?"

Sigh. Have to school the old man.

"Going straight north." Butch pointed in emphasis. "Then straight east"—another point—"then north then east." Additional points to underscore the first point. There. Got it?

Dad burst out laughing, the 'boy-are-you-dumb' kind and Butch's face blazed. "Where in the world do you get ideas like that? This road goes northeast, which means we ain't going straight north and we ain't going straight east, either."

Butch looked at him, lost.

Dad shook his head, "Boy, oh boy." Disappointment over this clumsy moron of an adopted son... should have left him in Germany. "Okay." Dad pointed through the windshield. "You know what a compass is, right?"

Butch, still in full embarrassment, answered cautiously, "Yeah."

"Good. You know what a compass looks like, right?"

"Well, yeah." And Butch rolled his eyes because if he knew what a compass was, then he knew what one looked like, okay?

"All right, smartypants, where's north on a compass?"

Butch smirked. That was easy. "Where the needle points."

"Yeah, that's the direction, but where is north on the compass?"

There was north on a compass? How can that be? A compass was just a neat round gauge with a needle. It didn't have any 'north' to it because it was right there in your hand, not north of you. This was, obviously, a trick question.

"You can't go north on a compass," Butch was back to smug. Nailed that one.

"What?" Dad was back to baffled.

"You can't go north on a compass."

"You sure can. What do you think a compass is for?"

"For finding north, but there's no north on it." Butch refolded his arms.

"Boy, are you messing with me?"

"No," Butch replied, exasperated, "There's no north on a compass. North is a place. How can there be a place on a compass? It's too small."

Jeez, dad!

Dad stared at him. "The 'N'," he said.

"Huh?"

"The 'N' on the compass. That stands for 'north.'"

Butch blinked. Oh.

"The 'E' on the compass, that stands for 'east.' North. East. Understand?"

"Yes." Butch answered slowly, feeling as stupid as dad thought he was.

"And 'S' is 'south' and 'W' 'west.' Understand?"

All right already.

"Do you understand?" dad insisted, belligerent.

And Butch was quick to assure. "Yes, yes, I understand now."

"Good. Finally." Dad shook his head to emphasize the burden of a retarded son. "Now, you know where it's got 'N' and 'E' printed on a compass, right?"

"Yes." Could we just get on with this, please?

"Well, we're driving in between the N and the E. That's northeast. North by east," and dad punctuated that last with three separate hand spears toward the windshield.

Butch frowned and visualized the compass and the letters and then thought of a map, like the one folded next to him, and a light went on. "Oh," he said tentatively, then "Oh!" with more conviction and felt suddenly brilliant, scales falling from eyes. He smiled happily, "Now I get it!" He pointed out the front of the car, "That's northeast!"

"Riiiight," dad said, telling Butch how slow he was but, so what? He now understood a complexity. There were more to directions, Tommy, than even you knew.

He blinked at the sun. Direction wasn't just a matter of 'north' or 'south' anymore; there were subtle gradations. Move one line off and the course is different, leading to bears. You leave the road and stumble into woods and the road could be twenty feet away but the woods block it and no one would hear your screams except the bears. Butch shuddered. Just one line off. It was really important to know where you were going.

Butch looked at dad. He was in the air a lot, flying all over Oklahoma for the Army and had flown in Norway and even flew President Eisenhower to Mexico once. If he'd been one line off, they'd never have gotten to Mexico and bears—are there bears in Mexico?—would have eaten Eisenhower. But dad knew the compass, so they arrived safely. 'Course, dad probably could see Mexico from way up there.

"It's called a rose," dad said.

Butch stared at him, surprised by this utterly irrelevant statement. "What?"

"The north and south drawing on the map?" Dad gestured with his cigarette at the one lying on the seat between them. "A compass rose."

Butch pulled the map to him and opened it, searching. Dad's calloused finger appeared and settled on a spot, "There," he said.

It was just a thick black line that bulged slightly in the middle and had a stylized 'N' on top of it. More reed than rose, but add the other directions and, well, it flowered.

"I always liked that," dad said.

Butch looked at him. Dad had a small, satisfied smile. Butch decided he liked it, too.

"Dad?"

"Yeah?"

"Where we going?"

"Nashville," he said simply.

# CHAPTER 13

They gradually came back east, Butch confirming the turn by shooting north. He wished he had a compass to follow the needle swing, but opening the map and orienting the rose was a decent substitute. Good ole rose.

Dad slowed considerably when they hit the long bridge over Lake o' the Pines, his head swiveling at the water and reedy banks on either side like an anti-aircraft battery. Thank God no traffic, because he crossed the middle line several times.

Any minute now, they'd stop and fish. Dad never passed up the opportunity, taking advantage of any situation to get out there and cast a line or two. One night he had them dress in their pajamas and took them to the Mt Scott Drive-In, which they all thought was neat until he put a bucket of crawdads, snapping and squalling, in the back of the station wagon. During the movie, an occasional crawdad snapflapped its way out of the bucket and over their heads, landed on the floor and advanced on their toes, claws extended, and they screamed and pulled hasty legs up until dad reached back, grabbed the creature and flung it back into the bucket, telling them to shut up. Dale sat outside until the movie was over. Days of Wine and Roses, yeah, that was it. Afterwards, dad drove to Lake Latonka and took the bucket and some poles and a flashlight into the pitch blackness while they all scrunched and fought with each other trying to sleep in the car, scared of the dark and the beasts prowling outside, Mom's assurances notwithstanding.

So he'll probably stop here, too.

But no, he didn't, although he drove so slowly a tractor ahead of them managed to stay ahead for the last third of the bridge. Butch did a silent whew. Not that he wouldn't mind a driving break but dad made fishing an ordeal, a marathon casting session sometimes lasting all night and always found something to get mad about, either the way Butch tied his line or held the pole or lost a fish.

But he got a break, anyway, when dad whipped into a beat-up Texaco station—"You can trust your car to the man who wears the star"—at the end of the bridge and eased next to a pump. "Gotta pee?" he asked.

Butch nodded.

"Okay." He handed Butch a quarter. "Get a soda and candy bar, if you want. But don't waste time."

Butch gasped at the sudden riches. Oh boy! Wonder if they have comics? Go look! He dropped out the door but, wow, his legs were really tight and he rubbed them vigorously as he crouched between the island and the Rambler.

Dad stepped around the back, stretched, then noticed Butch. "What are you doing?"

"My legs are crampy."

"Well, walk it off. You're wasting time." Dad turned back to the road, pulling at his shirt pocket for a Raleigh.

"Hep ya?" An attendant, whose suspender-laden belly preceded him by a good two seconds, stepped through the island and bumped Butch, who teetered but managed to stay upright. The attendant didn't and stumbled down the other side.

"Would you watch what you're doing?" Dad roared and was suddenly there, talons extended and grasping Butch's arm. "Ow!" as dad manhandled him past the pump. "Shit fire, boy!"

"S'alrite, I'm alrite there, mister." The attendant stepped clear, looked at dad with a shocked face. "Ain't no harm done. Boy's okay."

Dad gave the attendant a sidewinder look and Butch felt the tension flow back through dad's arm, taut and hard and dangerous. He held his breath, terrified. Dad was going to kill the attendant.

He suddenly released Butch, stood straight up, and glared. "Fill it up," he snarled, "and check the oil." Dad stalked toward the road, savagely pulling a cigarette out of the pack.

Butch rubbed his arm, gauged dad's distance and stance and

figured it was okay for now. He looked at the attendant. "Sorry, sir."

"S'alrite, boy." The attendant was probably dad's age, straw-haired and red-faced under a beat-up golden Panama with a jaunty red band. He had decades' worth of sunburn, making hair and Panama a complement—man as contrast of yellow and red. All lines flowed to that ample belly, a proud construct even the man's brogans regarded with awe. His neck took on the belly's declination and became its foothill. Man collapsing into stomach.

The attendant regarded Butch with brown eyes just a shade off sunburn themselves, and then looked to the side. Butch noticed a boy there, obscured by the Jupiter of the man's stomach. Probably pulled along by its gravity. Butch stared. Not a boy, a teenager, probably fourteen or fifteen, but so slight that Butch wondered if the belly transferred mass, like a star and its dwarf companion. He was a scarecrow with too-big denims and an amazingly white T-shirt with a snuff can rolled up in one sleeve, thin hair shaved almost down to the scalp. He looked at Butch with blue eyes brighter than his shirt and Butch had a sense of ponies running wild along riverbanks.

"Djew hear?" Belly asked. The teen nodded, "Yup," and stepped easily past Jupiter. Butch watched in amazement as the teen pulled the Rambler cap and draped the gas hose and switched keys and pushed buttons. It looked so expert and technical.

Jupiter, a half-worried smile on his face, gently nudged Butch and gestured at the building. "Bathroom's thar." Butch located dad, who stood almost on the road, cigarette dangling, staring back toward the lake.

Better attend.

It was a brick gas station, the overhang slapped carelessly onto the front. There was barely a car's width between the station door and the pump island. A couple of red freezers with 'RC Cola' printed on them flanked bug-and-dust streaked picture windows built as giant half ovals into the brick walls. Some wooden crates, randomly filled with empties, tossed next to the freezers; a rusty oil can peeked from behind. Butch peered around the side at a tin shack abutting the rear of the building. A few patches of grass fought for their lives among the dirt and rocks serving as a yard.

"Thass right, that way," Jupiter called, gesturing toward the shack. Butch stepped around. As he cleared the building, the sun smacked him with heat and light. He squinted and saw a paint-peeled knobless door half ajar on the shack. Must be it.

It was smelly and dark in there and Butch, fearful, sidled up to a brown-stained toilet filled with rusty water. Good place for snakes, especially since the door wouldn't shut all the way, and Butch kept watch for movement but no rattler came out to investigate the watering sound.

He finished and stood at a broken sink that was draining a thin stream of cold water from the tap, a cracked and brown-speckled mirror over it. Butch peered at the glass, making himself out between the specks—face as shotgun art. The cracks divided his features along odd fault lines: nose falling apart at the nostrils and right eye lower than the left. He grinned and watched part of his lip merge into his nose and become a separate entity. What if he really looked like this? Girls would shriek and run away from him; boys would beat him up. But on Halloween, he'd rule the streets.

He was considering the merits of that when he noticed a thin metal box fastened to the wall halfway between the sink and the corner. It was rusty and dingy and hard to see. He stepped up to it and squinted at the "25c" clearly written there, red on white, but twenty-five cents for what? He brushed some of the dirt off the front, even though the rust irritated his fingers.

A picture. Butch stared.

A blonde woman, like Mamie Van Doren, knelt on a bed, wrapped in a sheet that flowed across her shoulders and down her boobies, revealing the valley in between, then fell between her legs, which stuck out on either side. Her mouth was open and the expression on her face was… excitement, startled, thrilled, what?

Butch's stomach seized.

He had seen naughty pictures before. Dad had a pen that, tapped properly, dropped a woman's bathing suit so that she was standing there sideways, naked and winking. Dad also had playing cards with pictures of other Mamie van Dorens wearing very few clothes and carrying long cigarette holders, at least that's what Butch glimpsed before dad snatched them away. And, of course, the Coppertone girl.

But this blonde woman looked like she was waiting for something, and Butch knew immediately for what.

The Wicked Thing.

Butch blinked. Dad said "get a soda and a candy bar... if you want." So he could use the quarter anyway he liked, get two Marvels or one Special or even five Push-Ups.

Or a picture of an almost naked girl.

No contest.

Butch dug viciously into his jeans, seeking the quarter... there! He put it in the slot and heard it fall, but nothing happened. He frowned and peered at the machine. There was some kind of handle in the middle. Butch grabbed it and twisted. It was hard to move and he slipped and the knob dropped back a bit. Great, messed it up, but it suddenly gave way, unbalancing him. Something went thunk and he felt around at the bottom until he found an opening. He touched some kind of thin cardboard and pulled it out.

An envelope. Butch scrutinized it in the dim light. "French Tickler" was on the front. Was that the girl's title? Butch flipped it over but it was the same on the back along with a hard word Butch didn't recognize: Prophylactic.

So she's a professional French Tickler, hey?

Oh, boy!

Butch fumbled with the tab and pulled the envelope open. He blinked. No picture, but something plastic, and Butch fingered the top of it.

What the heck...

A balloon?

Butch stared at it, all folded within itself.

You've got to be kidding.

He'd just spent a small fortune for a balloon? Might as well have thrown the quarter down the toilet.

"Hey!" Dad's voice cut through the door from somewhere outside and Butch jumped, almost dropped the envelope. He shoved it hard into his pocket then turned, breathless. Dad wasn't there, thank God, but could be rushing over right now to see what Butch was doing and what the hell is that in your pocket? Better get moving. He pulled open the door and ran down the side of the station.

"'Bout time!" dad yelled. He was in front of the Rambler glaring at Butch while handing some bills to Jupiter, who studied them carefully. Butch hurried over but Jupiter blocked his path. Dad was just one more wrong-rub away from detonating and

Butch hovered, desperate, seeking an opportunity to pass.

"Ya go," Belly said, handing back some coins which dad briefly examined then palmed, heading towards the driver's side. Belly did not move and Butch's eyes widened. The wrong-rub was imminent.

"Pa, you in the way," a voice spoke from the side. The skinny teen behind the pumps had observed Belly's blockade. Belly shuffled, looked back at his son and then saw Butch. "Oh, sorry there, little man, didn' see ya," and stepped aside to give Butch room. With relief, Butch grabbed the door handle and pulled it open. Dad was fooling with a cigarette and hadn't noticed the delay. Yet.

"Y'all right?" the teen asked quietly. Butch stared at him and knew the question was genuine. It deserved a genuine answer.

"No," he said, and got in.

# CHAPTER 14

It was safer to sleep so Butch did, waking when the car stopped. He opened his eyes and peered through a dust cloud swirling past the windshield. They were parked against a big metal diner. A couple of weathered farmers sat in a picture window right over the hood; they leaned on their fists and stared down at Butch like he was a bug walking across their plates.

"Where are we?" he asked.

"Texarkana," dad said, opening his door, "Lunch."

Butch perked up. Okay, eating out, always good, and he jumped onto the crap covered parking lot, immediately hammered by heat and dust. He coughed and scurried behind dad up the steep wooden steps through the glass door. Stepping in, he let out a delighted sigh. Air conditioning! He closed his eyes and savored the cool.

"Seit ware yew wan," a short, dark waitress wearing a yellow-and-stained uniform, tough looking with a load of freckles, waved from the register. She didn't smile and didn't look at them —an automatic response to the little bell over the door, Butch supposed. Dad headed down the booths. Some old guys at the counter turned and nodded and dad nodded back. The two farmers, still on their fists, watched Butch as he passed. They didn't nod.

Dad chose the last booth and pulled out the menus while Butch played with the jukebox flipper. Jim Reeves, Tammy Wynette, George Jones...

Of course. Bumpkin diner.

The waitress suddenly appeared. "Chawl wancha trink?"

Butch stared at her, baffled. "Coke," dad said and Butch understood. "Pepsi." She wrote notes and slipped off but was back moments later with two glasses and straws. Dad and Butch started peeling the paper, then looked at each other. Zip! Two straw missiles flew across the table. Dad's clipped him in the hair but he got dad full in the shoulder. Great shot. They both grinned.

"Chawl tweat?" The waitress again but Butch got it this time.

"Hamburger," he said. "Cheese sandwich," from dad, and she stalked off, dad's eyes on her walk.

"That all you ever eat?" Dad asked when the show ended.

"Yep," Butch said with full conviction.

"Why don't you have some eggs or something?"

Butch expressed his opinion. "Yech."

Dad chuckled. "They ain't that bad. You eat 'em for breakfast."

True, but irrelevant. "I have other things with them, like toast and jelly."

"Oh, I see." Dad looked off. "It's gotta be somethin' sweet before you eat it?"

"Hamburgers aren't sweet."

"I'm talking about eggs. You gotta have something sweet to eat them, don't you?" Dad sounded irritated. No surprise—all grownups complained about kids eating sweets. 'It'll ruin your appetite'... silly adult talk. Butch's dinner had never been spoiled by a pre-meal Hershey bar or Butterfinger. They were actually stimuli because he didn't have to worry about saving room for dessert, which, also, had never been a problem. Adults simply couldn't stand kids enjoying themselves.

"I don't like them alone." There, settled.

Dad snorted. "You know, when I was a little kid, it was a treat to get an egg."

Butch found this slightly implausible. "A treat?"

"Yeah, a treat. Mawmaw used them for cooking and we didn't get one unless we got it ourselves. So we had to find the hens' nests and chase them off."

"Didn't they peck you?"

"Well, sure, but it didn't hurt."

Butch found this completely implausible. Dad said nothing hurt, even the belt while you were screaming.

"You know how I ate them?" Dad had an evil gleam in his eye and Butch braced. He wasn't going to like this.

"No."

"I'd just suck it right out of the shell." And the evil grin burst forth.

"Eeeeeeew!" Butch doubled over, pleasantly revolted, his voice and action letting dad know how sick that was. The farmers shifted heads, but not hands, to look at Butch and the old guys turned their wheel seats and frowned, but Butch couldn't help it. Information like this required a proper response. "Why'd you do that? Why'd'nt you cook them?"

"Pipe down," dad ordered, but he was obviously pleased with the effect. "If I didn't, I wouldn't get it."

"Huh?"

"One of my brothers would steal it or one of my sisters would break it so I couldn't have it."

"Why'd they do that?"

"Because they were hungry, too."

Butch blinked, not sure he was getting this. "Why an egg?" he asked. A peanut butter sandwich or an Almond Joy or even a jellybean—yuck—was better.

"'Cause we had no other food. You know about the Depression? No? You ain't got to that in school yet? Well, we were poor. We had no money. I stopped school in the third grade so I could work at the ice house. I'd get a sack of potatoes for hauling ice. That's all I ate all week."

Butch stared at him, open-mouthed. "Just a sack of potatoes?"

"Yep." In a strange way, dad looked satisfied.

"You were that poor?"

"Yeah, we were that poor," and dad was irritated again, as though Butch had made fun of him or something. "I ate those potatoes all week. I had to fight my brothers and sisters for them. You didn't fight, you didn't eat."

Butch pictured that dinner scene—Mawmaw approaching the table with a steaming plate of potatoes, eyeing her brood warily while they similarly eyed each other. She set it down and suddenly knives flashed, fists flew, chairs and plates thrown, a head busted open, a bleeding sister sank unconscious to the floor while the others roiled in a whirlpool of vicious biting and scratching. The survivors gorged on the spoils while their vanquished siblings whimpered and groveled and made pathetic attempts to get scraps.

Good Lord.

"You really had to do that?" Butch was awestruck.

"Yes, I really had to do that!" and dad was flat out mad now, making Butch recoil in confusion. "You calling me a liar? What do you know? You don't know how good you got it. You don't have any appreciation at all. You wouldn't last a day without a Snickers bar or a TV show or your mommy wiping your ass."

The words burned and Butch couldn't, for the life of him, figure out what brought them on. He'd just asked some normal questions! Man! Far too many hair triggers on dad's gun. "I don't mean nothing," Butch tried to explain.

"'Don't mean nothin',"' dad mimicked, "You never mean nothin'. What do you know? Stick your nose in a book all day. Wish I had time to do that. Wish I could just sit around all day and read, but somebody's gotta do all the work. Sure won't be you."

Butch felt sick, unable to respond. What could he say? He didn't want to work in an ice house—it sounded hard and dirty and cold. Besides, he didn't have to. They had plenty of food and a place to live and he wasn't in death matches with Art and Cindy and Dale for a plate of scraps; well, at least he wasn't before they left, but, now… hmm. Maybe dad was saying Butch had to give up hamburgers and reading because their very survival was at stake. Butch looked up and down the diner.

Work here?

What would he do? Mop floors, clean dishes, take out the garbage, all for a sack of potatoes at the end of the week? He'd sleep under a table and dress in cast-off towels and aprons and everyone would laugh at him. The Texarkana kids would all come over and jeer and push him around and take his sack of potatoes. And every day dad would yell that he wasn't working hard enough and he was a disappointment and they were going to starve.

Butch took in a frightened breath.

Dad glowered at him but didn't say anything. One wrong word, one little protest about their changed situation and Butch'd get a backhand. Best to disappear. He studied the torn Formica on the tabletop.

"Burg, shees." The waitress placed their food. She went away and came back with new sodas then went away again. A pile of potato chips and a pickle sat next to the steaming hamburger open on some white buns that looked more appropriate as dinner rolls.

Dang, should have ordered fries.

Butch put on way too much ketchup and attacked. He beat dad by about five minutes, basically inhaling his food, even the potato chips, as greasy as they were.

Deelicious.

He smacked his lips, searched out chip fragments, and considered ways to get dad out of this mood. What to do, what to do?

Ah, yes, of course, appeal to his expertise. Adults liked to be consulted, liked to school young pups like him. "Dad?"

"Humh?" dad, not looking up, answered around his sandwich.

"What's a French Tickler?"

Dad actually choked, a combination of laugh and exclamation of surprise filtered through cheese and toast. Butch immediately knew he'd stepped into something, but it wasn't necessarily bad. He leaned forward with some expectation.

Dad got hold of himself. "Where in the world did you hear that?"

Butch gauged him: high amusement on his face, but with a seediness that made Butch wary. Tread carefully, old pal. "I read it."

"Where?"

"On a coin machine."

"Where was it?"

Butch gestured back behind them. "At the gas station."

"You mean near the lake?"

"Yes."

Dad nodded, "In the bathroom?"

"Yes." Butch furrowed his brow. How'd he know that?

Dad nodded again and the smile on his face broadened. "Lordy," he chuckled and shook his head a bit. "Well, son, all I can tell ya, it's not something for kids."

"But, what is it?"

"It's something for grownups."

Butch let out an exasperated breath. Circular answers explained nothing. "So why does it tickle and why is it French?" It's just a stupid balloon, after all.

Dad burst out laughing, true mirth, trying to stifle it in cupped hands but failing. Butch was perplexed. Dad was, obviously, laughing at his ignorance and that hurt, but he was so enjoying it that Butch couldn't help smiling. "C'mon, dad!" he giggled and that just made dad laugh harder. Which, apparently, was forbidden in the diner because everyone stopped their eating and looked at them, disapproving.

All right, time for exhibit A. If dad was confronted with the artifact, he might be more forthcoming. Butch reached into his pocket, clasped the cardboard, about to pull it out...

No, Frank Vaughn said. Don't show your dad. Don't let him know you have it.

Too startled to be afraid, Butch asked, Why?

Just don't do it, Frank said.

A warning Butch couldn't ignore, and the more he considered it, the more correct it seemed. Right now, dad's mood was better; he was laughing; he'd forgotten his ice-house potatoes. The rest of the trip would go smoothly. But showing the envelope might well dash all that. At the very minimum, dad would know he'd misspent the quarter.

He reversed his hand and discreetly pushed the cardboard deeper.

"Oh, my, my." Dad wiped his eyes with the back of his hands and looked at the other diners eating again, but in the odd position of turned around and watching them. "Boy, you do say the wildest things. So tell me, what do you think it is?"

He shrugged. "I dunno. It makes women excited?"

Dad's jaw dropped. "Boy!" he snapped, "Where'd you get that idea?"

Startled by dad's sudden concern, Butch silently thanked Frank for urging him to keep the envelope hidden. "Because there was this picture and this naked blonde woman was real excited about the French Tickler—"

"Lawrd, mah Lawrd ib hebn!" a voice screeched next to them, causing both to jump. The waitress had approached unseen. "Wakina talg, wakina talg furra buoy! Nah Curisshun, nah Curisshun adal!" She waved her arms, pulling in the other customers. The frowns around the diner deepened.

Best Butch could figure, she was saying something wasn't Christian. Dad stared at her, blinking, but apparently had an easier time following her patois than Butch. "Now, look here!" Dad was red and getting redder. "You ain't got no call—"

"Eyuh caynt zay sin hyeah!" The waitress, arms akimbo and just as red as dad, became even more inarticulate. "Wea jus donch avit, wea jus donch!" and she glared at dad.

Dad turned purple and his eyes glistened and Butch pressed back as hard as he could because he knew what was coming. If the waitress survived dad's first blow, she wouldn't the second. Berserker dad would then kill everyone within a ten-foot radius, including Butch, before he realized what he was doing. Then he'd kill anyone left to get rid of the witnesses, drag their bodies out back and bury them. No one would ever know. Dad would disappear somewhere in Arkansas, living alone and brooding in some mountain cabin, stealing out every once in a while to murder again. Butch held his breath.

Any second, Frank, I'll be joining you.

But dad didn't reach out and pull the waitress's head off. Instead, he reached into his wallet and threw five dollars on the table. "We're leaving!" he snarled and stood, forcing her back.

"Eyuh take it, eyuh take it, ah ayn touchen it!" she yelled, pointing fiercely at the money.

Dad blinked only once. "All right," he swept the money into his fist and stepped beside her. At that moment, she realized how big and strong dad was and she quailed, moved back out of the way. "Let's go, boy," he gestured at Butch, who didn't hesitate. He slipped in front of the waitress without looking at her, more wary of an aroused dad.

Dad grabbed his hand and strode down the diner, dragging Butch behind. One of the old guys at the counter stood but dad glared him back. The two farmers kept chins on fists but Butch saw murder in their eyes and was fearful. What if they attacked? But they stayed seated, thank God, heads turning to follow Butch's progress. A big fat guy with a three-day stubble, dressed in a white apron and T-shirt, stepped out of the back and looked at them, more bewildered than anything. Must be the cook. Butch wanted to tell him his hamburgers were good, but thought it best to say nothing.

"Goan, goan!" shrieked the waitress, following them at a safe distance. Dad set his jaw, picked up the pace, and almost yanked Butch off his feet. They went through the glass door so hard Butch thought it would break. "Get in," dad ordered as they approached the car and Butch ran ahead and jumped inside, beating dad by a few seconds.

Butch looked up. Everyone was at the window: the farmers, of course, and the cook and the waitress and the old guys and two other women Butch hadn't seen before. The waitress gesticulated and mouthed and Butch guessed she was explaining things. He wondered if the others needed a translator. Judging by the way they all stared at Butch, their eyes hard and merciless, no. He whimpered.

"GO! TO! HELL!" Dad yelled each word, sticking his head out to get the proper emphasis, then gunned the engine. He backed around hard, aimed the rear of the car at the diner, then floored it, filling the air with dust and gravel. The Rambler spun out, fishtailed onto the road, and they roared, just roared, away. Butch looked back but couldn't see the diner because of the dust cloud.

Butch surreptitiously watched the rage flow across dad's face for a good three minutes before it softened. That coincided with dad's speed; as they slowed, he calmed. Once they were back down around seventy-five, dad'd be okay.

Didn't take long. Dad actually hummed after a minute, then smiled and chuckled aloud. He suddenly slapped Butch on the knee. "First time," he announced, "I ever got a free lunch off a French Tickler." And he laughed.

His knee stung because dad hit him too hard, but Butch was relieved. He wasn't in trouble. Might even have done something good. Butch laughed with him, even though he had no idea why.

# CHAPTER 15

"We're coming up on the Mississippi."

Butch jolted out of the road coma induced by dad's country music somewhere near Little Rock. What? He pressed against the dash, clawing for a look. The Mississippi! Ohhhhh EM-EYE-ES... ES-EYE-ES... ES-EYE-PEEPEE-EYE... Butch hummed the *Madcap* spelling song under his breath. Wow, he was actually going to see it! Half of him wanted to scramble backward and grab *Tom Sawyer* out of his bag and read random passages as they crossed, but he was too afraid he'd miss it.

They entered a high iron bridge and it took all Butch's restraint to keep from hanging out the window by his feet. Some kind of railing kept getting in the way, along with his shortness and the passenger door, but he still caught long glimpses. All that water! So wide! So big!

Barges and tugs crossed rather languidly below and he peered hard but, no, no raft. Disappointing. People ran up and down on tugs and barges and in little boats zipping between them but they weren't chewing on long-stemmed weeds or wearing straw hats and overalls and going barefoot. Had on jeans and torn shirts, mostly. They looked mean and mad, too.

Butch frowned. They shouldn't be there. This was Tom and Huck's river, a hundred years out of their time, yes, but still theirs. Tom on his raft, drifting the day away, catching six-foot-long catfish, pretending at pirates, watching out for Injun Joe. Couldn't do that now; all the traffic down there batting him about, the mean people on the little boats sidling up to steal the catfish, and he'd probably run into real pirates.

Everything's gone, Tom. But somewhere on an island no one's been to since the steamboats, there's a bare footprint, kid-sized, a hidden campsite and the waft of a corncob pipe. Butch smiled and sat back.

"Wacha think?" dad asked.

"Great," he said, knowing his thrill showed.

"That it is. For a minute, it looked like you wanted to jump in there."

Butch shrugged, "I just wanted to see it."

"So you have now. And wacha think?"

What could he tell dad, that some laughing kids were slapping his back and inviting him for a swim and a run to the cemetery to chase away warts? Or go whitewash something? He glanced at dad and wondered if he'd ever read Mark Twain. Doubtful. Dad read nothing.

"Great," he repeated and dad left him alone. Good. He didn't think he could really explain why he had a bounce in his chest. They reached the bridge's end and he watched the river disappear among piers and warehouses and docked barges. An old black man stood by the side of the road in an open blue shirt and Huck's straw hat, laughing as he waved a string of fish at them. Butch beamed. The black man knew.

They cruised through the center of Memphis. Lots of people walked around, lots of them black, which surprised Butch. He had never seen so many black people in one place. Was this a black city?

"Elvis lives here, you know," dad said.

Big deal. Butch wasn't all that knocked in the head with Elvis. Dad had taken them to see *Blue Hawaii* and *Girls! Girls! Girls!* at the drive-in, but they had bored Butch to the point of falling asleep. "I don't like Elvis," he said.

"What?" Dad had that tone Butch couldn't decipher, a mix between astonishment and leg-pulling. He figured out which from the follow-up questions—one got him a beating, the other, a laugh.

"How can you not like Elvis? Elllvisss! Elllvissss baaaaby!" Dad fell into his impression of a black woman, high falsetto and weird accent.

So, it's to be a laugh.

Butch giggled, which only encouraged dad to throw in some hip shaking, very hard to do while driving, and that made Butch giggle more and then he was downright laughing because dad was just terrible. Butch loved impressionists, like that Frank Gorshin guy who was really, really funny the night the Beatles came on Ed Sullivan. Dad was not Frank Gorshin.

They laughed their way right out of Memphis, dad discovering that a bored almost-ten-year-old was the easiest of audiences so kept his single act going with even more outrageous iterations. Butch was willing to be that audience but, after a while, he got it—girls went crazy for Elvis, like they went crazy for the Beatles, making Butch mad because he couldn't hear them play, and there was no reason, dad, to belabor the point. They were driving among hills and woods and the occasional river by then and it was getting dark.

"Dad, where we going?"

"I told you, Nashville," he said.

"How far is that?"

"Did you see the last mileage sign?"

Oh, great, another test.

He sighed inwardly, tired of this before it even started. "No."

"Then you need to wait for the next one."

Fine. Butch crossed his arms. He'd play along to keep dad's mood. Meanwhile, let's go billboard hunting. He peered at the quickly-becoming-gloomy side of the road. SEE AMERICA FIRST! commanded one above a picture of a man and woman beaming at the world from an open convertible. Well, Butch was certainly doing that. He'd been to the Mississippi and was coming up on Nashville, the capital of country music, which he figured to be wall-to-wall cowboy hats and too-tight-jeans and flouncy blonde hairdos.

Ugh.

There'd be so much 'howdy'-ing and 'y'all'-ing that no one would hear anything else, and if Butch said "Rolling Stones," the whole city would come to an abrupt and astonished halt. He smiled at that.

Up ahead, a green road sign approached, which should mean a pretty quick answer for dad, thank God.

Okay, still light enough to read... Jackson, no, no, don't care, Lexington. Hey, isn't that in Massachusetts? Ah, yes, there,

Nashville. Two hundred thirty miles.
Two hundred thirty miles?
"Is that right?" Butch asked.
"Yep," dad answered
"You mean," he was perplexed, "we're gonna drive all that way?"
"Yep."
"Tonight?"
"Yep."
Speechless, Butch stared at dad.
Are you out of your mind? That's gonna take at least two days! We're not stopping for two days? No supper? No hotel? No sleep?
"What's the matter," dad asked Butch's astonished face, "You need to crawl into a bed, little sleepy-bye baby? Do I have to stop and get you a crib? Huh? Need your diapers changed, too?"
Butch flamed but, hey, they've been driving since, what, sunup? Dad expected him to sit here for three or four straight days, skin sloughing off from lack of food, eyes turned in his skull from lack of sleep? Never to see *Jonny Quest* or *Hullabaloo* or any television again?
And just why in the blue blazes were they going to Nashville, anyway?
All good questions. But dad had made it a baby issue so he couldn't ask them. "No," he answered, sullenly.
"Well, all right then. You need to go sleepy-bye, you just go right ahead. 'Course, you do that, who's gonna keep me awake?"
Butch had a sudden vision of himself curled up in the passenger seat while dad, his eyes getting heavier and heavier, drifted out of the lane into an oncoming truck that hit its air horn, jolting both of them awake, dad yanking the wheel and careening off the side of the mountain, the Rambler tumbling over and over a half mile to the rocks below and exploding on impact.
"Once you get here, it's not so bad," Frank Vaughn whispered in his ear.
Butch paled. He pinched himself hard. No way he's sleeping.
They gassed up at the next exit, the attendant putting the "Closed" sign in the window as dad and Butch emerged from the bathroom. Were all the gas stations closing? How would they get to Nashville? Butch glanced at dad to see if he now realized they

102

weren't going to make it, but dad remained impassive and purposeful as he strode to the car. Butch looked longingly at the Scottish Inn across the road.

"Think I'm made of money?" dad asked as they tore out of the parking lot and got back on 40.

Butch said nothing. After a few minutes, dad reached into his pocket and threw a Butterfinger on Butch's lap. "If you're hungry, eat that." Butch was, and he did, but it was just temporary. Maybe if dad had about ten more, he'd be okay.

It got dark quick. Dad flipped on the lights and the dashboard made everything green. The world became a tunnel of head-lit Interstate, the occasional speed sign looming and flashing by, too fast for Butch to read. Billboards hulked by the side of the road, their messages lost in the dark. Butch watched them narrowly, not sure what powers they acquired at night. There were lit ones from time to time advertising hotels umpteen miles ahead…

Seeing this, dad?

…but Butch dismissed those. It was the wild, abandoned billboards standing silently in the fields, only incidentally picking up a bit of headlight to register their presence, which concerned him. They shed their man-imposed burden of advertising at night, their true, hateful natures emerging. They'd love nothing more than to eat a little boy. He shuddered.

Butch fought billboards for what seemed hours.

"I gotta pull off," dad suddenly said, matched with a bit of vehicle swerving to the right. "I'm getting too sleepy. You're not doing your job."

Butch goggled at him. Job? What was he supposed to do? Pinch him? Yeah, right; he'd lose an eye. "How do I do that?" he asked, helpless.

"Talk to me."

"About what?"

"Anything."

"Anything?"

"Anything at all."

Okay, well, there were certainly things they could discuss, like why they had to get to Nashville tonight, but that seemed a dangerous subject. Pick something safe… ah, "Did you have comic books when you were a kid?"

"No. I didn't have any. I didn't have time for them. I had to work for my supper."

Ack! Back off, back off now! "How 'bout baseball cards?"

"Yeah, we had those."

*Whew.* Butch mentally wiped his brow. "Which ones?"

Dad shrugged, "I don't really remember. They were Goudey cards."

"'Goody?'" What, only goody-goodies could have them? Then how did dad own them?

"Yeah, that was a gum company. I had Babe Ruth."

Butch's eyes rounded, "You had a Babe Ruth baseball card?"

"Yeah."

"Do you still have it?" Butch held his breath.

"Sheeyit, no. I lost that when I was still a kid."

"Oh," Butch couldn't hide his disappointment. "Why?"

"A Babe Ruth card is big points. I could probably get ten or fifteen other cards for it."

"Points?"

"Yeah. The bigger the player, the more points you get. Mickey Mantle is ten points, so is Drysdale. Kuzava's worth one."

"Is that what you do? Trade for points?"

"Yep," Butch replied, "What'd you do with yours?"

"Nothing. Just looked at them."

"That's it? You guys didn't trade them?"

"Well, yeah, we traded ones we didn't like for players we did, but not based on points or anything. It was just who we liked."

Butch nodded. "Yeah, I do that with comic books. I really like *X-Men* and *Sgt Rock* and *Nick Fury*, so I'll trade my *Batmans* for them."

"Comic books," dad sneered, "Stupid." Butch smacked himself mentally and sank lower and the silence built until dad suddenly said, "All we had was comic strips."

Hello? Butch sat up. "Like in the Sunday funnies?"

"Yeah, those. *Krazy Kat*, I liked him. And *Dick Tracy*."

"*Dick Tracy*? You had *Dick Tracy* when you were a kid?"

"Yep."

Butch marveled. "I didn't know he was so old."

Dad snorted. "Y'all didn't invent everything, ya know."

"Yeah," Butch agreed. "So, is it the same?"

"What? *Dick Tracy*? Yeah, about the same. He didn't have

wrist communicators or the flying things, though."

"Really? How'd they get around?"

"Cars," dad said simply. "He was on the radio, too."

"You mean like walkie-talkies?"

"No, no, I mean, *Dick Tracy* was a show on the radio."

"Really? Did you listen to him?"

"When I could. We didn't have a radio until just before I left."

No radio. Butch mulled that. If you didn't read and didn't go to school and worked all day just to get food, what did you do at night? Probably nothing. Probably just slept. Butch could see dad at twelve years old, dressed in overalls and Huck's straw hat, no shoes, torn shirt, dirty face, dragging himself up Mawmaw's porch, exhausted, a sack of potatoes over his shoulder. Too tired to eat, he just curled up on a burlap bag and was immediately unconscious, waking up with the rooster's crow, eating a raw potato while stumbling to the ice house where he hauled 500-pound blocks on his back. Butch's eyes widened. What a horrible life.

"When'd you leave?"

"Hmm?" dad had been gazing off to the side. "Oh, when I was sixteen."

"Sixteen? You left home when you were sixteen?" Butch was astonished. Wasn't that illegal? Sure opened up some possibilities if it wasn't.

"Yeah. I joined the Army."

Wait a minute. "You can't join the Army when you're sixteen," Butch said, smugly. He had dad now. You had to be at least thirty.

"You can if you lie about your age."

Butch's eyes popped. "You did that?"

"Yep." Dad sounded smugger than Butch had.

"And you didn't get into trouble?"

"Nope."

"How?"

Dad chuckled a bit, "Different times, back then. It was 1938. The Army thought we were going to be in a war with Germany before too long, so they didn't check too closely."

"So you joined to fight the Germans."

"I joined before the Germans."

"Huh?" Butch's jaw dropped. "You were in the Army

before?"

"Yep. Three years before."

Butch was stunned. Everyone's Dad had been in World War II. Tommy's dad had been in the infantry. Lynn's dad had been in the Navy. Frank Vaughn's dad probably was, too, although he didn't seem as old as Butch or Tommy's dad. "Was he?" he asked Frank, but got no answer.

Everyone joined the Army to fight the dirty Krauts. It never occurred to Butch that someone would be in the Army before they needed to be.

"So, then, well..." Butch wasn't quite sure what he wanted to ask.

"What?"

"Well..." He paused. "Weren't you scared?"

"Scared? Of what?"

"Being away from home."

Dad was silent, surprising Butch. He figured dad would laugh some derisive comment about only babies being scared and did he want his mommy, but nothing. He peered at dad, trying to make out his expression in the green light.

"No," he said softly, after a moment, "It was actually good."

Butch thought of straw-hatted dad with the exhausted face struggling to get a potato before his brothers did.

Yeah, maybe it would be a good thing.

"I missed Mawmaw, though," dad added, just as softly.

Butch's breath stopped. Oh, God, dad, why'd you say that?

Suddenly, clearly, Butch missed Mom. Tears welled and he struggled against them. He didn't think dad, alone in a bunk in some barracks on some forsaken Army base, ever cried when he thought of Mawmaw. But here Butch was, on a dark highway under skies he'd never seen, in woods so remote and empty that parts of it were still untrod by humans, a million miles away from Mom and racing farther away with each minute.

Dad, let's go home. Let's just turn around and go home. There's nothing out here. There's nothing in Nashville, nothing anywhere, so why do you want to feel as alone now as you did in 1938? You don't have to. There's no one grabbing the potatoes off your plate. You can have all the potatoes you want, and we'll be better; we'll stop saying things to make you mad and laughing too loud and playing instead of working and we'll get jobs and give you the money because it's only fair since you had no money when you were a kid. And I'll stop being a bookworm and I'll play baseball better and learn football and how to fix things. You'll be proud. You'll be happy.

Let's just go home.

"I gotta pull off," dad said, and they did, taking an immediate exit. Now a whole lane closer to the billboards, Butch watched them fearfully as they drove along a country road.

"Good," dad grunted and Butch saw a rest stop in the headlights, a little pull-off with a trashcan and picnic table. Dad eased the car next to the table and shut the engine and lights off.

"We'll take a little nap," he said.

"Here?" Butch knew he sounded scared.

"It'll be all right," dad, surprisingly, didn't make fun of him. "There's no one around. We'll sleep a couple of hours, then go on."

Butch looked at the dark pressing against the window. No one around, but that wasn't the problem. Roused by the car, the billboards were moving slowly, hungrily, toward them. Butch locked his door.

"You gotta pee?" dad asked.

Sure, but if dad thought he was getting out of the car..."No."

"All right," dad settled in, saying nothing.

Butch stared out. There was no way he was going to sleep.

# CHAPTER 16

"Wake up."

Huh, what? Butch blinked and got an eyeful of sun and trees. So, he had fallen asleep, despite the billboards, and was unscathed. Jesus Himself must have stood by all night, keeping the monsters at bay. He sent a quick "thank you" heavenward.

"Let's get breakfast," dad said and pulled his door latch, a sound like a pistol shot. Butch rolled out, almost hitting the picnic table with the door. First light blazed through the line of trees stretching around them, making the park golden. Robins and orioles were flying madly about, chirping and happy and vigorous.

He smiled. Good ole birds.

Dad had opened the tailgate and rummaged around in the back. Butch ducked in between dad's efforts and grabbed a few *Tales of Suspense*, dropping them on the car seat for later. The Interstate rose to their left, the country lane paralleling it. Butch could see the tops of big trucks winding past.

"What are we having?" he asked.

"C-rats," dad said as he fished among the cases.

All right!

But, first things first. Butch looked around but didn't see anything that looked like a bathroom. "Dad, I gotta go pee."

Dad pointed past the picnic table. "Go up there," he said.

Butch saw a dirt track running into the woods and curving out of sight. He'd have to pee outside? Guess so. He walked up the track, which looked like a tractor made it. The mad-happy birds converged in a triangle of pines and Butch wondered what it would be like to fly from branch to branch and sing all day. And eat worms, don't forget. Yuck.

He didn't want to get lost, so he went only far enough for good tree cover while keeping the car and dad in sight.

He pulled his pants down and aimed at the weeds, attacking grasshoppers and ants with the stream. Cyclops smiting the evil Bug World. Sure had to go, didn't he? Well, yeah, he'd been holding since last night.

A horn sounded and Butch looked up, startled. A pickup truck passing by on the country lane had a couple of people inside waving and hooting. At him, Butch realized. Dad looked at the truck and then back up the dirt track where Butch stood, pants around his ankles, moisturizing the world. Butch could see dad's grin from here. Oh no; he hadn't walked far enough and now everyone driving by, even girls and old ladies, could see him butt naked and peeing.

Trying to shrink down behind a tall weed, Butch finished as fast as he could and hastily pulled up his pants. Beet red, he walked back to the car, relieved no other trucks passed by and that the honking one was gone. Dad watched him as he approached. "Caught with your pants down, huh?" he said, then laughed.

Great, just great. Before noon, the story of the naked-butt pee-boy would be all over Tennessee. He'd walk into a diner and all the patrons would stand and point. The police would arrest him and parade him up and down the street, "This heathen pees outside!" He sure hoped dad drove straight through without stopping.

Dad handed him an open C-rats can, ham and eggs, and Butch took it, spooning the mixture into his mouth. Not bad, even cold. C-rats ham had a pleasant smoothness.

"Want some ketchup?" dad asked and Butch nodded, so dad squirted some of it from a packet onto the side of the can. Butch ate that up and then looked at dad expectantly. Sure enough, dad handed him one of the round chocolates found in every C-rat can and Butch peeled off the aluminum, very content. There was a rankness to it that no one else seemed to like but which Butch thought delicious. He licked his fingers.

Sated.

Dad handed him a canteen and Butch drank the water, hardly spilling any of it.

"Brush your teeth," dad ordered, and Butch fished around in his suitcase until he found his toothbrush and dad squeezed a little Crest on it. He attacked his gums and then rinsed with the water dad poured into his hands.

Dad had Butch gather all the trash and he ran over to the can next to the picnic table, stopped about three feet away and jump–shot the paper bag.

Score.

Butch felt pretty good as he slid into the seat. Dad started the car and backed away, pulling onto the lane and accelerating toward the Interstate. "Keep America Beautiful," Butch said.

"What?"

"Keep America Beautiful. Don't litter. That's why you made me throw the trash away."

Dad glanced at him as he pulled onto the ramp. "It's what you do with trash."

"But it still Keeps America Beautiful."

"But that ain't the reason. You don't leave trash lying around. It looks bad."

"You're still Keeping America Beautiful."

Dad shook his head, "You hear a slogan on TV and you're all for it. 'Keep America Beautiful. Munch a Bunch of Fritos… Corn Chips.'" Dad semi-sung that last.

"I like Fritos."

"Because of the slogan."

"No. I like Fritos for themselves."

"No, you don't. You wouldn't even try them if it weren't for the slogan."

Butch considered that. Had he heard the jingle and then wanted a Frito, or tasted them previously and the slogan was icing? He couldn't remember. "I guess."

"You guess. How 'bout this one? 'Let your fingers do the walking.'"

Butch smiled. "The Yellow Pages."

"Right. And you used them, too, since you heard that."

True, but, again, Butch was unsure of cause and effect. He liked the little cartoons of happy tow trucks and plumbers and, yes, may have, once or twice, hummed the jingle while letting his fingers do the walking. "I like the pictures."

"Uh, huh," dad said.

A few minutes went by as they reached speed and Butch checked billboards, suspicious. Nothing he could see. Didn't mean they were innocent.

"I'd walk a mile for a Camel," he said, as the appropriate ad whipped by.

"Hmm," dad grunted, then, after a pause, "Quick as a wink you're in the pink."

Butch immediately got a vision of the Pepto Bismol words flowing down the stomach outline on TV. "Things go better with Coke," he sang.

"Mabel, Black Label," dad responded, and they were off. They ran through the drinks and the cigarettes and both joined in a rousing chorus of "Mm! Mm! Good! Mm! Mm! Good!" and were fairly convulsed by the time the sun had made it completely over the hills.

"See the USA in your Chevrolet," Butch sang and dad suddenly quieted. Butch looked at him. Dad was tight-faced and stared down the road. Augh! should have said "Rambler" instead of "Chevrolet." But what rhymed with that? Gambler? Hambler? What's a hambler?

"We're stopping for gas," dad announced and they quickly pulled up a ramp to an Esso station perched at the top. "Go use the bathroom," dad said, and Butch slid out. He didn't really need to go and certainly didn't want to run into someone who knew the naked-butt story, but it was a chance to explore.

It was a really nice bathroom, all shiny and clean, a pleasure to pee there, so Butch made the effort. He looked around surreptitiously but no, no French Tickler machines. He finished up and played in the sink for a moment then went outside.

A couple of big trucks idled near some far pumps and people walked around. Butch stood, smelling the gas and oil and morning odors, liking them. A big fat trucker with red suspenders lumbered by. "Mornin', boy!" he called out and belched his way inside the bathroom. Butch giggled. This place was all right.

"My turn," dad said, pushing open the door. Butch wondered whether he should follow but that seemed a little strange. There was a store inside the gas station, so he went in. Tires hung from the walls and a guy in a blue jumpsuit with "Ed" stitched on his chest stood behind a counter ringing a cash register. White shelves had oil cans and air filters and cords arranged neatly on one side and candy bars on the other. Butch lingered. He wouldn't mind an Almond Joy. He felt his pocket but the only thing there was the envelope.

Dang.

Frowning, he explored the floor for a loose dime and bumped into...

a rack of comic books.

His heart almost stopped. Here, in the middle of nowhere, comics. He spun the rack—*Rawhide Kid, Daredevil, X-Men...* great! He had all these issues, though, so he thumbed behind them. *Doctor Fate* and *Hourman*? Look okay, even if it's DC. Charleton Comics, *Captain Atom*? What's that and who is he? And here we have... *Spiderman* #25, Captured by J. Jonah! Butch's heart did stop. In a gas station thousands of miles from home, a new Spidey.

Thank you, God!

"Hep ya?" Ed looked at him from the register, not unfriendly.

Butch held up the *Spiderman*. "How much is this?"

"That'll be fifteen cents." And Ed started ringing it up.

Fifteen cents? Robbery! Butch started to panic, "Wait! I have to go get my dad."

"'kay, son, but put it back until you get the cash." Ed turned to some paperwork.

Which prompted even more panic. What if someone else got it before he did? Butch looked around wildly but there were no other kids in sight. Better hurry.

He expected to see dad coming out of the bathroom, but he wasn't there. Butch poked his head inside, "Dad?" An old man with thick glasses peered at him from the urinal. "Nope," he said and Butch made a hasty retreat. He looked around but no dad so he ran back to the car but not there, either. Where'd he go? Had to find him fast because another station wagon pulled up across the way and that meant kids with money who'd get his *Spiderman*.

Butch zipped around the islands and through the mechanic's bay but no dad. He stopped, frustrated.

C'mon dad! You can't just leave me out here like this.

Could he?

A chill went through him.

You know, he could. In the storybook world, moms are wonderful and loving and dads protect kids from traffic and gypsies. But in this world, moms give their baby boys to other families and beat them to death with baseball bats. So what prevents a dad from simply leaving a bothersome child like Butch at a gas station, no food or clothes or water or money to call home and ask Mom to save you?

As if she would.

He'd be found by one of those big fat policemen who was always laughing but nothing was funny and they'd throw him in a workhouse where he'd wear striped clothes and file down rocks or mix cement, something hard and sweaty to do, and the other boys would beat him up and steal his gruel. No one would ever know what had happened to him. Years from now when he was old, thirty or so, they'd let him out, but he'd only have a fourth-grade education so he'd have to join the Army to get food and he'd live in a foxhole and the sergeant would beat him up every night and he'd get sent to die in Vietnam.

A sob escaped him. Dad! How could you do this to me? I chose you! I'm the only one who did, and you leave me? He turned, stricken, and looked at the Rambler still parked at the pump...

Oh.

Idiot. Dad might leave him, but not the Rambler. So, he's around here somewhere.

Butch walked around the other side of the store and there dad was, inside a phone booth on the corner, talking. Was it Mom? Hopeful, Butch slipped up behind, but dad saw him and waved him back.

"Should be after eight sometime," dad said, smiling, animated.

Yep, Mom. What did he mean, after eight? Butch guessed that's when dad would call back, which meant Butch could talk to Mom, too, and he felt a little surge. Come to think of it, couldn't he talk right now? But dad had already hung up and stepped out.

"Was that Mom?" Butch asked.

"No," dad replied absently, feeling in his pocket.

"Then who?" Some old war buddy in Nashville? They were going to drop by, maybe stay the night, which was infinitely better than sleeping in the car, as Butch's stiff neck reminded him. They must be a lot farther from Nashville than he thought if they weren't going to be there until eight.

"None of your business," dad said, pulling out his wallet.

No problem. He'd find out when they stopped at the guy's house. Maybe he had kids Butch could play with. Dad counted his money, and Butch didn't hesitate. "Dad, can I have a quarter?"

"What?" Dad looked up sharply. "I gave you one yesterday."

Butch froze. "Uh, I spent that."

"On what?"

"The soda."

"I didn't see you bring a soda back to the car."

How could dad remember that?

Butch gulped—he was dead. He'd never been a good liar and dad would demand an explanation and Butch would have to show him the Tickler and that would be it. Possession of the Tickler, whatever it was, constituted a mortal offense, at least based on the waitress's reaction.

And Frank's warning.

The Tickler was like having the proceeds from a bank robbery or the answer key to a test. Dad'd remove Butch's head, no hesitation.

Think of something. Quick.

"I drank it in the store." Butch hoped his trembling wasn't noticeable.

"Mighty fast drinking," was all dad said and Butch felt a spark of relief, quickly dashed. "Where's the rest of it?"

"Rest of it?"

"The change."

"Oh." Dang it! There'd still be fifteen cents left over. "I had some ice cream and some candy, too."

"You had all that in the store? Lordy, boy, what'd you do, stuff it all down in about three seconds?" Dad looked at him, incredulous, and Butch assumed the part, hanging his head.

"I was hungry."

"I guess you were. Whachew want the quarter for?"

Here it comes. "Comic book," he muttered and held his breath.

"Comic book?" Dad was contemptuous. "A comic book? Don't you have enough already?"

"It's new."

Dad stared at him and Butch's lip quivered as he kept his head down.

C'mon, c'mon, wasn't he appropriately craven? Enough

humiliation, cough up the quarter.

"Comic book," dad sneered as he dug into the wallet's change purse and slapped the quarter, a little too hard, in Butch's hand. "Hurry up. We're leaving," and stalked away.

Butch's heart sang, followed quickly by panic as he hurried inside. Sure enough, there was some chunky kid idly looking through the rack. Butch spotted the *Spiderman* one slot away from Chunky's grubby hands and he didn't hesitate, walked up, peeled it out and made for the register. Chunky watched him with mild surprise then turned and trilled, "Hey, Dad!" to some nearby adult wearing shorts and a fishing hat, "Can I have a comic book?"

"Sure," Fishing Hat said offhand and Butch's jaw dropped.

That's it, you just ask for it and get it? Butch looked back at Chunky Boy as Ed rang up the *Spiderman*. Easy for you, isn't it?

He slipped the change into his pocket and gave Chunky a hateful look as he walked out. Chunky responded with only mild interest.

Dad drove down the ramp and back out on the Interstate. "Get what you want?" He couldn't hide the ridicule.

Butch nodded, already examining the cover.

"Where's my change?"

Butch chilled. Slowly, he reached into his pocket.

Don't pull out the Tickler, whatever you do.

Carefully, with almost surgical precision, he fingered the nickel and five pennies and quietly put them in dad' s outstretched hand.

"What's that in your pocket?" Dad asked.

Oh no. Oh no, Lord, no, please don't let this happen. "Baseball card," Butch breathed.

"Oh," dad said. And nothing else.

Butch thanked Jesus for His daily miracles and threw in a distraction, just to be sure. "Dad, where we going?"

"I told you, Nashville."

"What are we doing there?"

Dad shrugged. "Driving through."

# CHAPTER 17

Butch was in his umpteenth reading of *Spiderman* by the time they got to Nashville and he barely noticed the city at all. Flash Thompson bullying Peter Parker was far more interesting. He had to puzzle out some of the words, wishing Tommy was here to make it easier, but there was satisfaction in finally getting it.

They didn't stop in Nashville, which blew Butch's theory about the war buddy and raised questions about the phone call. Butch wondered, for about a second, if he should enquire about this, but a rare burst of common sense overtook him.

They stopped for lunch somewhere past Nashville and Butch had a cheap hot dog because he didn't want to cost dad any more money than necessary. Economies like that placated the beast. He quietly read his other comics while dad worked the country music channels with almost savage joy, chasing down Loretta Lynn. More placation.

"Virrrrginny!"

Startled, Butch looked up from Sergeant Fury's death grapple with the Red Skull. They were passing a big "Welcome to Virginia" sign, with a picture of a cardinal on it. Butch liked cardinals and followed the sign until it was out of sight. The road diverged a bit here, part of it going straight and part of it looping.

"We're in Virginia?" Butch asked.

"Yep."

Butch looked at the rolling, green hills. "Neat!" he said.

"Yes, it is." Dad looked satisfied.

'Neat' didn't nearly express it. This was the land of the Civil

War, which Tommy and Butch re-enacted in the backyard, Tommy using a double-lawn rocking chair, all rust and sharp edges, as fortification against Butch's intrepid, but ultimately unsuccessful, assaults. Tommy would let him scale the works and then bayonet him a few times before the inevitable fallback. Gettysburg, Sharpsburg, Petersburg, they did them all, Butch sometimes in the guise of Robert E. Lee. Great fun.

Should bad weather force them inside, they set up epic battles on Tommy's garage floor. Tommy had a lot of Civil War soldiers, both Reb and Yank, which Butch supplemented with enough WWII infantry to make a fairly credible opposing force. Tommy also had cannons, which he split with Butch, and some cavalry, too, and the war raged all afternoon. 'Raged' was a pretty good description because they invariably got into heated arguments about which line caused what casualties and whether cavalry could actually penetrate flanks like that. 'Course, when Fourth of July rolled around, those arguments became academic. They hurled Black Cats and Torpedoes at each other's forces until one was obliterated. Very fair.

Wouldn't be doing that this Fourth.

A rather sad thought, but Butch dismissed it for the greater interest of nearby battlefields. Dad had turned off the Interstate and was on a side road, 11. Butch scrutinized the signs: Abingdon, Wytheville, Atkins… none of them were familiar.

"Dad, were there any Civil War battles fought around here?"

Dad checked his mirror as he swung onto 58. "Don't think so."

"Oh."

Dad, surprisingly, read the disappointment. "But this is the Shenandoah Valley."

"Really?" Butch brightened and resumed his scrutiny. A Jimmy Stewart Civil War movie called *Shenandoah* was coming out soon. He'd seen the trailer during *Mister Moses* and it looked real good, especially the battle scenes. There were kids in it, so it was doubly worth seeing. If they ever stopped long enough to find a movie theater, he'd have to ask dad to take him. And dad probably would. He liked war movies, too.

"So where's the river?"

"What river? The Shenandoah? Hell, that's at least a 100 miles from here."

What? "Then why is this the Shenandoah Valley?"

Dad threw a cigarette out the wing and lit another. "Because the river is in this valley."

"How can that be, if it's 100 miles away?"

Dad chuckled a bit, "Because the valley is longer than the river."

"Oh." Butch considered that. Apparently, there didn't have to be a one-for-one relationship between name and feature. Seemed somewhat of a gyp, but understandable. If you had to name a valley, a nearby river worked. So, if he didn't actually get to see the Shenandoah, he could at least tell Tommy he'd been in its namesake. That would be worth points.

But how to collect them? Could call; Elgin 34719—he recited Tommy's number silently. Long distance calls cost a lot, though, and he didn't think dad would allow it. Ah, he could write a letter! Butch squirmed in delight. He'd tell Tommy all about his travels in the Valley and Tommy would write back all jealous…

Write back? To where?

Butch blinked out the window. Good question.

Suddenly, the Valley wasn't this graceful, staid place of historical significance, but a labyrinth of unknown roads, mysterious hills, indifferent woods. Butch didn't know these towns or these people, what was nearby, what were the far points of reference. In Lawton he knew Mt. Scott and Cache Boulevard and Oklahoma City, could place himself in that sphere, but 'Route 58' and 'Abingdon' meant nothing. He couldn't tell anyone where he was. Tommy could not find him. Nor Mom, nor Cindy.

If something happened, say the car plunged down one of these embankments and dad was crushed to death against the wheel but Butch survived and managed to get back to the road, gasping, swaying with the effort, would anyone stop? They'd know he Wasn't From Around Here and cast dismissive glances as they drove by. Should he manage to locate a phone, what would he tell Mom, presuming he had enough change to make the call? "Mom! I'm in the Shenandoah Valley! Where the Civil War was fought? Come get me!" but she wouldn't know exactly where and a fat policeman would put him in the workhouse. Lost. Forever.

Butch cast a panicked eye at the side of the road. A moment's inattention would undo them. Disappeared somewhere in the Valley, Mrs. Deats, that's all we know. We'll eventually find the bodies and ship them home to you.

Keep the old boy awake. "Dad?"

"Hmm?" he was lighting another Raleigh.

"Where are we?"

"I told you, Virginia. The Shenandoah Valley."

"I know, but..."

"But what?"

Butch was stumped. He was trying to ask a metaphysical question with unsuited words. He wanted to know if he was safe, if this feeling of drift, of aimlessness, had a purpose. Were they actually going somewhere? Would Butch get a life back? Would he get an address and exchange letters with Tommy?

"Where we going?"

Dad took a puff. "Newport News."

Butch's brow furrowed. "What's that?"

"A city. You'll like it. It's on the ocean."

The ocean? Butch's brow unfurrowed. Now, that's different.

He'd seen the ocean before, in New Jersey when they visited Mom's parents, Nanny and Pop-Pop, and he and Cindy were really, really young, long before school and Tom Sawyer even existed, and they both ran like madmen through the waves and gulls and brown sand, shrieking with the exhilaration of spray and sun and emptiness. Art stood befuddled in the surf, but Butch and Cindy knew what to do and kicked water and made castles and threw sand and buried each other. They both cried when Pop-Pop said it was time to go. The ocean was great.

"What are we going there for?"

Dad shrugged. "Look for a job."

"You're going to get a job there?"

"Gonna try."

"Is that where we're going to live?"

"Maybe."

Butch sat back. Live in a city by the ocean. He'd sail and catch big fish like *The Old Man and the Sea* but he wouldn't let the sharks get his. He'd cast a net and haul in shrimp and wear a cap and bell bottoms. The crews of great ships would wave at him as he played about in his little sailboat, expertly dodging wakes. He would write letters to Tommy and Cindy every day, telling them about his maritime adventures.

"Will we have an address?" Butch asked.

Dad let out a little chuckle, "Well, yeah, we'll have an address. Why?"

"I have to write letters," he said.

Dad stared at him for a moment, then turned to his driving. The road slipped in and out of hills and small rivers, but now with direction. They were going to the ocean. Butch wasn't lost anymore.

# CHAPTER 18

"Wanna see the ocean?"

"Huh?" Butch started, disoriented. A quick glance around... oh, okay.

He was in the car, comics on his lap and one or two on the floor. Must have fallen asleep after that Sinclair station somewhere past the Valley.

"Look there," dad said and pointed out the windshield.

The road rose to a gray line in the middle of the horizon that really shouldn't be there.

Butch squinted. What the heck was that? Oh, it's water. A couple of ships floating there helped define it. "Neat!" he said.

They approached the top of the road and now Butch could see a lot more water arrayed to their right and front, and a lot more ships, all rusted with smoke coming out of their stacks, complicated works along their tops and a lot of big boxes stacked here and there. The ocean went on forever, dots of ships in the distance, all gray, no blue in sight, maybe because it was so late. The sun had already gone, the afterlight turning the water into silhouette and shadow and cloud. Indistinct, dismal.

As was the land. Factories and docks and warehouses, dingy and haphazard, built on a whim. There was little activity; no trucks, very few people moving around. Butch figured everybody had gone home for the day.

They descended now and Butch gasped. A huge tunnel loomed, yawning and hungry. Feeble lamps arrayed along the top didn't help. The entrance to hell and they were heading right for it.

"You afraid?" Dad sneered.

Butch shook his head no. Such a lie.

"You been in tunnels before," dad observed.

True. There'd been a real long one when they drove from Oklahoma to New Jersey to see Nanny and Pop-Pop. 'Course he'd been with Dale and Cindy and Art and there was protection in numbers. To avoid accusations of "'Fraidy cat!", they'd all held their breaths and acted like it was nothing. They'd emerged unscathed and it had been kind of neat, overall, so what was different?

He was doing this on his own, that's what.

The tunnel swallowed them and they were in darkness, the feeble lamps doing absolutely nothing. Dad put on the lights but that didn't do much more. Butch watched the passing tunnel, wide-eyed. A walkway ran down it and signs flashed by so this wasn't as bad as a real cave, like Carlsbad Caverns, which had been black and eternal, a place where dragons lived.

And bats. Jeez, lots of bats.

He remembered one skittering between Mom's feet on the walkway, giving her a heart attack. They'd sat on benches in front of a monstrous black opening the guide called the Bat Cave, and Butch felt small and eatable. A dragon, three or four dragons, could easily fit in there although the guide assured him it was just bats which, of course, can eat you, too.

At sunset, they stood near the entrance and watched as the bats burst out, whirling from the cave in an unending, squeaking line, all the vampires in the world stretching from the cave to the horizon, a dark underscore to the emerging stars. Dad said some of them made it all the way to Lawton, which Butch found extraordinary. After that, every bat he saw came from Carlsbad.

"Dad, are there bats in here?" he asked, shivering.

"Maybe, you never know," he answered, but Butch detected amused cruelty in his voice. Dad wanted to scare him.

"Right," one of Butch's rare opportunities to apply sarcasm, and he suddenly felt better.

"You know, we're under the ocean," dad said.

What? Alarmed, Butch peered upwards, the gray ceiling faint in the light. The ocean was above them? "How deep are we?"

"Pretty deep," dad said, "The ships go right over the top."

Butch's jaw dropped. "Don't they hit the tunnel?"

"Sometimes."

Butch stared at him, aghast. "Ships hit the tunnel?"

"Yeah, like I said, sometimes. You can see it if you're standing on shore. The ships will jolt and you know they've just hit it."

"But," Butch spluttered, "they'll crash through!"

"Nah." Dad flipped his Raleigh out the wing, sending sparks flowing down the car's side. "They don't hit it that hard." He paused. "Usually."

Butch half expected the prow of a ship to suddenly burst through the ceiling, forming a wall directly in front of them as the entire ocean poured in behind. They'd slam into it and Butch would struggle out the door as dad screamed "Run!" but the black freezing water would grab his legs and knock him off balance and he'd be swept under the ship as it kept going, scouring its way through the rest of the tunnel, the massive propellers coming closer and closer...

They cleared the tunnel and ascended a long flat road with the ocean on either side. Butch let out a breath of great relief and glanced furtively at dad, who had a half smile on his face. Butch flamed. Dad got him, after all.

They drove, crossing occasional bridges that gave a good view of the water and the land on either side. "This is Hampton Roads," dad said, "where those Civil War ironclad ships fought."

The Merrimac and the Monitor! Butch pressed his face against the window, trying to make out as much detail as he could. More points from Tommy.

The next thing Butch knew, they were in an honest-to-God city. Buildings and stores pressed against each other on both sides of the narrow street and lots of buses and cabs and people running about. He stared, round-eyed. Downtown Lawton, once past the A&W where Dale worked, was pretty busy, but this was magnitudes above that, almost like New York City. "Dad, is this Newport News?"

"Yep." He waited patiently behind a bus, then turned a few times, doubling back, and it became apparent even to Butch that he was looking for something. A clock in a store window showed a bit past eight.

"Where we going, Dad?"

"A friend of mine's."

Inadequate information and Butch gathered breath for more questions, specifically what friend, where do you know him from, what are we going to do here, what am I going to do here, can I call Mom? when dad said, "Ah," and pulled over quickly, into a parking spot.

"C'mon," dad said and got out. Butch opened his door wide and a horn sounded. Startled, he pulled it back, realizing he had almost smacked a car going by. The driver glared at Butch and he ducked his head, embarrassed. Real rube, wasn't he?

"Stop wasting time," dad snapped and Butch pushed out, cautious this time and scurried around the front of the car. Dad was under a green and white awning, his hand on the knob of a shoe repair shop. News' Shoes—'Newport News,' get it?—was blazoned in yellow above the awning, with the Cats' Paw logo on one side. Two big windows flanked the entrance, both filled with shoes progressing from utter loss to shining, pristine examples of the cobbler's art. Butch figured this demonstrated News' restorative capabilities. Lights blazed inside and Butch saw people in there, a couple of them sitting on big, elevated leather chairs braced against the left wall. Others sat in regular chairs facing the elevated chairs, watching an old black man bent over the shoes of the elevated people. Butch frowned. Were they getting their shoes fixed?

They went in, a little bell tinkling overhead. The customers gave grunts of greeting. Dad grunted back. Fat old white men wearing suits, gray hair framing red, veiny faces and rheumy eyes, sat in the elevated chairs. The regular-chair people were all about the same, except for a black kid, maybe fifteen, with very short hair and a very smooth face, who stared solemnly at Butch. Butch raised a hesitant hand in greeting, but the black kid just furrowed his brow.

"Evenin', gentlemen." The black man stopped popping a cloth on a nice set of burgundy brogans worn by one of the elevated and turned, smiling.

Uncle Remus, Butch immediately thought. Kind, coal black shiny and wrinkled face, white white hair, and mirth in his eyes— all they needed was orchestra swell and 'Zip-A-Dee-Do-Dah.' Butch shook his head in amazement. Such people really exist.

"You be wantin' a shine, youngster?" Uncle smiled down at Butch and all the old white men looked at him.

Butch was on the spot. "Uh," he said and turned out his Keds.

"Well, I don't 'spect so!" Uncle laughed and everyone else joined in and Butch realized he'd done well. He warmed and smiled at Uncle. "Maybe later." That got some appreciation, but not as much. Don't push it, Butch decided and slipped in behind dad, heading toward the back. He glanced at the black kid, who ignored him.

Dad stood at a long counter that separated a large room from the shoe shines. Worktables and shelves filled with shoes tagged with too-long strings were stacked all the way to the back. The smell of leather and polish hung like a fog and the high whine of a machine cut the air. Butch saw a grizzled, swarthy man sewing a boot together on a heavy sewing machine placed next to a curtain. Another swarthy man, younger than the sewer, sat next to him, tapping nails into the bottom of a slipper mounted on a metal saddle. "Sim?" the older swarth asked as he looked up.

Butch furrowed his brow. Sim who?

"Is Dorey here?" dad asked.

Dorey? Butch looked at dad. Who's Dorey?

Before the swarth could answer, the curtain parted and a woman stepped out. She looked at dad and smiled warmly. "Owen," she said.

"Dorey," dad responded, a small smile on his face. "We made it."

"So I see." She raised a hinged portion of the counter, passed through it and kissed dad lightly on the cheek.

Butch looked at her. She was tall, almost as tall as dad, with black hair cut close around her head like that Twiggy model. There were smiley lines on her face. She had dark eyes, maybe brown, hard to say, and an olive complexion. Italian or something. Very slender, virtually no boobies at all, which Butch found a surprising thought.

She turned to him. "You must be Butch," she said, holding out a hand.

Butch took it, too surprised to do anything but stare at her. "Rob was right," Frank whispered in his ear.

# CHAPTER 19

A woman's contralto floated across Butch's dream. "Wake up, sleepyhead. What do you want for breakfast?"

"Mom?" Butch muttered. Couldn't be. He was in some apartment thousands of miles away from her. Unless magic was real and dreams came true...

"Wrong guess," the contralto said gently.

Butch opened his eyes. Dorey, dressed in a pink velour-like bathrobe that looked really comfortable, was at the foot of the couch. So, no magic. But Dorey had a little smile on her face and compassion in her eyes and Butch decided he liked her.

"Sorry," he murmured. The little smile grew big and genuine. A real sense of fun, Butch concluded and liked her even more.

"That's all right. Would you like waffles?"

"Well, yeah!" There is magic, after all.

She laughed, "I thought so. Get cleaned up and they'll be ready when you're done."

She turned away and Butch discreetly put on his jeans before heading to the bathroom. You're not seeing my underwear, lady. He did his business and found his toothbrush next to dad's kit and cleaned his teeth and splashed his face. Okay.

He stepped out. Ahh! Not only waffles but bacon, too! Follow your nose, the nose always knows! But the beigeness of the place disoriented him. A long living room with fluffy brownish carpet and an off-white overstuffed couch—last night's bed—stretched before him. A tan blanket drooped half off equally tan couch pillows, still dented with his skull. A painting of dark-brown swirls that didn't form into any image Butch recognized hung over the couch, flanked by two smaller versions of itself; those, in turn, were bracketed by light brown candles inside copper sconces. Thin cream curtains billowed in the light breeze of a tall white fan oscillating in the corner and occasionally revealed a window. It was like living in a Twinkie.

He stepped between two shapeless beige chairs guarding an opening on the right from which sunlight beamed and bacon sizzled. Dorey stood at a stove. "Take a seat," she said cheerily and Butch pulled out a white wooden chair placed against the off-white wooden table. Aunt Jemima greeted him from the center of the table and Butch stared, hoping she'd wink.

"Here ya go." Dorey put down a plate before him and Butch was suddenly starving. Instinct was to grab the fork and fall to, but he didn't know this woman so he looked at her sideways.

"Go ahead, it's all right." She smiled and that was enough protocol.

As he devoured, she sat down opposite and opened a Metracal. "Been awhile since you had a home-cooked meal, isn't it?"

"Five days," Butch answered between bites. Mawmaw's didn't count; she said home, right?

"Five days," she mused. "Are you all right?"

Butch, a bit startled by the question, kept things neutral. "Yes."

"Are you homesick?"

Was he? He'd been torn away from Cindy and Mom and Tommy and a summer of swimming and playing army in the snakey field across from Carl's and devising new X-Men adventures and riding his bike down the murderously steep hill next to the house. He'd never see B.C. Swinney again, nor Mom, nor Jonny Quest.

And a dead kid talked to him.

Not homesick. In shock.

"No," he replied and wondered if he was convincing.

Apparently so. She nodded and brought more waffles until he sighed contentedly. "That was really good," he said.

She smiled. "Would you like to watch TV until I get everything cleaned up?"

His heart leaped. Oh, well, yeah!

It must have shown because she laughed and turned on a white portable Admiral sitting on the kitchen counter.

Hallelujah!

She showed him how to tune the channels and tidied the kitchen as Butch maneuvered his chair into prime viewing position. The set warmed up in time for Butch to see the Captain getting pelted by a shower of ping-pong balls and he laughed, although he missed Moose's actual joke.

"Your dad left early," Dorey said, pouring Vel into the sink.

Oh yeah, dad. He'd disappeared last night as Butch gratefully fell on the couch into a dead sleep. Man, who'd'a thought riding in a car was so exhausting? Come to think of it, dad had pretty much disappeared from the moment Dorey kissed him in the shoe shop. Butch hadn't really looked at him since then.

"Where'd he go?" Butch asked.

"To the airfield about a job."

"Oh." A job at the airfield. That implied they were staying.

She must have read his mind. "He's just checking. He's not sure he'll take it." She looked at him, worried.

Uh-oh, did he give her the impression he didn't want to stay because he didn't like her? Augh, an inadvertent insult!

"He likes to fly," Butch said.

There, an indication dad would take the job and they would stay, maybe even here with you, Dorey. No need to feel insulted.

It worked. She smiled, "I know. He's like a kid up there."

Butch's eyebrows rose. You know?

"Have you ever gone up with him?" she asked, missing it.

"No. They won't let us fly on Army helicopters."

"Oh, that's right," she said absently and reached for a cigarette. Kools, Butch noted.

"You don't smoke Raleighs?"

"No, they're too harsh," she said, drawing the first puff.

"You can get stuff with the coupons."

"They offer the coupons to offset the taste."

Hmm. Make a mediocre product palatable by offering something else. Like Batman comics carrying extra stories in them.

"You're not smoking, are you?" she asked suspiciously.

"No!" Butch giggled that into about three syllables. Ludicrous. He was way not old enough.

She smiled, "That's good. It's a bad habit."

Butch forewent the obvious question because he already knew the answer—it relaxed you, tasted good and, most importantly, marked you as a grownup. He still had no inclination to smoke, though. It seemed like a waste of time.

"So what grade are you in?"

"Fifth."

"You just finished fifth?"

"No, I'm going into fifth."

"Hmm." She took another long puff. "My nephew, Johnny, is going into sixth. He's coming over today, along with his sister, Marianne. She's going into seventh. Would you like to play with them?"

"Sure," he responded, noncommittally. He'd see when they got here.

"Okay," she ended the cigarette. "I'm going to finish the kitchen and then do some vacuuming. You can keep watching TV."

Butch smiled. Deal.

# CHAPTER 20

"Hi, I'm Johnny," the boy said. "This is my ugly sister, Marianne."

Butch giggled, more so when Marianne, rather good-naturedly, socked Johnny in the arm. "At least I'm not stupid," she said.

"Who says?" Johnny came back and there ensued a rather riotous insult exchange that had Butch rolling.

"All right, all right," Dorey called from the kitchen where she was making hot dogs, "Stop that or I'll call your Mom."

"*Phhppt!*" Johnny indicated how seriously he took that threat.

Butch held his side. He grinned so much his face hurt. These guys were all right. Johnny was skinny and narrow-faced, everything rising from the sides of his head like a mountain ridgeline to the middle of his nose, merry blue eyes dancing with devilment capped it. Marianne was flatter-faced and taller and her mouth had a permanent sardonic twist while her brown eyes were cooler, but she possessed an equal air of devilment. Butch was in for a great time.

"So what do you like?" Johnny asked.

Butch did not hesitate. "Comics."

Marianne rolled her eyes but Johnny nodded and said, "Cool."

Cool? Butch blinked. Maynard Krebs said that, Mike said that, flower children did, too, but not a lot of others. Everyone Butch knew said "Neat." "Cool" was a different take. A good one.

"Marvel?" Johnny asked. Butch nodded, and Johnny waggled

his hand. "Eh. They're okay. I like *Mad*."

"Yeah," Butch agreed, "*Mad*'s great. I like Spy vs. Spy."

"Don Martin."

"Yeah! Lighter Side," and they were off, fold-ins and Scenes We'd Like to See and Gazoonked and "What-me-Worry?"-ed each other until they were absolutely convulsed.

Marianne shook her head. "Nerds."

Johnny jerked a thumb. "Don't listen to her. She reads *Confidential*."

"Oh, no!" Butch giggled, "Will Liz and Sammy run off together?" He was pleased how much that cracked Johnny up.

"Idiots," Marianne muttered and stalked off, disappearing into the kitchen.

Butch felt strangely cut by that, but Johnny said, "C'mon!" and Butch followed him out to the foyer where Johnny dug into a knapsack. "Here it is," he said and pulled out…

…a GI Joe.

An aura of golden light beamed down from heaven while angels sang, "Ahhhhhh!" An honest-to-God GI Joe! Butch took it reverently from Johnny's offering hands, cradling the black-haired Joe, dressed in Marine fatigues with an M-1 and a backpack, the cheek scar shining red in the golden light. "Wow," Butch breathed.

"You got one?" Johnny asked.

"No." Butch shook his head sadly. "My dad says they're dolls and only girls play with dolls."

"Grownups," Johnny snorted, summarizing adult obtuseness. "Use that one," and he reached into the knapsack and pulled out another GI Joe, the Army MP version.

The light intensified and the angels sang louder. "You have two?"

"Yeah," Johnny said absently as he fished around for Joe pistols and entrenching equipment and rifles. Butch concluded Johnny was kid royalty, luckier even than Tommy, who had model airplanes and games and a million comics and toy soldiers but whose father shared dad's viewpoint about Joes.

They played in the foyer, one Joe becoming Nazi or Russian as necessary. They stopped and ate hot dogs, enduring Marianne's scathing commentary regarding "boy dolls," Butch and Johnny countering with "action figure." Dorey laughed and pitched into either side as the argument faltered, encouraging more than teasing, which raised her stock even more. Then they returned to war. Marianne, surprisingly, joined them, adding Barbie as a nurse and sometimes fifth columnist.

It was so absorbing a day that Butch was startled when the door swung open and dad stood there, blinking. "What's going on?" he asked suspiciously.

"Nothin'," Johnny answered breezily, barely glancing up. Johnny's easy dismissal of dad and Marianne's downright ignoring him startled Butch even more. Didn't they know he was the Beast?

Dad's eyes narrowed as he took in their play but said nothing, glanced over Marianne and Barbie then, with a slow shake his head, strode off to the kitchen. Butch watched him sideways, wondering if he would turn back with merciless ridicule about sissies and play-babies, but, no, kept going. With an eye out for danger, Butch continued the game. Marianne frowned at him, picking up the sudden hesitancy that Johnny missed.

"Time to go!" Dorey sang breezily as she came out of the kitchen.

"Awww!" all three responded, Marianne just as emphatic. That was pleasing. Things were packed and Johnny and he exchanged giggles over some remembered maneuvers and Marianne added eye rolls but there was something less insulting in them now. "See ya later," Johnny said as he tripped down the stairs. Marianne merely waved but also gave Butch an appraising, and somewhat disconcerting, look. Out the door and gone.

"Have a nice time?" Dorey asked.

"Yeah, I mean, yes, ma'am, I really did." Butch looked up at her. "Thanks."

She smiled, genuinely pleased. "You're welcome. We'll see if they can come back tomorrow," raising Butch's hopes.

He followed her back to the living room where dad sat smoking, a half-empty glass of beer in front of him. "Have fun?" he asked, with contempt.

"Yes," Butch replied, wary.

Dad nodded and puffed and Butch slid into a chair beside him, keeping some retreat distance. "Did you get the job?" he asked.

"No," dad said, drinking more of the beer. Butch eyed it. "You want some?" Dad asked and Butch nodded, taking the glass and sipping.

"You drink beer?" Dorey stood by the table open-mouthed.

"Tastes good," Butch said.

"I let him have a little," dad said absently.

"Oh," Dorey turned and attended to something then looked back at them. "I can't get over how much you two look alike."

It was said so sweetly that Butch forewent the impulse to laugh. Obviously, Dorey, it's impossible for Adopto-Boy to look like Adopto-dad, but it would be rude to point that out, so Butch remained impassive and noted that dad did, too. How 'bout that? They were actually sharing a thought.

"You ready?" Dad asked and Butch looked at him to ask for what, but dad was on Dorey.

"Yep," she said cheerily and hooked a purse over her shoulder as dad levered off the couch.

Dorey noted Butch's alarm. "We're going to the shop," she said.

"You're going, too," dad added.

# CHAPTER 21

"Hello, young'un!" the old black man greeted Butch as he strolled in behind dad, "Did you come back for that shine?"

Butch dutifully turned out his Keds and the black man shook his head, still smiling, "I guess not."

Dorey laughed, "Uncle George, this is Butch."

Uncle George made a bow and extended his hand. Butch took it. "Pleased to meet you, Butch," and shook vigorously.

Butch smiled, quite taken with his manner.

"This here's my grandnephew, Ronald." Uncle George gestured at the same black teenager sitting in the same chair, who regarded Butch with indifference. Butch waved shyly and Ronald gave him a barely perceptible nod.

Uncle George frowned, as if about to say something, but the doorbell tinkled and they turned. A black girl, maybe fifteen, very slim and very pretty, stood there glaring at them all. Ronald leaped to his feet and joined the girl, both sailing from the store with an air of youth and excitement, the girl leaving behind another glare.

"That Louisa," Uncle George chuckled, "she's something. Got that Ronald wrapped around her little finger. Don't let that happen to you, young man," Uncle George warned Butch, sternly.

"No, sir," he replied solemnly. The old fat white man Uncle George was shining up said something and they both laughed and Uncle turned back to his business. Dad and Dorey had already moved to the back and Butch followed in their wake.

Dorey sat behind an old rickety desk piled high with yellow papers, a black telephone on one side. She had books open in front of her, writing from one to the other.

Ledgers, Butch thought.

Dad sat in front of the desk on a folding chair, reading a paper.

"*Filho*," someone said.

Butch looked. The same swarthy old man as last night sat behind the same sewing machine, his face creased and recreased by smile wrinkles. Butch guessed he was in his sixties.

"*Vindo, vindo*," the old man waved him in.

Butch cocked his head. "Huh?"

"He's telling you to come over, he wants to show you something." The younger man was stacking shoes in the corner.

"Oh," Butch said and, warily, slipped under the counter. The old man grasped Butch's shoulder with steel fingers and pulled him next to the bench. He placed a small nail against the sole of a shoe propped on the iron saddle and expertly hammered it in. He then spoke rapidly, gutturally, in a language absolutely incomprehensible and gave Butch the hammer and a nail. "*Prueves*."

Butch looked at him. "He wants you to try," said the young man.

"Oh," Butch said and the old man nodded in encouragement. Butch lined up the nail and was about to strike.

"No, no," the old man said and moved Butch's hand to readjust the nail's position. "Okay," he said and Butch tapped it in.

"Good, good!" the old man beamed and let off a long stream of that same alien language to the young man, who chuckled. "He says you're a natural."

"Thanks!" Butch smiled at the old man who smiled back and handed him a whole bunch of nails, talking gibberish the whole time. With the old man guiding, Butch nailed the sole to the shoe, earning various foreign words of either encouragement or admonishment, he couldn't tell. The old man adjusted him with his steel grip and Butch's arm quickly went numb. The young man must have noticed because he spoke sharply and the old man's grip relaxed and he spoke apologetically.

"Papa doesn't know his own strength," the young man said as he lifted up a load of shoes and hefted them onto the shelf.

"That's okay," Butch said to Papa and returned to the task.

"Put him to work, huh?" dad said and Butch looked up to see

him by the counter watching Papa. "'Bout time someone got some use out of him."

Butch supposed it was a joke, but he flamed with embarrassment, anyway. Papa smiled and said some things but dad had already turned away. The young man frowned and did not translate.

It didn't seem like fun after that. Butch finished the job, handed the hammer back and moved away from the bench. Papa implored him to stay, promising to show him other things, Butch guessed. He went into the office. Dad was reading the paper, again.

"Is this your store?" Butch asked Dorey.

"It sure is," she said, flipping a page of the ledger.

Butch was impressed. "How'd you get it?"

"Bought it."

Even more impressive. Butch figured it had cost about a million dollars. "Wow."

She smiled. Dad folded the paper down and looked at him with annoyance. "Stop bothering people," he snapped.

Butch shrank reflexively. Dorey looked surprised. "It's all right. He's not bothering me."

"Yes, he is."

"No really, it's fine," she said, perplexed, like Mom with dad's moods.

Dad glanced at her then stared at Butch, warning. He returned to his paper and Butch took that opportunity to slip out the door. Papa said something and gestured, but Butch shrugged and walked all the way back to the front. He slid into Ronald's chair.

Uncle George was working the shoes of another fat white man, both in animated conversation over baseball. Butch leaned forward, picking up the rhythm of the talk and the shine rag.

"Don't know how the Reds are gonna make things better," the fat man said, contemptuously.

"I dunna, either," Uncle agreed, with rag pops, "We did pretty good with the Senators, pretty good, but you gotta admit, we're playing in a better league now."

"Yeah, Uncle, that's true. The Pilots got some real competition now, but I don't know. The Reds."

Uncle laughed and popped and turned to Butch. "You follow

baseball, boy?"

"Sure."

"Who's your favorite team?"

"Yankees."

The fat man snorted. "Yankees? I thought you followed baseball!"

"They're still pretty good."

"Maybe Whitey is, but the rest of 'em..." and the man waggled his hand.

"Now, come on there, you kickin' 'em when they'se down," Uncle said and Butch wondered why his speech changed.

"I suppose," the white man conceded and the talk went on to boxing and the Olympics and Butch tuned out. He looked through the magazines, happy to find an old Atlas comic with a bunch of unknown superheroes in it, including one guy who was learning to be a barber and shaved off his boss's hair so he could get fired, get into costume, and fight some big monster. Butch laughed.

That killed ten minutes. Five minutes more died watching Uncle George pop shoes with that pleasing rhythm. Butch started swinging his feet to it, enthusiastically at times, which drew frowns from waiting fat white men. He stopped and stared out the window. It was nearing sunset and gray and busy, the way a big city's streets should be, and he felt an urge to join it. He stood and moved to the door.

"Where you goin', young man?" Uncle George asked his back.

That surprised Butch because he'd thought Uncle was absorbed in his work. "Nowhere," he intoned.

"Don't get lost," Uncle said and Butch smiled as he slipped outside.

Butch stood under the awning. The street was made of taxis and buses, the sidewalks of hatted men in suits carrying briefcases and high-heeled, smartly dressed women carrying leather purses. They ignored Butch. Other men, wearing overalls or work pants and steel helmets and carrying lunch pails, didn't. "Hey, boy!" they said or "Youngster!" as they passed. Butch smiled. The overalled seemed in a better mood than the suited. The overalled swung their pails and laughed and smacked each other's backs and Butch guessed their mood extended to onlookers.

There was a jewelry store right next to him and Butch idly

gazed in the window. Rings and bracelets and watches. The watches were nice, but they were $10.00 and up and there was no way he could get that from dad. Butch jingled his pocket around the cardboard envelope and figured he still had a dime and some pennies. What could he do with that?

The sun burst out, bathing the street in red as Butch looked up and focused on a sign only three stores away: Downtown News Center.

Well, waddya know?

There were lots of newspapers stacked beside each other inside the door. Butch looked them over but didn't see a Lawton paper anywhere. New York and Philadelphia ones, though, how 'bout that? "Hoodlum, 17, Seized as Slayer of Boy, 15" read a headline and Butch's eyes widened. He remembered the knife fight in *Rebel Without a Cause* and figured it was something like that, especially with the word 'hoodlum.' If mothers could kill their children, teenagers could kill each other.

He moved to the magazine rack, which had *McCall's* and *Look* and a bunch of others fanned out. He wondered if there was a new *It's All in the Family* and reached for the *McCall's* but his eye caught something on the lowest shelf and he stopped.

*Creepy.*

Oh, man! Butch dropped to his knees and stared at the cover, open-mouthed. A boy sitting at a desk was looking at a desiccated vampire walking through his bedroom door. Oh, just way too... cool. Not neat. Cool.

He pulled it out and flipped it open. Wow, a comic book! He thrilled. Scary comics, with real grisly drawings! Butch was in heaven.

"What are you doing?"

Dad.

Butch shook in sudden fright, set up for it by the scary story he was reading. "Nothing."

Dad's claws dug into his shoulder and yanked him to his feet, "Oww!" Butch yelped. Dad shook him hard, "Who told you to go outside?"

"No one... I was just..."

"Just what?" Dad was red and murderous. "I knew you'd be here sticking your nose in some damn comic book," and he struck the Creepy from Butch's hand.

"Hey!" a voice called out. They both looked. A big-bearded, dark-skinned man sat behind a counter almost hidden by stacks of magazines and newspapers. "That's merchandise!"

Dad stared at the man, his jaw working. He dug into his pocket and flung some change at the counter, the man drawing back in surprise. "Pick it up," dad snarled and Butch scooped the Creepy on the fly as dad dragged him out of the store and into the street.

It was dusk now and some lights were coming on, but the traffic hadn't slowed. Some of the pedestrians parted the way and gazed at Butch, first startled then angry. Obviously, based on dad's fury and the way he pulled Butch along, he was a bad kid. He hid his face in shame, only looking up as dad yanked him forward every third or fourth step. Yes, he was bad. He'd cost dad unnecessary money and was crying, the worse thing a boy could do. Butch put all his effort into stopping the tears but he wasn't having much success.

Dad wasn't done. "Who said you could go out?" he snarled.

"No one," Butch blubbered, "I was just bored. I just went out to see."

"Bored? I'll *bored* you!" and his hand dug harder as he pulled Butch off his feet.

"I told Uncle!" That wasn't quite true. He assumed his leaving had Uncle's tacit approval.

"Told Uncle? You think that's okay, telling some damn nigger?" said at the moment they cleared the shop's door.

It was like one of those scenes in *The Danny Thomas Show* when someone says something too loud at the most inopportune moment. Everyone froze. The fat white men all stared, open-mouthed. Some even dropped their newspapers. Uncle George didn't look surprised. He looked hurt.

Butch wanted the floor to open so he could drop in and traverse the earth to some deep, dark, unknown center where no one could blame him for dad's hateful words. Dad turned beet red and his jaw worked as he stared Uncle down, but he didn't back up and didn't apologize. It couldn't get any worse.

And then it did.

"Who you callin' nigger?"

Butch didn't recognize the high-pitched woman's voice singing anger and offense in an off-rhythm. He looked past Uncle to the back of the shop and saw its source.

Louisa.

She stood there in complete fury. Butch didn't know black people could turn red, but she sure had. Her face was twisted as though someone had closed it with a corkscrew and she leaned forward like a tiger poised to rend prey, her murderous eyes fixed on dad. Ronald stood a bit behind her, open-mouthed, stunned, staring at his girlfriend as if she had already committed the murder her face intended.

All the fat white men, dad, Uncle, and Butch, stared at her with equal astonishment. She was a superhero who could paralyze with her voice. They were all fixed in place by the power of it.

"Who you callin' that? You callin' Uncle that?" and her voice actually got shriller and louder. Butch was amazed. "Don't you be callin' him that! He a better man than all you put together, shore put up with too much of y'all white people's shit," spat with pure venom.

Butch gasped. A girl actually said that!

"He do all your shoes and you throw him a dime and calls him nigger?"

She was just getting started, Butch could see. Apparently, she possessed great stores of condemnation available for such occasions. Butch thrilled. He was going to learn a lot.

But things happened. Ronald grabbed her by the wrist and whirled her around mid-sentence. "Come ON!" he yelled and practically yanked her out the back door past the stunned Dorey, who had emerged to see about the fuss. The door and the outside did not diminish the tone and violence of Louisa's words, carried to them even as Ronald ran her away.

"Black bitch!" Dad roared and let go of Butch and took dragon steps after them, only to be intercepted by Uncle, who stood in his way, head lowered, a placating smile on his face, but implacable. "Suh," he said, low, "she doan know bettah. She an ignorant little girl."

Butch was certain dad would tear Uncle in half but there was a movement and a balancing and, somehow, Uncle kept dad back and unable to gain strength, all the time smiling and soothing with his new voice and cadence.

"Iss the young'uns today, ain't got no respect, ain't been proper raised. Ise tole her momma, overs and overs, suh, dat she be a wild child, needs a hand to her, but she just go off and ignorin' me and you see, suh, what be the result." Uncle bobbed and weaved with dad's motion and played his anger across a broad spectrum, diffusing it.

"Well somebody oughta take a hand to her, that's for sure," dad said but Butch read the waning tones and knew the crisis was past. Dad was settling, evaluating, maybe even thinking he'd been a little over the top. If they were home, he'd sulk in the arbor for a bit and then take everyone to the Drumstick for hamburgers and ice cream. Butch realized Uncle sensed the same thing. He even gave Butch a slight wink.

"What on earth is going on out here?" Dorey, flabbergasted, asked from behind Uncle.

Quite exciting, Butch concluded. And he even got a *Creepy* out of it.

# CHAPTER 22

"Hey, wacha doin'?" Johnny called out as he and Marianne cleared the landing.

"Nothin'," Butch replied, fixed on the television. Lucy, the *Vitavetavegamin* episode. Pretty funny.

"Let's go downtown," Johnny said.

That got Butch's attention. "Huh?"

"Yeah, see a movie at the James."

"Huh?"

"You said that," Johnny observed and went into the kitchen, digging through the cabinets. Marianne plopped next to Butch on the couch. "I know this one," she said, meaning Lucy, "It's hilarious."

"Yeah, it is," but Butch no longer saw the show, because his heart had leaped into his throat as her shorts brushed his.

Oh man, sitting next to a girl!

He trembled a bit. If she noticed, he'd simply die.

Johnny passed out Fig Newtons and they ate, Butch forcing the cookie past his heart to keep appearances. "Hey!" Johnny said, picking up the *Creepy*, "Where'd you get this?"

"Newsstand."

"Your dad let you buy it?"

"Sort of." Johnny seemed content with that as he leafed through. Good. Butch really didn't want to explain.

Marianne giggled as Lucy reeled and Butch split his time between TV and her. Man, she was a really fun girl. More fun than Cindy... a traitorous thought that led to momentary guilt.

Momentary.

"So, movies?" Johnny asked, putting the Creepy down

"Now?" Butch asked.

"Sure."

"They have movies at lunchtime?"

"Yeah! Jeez, where you from, the country?" Johnny grinned.

Butch flushed. "Oklahoma."

"The country," Marianne concluded and shifted to get another Newton, bringing her shorts directly into contact with Butch's leg.

Oh, good Lord.

"I don't have any money," Butch said. He doubted his dime and pennies would cover a ticket, much less the required popcorn. Dad had left this morning in a snit, conveying his intent of an all-day job hunt with the minimal words necessary. Given the events of last night, Butch thought it best not to mention his lack of funds. Dorey left right after, telling Butch to expect Johnny and Marianne. He figured it would be another day of Joe and Nurse/Mata Hari Barbie, so he'd amused himself in the interim with the third and fourth reading of the *Creepy* and whatever he could find on television. But he was getting bored. Noon-time movies sounded good, but the means, the means.

"Yeah, we know," Johnny said, balancing a Newton on his nose. "Dorey called Mom and told us to bring enough to cover you."

Butch was astonished. "She did?"

"Yeah," Marianne said, patting his leg, "We're set."

Butch almost died right then but recovered sufficiently, "Uh, how we going to get there?"

"Bus," Johnny said.

"You guys ride buses?"

"Sure. Don't you?"

"No. Never."

"First time for everything," Marianne patted his leg again, harder.

Die? No way. Too thrilling.

"Time's a-wastin'. 'S'go," Johnny ordered.

They were all legs and arms and elbows down the stairs, slamming the door behind. They cut across the apartment quad, playing dodge car through a couple of streets. The sun was up and filled the day with summer strength and no school and no parents or sitters. Free. Butch raised his face to the sky, reveling in the heat. So good to be alive.

They stopped in the middle of a grass-covered island. "Here," Johnny said, handing him fifteen cents.

"That's how much movies cost?" Wow. Dirt cheap. Maybe he DID have enough.

"No, stupid," Johnny said, "That's for the bus. The movies cost seventy-five cents."

"Oh," Butch said, feeling stupid. Marianne shook her head and he felt small, too.

A bus pulled up, huge and green with a yellowish arrow painted on the front, wide at the top and tapering off to the license plate. The door opened on a hinge and Johnny tromped up, followed by Marianne and a more hesitant Butch. The driver wore a gray uniform and billed cap, just like Ralph Kramden, except he was skinny and a lot older. Johnny threw his money at some machine sitting by the driver and so did Marianne. Butch watched the money fall down through a port. Fascinating.

"Okay," Johnny said.

"What do I do?"

"Put your money in the top."

Butch peered at the machine and saw a coin slot there. Carefully, he put in the dime and the nickel, watched them fall down. The patient bus driver smiled. "Now what?" Butch asked.

"We sit," Johnny said, "When we get where we're going, we pull the rope."

"Rope?"

Johnny pointed at the bank of windows and Butch saw a rope strung along the top. He guessed that operated the brakes. "Wow," he said. The driver still smiled at him. Down the aisle, seven or eight other passengers, mostly women in flower dresses and hats, smiled at him, too. "I've never been on a bus before," Butch apologized to the driver.

"It's okay, son," the driver said, "First time for everything." He pulled a lever and the door hinged back and the bus started up.

They sat on the sideways seats and Butch craned about to look at the passing houses and apartments and cars. He was hopelessly lost, but it didn't matter—the bus would take him where he wanted to go. The bus made him free. On a free day in summer.

Cool.

Johnny and he babbled happily about the Creepy, discussing the artwork and the stories while Marianne rolled her eyes. Girls don't like gory stuff, Butch knew, but if Marianne thought *Vitavetavegamin* was funny, then maybe they had other common grounds. Perhaps gentler comics?

"Do you like *Millie the Model*?" he asked her.

She grimaced. "Not really," then looked at him with amusement. "Do you?"

"No," he snorted, covering that he did, indeed, read it from time to time. "My sister does."

"You have a sister?" Marianne was interested.

"Two. Dale's the oldest. She's going to college. Cindy's my other sister."

"How old is she?" Johnny asked.

"Ten."

"Ten? I thought you were ten." Marianne pointed out.

"Almost." He paused. "What's today?"

"Tuesday."

"No, what's the date?"

"It's June 15."

"It is?" A chill ran through him. "Then it's tomorrow."

"Your birthday's tomorrow?" Johnny asked.

Butch nodded. Oh, man. How had he lost track?

"Whacha gonna do?"

"Dunno," Butch shrugged. Such an important birthday, and he was going to spend it alone on the couch while dad was out looking for a job and Dorey was at her shop. No presents, no party, no kids to play with; that is, if Johnny and Marianne couldn't come over. Not fair. Not fair at all. He felt justified tears rising but suppressed them. Later.

"How can you and your sister be the same age?" Marianne pressed the point.

"She's not really my sister."

"Huh?"

"I'm adopted."

"Huh?" they both said at the same time, suddenly fascinated. They examined Butch like he was some new species. "Really?" Johnny asked.

"Yep. My Mom and dad were in Germany and they didn't have any sons then so they adopted me. I'm German," he added proudly.

"You're German?"

"Um-hm."

"A real German." Johnny dipped an approving head. "That is so cool."

Butch warmed.

"You know who your mother is?" Marianne asked.

"Nope. Saw a couple of pictures of her, though."

"What'd she look like?"

Butch shrugged, flashing on the slides. "A woman," he said, noncommitally.

They both stared at him for a moment and the talk went back to scenery and TV shows, but Butch couldn't shake the feeling that he was now lesser. Why? His adoption was sensible—the sonless Deats' swap out the destitute German mother. Not his fault Art negated the whole deal. It was like buying a used car; you're stuck with it.

But there was a sordidness here. Mothers just don't give their sons away. Mothers die first, then the son goes to the orphanage and Daddy Warbucks sees him and takes him home. So why did she? Were things really that bad in Germany? That's what Mom said: Real Mom's family all killed in the war, including her husband—Dad. Wonder who he was?—and what could she do with this boy? She couldn't feed or clothe him, but there was this kind, conquering, American family. If they raised her son, he'd eat and have clothes and no longer be a beaten, loser Nazi but a Yank, a winner, the best people. So, tearfully, with a broken heart, she gave up the last member of her family and wandered away to die in some rubble-strewn alley or maybe on the banks of the Rhine, cold, friendless, whispering his name, "Butch, Butch."

He caught his breath.

"You all right?" Marianne asked.

"Yeah, yeah," he said, wiping his eyes quickly with the back of his hand.

"Pull the rope," Johnny ordered.

"What?"

"The rope, the rope!" Johnny gestured frantically and Butch grabbed it and yanked for his life. A bell tinkled but little else happened so he pulled again, wondering how long before the brakes engaged. The bell kept ringing. "I heard you the first time," the driver called back.

"Let go of it, Goofus!" Johnny ordered and Butch did, confused. They were slowing down, but not enough. "I thought it was supposed to stop," Butch said.

"It has to reach the bus stop first. We can't just get off in the middle of the street, ya know." Marianne's tolerant tone was belittling and amused.

So, the rope didn't operate the brakes, just a little bell alerting the driver. Why didn't they explain that?

The bus hissed and stopped completely, the door hinges squealed and Butch headed toward the front. Johnny grabbed his shoulder and turned him. "This way," he said, heading toward a set of swung-open doors in the middle of the bus. How'd Butch miss those? Easy, they were the first persons leaving. Butch looked back at the bus driver watching him in the rearview mirror. "Sorry," he said and the bus driver waved and the ladies smiled at him and each other and he knew, as soon as he cleared the doors, that he was country.

They were on a busy street, cars and taxis and, Butch swore, the same people from last night. Johnny pointed across at a theater. "We're going there," he said. "Aunt Dorey's store is about two blocks that way." Gesture to the left.

They went to the corner and waited for the light and crossed with a bunch of dressy ladies wearing sensible pumps and little berets, interspersed with hatless young girls, hair loose and free, teenager style. They cut back and stood in front of the posters.

"Hey, it's *The Sound of Music*," Marianne sounded pleased. Johnny made retching sounds that Butch quickly imitated. She looked at them, annoyed. "What, then?"

"Let's go see what's at the Palace," Johnny walked down the street. Marianne made an exasperated sound but fell into step and Butch followed. They came to another movie theater and stopped at the display.

"*Doctor Zhivago*," Johnny said. Marianne pursed her lips and studied the poster. Butch did, too. Obviously some kind of love story, but there were soldiers and cavalry in the background so, war scenes. Something for everyone. They looked at each other and shrugged their shoulders. Johnny bought three tickets and passed them out. They went inside and Butch almost floated off his toes at the sudden rush of air conditioning. The usher took their tickets and opened the rope and they went into the auditorium.

The movie didn't start for another hour and they were showing *Bugs Bunny* cartoons. Road Runner, *meep meep*. Butch laughed as Wile E plunged a mile or so off the cliff, looking back at them most distressed. Kids ran around and Johnny stopped to talk to two or three of them.

"You know those guys?" Butch asked Marianne.

"Some of them." She waved a dismissive hand. "Let's sit down."

They did, in the back, and Marianne sat right next to him without skipping a seat, which was somewhat startling. She leaned forward and started laughing at the latest Acme gadget. Butch leaned forward, too.

A few more *Bugs* came on, including the absolutely hilarious "wabbit season" and Butch was just about falling out of his chair. Johnny had joined them and socked Butch in the arm at the funniest parts, which was okay.

A *Three Stooges* came on and he and Johnny were entranced. Marianne shifted and said, "I'm getting popcorn," something they acknowledged with a grunt. *Men in Black* had them both helpless with laughter and they were "*Nyuck-Nyuck*"ing each other when she came back, snorted, and passed out greasy striped bags.

The movie started. Pretty confusing. About twenty minutes into it, Butch wondered if checking out the lobby pinball machines might be in order, but then the old doctor threw back the woman's covers, almost revealing her butt, so he decided to stay. Wise decision, because cavalry rode the demonstrators down and the story picked up. By the time they got to WW1, Butch was fascinated. Intermission came and Butch raced to the bathroom and back, not wanting to miss a moment.

*Zhivago* ended and Butch, completely blown away, played over and over the last scene of the daughter and her boyfriend walking into the sunset... or across the top of the dam. "Let's go," Johnny said.

"I want to read the credits," Butch replied.

"You do?" Johnny looked at him like he was crazy. Marianne said nothing, just cocked her head.

"Yeah, I do," he replied and Johnny stared then shook his head and sat back down. "We're getting milkshakes," he pointed out.

"Okay," Butch waved him down. "In a minute."

They stayed until an usher frowned, then exited out the back onto a side street. Butch was disoriented, but Johnny knew where they were and guided them through an alley to Washington Avenue.

"That movie was too long," Johnny complained.

"I liked it," Marianne said, "but you're right. Almost put me to sleep."

"I loved it," Butch breathed.

"You did?" they both said simultaneously.

"Yeah, it was great. Just great."

"How could you like it?" Johnny balance-walked on the curb. "It didn't make any sense."

"I know. I didn't really get what was going on. But," he paused, taking a breath, "it was like, they all had this great life and they all loved each other and then all these things just happened. Just out of nowhere. Wasn't their fault. Yet they lost everything. Lost each other." Butch couldn't say any more.

Johnny windmilled off the curb, stood up, and laughed at Butch but Marianne socked him hard in the shoulder. "Shut up!" she yelled.

"Oww! What was that for?" Johnny almost sat down in the street, rubbing his pulverized shoulder and stared at Marianne, who glared at him fiercely. She looked at Butch strangely then flounced away, heading toward the Jackson Restaurant.

Johnny tried to put his shoulder back together and the two of them stared after her, dumbfounded. "Women," Johnny sneered, and they followed.

They finished their milkshakes and threw napkins at each other until the old mean cook in the back yelled, so they left. It was still afternoon but getting busier and they headed toward News Shoes.

"Uncle!" Marianne squealed as they walked in. He was sitting quietly in one of the shine chairs, fanning himself with a newspaper. "Well, young'uns!" he said and Marianne gave him a big, hard hug. "What y'all been doin'?"

"Movies," she said, "Milkshakes."

"Well, ain't that nice?" Uncle smiled and nodded his head, "Y'all be enjoyin' this summer vacation."

"Oh, we will," she said airily and headed toward the back where she started talking to Papa and son. Johnny followed and Butch shuffled a bit, absorbed by the Cat's Paw logo in the window. Uncle stared at him. He reddened and ducked his head, still embarrassed about last night.

"You awl right, boy?" Uncle asked.

Butch nodded, unable to meet his gaze.

"I worry 'bout you," Uncle said.

Butch looked up, surprised. "You do?"

"Yes, boy, ah do. See, I dream things."

"Huh?"

"They'se just dreams, but they tell me things. They tell me you got sorrows ahead of you."

Butch jolted. "What?"

"I don't know what they are, can't tell." Uncle shook his head. "But, they made me sad." He peered at Butch. "You got somebody followin' you around, too."

Butch was full out scared now. "Who?"

"I don't know. Seems to be some boy. He all alone."

Butch immediately knew who it was. "Frank Vaughn."

Uncle considered, "That might be him. Don't really know."

Butch breathed. "It's him. He talks to me sometimes. His mother killed him."

"Oh," Uncle clucked, "That explain why he all upset. Now, don't you get all scared," he said, putting a hand on Butch's suddenly trembling shoulder. "He ain't no ghost. He a dream. But that might be why you got some sorrows ahead."

Butch backed out of Uncle's grasp, "What do you mean?"

Uncle shook his head and started arranging his polishing tools. "I dunno, son, I just don't know."

Butch was stunned. He stared at Uncle's back, not certain what to say, half of him thinking Uncle was getting back at him for what dad said and the other half thinking Uncle was in touch with spirits. After all, hadn't Uncle seen Frank?

A hand fell heavily on his shoulder and he shrieked.

Johnny stared at him. "What's with you? C'mon, let's go look at magazines before Aunt Dorey takes us home."

# CHAPTER 23

Foggy, cloud-shrouded evening, the purplish sunset adding to the murkiness. Everything was hazy and blurry. Butch stood beside a real nasty bog, cypress trees leaning wrongly out of the water. On the other side, a boy sat crying on a stump.

Frank Vaughn.

"Hey!" Butch called, and Frank suddenly stood right next to him, tears streaming. He didn't look dead.

"I don't like this place," Frank said.

Butch looked around nervously. "Don't blame you." He stared at Frank. "Thanks for helping me back at the diner."

"I'll always help you," Frank said, "Anytime you need it, anytime you call." Frank's tongue fell out of a hole in his jaw. "By the way," he said, stuffing it back inside, "happy birthday."

Butch opened his eyes. Dad stood over him. "Happy birthday." He thrust out a box.

From terror to ecstasy took a moment and Butch didn't move, didn't speak. Dad frowned. "What's the matter? You don't want your present?"

Present? "No, no, I mean, yes!" Butch said hastily, sitting up, "I wasn't all awake yet."

"Are you now?"

"Yes."

"Good, then open it. I ain't got all day." Dad shoved the box at him.

Butch took it. Heavy. A model? Had to be, and probably a real big one, judging by the weight. He tore off the wrapping.

A GI Joe Official Footlocker. Which meant inside must be…
GI Joe.

The one-note heavenly chorus of joy reverberated through the living room. "GI Joe," Butch breathed. He paused to catch the trailing end of the chorus. "GI Joe," he said again.

"Knew you wanted one," dad said, "Hope that's it."

"Thank you, thank you so much!" Butch almost fainted with ecstasy as he flipped the locker open. There, the blond Joe in his bland green fatigues, eyes ready, the ultimate fighting man. What are your orders, sir? We're going to vanquish the Chicoms, Joe. Then the Russkies. Then Hitler. Butch noticed another package in the wrapping and pulled it out. A mess kit, oh man, but, wait, there's more—field pack and shovel, M1 Rifle set, and, unbelievably, the frogman suit.

Speechless.

Dad sat for a minute watching him. "Must be it. Well." He stood. "Enjoy your doll."

"Action figure, dad."

"Yeah, action figure." He shook his head and went into the kitchen.

Butch pawed through the locker and found the manual, which showed how to dress and position Joe. He worked on that and stood him on the table.

America's Fighting Man, GI Joe.

Wow.

Ten thousand miles away from home, no Mom, no Cindy, no party. He was tangled in a sheet on some nice lady's couch, and Frank Vaughn was following him around.

So what? He had a Joe.

Butch played with it until dad yelled to get cleaned up. He took everything into the bathroom, opening the frogman's outfit and holding the air tanks underwater to see what they'd do until dad pounded on the door and told him to hurry his ass up, breakfast! He crammed everything, still wet, back in the footlocker, taking note of the diagram on the inside front cover. Have to set things up later.

He stepped out and was immediately hit by waffle odor. Twice in one week? Ah man, perfect. Dad looked annoyed as Butch slid into a kitchen chair, but returned to his paper.

Whew.

"Happy Birthday!" Dorey beamed at him from the stove.

He smiled, "Thanks!"

"The birthday boy gets a special treat," she said and he started because those were Mom's words. "Here." She laid waffles, covered with whipped cream and strawberries, in front of him. What the heck? Butch studied them dubiously.

"Oh," Dorey sounded worried, "You don't like strawberries?"

"Well," Butch paused. Dad was looking at him with rising murder. Gulp. "Uh, I never had them on waffles before."

"It's like strawberry shortcake. You like that, right?"

"Yeah." He did, but that was shortcake; these were waffles. But he didn't want to hurt her feelings, or, more importantly, get killed, and took a tentative bite. Then another. "Hey, these are good!"

Dorey smiled and went to make more and Butch happily demolished his plate while dad crawled back into the classifieds.

All's right with the world.

"Johnny and Marianne are coming over later," Dorey said as she laid down another plate fit for destruction.

"Can I call them first?" Butch asked.

"Sure. Why?"

"I want to make sure Johnny brings his Joes."

"Oh, okay," she laughed, "I have to call my sister, anyway. I'll mention it." Butch nodded. She was really, really nice. Let's say she married dad, acquiring Adopto-Boy as part of the package. Butch would never be a lesser in her eyes, even if she had her own son with dad. She'd make strawberry waffles for them both and buy them lots of Joes, an army's worth, since she was rich. Dad would finally be made of money. Butch would stand up for his new little brother (a better one than Art) and fight off bullies and all four of them would happily sail the nearby ocean… he stirred uneasily. This line of thought felt treasonous.

"Here you go," Dorey laid down more of the never-ending waffles. Dad tore absently into his breakfast while examining job prospects. "Real good!" Butch commented around his fork.

"Mouth full," dad warned.

"It's okay," Dorey soothed and turned back to Butch. "So, what do you want to do today?"

The answer popped into his head immediately, maybe spurred by the treasonous thoughts. "I want to call my Mom," he said.

Dad folded the paper down and stared at him. "No."

"I want to call Mom," Butch repeated.

"I said no."

"I want to call Mom," Butch did not change his voice nor raise it, but on this, he was determined.

"It's too expensive," dad snapped, the murder rising again, but Butch didn't care. It was his birthday, dammit! Wow, he'd just thought 'dammit!'. He should get what he wanted. And he wanted Mom to know he wasn't a traitor.

Dorey interrupted, "You can call from my phone tonight when the rates are cheaper."

Butch looked at her, admiration rising in his chest. That's it, all decided, and by Dorey. Wow. "Okay. Thanks, thanks so much."

Dad stared at her. She calmly returned his stare. "Fine," he said after a moment and snapped the paper open. Dorey said nothing, cleared away plates. Butch watched her. She didn't take any crap, did she? Of course not; she owned her own store and had her own money and car and apartment. Didn't cower like Mom did. Like Butch did.

Very cool.

# CHAPTER 24

"A frogman suit!" Johnny's face lit up.

"Yep," Butch said proudly. Marianne rolled her eyes so high they were in danger of sticking to her brain.

That bothered Butch. What's wrong with a frogman suit?

"Well, what are we waiting for?" Johnny grabbed his backpack and headed to the bathroom, the frogman Joe in tow. Butch followed, concerned. Marianne stayed behind, turning on *The Guiding Light*. Stupid soap operas.

Johnny filled the tub and, reluctantly, relinquished control to Butch, who dived Joe. The tanks filled with water, as did the red rubber mask, but Joe can push through it. Butch laid demolitions along the tub while Johnny's Joes, Nazi guards all, vainly tried to find them. They got into a hellacious firefight when Butch's Joe emerged from the water. The submarine pens then blew in a series of spectacular explosions, aided by Johnny's and Butch's sound effects.

"I'm bored." Marianne stood in the doorway. "Let's go to the movies."

"See what?" Johnny asked as Butch stripped the Joe while hiding it from Marianne. Can't embarrass a war hero.

"*Shenandoah*," she said.

Johnny made a dismissive sound but Butch's head popped up. "Really? That's playing?"

"At the Paramount."

"That's farther away," Johnny said.

"So? Bus goes right by it."

155

"Ah," Johnny waved that off and armed his Joes with grenades. "This time, Joe," he said in a German accent, "you will die."

Butch giggled then looked at Marianne. Her eyes stormy, challenging, she said, "My treat, birthday boy."

No contest.

"Let me get my money." Dorey had given him a dollar before she left, which was after dad had left. Funny, they didn't speak to each other. Or maybe not so funny; par for the course in Oklahoma.

Johnny looked at him in utter disbelief. "You're going?"

"Yeah," he said, closing the footlocker. "Let's go."

"I don't want to."

"Then, stay here." Marianne threw a dismissive hand and flounced out, decision made.

Lots of that going on with the women in this place.

Butch ran for the dollar and followed her to the stairs. "Hey!" Johnny appeared behind them. "Don't make kissy faces!" He placed the back of his hand to his lips and made really obscene noises.

Marianne plowed him right in the chest, driving him into the wall. "Ow!" he yelled, slipping down to his butt. She tromped down the stairs, face furious. Butch hesitated, the implications of kissy-face sinking in, then tromped down the stairs after her.

He caught up and they walked, wordless, to the bus stop. After a moment, she muttered, "Brothers."

Butch sympathized. "My little brother is a pain, too."

"I'll bet you're a pain to your sister."

Butch shook his head. "No. We get along great. I..." and he caught himself before saying 'love her,' "...like playing with her."

"I like playing with Johnny, but he's still a pain."

The bus slid up and they boarded. Butch placed the coins with no hesitation. Veteran, now. It was the same bus driver, who smiled in approval. Butch swore the smiling passengers were the same flower-dressed ladies.

They got off at the Paramount and stood in front of the poster. "Looks good," he said.

"Eh," she responded, "We'll see."

She bought their tickets and handed him one and they went inside, stopping at the popcorn stand. Butch got a big buttered bucket, a giant Hershey bar and a giant Coke, securing the forty-five cents change for later. Maybe Newport News Center had the latest *X-Men*. Marianne took the bucket and marched into the auditorium, Butch in trail.

The same kids as the Palace but different cartoons: *Popeye*. Good. She selected a row in the back and moved toward the middle. Butch hesitated. Sitting next to a girl? By himself? It wasn't like *Doctor Zhivago* because Johnny had chaperoned. What to do?

"Here," she ordered, patting the cushion beside her, and that settled it and he scurried over. "No funny business," she warned.

Funny business? What did that mean? Johnny's kissy noises suddenly filled his ears and he flamed. "No," he agreed.

"'No what?"

"Funny business."

She stared at him. "You think I'm going to do that with you?"

"No!" he was horrified. "I mean, I'm with you. Not like that, I mean, you're right, no business."

She shook her head. "Boys."

Butch settled, vitally aware of her blue shorts, tanned legs, white-flower blouse cut down the neck, and warm arms balancing the popcorn between them. Disturbing. They kept brushing each other's hands in the kernels, electric, Butch's fingers recoiling but right back there in moments. He glanced at her every time they brushed but saw no reaction and he was a bit ashamed over the surreptitious charge he was getting from this. But, just a bit. The finger-brushing continued when he broke open the Hershey and it was all too exciting. He barely saw the cartoons, even a rare *Bettie Boop*. Marianne leaned into it with delight.

The movie came on and Butch was of two minds, entranced by the story, entranced by Marianne. The last time he'd felt this much roiling was as Lynn's partner for backyard under-the-blanket ghost stories. He'd been so fixed on Lynn's hand locked over his blanket covered fingers that he missed the scream cue. He was similarly confused when the lights flashed on and crazed kids flung themselves down the aisles. What world was this?

She nudged him. "Let's go, dummy."

They hit the sidewalk, gasping from the sledgehammer sun, and headed toward Dorey's. "What'd ya think?" Marianne asked.

"About what?" Their hand jive?

157

"The movie, moron."

Oh, right. "I liked it," he said, not really sure what he meant.

"What'd you like about it?"

"Well, it was scary, with the war coming and them having to go look for their brother and those three crook Yankees and what they did to the older brother and his wife and then the little brother showing up at the church... I felt so bad for them all. It was like *Doctor Zhivago*."

"Huh?"

"You know," Butch's hand fluttered in the air, "They had these lives and things come along and just tear them up. It isn't fair."

She looked at him. "You really like movies like that, don't you?"

"Yeah, yeah I do." And he liked sitting in the dark next to her with their fingers glancing in butter and chocolate while the screen people danced big and colorful as things intruded, things unlooked for, breaking the dance. You're a doctor with a growing practice and a loving wife and child and a funny old father-in-law but the Commies take it all away because they can, and you find, in the middle of war and ruin, a woman who isn't your wife but she's alive, so alive, and you need her because your old life died and then you do, broken, alone, a hand reaching out to a phantom on the street. Or you have a farm and grown sons and feel the power of what you've made but armies take your sons and your land and everything you ever worked for and you are reduced and broken and have to salvage what you can from what's left.

Just completely unfair.

"You all right?" she asked.

He pressed his eyes, wearied by the sun's brightness and everything else. "Yeah," he said.

They stopped at Jackson's, where the mean old cook served milkshakes and glower. Marianne treated, more of her birthday boy attitude, and then they went to Dorey's.

"Uncle!" Marianne ran to him, dodging the polish rag for a hug. Must be a routine.

"Young'uns!" He smiled and it was cool and leathery and polishy in the shop and Butch felt relieved somehow. "What y'all been doin' on this hot, hot day?"

"Movies."

"Is that right? Well." He flipped the rag expertly at the shoes of a fat white man patiently reading a paper. "And where's the other one?"

"That idiot stayed home playing with GI Joe." Marianne rolled her eyes to accentuate her disgust.

"Oh," Uncle paused. "So you two on a date?"

Uncle might as well have thrown polish at them. "No!" they simultaneously exclaimed, horror bulging their eyes and dropping their jaws and they took inadvertent steps apart.

Uncle grinned. "Seem like it to me."

"Ack!" Marianne said and flounced off. Butch hesitated, not sure how following her would be read. Uncle grinned bigger and the fat white man started chuckling. He ran.

Marianne was sitting next to Papa, who was speaking his incomprehensible language while showing her how to sew up a boot. The curtain was open and he saw Dorey sitting behind the desk. She motioned him inside.

"Hi," he said.

"Having a good time?"

"Yeah. Marianne treated me to a movie and milkshake. For my birthday," he added. Important this remained neutral.

"Oh. Where's Johnny?"

"Stayed home."

"Oh." She paused. "Would you like to call your Mom?"

"Sure." Butch furrowed a brow. Dorey already knew that.

She gestured at the phone. "Go ahead."

"What?"

"It'll be fine. You can call her now," and she gestured again.

Concern flooded through him. "But, won't it cost too much?"

She smiled. "That's your dad talking. It's not that expensive. Consider it a birthday gift."

Hmm. Birthday gifts covered all objections, even about money. Besides, dad couldn't complain if someone else was paying for it. "What do I do?"

"What's your phone number?"

"Elgin 3, 2234."

"Do you know the area code?"

Butch was dumbfounded. Why would he know that? He'd never called anyone long distance. Guess this was over and his face fell.

"Never mind. The operator will know it." She stood and waved him to the chair, picked up the phone and dialed "O" and passed numbers. "Your code's 405," she informed and Butch tucked that away. She handed him the receiver. "It's ringing."

Butch listened to the soft "brrr" of a distant phone, static popping and swelling. Tommy had told him sunspots caused that and they could get so bad TV shut down and planes fell out of the sky. Butch wondered if sunspot energy could burst down the phone line and fry him, like Electro.

"Hello?" someone said on the other end.

Butch's heart skipped and he looked frantically at Dorey. She smiled and nodded encouragement. "Hello?" he said.

"Hello. Who's this?" It was a girl but the static masked the identity.

"It's Butch."

"Butch? Oh my God! Butch! It's me, Dale!"

Never before had Butch been so happy to hear her. "Hi! Hi! Jeez, hi! I thought you were going to California!"

"I was. I am. But not until August. I'm staying to help Mom."

"Help Mom?"

"Yeah, you know, with things," her voice trailed off and Butch suddenly did know. Breaking up a family involved a lot of detail, stuff to move and people to notify, other mysterious adjustments. It was a very good thing that Dale was helping and he told her so.

"Well, thank you, that's really sweet." She paused. "Do you want to talk to Mom?"

"Is she there?"

"Yes."

"Well, yeah!" he almost shouted. Oh man!

"Wait, I'll go get her," and there was background shuffling and shouts of "Mom! Mom! Butch is on the phone! Yes, Butch!" and more shufflings and other voices, shriller, approaching with Doppler effect and that just had to be Cindy and Art and he thrilled again. Funny he could hear everything so clearly. Excitement must block sunspots, like Spidey smacking Electro with webbing.

"Here she is." Dale again. "Happy birthday, kid."

The phone changed hands. "Hello?"

"Mom?"

160

"Butch! Oh, my God. Happy birthday! Are you all right?"

He warmed in a way he hadn't for the past several days and the heat climbed his heart and battered against his eyes, filling them. Dorey was quietly watching and he turned away, afraid she'd see. "I'm fine," he said, "I'm okay. How are you guys?"

"Oh, we're doing just fine, just fine. Everyone wants to talk to you. Did you have a good birthday?"

"I sure did. I got a GI Joe and Marianne took me to the movies."

"Who's Marianne?"

"She's my friend." Emphasis on the 'friend' part because this must remain neutral. "She's Johnny's sister but he didn't want to go, so we just went ourselves."

"Oh, that sounds nice. I would have sent you a present and a card, but I don't know where you are."

So, he *was* lost. "I'm in Newport News." Not lost anymore.

"Virginia?"

"Yes."

"How long have you been there?"

He shrugged, which, doofus, Mom couldn't see. "I don't know, a week, maybe."

"Where are you staying?"

"With Dorey," he blurted.

And knew, right then, he had made an irrevocable and fatal error.

"Dorey?" Mom paused. "Who's Dorey?"

"A friend," he said, weakly.

"Friend," Mom said it with no particular inflection, but she might as well have screamed or cried or raged. Butch felt a desperate sense of failure, as if he'd just given up the Avenger's secret location. "Where's your dad?"

"Out."

"Doing what?"

Again, the invisible shrug, "I don't know. Looking for a job, I guess."

"A job? Is that where he's planning to live?" Pause. Then Mom's hand reached through the phone and slapped him. "With Dorey?"

He looked at Dorey, but she was busy with something on the desk. "No," he said, lamely.

161

"I'll bet," Mom snorted in that tone of bitterness and murder she used with Lynn's mom during the kitchen table sessions. "Is she nice?"

"Yes."

"Treat you real good?"

"Yes."

"I'll bet." Another pause. "Did you have a birthday party?"

"No."

"You would have if you'd been here."

*Phzzzt!* Electro fried him where he sat. His breath died. Yes, he would have. Tommy'd be there and Chucky and maybe Dale from across the street and Art and Cindy, of course, and there'd be cake and ice cream and Pin-the-Tail and Bingo and little presents for the kids who won but he'd get all the cool stuff—a GI Joe, no, two Joes, a Joe jeep, a pile of comics, and Operation or Monopoly...

He'd really screwed up going with dad, hadn't he?

"I gotta go," Mom said.

*Phzzt!* Another blast from Electro. "But..."

"I'm sorry, I gotta go," and Butch heard Cindy's soprano of protest in the background. Wait, Mom, he had to talk to Cindy! "But..." he said again.

"I'm glad you had a good birthday," and she hung up, cutting Cindy in half. Him, too.

A stone in the middle of his chest pounded against the linings of his heart. The only relief was to burst out crying, but no way. No. Way. He fought hard, beating the stone back, forcing it to his stomach. Quite a struggle, and it left him mean.

He looked at Dorey. She gazed at him with eyes large and sorrowful. If he had a gun, he'd shoot her right now. "It isn't right," he said, bitterly.

She blinked. "I know," said softly.

"It's just not right," he repeated, venom in his voice and red in his eyes.

"I know," her repetition, just as soft, "It isn't."

"What's not right?" boomed dad from the doorway.

The stone came back hard, but it was the stone of terror and Butch was a wrong word away from execution, especially if he mentioned calling Mom. He gave Dorey a desperate look and she nodded imperceptibly. "Vietnam," he breathed.

"Vietnam?" Dad snorted, "You been listening to beatniks? 'Course it's right." He flopped into the chair opposite, grieved by his Commie-loving son. Butch sent a silent prayer of thanks to the ever-watchful Jesus.

"Got a surprise for you," dad said, his hands folded and his eyes unreadable.

Butch's brows rose. Another Joe?

"Found us a place to live," he said. Butch started. Huh? He glanced at Dorey.

She looked like she'd just been slapped.

# CHAPTER 25

"Up there." Dad gestured at some wooden stairs precariously attached to the paint-flaked and rickety building they'd parked behind. Much too much distance between steps and Butch hesitated. "Go on," dad snapped, as he messed with something in the back of the Rambler "The door's unlocked."

Orders were orders, even suicidal ones, and Butch clutched Joe as he mounted. More like a ladder than stairs and he was out of breath when he got to the landing; no dashing up and down this. The washed-out graying platform bent a bit under his weight: collapse, followed by a long fall onto a rusted-out Ford sitting in a little weed-covered alley. Impaled on the broken steering wheel, ma'am.

Hastily, Butch cleared the threshold and stood in the door, peering about. It looked like a motel room. Dust-laden light from two floor-to-ceiling windows barely covered with paper-thin brown curtains striped the place. He sneezed. The brick wall of the building next door loomed behind the curtains.

A gigantic iron bed, covered with a torn white blanket frayed along the floor, jammed the wall immediately to his left. Butch watched a couple of dust bunnies flee underneath. A white-columned room divider against the end of the bed had a 12-inch T, thank God, set in a gap. Beyond was a sink big enough to hold a horse, with a hotplate and rusty refrigerator next to it. White cabinets ran around the top of the sink. An open door next to the kitchen revealed a tub and toilet. Two peeling chests of drawers, flanked by two dining chairs, were on the right wall. Both chests were probably identical at one point but random abuse had made them distinct. A faded painting of a river with a couple of cows drinking from it hung on the wall above the chests.

Not bad, not bad at all.

"You done up there?" Dad, irritated.

Butch dropped Joe on the bed and scurried, carefully, down the stairs. He helped unload, struggling with dad's duffel and suitcase and one of the K-ration cases. Man, heavy. How'd they lug 'em around a battlefield? He asked dad that.

"We only carried a coupla cans at a time." Dad placed boxers in one of the chest's debris-filled drawers.

Well, Jeez, then why'd you make me haul an entire case? Discretion changed the question. "What'd you do with the rest?"

"Filled up the 36s with 'em and ran for the border."

"What border?"

"Germany," dad said as he unclipped the duffel bag and pulled out shirts.

Butch, goggle-eyed. "Really?"

"Sure." Dad caught Butch's astonishment. "Fought across France to get there."

This was more than dad had ever said about the war. "What was it like?"

Dad shrugged, laying his shirts in another drawer. "It was rough. Put your clothes away."

Butch stuffed some of his shorts in the other chest but wanted to keep this going. "So, did you get shot at?"

"Oh yeah, a lot," dad said absently as he sorted socks. "I was in a jeep."

"A jeep?" Weren't those for generals?

"Yep. I was in a scout platoon. We had a fifty mounted on the back, and it was our job to get ahead of the tanks and see what was there. The Germans didn't like that much."

Butch laughed, "I'll bet!"

"I was in the middle of the biggest tank battle in the war in that jeep."

Butch stared at him. "No way."

"Yeah, I was. Arracourt. In France. I was just driving along when all these tanks showed up. Had to jump into a ditch. I tell ya, I was never so happy to see the Air Corps in my life."

"Why?"

"They rocketed the German tanks. Thunderbolts. Saved our asses."

"Were you hurt?"

"Nah." Dad slung his empty bag under the bed. "Never got hurt the whole war. One time, I was leaning out of an airplane and a piece of shrapnel cut my shoulder. That was it."

"Really?" Butch was impressed. "Did you get a Purple Heart?"

"Nope. Paperwork got lost."

Butch decided to draw a scar across one of Joe's shoulders. More authentic. "Did you drive one of those jeeps in Korea?"

"Uh, uh. Drove a tank."

A tank? Wow! "Did you shoot it a lot?"

Dad laughed, "You betcha. So many Chicoms swarmed over us we had to hose each other's tanks down."

Butch had a sudden vision—hordes of screaming Chinese, three and four deep on top of a tank, pounding it with their rifle stocks while dad calmly drove up and machine-gunned them.

"So why'd you start flying helicopters?" he asked. Seemed more fun to drive a tank.

"'Cause I could."

"Is it better than a tank?"

"Yep."

"So why'd you retire?"

Dad pulled out a cigarette. "They wanted me to go to Vietnam." He took a long puff. "I figured two wars was enough."

That sounded a little yellow. Butch pictured John Wayne standing in a tent entrance with that "you're a coward" sneer on his face. On the other hand, a third war was pushing your luck.

Dad broke open a couple of K rations and got a ham stew boiling on the hot plate. Butch worked some ice out of the frozen-over freezer to make cold water. A fold-up table leaned against one of the kitchen walls and dad set it up and spooned out the stew. Pretty good, but needed cornbread.

They threw away the paper plates and dumped the silverware in the giant sink and dad told Butch to wash them. Butch had done dishes under Mom's close supervision, but on his own?

Rise to the occasion, bucko.

He located an open bottle of Joy behind one of the rusty pipes under the sink. Good place to harbor snakes or big spiders

166

and he steeled and made a quick grab, stepping back fearfully. The only thing that chased him out was a shabby cloth, fortuitous because it now became his dishrag. He ran water and poured Joy on the rag and was pretty proud of himself when he figured out how to get silverware clean.

Nothing to it.

"Stop wasting water," dad growled.

"But I gotta rinse."

"Turn it off and on, then."

Oh.

Dad started going through the TV channels. Butch watched intently. Channel 3, Norfolk; Channel 6 was too fuzzy; Channel 8 was better, some place called Petersburg; Channel 10, Portsmouth; Channel 12 was Richmond and also not bad; Channel 15 was educational. Blech. So, five channels, if you count the educational one. Blech. Two more than Lawton, and he had ABC, NBC, CBS. Set.

"I don't want you walking around this neighborhood," dad said.

Butch was struck. That had been a plan for later. "Why not?"

"Because you might get lost."

Good point. How to fix that?

He could explore in stages, keeping the apartment in sight until he established other landmarks. Or he could blaze a trail like the Hardy Boys, although there didn't seem to be a lot of trees around for cutting notches. Maybe he could leave marks on telephone poles. Would he get in trouble?

"You don't know these people," dad added.

"Are they bad?" Butch asked.

"Dunno. But you don't want to find out."

Another good point. Dad tapped the bed to test springiness. "I'm taking a bath," he announced. He grabbed some clothes and closed the door to the bathroom, which didn't latch all the way so Butch would have to time his usage for maximum privacy. He looked around the channels. News, mostly. There was some big attack in Vietnam and Butch watched the footage curiously.

Sure is a lot of fighting, but we'll get those Commies.

They then went to Ed White's spacewalk and Butch was riveted. He'd missed it initially because they'd been traveling but replays were good. Commercials followed...

*Jonny Quest* was on tonight.

Oh man. Oh man oh man oh man. How long had it been? A week, two?

Seemed like a month and he almost dropped to his knees, yearning like an addict for the needle.

What time, what time?

He stared frantically as Race threw the frogman.

What time, dammit! He barely noticed he had cursed.

Seven o'clock..

He sat back. He now knew time and channel. The universe was in harmony. Television Zen

"Take a bath," dad ordered. He was drying his hair vigorously with his T-shirt.

Oh, no. "Are we going somewhere?"

"Yeah, back to Dorey's."

Oh, no. No TV. No *Jonny*. Sitting around the shoe shop watching Uncle, bored out of his mind.

"Dad?"

"Yeah?"

"Can I stay here tonight?"

Dad looked at him. "You mean alone?"

"Yeah."

"What's the matter, you don't like Dorey or something?" Menace in his tone.

"No, no," Butch said, hasty to dispel that notion. "I like her. She's real nice. It's just the shop is boring."

Dad looked at him suspiciously, eyes narrowed, and then glanced at the TV. Something flitted across his brow. Expectation?

"You sure?" dad asked, softly.

Hope soared. "Yeah! I'm sure! I won't make any noise or a mess or anything."

Dad considered and Butch held his breath. "All right," he said, nodding and Butch could have leaped for joy right then. "Don't go out. Don't leave all the lights on. I'm not made of money. You get hungry, open a can. There's a can opener in the drawer."

Dad grabbed a few things and placed them in pockets and moved some things and Butch followed him around a bit to throw off any lingering suspicions but dad seemed content. He went to the door, stood, and looked at Butch again. "You sure?"

"Yes."

Dad nodded and turned the handle. "Dad?"

"Yeah?"

"What time is it?"

Dad looked at his watch, "Six o'clock." he said. He stared at Butch a moment. "Don't go out," and was gone.

As the door closed, Butch calculated. An hour. He rubbed his hands, Snidely Whiplash-like. Good.

# CHAPTER 26

K-ration chocolate and crackers and ice water — a royal feast. Butch sat back against the pillows, quite satisfied. It was dark, the feeble lamp next to the bed good only for marking territory but he wasn't scared. Seemed a quiet place, the occasional passing car and distant siren the only sounds.

He was still in *Jonny* thrall: four shows ago and a re-run at that, but what a re-run, the very first episode ever—laser beam in the Sargasso Sea. Pre-Hadji *Jonny*. Man. *Twelve O'Clock High* was on right now, but he was only half-watching. He kept replaying the way Jonny threw the lizard man over his shoulder. Judo. If Butch knew judo, no one would bother him.

He'd walk into his new school and some big bully grabs his collar and, *whoosh*! Upside down against the lockers, stunned. Butch brushes his hands as the girls go "Ooooo!" and the boys crowd around, "Howja do that, howdja do that?" and the bully slinks away. But, like Joey in *The Happy Hollisters*, the bully'd seek revenge and eventually catch Butch alone, with three other bullies as backup. Butch tries not to fight but they'd call him chicken and push him and then *whoosh*! Three thrown bullies, crying and running away. The head cheerleader takes his arm and he'd walk her home.

Man.

He made a judo move while lying there, his fingers brushing his pants pocket and the envelope inside and he idly pulled it out. He shook the plastic roll onto his chest, grabbing it as he sat up. By now he was an expert unfurler and he picked at the little nub

170

until his fingers gained purchase. He studied it for about the millionth time, frowning, still baffled; form wasn't conveying function. It had all the hallmarks of a balloon and he'd tried to blow it up a few times but couldn't. The opening was too big and wouldn't hold enough air to tie off. There were these odd little bumps arranged sequentially around the balloon that looked like Stingray bike tires but that just deepened the mystery. Butch ruminated. The Tickler came out of a machine with an excited blonde on it, inferring a grownup function that Butch probably wouldn't realize for at least twenty more years. No way he could hold on to it that long, so had to do *something* with it. After all, this was a quarter's worth of product. Maybe a water balloon. He looked at the sink.

The apartment started shaking and there was thunderous noise on the steps.

Oh man, someone was coming up!

Panic fluttered his stomach but he had the good sense to collapse the Tickler and stuff everything back in his pocket. A key scraped the lock. Butch held his breath, suddenly realizing he was alone in a very dark apartment. He looked about frantically. The windows were too high—he'd already checked—and, anyway, there was the whole steering-wheel-impaling thing. Might be his only option, though, and he gauged the distance he'd have to run before the slavering monster burst inside…

"Hello, boy!"

Ah. Not a slavering monster. Just a dad monster. Butch relaxed, was kind of glad, in fact, because he was getting lonely.

"Dj'ave a good time?"

Butch frowned. Was that a tone of sarcasm? "Yep," he said, cautiously.

Dad shook his head and stripped off tie and shoes and lit a cigarette. "Just watching television," he observed. Butch braced for the old criticism about how much time he wasted in front of the idiot box. Like he should have a job or something.

Change the subject. "Did *you* have a good time?"

Dad grinned. "Oh yeah," and the leer made Butch wary.

"Here," dad said, "Brought you a snack," and he tossed a Payday on the bed.

Well, well. Butch picked it up, rather pleased, as dad got undressed. Butch couldn't help staring at the unsnapped underwear slot where dad's peepee hid. He couldn't see it because of the dark, thank God. Naked wieners were disturbing, something ugly and sordid about them. The occasional flash of them in bathrooms had disclosed his was different; he still had skin. That's because he was German, according to dad. Okay, Germans were odd — everyone knew that. But it set him further apart.

Butch gobbled the Payday and pitched the wrapper into the trash and then did his bathroom business. He came out and saw that dad had already climbed into bed. Making sure to hide the front of his underwear, he did, too.

"You going to leave the TV on?" dad asked.

Well, yeah, he'd planned on it. The highest luxury ever conceived was to lie in bed and watch TV while drifting off. But, apparently, not to dad, so Butch skipped out of bed and switched it off and scampered back.

"Light?" dad asked.

He skipped out of bed again and pulled the cord but didn't skip back because, man, dark. He walked cautiously until he bumped into the mattress, then got in.

"So, that little girl," dad said.

Little girl? "You mean Marianne?"

"Yeah, that one, Dorey's niece. She's kinda cute."

Butch grimaced. Here comes the teasing. "She's all right."

"She's a little more than all right. She's good looking." Dad had the leer in his voice and Butch steeled. Any minute now...

"She your girlfriend?"

Bingo. Stop for more than half a second to talk to Lynn or Debbie or Maria and wham! the ever vigilant kids sing-songing "Butchie's got a girlfriend!" followed, inevitably, by, "K-I-S-S-I-N-G, first comes love then comes marriage..." Gawd, and he'd run, protests shredding from his lips, shameful because, well, yeah, he *did* like Lynn. Maybe even Debbie, although she was a bit chunky. He'd had a lot more close physical contact with Marianne than with them. They'd even been on a date; at least that's what everyone thought.

"No," he said in the tone of playground shame.

"Well, she should be, she's cute." Dad paused. "You know what to do with her?"

Do with her? What's that mean? An uneasy feeling stole over him. "Huh?"

"You know." Dad leaned closer and Butch could smell Aqua Velva and cigarettes. "What you do with girls."

"Kiss them?" Butch felt fairly confident this was the direction they were taking, although the only girl he'd ever kissed was Cindy, on the cheek. But at least he knew what dad was talking about.

"Well, yeah, that's a start."

Butch was momentarily puzzled, but then caught on. "Oh, you mean hugging them, too."

"Well, yeah, that too, but, I mean, after."

After? You go home or watch TV or... oh! "Walking holding hands," he said confidently.

Dad paused and Butch pictured his face, a look of amazed, amused contempt. "Boy." Ah yes, there, the ridicule. "For someone who reads all the time, you sure don't understand much. I'm talking about sex."

Butch was instantly mad. "I know what sex is!" he retorted rather hotly.

"You do?" dad sounded surprised, then immediately suspicious. "What is it, then?"

"Whether someone's a boy or girl." Didn't know what sex was. Sheesh.

Dad clucked annoyance. "No, dummy, I ain't talking about that. I'm talking about where babies come from."

The insult was lost in the sudden intrigue. Baby origin, one of those universal mysteries whispered about with much looking around before information was imparted. Butch had heard them all —the stork and the rabbit and the baby under the cabbage leaf. Well, the cabbage leaf one had actually been a fairy tale in the blue SRAs, but it was of the same false genre because babies grew inside mommies and came out when ready. Dad's tone, though, implied something more, the Wickedness flapping about it.

Dad pulled himself closer, his lips against Butch's ear, stubble rubbing his lobe raw. Butch held his breath, wondering what secret was so terrible that dad had to whisper even when there was no one else to hear it. The flapping became the frantic pounding of a thousand wings. "Babies come from men and women having sex." Dad was gleeful. "And sex is you putting your dingaling inside where she goes to the bathroom."

"What? What?" Butch was simultaneously floored and

fascinated. An image of the Coppertone girl's bottom immediately leaped to mind, and he couldn't imagine how his dingaling could go in there.

"Remember when you asked me about that French Tickler?"

Dad's voice still gleeful, still on this astonishing topic, as Butch's heart watered in terror. Oh no! Dad must have found it! Dad knew he had evil thoughts about half dressed blonde women who wanted French tickles and now, now, the judgment.

"If you don't want the girl to have a baby," lustful and sneering and whispering, "you put the French Tickler on your dingdong before you put it inside her."

Unbelievable, impossible, not true in any way. Just not. A sledgehammer stroke caused less shock. He had to hear more.

"Well, good night." Dad pushed away, humming a little bit and, in seconds, was sleep-breathing. Butch lay there, staring at dad's sounds in the dark, baffled, scared, a thousand questions on his tongue, but death awaited if he woke dad to ply them. The Wickedness spiraled down from its perch and zipped up his nose and raced down to the pit of his stomach and joined that twitchy, unstable feeling present when he looked at Lynn or when he'd brushed Marianne's popcorn hands. It pounded for release and his hand moved to shake dad's shoulder.

Are you crazy?

He froze. What dad had told him could be everything. He'd go to his death for no reason.

You've been briefed, soldier, now accomplish your mission.

His mind reeled, trying to flesh out the sparse info. No way he was sleeping now.

# CHAPTER 27

"Get up."

Butch was dreaming about warm, fleshy cacti that were trying to pierce his wiener. Disturbing and fascinating at the same time and he wanted to see it through.

"What?" he asked, bleary.

"I'm dropping you off at Dorey's. Eat your toast and get cleaned up."

Butch shook awake and crab-ran to the bathroom. He did his business and grabbed his pants, fingers brushing against the envelope. What dad said came roaring back and he pulled it out. Function now apparent.

"What are you doing in there?" dad yelled and Butch almost dropped the Tickler.

"Nothin'!" He jammed it back into his pocket, terrified dad would drop-kick the door to see.

"Well, get goin'!"

Jeez, what a grouch.

First thing in the morning grouch, so be warned. Butch finished breakfast and teeth-brushing in record time, but dad was still fuming and practically dragged Butch down to the bottom when they got to the stairs,

"Ow!" Butch said, twisting his ankle a bit.

"Stop screwin' around," dad snarled and flung him at the Rambler. Butch caught himself and scuttled around to the other side.

Careful, careful, careful.

He slunk in the seat and eyed dad warily as he started the car. "Where we goin'?" he asked.

"Told you, Dorey's," dad snapped.

"Why so early?"

"I gotta be someplace."

"Where?"

"None of your damn business."

All right, all right, and he ducked lower, then a thought flashed. "Did you get a job?"

"No. And stop asking me questions."

Shutup, shutup, shutup! But if you're not off to work, dad, then what's the godawful hurry? Questions queued at the back of Butch's tongue and made forays to the front, generating little clucks Butch was convinced dad could hear, impelling murder.

Shutup, shutup, shutup!

"Here ya go," dad said and Butch looked and they were at the apartments. Astonishingly quick. Dad barely waited long enough for him to grab his knapsack, the Holy Joe secure inside, before spinning off with a, "I'll come get you later." Butch watched him turn at the corner, gone.

What the devil?

He took in a big breath and decided this was one of those things so fraught with peril he best drop it. The issue will manifest, like dad announcing the divorce and stealing Butch away and leaving him alone and lost on the sidewalk of a strange woman's apartment. A nice woman, yes, but, still, a stranger.

What was happening to him? He looked at the street. Walk down it. Turn in the opposite direction dad took. Shoot the compass points, head west. Toward Mt. Scott. Toward home.

Butch paused. Considered.

He'd be eaten.

He walked across the courtyard and knocked on Dorey's door. She opened it. "Hello, Butch," she said flatly.

The voice, the dull eyes, head turning away: no real welcome here. He panicked. If she didn't want him here, then he was in big trouble. He had no idea where dad was, no idea where their new apartment was, no idea, frankly, where he was. He could hang around on the sidewalk until dad got back but the police might see him and wham! Orphanage.

Maybe walking home wasn't such a bad idea.

Genuine puzzlement on her face as she peered over him. "Where's your father?" Butch shrugged.

She frowned but it wasn't directed at him and a little surge of hope rose. "Well," she sighed, "come on in."

Butch almost fell to his knees in gratitude.

"Have you eaten?" she asked as he settled into the living room.

Be as little trouble as possible. "Yes, ma'am."

"Okay. Well, I have to go to the shop but Johnny and Marianne can come over so you guys play here."

Excellent. The decision not to go west was looking better and better.

Butch watched the tail end of *Captain Kangaroo* segue into *Lucy* and the chocolate factory episode. He was giggling when Johnny said, "Hey!" and he and Marianne flopped down beside him. All three were soon giggling.

"I'll see you kids later," Dorey called and she was keys and purse and flapping and gone.

"Bring your Joe?" Johnny asked.

"Yeah," Butch waved a general hand toward his knapsack. Apparently, Johnny was just checking for later because he made no move toward it.

The first commercial and the three of them, in unison, "Calgon, take me away!" accompanied by dramatic clasping of arms to breast and falling back against the cushions followed by ritual hitting of shoulders for simultaneous utterance. Butch looked at the pretty lady lying in the tub and felt something stir, the Wicked Thing moving a wing.

"Know what my dad told me last night?" Butch didn't mean for his voice to be so sly. He attributed that to the Wicked Thing.

Johnny stared at the pretty lady, too. "What?"

"What sex is." Damn. Still sly. And now he grinned evilly, too. What was this?

"Huh?" Johnny and Marianne.

"You guys know what that is?"

Marianne eyed him suspiciously. "Yeah."

"You didn't know before?" Johnny's tone edged on ridicule and Butch's guard went up. Perhaps he wasn't completely read up on this.

Johnny and Marianne shared a smile of contempt that they

turned on him and Butch was in trouble. Think fast. "Well, do you know what a French Tickler is?"

Got 'em.

Two sets of eyebrows rose and they exchanged concerned looks that told Butch all he needed. "I'll show you," he chortled and pulled out the envelope.

They stared and Marianne reached for it. "What's 'prophylactic' mean?" she asked, stumbling a bit, saying 'profi.' Butch bobbed a shoulder as if he knew and hoped they wouldn't press it.

"What's inside?" she asked.

"*Uh...*" he began but Marianne pouched the envelope and shook it. The plastic fell into her lap.

They all stared. "What is it?" Johnny asked.

"A balloon," Butch said, lamely.

"A balloon?" Johnny's brow furrowed. "Why do they call it a French Tickler, then?"

"I don't know."

"I thought you knew," Johnny accused and Butch was caught. He rallied. "I know what it's for."

"So what's it for?"

He hesitated, recalling dad's words. "So a girl won't have a baby."

Marianne held it up. "How's it work?" she asked.

"*Uh,*" again, hesitation and, again, the growing look of ridicule in their eyes. "You put it on before you have sex," he blurted.

"Put it on how?" Marianne asked.

Defeated. How could he say 'on my wiener' to a girl, especially one so cute that dad noticed and who now stared at him intently? His face grew warm. Done, exposed, humiliated... then the Wicked Thing flapped its heavy wings. "On my dingdong." He had changed the word to something more acceptable before proclaiming it boldly, loudly. And then grinned. Evilly.

"Hmph." Marianne regarded the plastic. "Show me," she said.

Butch was aghast. "What?"

"Yeah, show us," Johnny chimed, his eyes aglow.

"You mean, right here?"

"Sure," Johnny said, matter-of-factly.

Butch was paralyzed. Was this for real? "I can't do that."

"Why not?" Johnny asked.

"Well, I just can't," he said weakly and flapped a weak hand around in emphasis.

Marianne looked at him askance, challenge in her eyes. "Haven't you ever played doctor?"

"Well..."

"With your sister, right?" More challenge and Butch swallowed because, well, yeah, he and Cindy had.

"Have *you* guys?" he countered.

"Played doctor? Sure," she said, and she and Johnny passed knowing looks.

"But, I mean, all the way?"

"What do you mean by 'all the way'?" Marianne leaned toward him and he shrank back into the couch because, really, what did he mean?

"Uh, you know, showed yourselves." That's what he meant. He guessed.

"Yeah, we have," Johnny said.

"Really?" He and Cindy had never gone that far. "You really have?"

"Yeah, so, you can, too," Marianne sat back, expectant. Butch looked at her and Johnny and the anticipation there. The Wicked Thing's shadow flashed in their eyes.

He quailed. "I just can't."

Johnny sneered but Marianne was appraising. "Because of him?" she pointed at her brother.

Well, yeah, and you, and Cindy and everyone else in the world because you just don't go around naked in front of people. Just don't. It's embarrassing. And it's not right. Not even in a bathroom. Why do you think they have stalls, so you don't show your naked butt while you're peeing?

But Butch couldn't convey that to a brother and sister who had no compunctions about showing themselves to each other, so he simply nodded.

"Okay," Marianne said, "Come with me." And she grabbed his hand and yanked him off the couch, the Tickler dangling from her fingers, and dragged him down the hall.

Johnny, startled. "Where you going?" he called to her eager form and Butch's hesitant one. "Bedroom," she called back over her shoulder. Johnny jumped off the couch and spun around to follow but Marianne froze him with a "No!"

"But," he spluttered, "I wanna see how it works!"

Marianne stopped in half-drag, allowing Butch to regain his balance. "I'll tell you how after," she said. Then, in a scornful voice, "Boys don't show themselves to boys, idiot," and resumed the drag. Johnny was brought up short by that and Butch had an immediate sense of relief. Half relief, that is. He still had to deal with Marianne.

She practically flung him into the bedroom, Johnny still dogging them despite the admonition. "Stay out here," she ordered her brother and slammed the door in his desperate face. Marianne turned, her expression unreadable, arms crossed, head tilted. "Okay. Show me."

They were standing at the foot of an acre-sized bed covered in a beige summer blanket, two light brown night tables flanking the far end where light tan pillows in frilly covers leaned against a blond headboard. Two paintings identical to the nondescript brown swirls hanging in the living room overtopped the nightstands, and a mile-long dark-brown chest of drawers L-d to the left, various jewelry boxes and perfume bottles and even a wig stand strewn across the top, all reflected in a giant mirror that stretched from one end to the other. Barely clearing the end of the chest of drawers was an out-of-place metal and glass makeup desk with a modern looking metal chair pulled up to it, a mirror with lights all around it like in a Hollywood movie smack in the middle.

Butch inventoried the contents of the room over and over, anything to keep from looking at her.

She watched him expectantly for a few moments, then tsked, hooked her thumbs into her shorts and pulled them down, her Mickey Mouse underwear accordioned at her feet. "There," she said, with some triumph.

Butch was transfixed. She was... there was... nothing. Simply nothing. She was smooth and thin, a little line where her wiener should be and this did not make any sense at all. He didn't know what to make of it, didn't know what he was looking at, but, apparently, the Wicked Thing did, because it beat gleefully against his stomach and ribs.

Marianne was stock-still, absorbing his scrutiny with the

patience of an artist's model, but he could not figure this out. And he didn't know how to figure this out. Did he ask questions? Did he touch? What the heck do I do? So he fidgeted, trying to find a place to put his hands, and stared, hoping answers would make themselves apparent. After about six or seven days of this, she tilted her head and said, "Your turn," staring him full in the face, her eyes bold, challenging, a pulse in her neck.

Okay. That's that. Sarge says go, so we go. Slowly he unbuckled his pants, dropped them, and then pulled down his underwear. He hoped they were clean.

Her turn to stare for six or seven hours while Butch's eyes roved everywhere but at her. "Why you got your skin on?" she asked.

Butch's face flamed. "Because I'm German."

She shrugged. It seemed technical enough. "Here." Marianne handed him the plastic. He held it in his palm, regarding it.

"Well?"

Butch pulled at the nub and unrolled it and this action was interesting enough to distract her and give Butch the few seconds he needed to realize why, indeed, the end was so big. Smacking himself mentally, he pulled it over his wiener. The plastic hung there, barely staying on.

They stared, fascinated.

"Now what?" she asked.

"Well, uh." Dad's words came back. "You have sex."

Marianne pursed a lip. "Okay," she said.

Okay? "Uh," was all he could muster.

They both stood for a moment looking at each other. "What do we do?" he finally asked.

"I think we have to get in the bed. You're supposed to do sex in the bed. And you have to take of all your clothes." She peeled the pants off her feet and began working her way out of her blouse. "Turn around," she commanded and Butch did as hastily as being shackled by pants and underwear allowed. There were shufflings and the sounds of fabric wafting and then she said, "Okay."

Butch turned. Her clothes were in a pile at the foot of the bed and he stared at them stupidly. "Get in the bed," she said and Butch followed her exasperated voice around and could see the top of her head and eyes peering at him from the pillows, the blankets pulled all the way up. Carefully, he began to mount the foot while grasping the Tickler in place. "Take your clothes off first, idiot."

Oh, right, and he slid back down and disrobed, the Wicked Thing beating against his wiener and stirring things he'd never felt before and making him lose the Tickler in the process and he got it back on before resuming his climb, his naked climb, fully exposed to her evaluating eyes as he made his way beside her. He was sure his entire body was a deep, embarrassed red by now.

"Now what?" he asked.

"You have to get on top of me," she said, still maintaining eye contact

"Huh?" was all he could muster.

"To do sex. I think you have to be on top of me."

Butch threw legs and arms over until he had assumed the mountain climber pose, and was eye-to-eye to blanket covered face with her. "Now what?"

"Well, put it inside me."

"Under the blankets?"

"Yeah," said in a 'you're-a-dope' voice.

He turned a deeper shade of red, if that was possible, and wondered at the logistics. Did he wriggle underneath or take the blankets down, exposing her naked body? A girl, completely naked. The Wicked Thing was trying to rip its way out of his chest. Marianne looked… calm, accepting, her eyes shining.

Okay. Sarge says go, so we go. "You'll have to turn over."

"Huh?"

"Dad said it goes where you use the bathroom."

She stared at him then laughed out loud, which felt like a sword stroke. "You don't know anything about girls, do you?" She threw her arms down, unmasking her face and pointed down the bed. "The babies come out there."

Butch didn't see the connection.

"If that's where the babies come out," she said, patiently, "then that's where you have to put them in."

"Put them in?"

"Yes. Sex. That's where babies come from."

"I don't get it," he said and burst into tears.

She stared in full astonishment. "It's okay," she said and was transformed, no longer Vampirella drawing the Wicked Thing out of him, but Mom. "It's all right." She held him close, wrapping him in the blankets, and the Wicked Thing flapped away because Butch's misery was so complete. They remained like that for a while, Marianne soothing and him crying, the fear and frustration gradually dissipating.

They got dressed, not looking at each other. They made the bed so it looked like no one had been in it. Butch stuffed the Tickler down the bedroom trash.

"Ready?" she asked. He nodded and she opened the door and Johnny almost fell through onto his face. "Well?" he asked.

They looked at each other. Simultaneously, their hands came out to waist level and waggled. "Eh," they both said.

# CHAPTER 28

"Something happen at Dorey's yesterday?" Dad's voice, all suspicion.

Butch's blood froze. "No," he said, frantically fighting the lie's rising tone.

"Well," answering tone of disbelief, "Last night she said'd be a good idea if you didn't come over for a while."

Oh no. Dorey found the discarded Tickler. Which meant, in the next half second or so, dad will descend on him with claw and fang. Butch braced, several million apologies and explanations marshaling for launch—"I'm sorry! We didn't do anything! It's your fault! You told me about sex!"—and… nothing. He blinked at dad, who was fooling around with some stuff on the table.

Odd, unless… Dorey didn't tell. Relief, quickly followed by puzzlement. Why not? Maybe she was too embarrassed, her soiled niece and all. Okay, saved from execution, but he was now proscribed, unable to see Marianne.

Marianne.

He wanted to have sex with her again, for her to hold him and say everything was all right, again. The Wicked Thing reared back its scaly head and howled, a cry of grief and loss.

Probably shouldn't convey that. He shrugged. "Okay."

"No problem staying here?" Dad was at the door, already turned and gone.

"Nope."

Dad nodded and walked out and Butch heard him go down the stairs and the car start and pull away. It got quiet. Butch stood, wary. Might be a trick and dad would come roaring back, belt in one hand, club in the other, "You dirty boy!" and pound him into jelly. Minutes passed. Nothing. He was alone.

Alone.

"Marianne," the Wicked Thing sobbed through Butch's lips.

What was he going to do about Marianne?

What could he do?

Don't know. Nothing came to mind and he needed things to come to mind. Needed fuel to get things to come to mind, like the Cheerios Kid getting 'O" muscles, but he didn't have any Cheerios so made peanut butter toast and then turned on the TV for added inspiration. Some morning show, a couple of men sitting around talking about taxes, which Butch knew was a bad thing. He had done a bad thing, so he listened for a connection. Vietnam and withholding and literacy tests; he didn't understand half the conversation but all bad things were part of a bigger Bad, and sex with Marianne was right in there. The men mentioned JFK's assassination, another bad thing.

He remembered that day. Third grade. All the teachers were called to the office, prompting a room-wide paper airplane war.

Mrs. Ellis came back looking grave and they quieted. "Go home, children," she said in her gentle way and they looked at each other, puzzled, her gravity diffusing the joy of early release. He trudged into the yard. Cindy sat on the back porch. "Guess what," she said, "President Kennedy's been shot."

"Oh," he said and went in and made himself a sugar-and-butter sandwich.

The whole assassination thing turned out one giant annoyance—nothing on TV but solemn people intoning the same regrets for three days. The funeral was an interesting exception: that little kid, John John, saluting and Mrs. Kennedy, who was a real pretty lady, all in black and the horses and the caisson. But, come on already, and he told Mom, as she pulled a meatloaf from the oven, they needed to put the cartoons back on. Mom flipped out.

Jeez. The guy's dead, why get mad at me?

Finally, Sunday, they moved off Kennedy and put on a show about Lincoln. Butch watched, hungry for something different. Good story, too.

Now, the cloud of another bad thing. So when does he get his life back this time? Three days? Three months?

He changed the channels, but nothing, and gave up, pulling out some comic books: Thor's origin, Spiderman's, when Captain America became an Avenger and, of course, *X-Men* #1. Ten minutes later, he tossed them aside. Inspired.

Peter Parker and Steve Rogers and Scott Summers didn't sit around waiting to get their lives back. They went out and did stuff.

How 'bout you go out and do stuff?

Hmm.

He searched the chest of drawers and dad's side of the mattress, collecting about three dollars in change.

Jeez, dad, no wonder you're not made of money; you keep losing it. Add to what he had... $5.32. A fortune.

Okay.

He didn't have a key or any idea when dad was coming back but, you know, so what? I am Captain America. He closed the door carefully and went down the stairs and stood in the alley, looking over the old car. Not a Ford, a DeSoto, stripped to bare metal, the seats gone and mere shreds of tire on the wheels. It was up on blocks so someone was working on it and he looked around fearfully. Nobody around.

He walked out of the alley and stood, blinking. The morning sun poured gold down the street, quite dazzling and quite pleasant. Old houses with big glass windows were planted right up against the sidewalk, all of them with slivers of lawn bordering steep front steps angling to the doors. Big trees teetered precariously between the sidewalks and the street, shading things. Butch's apartment rested on top of an auto parts store with a couple of bare shelves in the window. A red "Closed" sign flapped on the doorknob, like that was necessary.

Butch saw a bus stop at the far corner. He headed over and leaned against the sign, yanking a couple of long weeds from the curb to play swordfight. He was so absorbed that the arriving bus startled him.

The bus driver, a jovial fat man, looked down from the seat. "Where you goin', son?"

Good question and the answer came to him immediately. "Movies."

The driver shook his head, "Wrong way, son. Wacha wanna do is go up two more blocks and catch the 39th Street bus, going west. You know what direction west is, right? Good, that'll getcha downtown." The driver paused as Butch craned his neck up the street. "Hell, son, get on, I'll take you to the corner."

Butch dug in his pocket but the driver waved him down, "No charge, son." Butch stood in the entrance, which was a very cool way to ride the bus. An old, fat, black lady in the back mildly regarded him.

"Here ya go," the door opened and Butch stepped out. "There." The driver pointed over his shoulder at a stop across the street. Butch dropped back to let the bus go. "Son," the driver said, "you comin' back here?"

"Yes."

"Do you know what street this is?"

Butch shook his head.

"This is Chestnut. The street you're going down is 39th. Get off at Washington, that's where all the movies are. You get back on the 39th bus heading east to come back here. Got it?"

Butch nodded.

"All right then." The driver pulled the door and airbrakes hissed and it was off, the black lady still regarding him as her window passed and the bus was a block away before Butch realized he hadn't thanked the driver. Next time.

Butch still had the weeds and kept dueling until the westbound pulled up. The driver stared at him like he was committing a crime and he nervously dropped the swords, boarded and paid. A couple of old ladies stared at him like his photo adorned a post office wall. He kept tight by the window, afraid of arrest for some obscure crime and afraid he'd miss the street.

He did.

Butch watched a street sign marked "Washington" pass by as the bus turned a corner. "Hey," he called out, "I need to get off!"

"Then pull the cord!" the driver called back. Butch yanked frantically and the bus stopped a block later and he ran off, avoiding the baleful looks of newly seated old ladies and the earlier old ladies and the driver. He walked back to Washington. Nothing looked familiar and a fluttery panic took hold. Was he lost?

An old man in white overalls was cleaning a store's big picture window. Butch walked up to him. "Excuse me, sir." He hoped his voice wasn't too quavery. "Can you tell me where the movies are?"

The man pointed with his squeegee down the street, then went back to his window. Butch didn't see any theaters. "That way?" he copied the man's point.

"Yes, boy, that way," the man said, irritably.

Jeez, what a grouch. Don't press your luck, bucko.

He walked. As the blocks fell behind, nothing looked right and his panic increased. The street numbers, though, decreased, 39, 38, 37, staving the terror. At least he could retrace his steps to 39th and Washington and the bus back to Chestnut, so maybe he was all right.

When the marquee hove into view, he was more than all right.

Made it!

Feeling accomplished, he looked at the posters and focused on *The Train*, with Burt Lancaster, starting in fifteen minutes. Made it! He got a ticket and went inside and bought some popcorn. The usual gang of idiots ran around grabbing each other and Butch smiled and took a back seat, watching them. He looked hard for Marianne and Johnny, but no luck. The cartoons came on. He settled.

It was a decent movie and Butch felt good when he walked out. The sky had clouded, but it was still bright and he blinked into focus. The clock over the bank said two o' clock. Dad had never been home before four o' clock, so he had time. He walked slowly toward Dorey's, getting to the corner in about ten minutes. He paused, eying the front window.

Go in, say "Hi, everyone!" only to have Uncle and the old fat men turn and stare, horrified. "You!" Uncle's accusing finger straight at him. "You evil, evil, boy! You dirty little boy!" Dorey charging out, face pulled back, all teeth and popped eyes, shrieking, "Dirty! Dirty! You ruined my niece!" and there's Marianne in the office, wounded, broken. "Dirty boy! Dirty boy!" all in unison, their fingers pumping in time with the chant, driving him onto the street where all the passersby join them and he is hounded, shamed, through the city.

Don't go in.

He held his breath. Exiled, branded, shunned, because of something he didn't understand—sex. The powerful urge, the wings fluttering in his stomach again, and he really, really wanted to see Marianne, but didn't dare. He'd crossed a forbidden, irrevocable line. Butch felt years of baseball games and summer afternoons and big floating clouds dissolve, their magic thinning, evaporating.

"You all right, son?"

Startled, Butch looked up at an older man in a tan suit and hat bending over and smiling. "Uh, yeah, yes, yes sir, I am."

The man's hand came down on his shoulder, a talon. "You sure, son? You look a little upset. Are you lost?" The man's eyes widened a bit. "Are you alone?"

"No, sir, I'm fine. I'm not lost." The brightening in the man's eyes turned Butch cold.

"Maybe you should come with me. We can look for your mother, together," and the talon gripped and there, in the man's hopeful tone and sudden shortening of breath, the Wicked Thing.

"No!" Butch shouted and dropped down like he'd seen Race do and wrenched out of the man's grasp. The man stepped forward, his face now dark, but one or two people stopped and regarded him. He straightened, gave Butch a long hard look, then walked away, adjusting his hat.

The stopped people looked at Butch just as hard but walked away too, and Butch stood there in the middle of pedestrian traffic, staring at Dorey's. He *was* alone, wasn't he? Truly, completely alone, vulnerable to men in tan suits who'd sell him to the pasha and he'd work forever in the kingdom's salt mines, never heard from again. He peered around for Tan Suit's return, but nothing, and headed toward News. He passed Dorey's, looking in the window.

Uncle was hard at work and the fat men read their papers. Ronald slumped in his chair watching Uncle. Louisa sitting next to Ronald, stared at Butch as he drifted by, the murder in her eyes so pure and hot it melted a hole in the glass. He ran.

He spent an hour leafing through News's magazines. He didn't want to spend his precious few coins on them, so he ducked the bearded guy's irritated stare and left. It now looked like rain and he didn't have a coat and dad would be real suspicious if he was all wet, so, best go. He slowed as he came to Dorey's, hoping Marianne was sitting there and would see him and come out and say, "I love you. Let's have sex." But the clouds and the light obscured the window and he couldn't see in, which didn't prevent them from seeing out, and the last thing he wanted was pop-eyed Dorey on the sidewalk leading the 'Dirty Boy' chant, so he ran.

He made it back to 39th as a bus came up. "Do you go to Chestnut?" he asked the skinny old man driving.

"You want the bus across the street, son," the old man pointed and Butch said "Oh" and changed sides. Good thing he'd asked, or he'd end up in Alabama or something.

The eastbound came and he got on and watched hard but passed Chestnut, anyway, so he frantically pulled the rope and got off a block down and walked back and found the apartment after only a few moments of disorientation. It was just as he left it, like no one actually lived here, the backdrop of some TV show. *Twilight Zone*, he decided. His suitcase and dad's duffel bag and the K rations were props.

And nothing had happened. No gypsies had stolen him off the street (although Tan Suit might be one) and no police or boogeymen waited in the apartment. He supposed it'd been an adventure, but a fairly meaningless one. He was a movie up, but almost two dollars down. He pulled out the remaining change and decided he had enough for a repeat tomorrow. After that, maybe he could just walk around.

This was going out and doing stuff? This was being Spiderman and Captain America?

Small origin, small powers. Nothing radioactive had bitten him, at least, as far as he knew. Only unusual event had been taking off across America with dad, which was hardly the birth of a superhero. He might be, at best, a lesser Sue Storm with a wimpy force field kind of like a bubble, riding buses and going to movies without really touching anything. Unharmed, unless Bad People like Tan Suit could use their evil powers to break through and get him. A vulnerability.

How do you counter it?

Butch picked up the comic books and researched. Thor had to be in contact with his hammer, except for the brief moments when he threw it. Spiderman could be killed, so could the X-Men. Having a power was no guarantee of invincibility; if anything, it stirred greater threats. His bubble must do the same. While it gave him enhanced abilities, like traveling alone on a bus, negotiating a strange city, and even gathering entertainment, it revealed him to potential enemies. He wasn't sure he could handle them.

One thing for sure, powers made you lonely. Like Spiderman.

He blinked. Lonely.

"You get used to it," Frank whispered.

Maybe, Frank, but he wasn't even supposed to be here. He should be coming out of the Ritz with Cindy and Art after seeing something like *Pinocchio* (which had scared him to death) or *101 Dalmations* (likewise) and going to A&W for floats, which he didn't like because soda and ice cream, ugh, so he had a milkshake. Dad always said something because those were more expensive but he couldn't help what he liked and maybe Dale was working which was cool even though she acted like a stranger.

A tear made it out, dropping off his chin. Lynn told him to count his tears; that's how many laughs he was due.

Someone owed him about a million, then.

He turned on the television. "Oh, baby, come oooooooooon!!" blared from the speaker.

Cool.

Butch watched as the opening segued into the Stones' *Satisfaction* and he sang along with it, vaguely disturbed by the lyrics. Yeah, Mick, neither can I, and if sex is what you're referring to, then I sympathize. Paul Revere and the Raiders did some skits and Butch was laughing when the stairs shook and dad came in. "What are you watching?"

"*Where the Action Is.*"

Dad peered at the screen. "What kind of show is that? Bunch of beatniks running around acting stupid?"

"Music, dad."

"Beatnik music." Dad made a dismissive wave but watched Dee Dee Sharp sing "Ride" as the Action Kids danced behind her. "What'd you do today?"

"Nothin'."

"Hmm." Dad rummaged through the K Rations and opened a couple of them while turning on the hot plate. "Well, you won't be sittin' around here watching TV all day anymore."

"Huh?"

"Tomorrow, you're going to the Boys' Club."

# CHAPTER 29

"Go in there."

Dad pointed at a fenced-in building that looked like a... school? What the heck? Summer school! He wasn't a retard! "What am I supposed to do in there?" Butch asked, more in protest than curiosity.

"Run around and be stupid, I guess. How the hell do I know? I ain't no damn kid!" Dad snapped.

Butch pressed his lips. Wonderful.

"Hurry up." Dad fiddled with the radio. "I'm late."

Hello? "For work?" Butch suddenly felt a bit hopeful. Work meant staying. Staying meant Marianne.

"No, not for work!" Dad yelled. "Just you never mind. Now go inside!" Dad's finger was a dagger so, for the sake of preservation, Butch got out. He looked back, more protest forming, but dad's face darkened so he opened the gate and walked in. Dad floored it. Butch watched him take the corner almost on two wheels.

Jeez, dad, can't wait to get away from me?

Feeling's mutual.

Butch was on the edge of a dusty playground filled with jungle gyms and swings and slides. A baseball field ranged off the back next to an outside basketball court. Lots of kids running around.

Okay, so a well-appointed summer school with an early recess. Still didn't make it right.

Butch went inside and walked down a narrow hall that

opened into a large room with pool and ping-pong tables scattered all over the place, each one enthusiastically occupied by several layers of kids.

What the hey?

A bored adult sat in an alcove splitting his time between a newspaper open on his lap and the goings-on. Behind the man was a rack of pool sticks so Butch presumed he was in charge of equipment, but that's about all he commanded. If this was summer school, then kids were running it.

Butch watched for a while, not inclined to join in because he was bad at table games. Face it; he was bad at *all* games. Drawn by the sound of shouting kids, he followed a hallway to a gym where hundreds of basketball players, jammed shoulder to shoulder, jostled and maneuvered and pushed for a shot at either of the two rickety baskets hoisted above the uneven wooden floor. There had to be about twenty or thirty individual games running.

How'd they keep it straight?

An adult in a sweatshirt and whistle yelled something incomprehensible every few seconds at the dozen or so scrums, none of which paid him any attention. Butch would have to run a gauntlet of games to reach center court.

Forget it.

Butch had no idea whose game was whose and, besides, he was exceptionally bad at basketball.

Another two hallways led out and he picked a very narrow one that felt like a tunnel. It emptied into a lunchroom, wooden picnic tables here and there, a number of kids eating hot dogs and popcorn. Butch spotted a little kitchen manned by an adult wearing an apron and a paper hat. Hot dogs fried on a gigantic stove against the wall, buns stacked on a table alongside mustard and ketchup bottles. A popcorn machine stood in the corner and Butch watched it blast kernels for a while.

"Hep ya?" Apron said. Breakfast had been a C-Ration chocolate bar, and Butch was a mite peckish. He pointed at a hot dog and the man deftly slid one into a bun. "Watcha wan onnit?"

"Mustard and ketchup."

The man complied and handed it to Butch, who turned. "Hold on, boy."

Butch stopped. Did he do something wrong?

"Dat's a dime," and Apron pointed at a price sign written with magic marker on cardboard propped against a sugar container.

"Oh." Resemblance to school ended at a free lunch. Butch dug down, the coins evading his grasp as Apron grew a little impatient but, finally, snagged a dime and brought it forth.

"Thankee."

Butch grabbed a miraculously empty table and ate while he pulled out the remaining coins and considered his wealth. $3.72: thirty-seven hot dogs, seventy-four bags of popcorn, combinations either way, two cents left over for gum, if available. He wouldn't starve, unless hidden charges for other things lurked around the corner, such as sitting or breathing. "That'll be a dollar, son, to use our bathroom." Butch giggled and then looked around guiltily. A couple of kids at distant tables glanced his way and then past, as if he wasn't there.

Oh, right, small powers.

The Invisible Boy got up and wandered around. It was like a space station in here, corridors running randomly in odd directions then flexing back to some central point that joined another set of random hallways. Needed a map. He picked an opening and, after a minute, spilled into an auditorium with a screen on one side and a bunch of fold-down chairs on the other. A noisy projector clacked through an old fifties science fiction movie about some people in a spaceship.

Cool.

Butch picked an out-of-the-way place and settled. It ended with the spaceship crashing back to earth, Butch watching in horror as the woman and the captain held each other and looked out of the porthole at the rapidly closing ground, faster and faster, then *ka-blam*!

Wow.

Butch stayed for a couple of more movies, all space ones, the best about some guys circling the moon. The wisenheimer's harmonica kept floating out of his hand and Butch wondered how they did that. Was it actually filmed in space? Rescuing the wisenheimer off the surface of the moon was very cool, but had to be special effects. No one's been to the moon yet, not even a film crew. Butch left when the crashing spaceship movie returned.

Somehow he found his way outside and decided a little playground silliness was in order. He weaved in and out of the monkey bars, seeking respite from the sun at the different angles.

Other kids flowed through but didn't see him. Of course not: the Invisible Boy. He tried using his force field to throw them off the bars, but it didn't work. Should be grateful for the one power, he supposed.

There was a shady and embracing tree on one side of the playground. Butch went over, patted the trunk, and sat down underneath. It was comfortable, moss and several decades of leaves providing a rather cushiony seat. Butch indulgently watched the other kids making fools of themselves.

"I wish I could play," someone said.

Startled, Butch looked over. Frank Vaughn sat next to him, dressed in a very nice suit. "Maybe you should change clothes," Butch suggested.

Frank looked down at himself. "They dressed me in this for the funeral. Now it's all I've got. Can you believe it?" He shook his head. "Moms."

Frank was due that touch of resentment, considering everything, so Butch didn't say how much he missed his own mom. "Maybe if you're careful, you won't get dirty."

"Hmm," Frank considered. "We could just throw a ball to each other, like we used to."

"Okay. Do you have one?"

Frank said nothing so they both sat for a while, watching the others. "What's it like, Frank?"

"What's it like being invisible?"

"Scary."

Frank nodded. "There you go."

Butch woke up. He watched the kids for a while longer then got up, brushed off, and walked back into the building. The theater had the ship crash movie again so he headed down some other dark, twisting corridors. Light streamed out of an open door in the middle of one and Butch stopped, curious.

He gasped. A library.

Butch stepped through the portals of heaven, embracing the smell of old, neglected books. The surprisingly large room had yellow walls with about eight or ten dark-wood shelves, perpendicular and parallel to each other, and equally dark-wooded tables marking the boundaries between. Fluorescent banks hanging from the white spackled ceiling flooded the area with reflected yellow light. One of the bulbs blinked like a store sign, but somehow that was okay. He caressed the nearest shelf, calming the novels, then gently wound through dispensing a random pat or two for assurance. A couple of other kids looked up fearfully but Butch turned invisible and they blinked and forgot about him.

Butch pulled a book here and there. Ancient 40s and 50s adventure stories he'd never heard of—*Jack Armstrong, the All American Boy*; *The Three Golliwogs*; *John Carter of Mars*—now, that one looked interesting.

*Tom Swift in the Caves of Nuclear Fire*. What the...? Butch took it, sat down, and began reading.

"Figured you'd be here."

Butch jumped. Dad loomed over him, angry, as usual. "I've been looking for you for twenty minutes. Next time, I'm just going to leave you."

That was chilling and Butch's eyes widened. "I didn't know you were looking for me."

"I told you be out front at four."

No he didn't. "No, you didn't."

"You sassin' me?" Dad went from loom to threat and Butch shrank. He looked around for help, but no one else was here. Unless they had all turned invisible.

"Let's go." Butch moved to put *Tom Swift* back on the shelf. "Leave it," dad snapped.

Sacrilege, but anger the library gods or get killed? He chose to live and slipped in behind dad, who stalked out, winding through the hallways. Butch thought they were lost until they suddenly emerged through a side door into the parking lot. How did dad know this building so well?

"Get in," dad growled unnecessarily because Butch had already slid across the seat.

Jeez.

They pulled out.

"Didja like it?" It wasn't a question and demanded only one answer; that is, if Butch didn't want to be thrown out the door.

"Yes."

"Good." Dad was satisfied. "You're going back tomorrow."

# CHAPTER 30

"Dad, can I have some money?"

"What for?" Dad messed with a flight suit he'd laid on the bed.

"Food," Butch said as he dried a dish. Telling a lie while doing something innocuous made it more plausible. He hoped.

"You mean you spent all that money I gave you for food already?"

You mean the quarter a day, Scrooge McDuck? Butch shrugged. "I was hungry." Not a lie since he'd only spent half the quarter, hoarding the rest, which meant a grumbly stomach by afternoon.

"Well, maybe you should stay hungry, teach you I'm not made of money."

Right, right, right. Butch patiently worked the few dishes; easy job, since they were living out of cans. He was slowly losing his taste for C-Ration chocolate, though. Worrisome. He doubted very seriously Mr. I'm-Not-Made-of-Money would buy something good, like Reese's Cups or M&Ms.

"Here," dad said and flung a couple of dollars on the bed then went into the bathroom. Butch scooped them up. Perfect. Now he had over five dollars. Half-starving himself all week had paid off.

He was dressed and waiting by the door when dad emerged and he watched for signs of suspicion but dad was distracted, probably about where he was heading. Not a job, Butch knew, even though dad hinted it was. Not to go fly, either, because the suit was still on the bed. Butch wondered what he'd been looking for in the pockets.

Fifteen minutes later, dad stopped in front of the Boys' Club. "What time are you picking me up?" Butch asked.

Dad's eyes got ugly. "What time have I picked you up all week?"

Butch mentally smacked himself. "Four o'clock."

"And have I told you anything different?"

"No."

"Well, then I guess it's still four o'clock, ain't it?" Dad glared. "Boy, for all your reading, you sure are dumb."

Right, right, right, but maybe, this time, not so dumb.

"Don't make me come look for you. Be right there." Dad jabbed a hand toward the gate.

Butch slipped out and stood quietly as dad roared off, watching him out of sight. He turned invisible and went straight to the library, grabbed *Tom Swift and his Jetmarine*, found his place, and started reading. He'd turned visible earlier this week during a playground obstacle race, having a pretty good time and losing, of course. Everyone ignored him when it was over. He'd been invisible ever since.

He finished the book and went to the kitchen and bought two hot dogs. The lunchroom was crowded and he sat down between two big kids who didn't see him but made room anyway and continued their talk about some high school football team, the Typhoons.

Good name.

Butch finished and threw away his plate and left the building, unseen. He stood outside the gate for a moment, getting his bearings.

Okay, corner of Jefferson and Hilton. He peered about. Ah, there. Bus stop.

Butch walked across the street. A couple of kids and adults meandering the Club yard glanced in his direction but didn't see him. After twenty minutes, he got fidgety, wondering if the bus stop was a joke and everyone was getting a big old laugh seeing him stand there like a doofus (but how could they see him?) when one finally showed. He turned visible in time to catch the driver's attention.

"Does this bus go downtown?" Butch asked.

"Waal, it shore doan!" the big man driving chortled, "Tellee what, yore goan rat way. Geed offn 39, towads wes', take dirdy-nyn bus, yew be awright!"

Amazingly, Butch understood all that and, smiling, dropped his coins. There were several black boys in the back fooling around and Butch strained to see if one of them was Ronald, but no. A couple of the boys caught him staring and gave back hard looks, elbowing their friends to participate, so Butch hastily turned invisible and they blinked and went back to each other.

"Ear yewgo!" the bus driver sang and Butch got off, wondering how the driver knew he was there and figured invisibility flickered if he didn't concentrate. Confirmed when one of the black boys made a face at him as the bus pulled away. The 39 bus came right up and he was soon at the theater.

It was still a half-hour before the movie, *Atragon, the Japanese Supersub*, so Butch waited under the canopy. It was melt-into-the-sidewalk hot, and he was grateful for the shade. No need to turn invisible; the heat kept everyone's heads down. He watched for Tan Suit, but figured he wouldn't show. Can't walk around on a day like this dressed like that.

The ticket lady finally opened the booth and Butch stood in line with some other kids, who ignored him. He looked for Marianne and Johnny, but no. Marianne wouldn't want to see this movie, so they were probably at the Palace. Butch didn't feel like walking down there because it might be something lame, *The Great Race*, maybe. He did feel like seeing Marianne, but this was a double feature. No contest.

Butch squirmed with delight as the cartoons ended and Atragon came on. Very cool movie but, even cooler, what followed: *The Evil of Frankenstein*. Peter Cushing was just the best mad doctor and the hypnotist scared Butch into open-mouthed terror at a few spots. Overall, good session.

It was even hotter outside, if that was possible, and the day's brightness had washed out. People staggered, as though the air was beating them savagely. Butch took in a breath to burn his lungs. It was Oklahoma hot, a day for the pool or running through lawn sprinklers then get some ice cream and retreat to Tommy's porch where they'd line up soldiers and idly shoot rubber bands at them. Cindy would come over and they'd play jacks for a while and then Tommy would get out his Slip and Slide, which was great until Butch hit a rock under the plastic and started crying.

Drift into Tommy's garage, setting up more wars and arguing about them while the sun glared a sullen retreat then go outside and lay on the cooling grass and star wish.

His next breath was a sob.

A clock sticking out of a wall showed two-thirty. Slowly, Butch oozed down the sidewalk. He stood in front of Dorey's. He couldn't see inside so he pushed open the door, blinking.

"Young'un!" Uncle's surprised voice caught him and he stared in that direction, eyes catching up. The old man was rubbing a rag through an open can of polish. The seats were empty.

"Hello, Uncle," Butch said, " Johnny and Marianne here?"

"No, they ain't about today. What you doin'?"

"Movies."

"Oh. How you been?"

"Fine." He hesitated. "We moved."

"I heard. Is it a nice place?"

Butch shrugged.

"Hm. Well, you ready for that shine?"

Butch looked down at his sneakers but there didn't seem to be a joke there anymore. "No," he said.

"All right, then." Uncle regarded him. "That boy still following you around?"

"Yes."

"Thought so. He don't mean no harm."

"I know," Butch sat down and picked at a *Life* magazine. "He's scared. And lonely."

"I think he ain't the only one."

Butch looked up, wondering how a grownup could feel someone else. Usually, they only felt themselves. Uncle not only touched spirits, but souls. "I'm okay."

"I know, son, I know. But, lonely," Uncle laid a gentle hand on his shoulder. "That's gonna be your way."

Butch stared down the long tunnel of Uncle's eyes. His own face, wreathed in blackness, stared back looking fearful and unhappy and lost. No other faces. No other shadows, not even a hint of Frank. He blinked and the tunnel got longer and his face older, a teenager, a young man, elderly, with no other face next to it.

"No," Butch whispered. But that tunnel was as certain as

Uncle's hand on his shoulder.

"Why, Butch!" Dorey's voice broke the spell and Uncle moved away, pulling Butch out of that long, miserable tunnel. "What are you doing here?"

Screech-eyed, Dorey would now lay hold of his neck and twist his head around. He stared at her, terrified, but didn't see any hate, just a mild surprise. Could be a ruse and Butch measured the door's distance, prepared to spring for it. "I was just walking by." He readied.

"Well, I'm glad you came in. I haven't seen you in so long." She sat down next to him and the rustle of skirt and waft of Avon was Mom's and the fear left him. Everything was okay.

"We live far." He figured that was the best explanation.

"Oh, I know, I know." She laid a gentle, reassuring hand, looked at him and hesitated. "How's your dad?"

"He's okay. He's"—Butch almost said 'out'—"working."

Might as well be wearing a "Kid is lying" sign. Change the subject. "Where's Marianne?" he asked hastily.

And Johnny, you idiot. He smacked himself in the head but too late, Dorey caught it.

She smiled a little too warmly. "She and her brother are in North Carolina, at my momma's. I'm sorry you didn't get a chance to see them before they left. She asked how you are."

And Butch had no secrets anymore and he wondered why Dorey was being so calm. Shouldn't she be snapping his head around?

But Marianne had asked how he was. A delightful warmth shivered him. "Tell her I'm okay."

"I will. I talk to them on the weekends when the rates are cheaper. So what are you doing down here?"

"I went to the movies."

"By yourself?"

"Yes."

She looked a bit astonished. "Do you live nearby?"

"No. I live off Chestnut. I came from the Boys' Club."

"By yourself?" she repeated, looking at him sideways. "Did you walk?"

"No. I took the bus."

"By yourself." It wasn't a question this time. "My, you have become quite the little man, haven't you?"

He flushed, confused and pleased at the same time. It was always good to be thought older than you were, but there was a tone in Dorey's voice, like her dog had run away or something. Butch's first dog, Sugarfoot, had run away and he'd been very upset. Still was.

She watched him for a moment. "Your dad doesn't know you're out here, does he?"

His heart leaped and he paled. He didn't say anything. Didn't have to.

She nodded, "All right. I have to go pick up some supplies. I'll drop you off." She stood with a no-nonsense air and Butch got up, too, no point in arguing.

She drove a Simca, which Butch always thought a cute little car, and he played with the door strap as she started it. "You have to be careful," she said.

"I know."

She shook her head, "I don't mean around here. Be careful with your dad." Butch looked at her, surprised. "He'd be very upset if he knew what you were doing. Maybe you shouldn't go out alone anymore."

Butch shrugged. "If I don't, I just sit around all day."

"Aren't you having fun at the Boys Club?"

He thought of telling her about invisibility. She seemed receptive but, hey, a grownup. "I guess."

"Okay. Settle for that, if you can."

They turned down 39th and Butch enjoyed the view from the funny windows. "Are you mad at me?" he asked.

"No. The buses are pretty safe. Be careful of the bad people." Butch flashed on Tan Suit. "The good people will help you." He flashed on the bus drivers. Except the mean one.

"I know. I mean, about Marianne and me."

She smiled. "I think it's cute."

Cute? Butch stared at her. What the... oh, wow. She didn't know, she had no idea! Relief coursed through him, and he almost fell to the floor. But then... what had dad been talking about? "Dad said you were mad because of..." careful, man "... something we did."

"What?" She furrowed a brow. "I can't imagine what that could be. I haven't seen your dad since you moved out."

Huh? Confusion took over. "But dad said the other night that

202

you didn't want me to come over for a while."

"The other night?"

"Yeah. A week ago." Something like that.

She shook her head. "I haven't seen him."

"But, he's been going out..." And he stopped. Way too late.

"Oh," was all she said and looked away, her lips compressed.

He closed his eyes, mortified. Way to go, stupid, you just hurt her real bad and she's been nothing but nice, even though you had sex with her niece. Sort of. "I didn't mean..." he said but was too far from the right words.

"It's not your fault," she toned. "I've known your dad for a while." She looked at Butch. "Don't be like him. Be someone else, someone who thinks of others first and how they feel. You do that, and you'll have everything you want."

She pulled to the curb and he got out. She smiled and waved and drove off.

Idiot! Forgot to thank her! He waved frantically at the disappearing car, hoping she saw.

Think of others first?

He blinked in the direction she'd gone. Dorey, that's how I ended up far from home, far from friends, all alone, wracked with guilt over Marianne and wanting her at the same time, confused and helpless.

Like Frank.

Tears flowed. In front of a Boys' Club was probably not the best place to cry and he tried turning invisible, but couldn't. Loss of control, he guessed. He grabbed his shoulders so they wouldn't heave, attracting playground predators. 'Don't be like him.' Not to worry, Dorey—he'd be as different as possible. He wouldn't be mean. He wouldn't hit. He wouldn't be dad, who was a complete jerk, who was a...

...bastard.

A bastard. He gasped and stopped crying. The forbidden word was a stark, hard line to cross. But, you know, it fit.

He wiped the crying evidence from his face to throw off the vultures, turned invisible, and walked inside. He beelined to the library and grabbed a *Bobbsey Twins*. At five minutes to four, he slapped the book closed and left. Dad was already at the gate, idling.

He got in. Dad's face was stone and the hate lights glowed in his eyes. Thank God Butch came out early—five minutes later and he'd be a bloody corpse on the sidewalk. Heck, there was a very good chance he'd be a bloody corpse in the car. He turned invisible.

They pulled up to the apartment and Butch watched dad warily, but he'd forgotten about him, so Butch trailed him up the stairs, staying out of reach. Dad looked through some papers and Butch put the bed between them, gingerly posing Joe in various warrior positions while keeping an eye out.

"Pack all your stuff up," dad suddenly said.

"Huh?"

"We're leaving in the morning."

Hope surged through him. "Are we going home?"

"No!" The fury reddened dad's skin and slitted his eyes. "We ain't! We ain't ever going back there. So just get that out of your goddamn head!" He turned back to his papers, all the lines twisted down.

Shocked, Butch stared at him. The word came back, presented itself in flaming letters.

Bastard.

# CHAPTER 31

They went south then west, picking up 158 in North Carolina as small towns and intersections blurred past. By ten o'clock, they reached Winston-Salem and Interstate 40 and dad drove faster. They gassed in Asheville and ate cold C-Rations in the parking lot. It was cool here; a breeze flowed off the mountains and Butch put his face in it.

Dad pointed at the rolling hills and peaks with his ham-laden spork. "They call those the Smokies,"

"Why?"

"Because, from a distance, they look like smoke."

True enough. The farther hills were smudges on the horizon easily mistaken for clouds of smoke. Maybe the first explorers strolling about here thought they were seeing the cook fires of great civilizations and felt stupid when it turned out to be mere mountains. A warning to those coming later.

They exited onto a confusion of roads and signs that would baffle the Russians. Sure baffled him. 64? 74?

"Georgia's over there," dad said.

Butch pressed against the window. Another state he could claim. "Where?"

Dad pointed left and Butch strained but saw no markers. Needed some big billboard hanging from the sky proclaiming "Georgia!" with an arrow pointing down so he could verify it.

They cleared Chattanooga and dad sang *Chattanooga Choo-Choo* for a good annoying hour afterward. Butch contemplated a leap from the car until dad finally switched on the radio. Even country music was tolerable after dad's improvisation.

"Where we going?" Butch asked.

"This way." Dad pointed down the road.

Funny. Real funny

Butch got drowsy and his head nodded. A thump woke him. They were on the shoulder, bumping along about half speed, and then came to a sudden stop. "Dammit," dad said.

"What's wrong?"

"The oil light came on."

Butch saw a red-lit oilcan glowing on the dashboard. "What does that mean?"

"Dunno yet," dad said and got out. It was sunset now and the day's spent heat rolled in, jolting Butch. Cars and trucks whipped by, shaking the Rambler. Butch opened his door and stood on the broken asphalt. "I gotta pee," he said to dad, who was fiddling with the front of the car. Dad pointed down the berm.

It was rather steep and Butch was pleased he made it to the bottom without falling. There were lots of old tires and soda cans scattered around. Good place for snakes. After assuring himself none lay in ambush, he looked back at the road. Didn't want to be naked-butt famous again. They were on an outside curve and the only thing he could see were the sides of trailers as the big trucks rounded it. Since he couldn't see the cabs, they couldn't see him. Whew. Hidden by angle and the growing dark.

Dark.

Nervously, he looked at the pinewoods opposite the ditch and wondered if bears lived in there. Or vampires. He swore he heard the sound of coffins opening, so he hurriedly dropped his pants, finished, and scrambled up the ditch on all fours. Safe. But, not really; he didn't have a cross or garlic. He peered at the woods, expecting a white face with bloody fangs to peer back.

Dad was looking down at the engine, hands on hips. "Dammit," he said.

"What?"

"The gasket blew. We can't drive." He wiped his hands on a rag and frowned at the engine, although how he could see anything with the sun down, Butch didn't know.

"So what do we do?" Butch kept his quaver to a minimum. Dad wouldn't buy the vampires-creeping-up-the-berm story. Until it was too late.

Dad looked at him. "What would you do?"

"Huh?"

"What would you do to get out of this? Save yourself?" Dad's 'you-dumb-kid' face grinned at him.

Great. Another one of dad's games where he proved Butch wouldn't live through the next five minutes if it weren't for him.

Bastard.

Butch made a frustrated gesture. "Get some help, I guess."

"How?"

"I don't know," frustrated-kid-whine, "Wave at some cars."

"Or." Dad pointed up the road. "You could walk up to that gas station."

Butch followed his point. Where the road curved to the left, a ramp led up a darkly green embankment to a blazing Esso sign. "Oh," he said.

Score one for the bastard.

It took them about twenty minutes to reach the top. Dad surged across the access road, leaving Butch behind. Fearing the encroaching vampires, Butch ran past a sign that read "Lacon, Cold Spring," forcing a car to quick-stop.

"Watch it!" Dad called from the front of the station.

Well, why didn't you stay with me, you bastard?

Dad was talking to a guy in a striped shirt and overalls wearing a red Esso hat. "Klemeth" was stitched over his pocket. He nodded at what dad said and walked over to a tow truck. "Get in," dad ordered.

Butch scrambled up and wedged in between the two adults. He stared at the levers and dials. Cool.

Klemeth drove the truck up the shoulder to the Rambler, getting a few annoyed honks from truckers in the process. He looked at the engine, nodded at what dad said, then hooked up the car, getting a few more honks.

"Can I ride in the Rambler?" Butch asked. Sitting in a towed car. Cool.

"No," dad said so he squeezed back into the cab and they rode up the shoulder again, Butch watching the Rambler as it bounced behind.

Cool.

Klemeth dropped the car in front of an open bay and he and dad pushed it in, Butch rendering a bit of assistance. The Rambler rose on lifts. It looked wounded up there, a soldier pulled off the battlefield for an emergency transfusion. Klemeth and a couple of other guys gathered underneath, poking and prodding. Surgery prep.

"Don't get in the way," dad snapped and stalked out.

There was no place to sit. Butch folded into a corner near the big doors, avoiding the drip cans and discarded rags. The whole garage was covered in oil, as if someone had painted it that way. He saw the imprint of his Keds wherever he stepped. The oil was alive, seeking human hosts. He wondered what he would look like as Oil Kid. Probably Buckwheat, but without the cool hair.

Klemeth and his crew poked and prodded some more, giving Butch an occasional baleful look. Maybe they blamed him. "Wadjew do, kid?" Klemeth asks, hate flowing out of his eyes. "Nothin'," Butch replies. The fat bald one with the cigar clamped in his mouth shakes his head. "That's a lie. We know you did somethin'. We're mechanics." The old guy with the mean, stubbly face leans down, sneering, "Tha's right, kid. So, why don't you tell us what the klavisrod is, how it connects to the stemsin, or are you some kind of sissy boy who doesn't know anything about cars and tools and manly things?" And they'd laugh and point and hit him.

Probably should leave.

There was an opening to his left and Butch sidled along until he stood opposite, then darted inside. It was an office, the oil motif continuing. Stacks of car magazines and Chiltons teetered on a metal desk, spilled across the floor, and leaned out of some dangerously balanced shelves along the wall. A rickety chair had a Chilton repair manual propped under one leg. A calendar on the wall flaunted a picture of a breathy blonde holding a large wrench and wearing very tight short shorts, leaning against a big tool carrier and looking back at Butch with a "kiss me" expression. Butch thought of Marianne.

A Philco clinging to a top shelf played a car commercial, "Come on down to Franklin Ford, we got the best deals in town, y'heah?" Then it broke into music—The Four Tops, *Sugar Pie Honey Bunch*.

Surprise.

Butch figured a bunch of yokel mechanics would be tuned to George Jones. "I can't help myself," he sang under his breath, "I love you and nobody else, do do do DO." "Sugar Pie Honey Butt" is how it sounded and Butch had a picture of a brown-skinned girl with a large, treacly butt shaking it while looking at him over her shoulder. He thought of Marianne again.

He hummed the song as he went outside, standing on an oil-covered walkway. Full dark now. Truck headlights popped around the Interstate curve and then roared past. The evening star blazed and Butch stared at it. Tommy told him it was a planet, but Butch wasn't sure which one: Jupiter, Venus, Pluto. It was the only pure light in the world, white and powerful.

Butch stepped down to the tarmac, a crumbly asphalt that looked like solidified oil, and walked to the edge of the berm. Butch followed the windings of trucks and cars below. Their headlights were yellow and mean and insignificant, nothing like the evening star, and he switched between them. The star was beautiful. He'd like to go there.

He turned and saw dad inside a telephone booth, red and gesticulating, obviously mad. Curious, Butch walked up, stood outside the door which didn't close all the way. "I don't care!" dad shouted, "I don't care about that at all. You shoulda thought about that before I left!"

"Is that Mom?" Butch asked, "Can I talk to her?"

Dad glared, his eyes murderous and stunning, knocking him back. Then the screaming started, murderous and stunning, and Butch stood there, open-mouthed, shocked. It was about money and fault and stupidity and who was to blame for what and who was more of what than the other and dad might as well have reached through the phone and lashed Mom, just lashed her, in frenzy and pain and hate. He slammed the phone down and stalked off to disappear inside the bay.

Butch stepped inside and gently picked up the phone. Nothing. He walked back to the berm and took in the headlights and star, and cried.

After a while, he went back to the station. The car was down but the hood was up and dad was talking to the three mechanics. Dad shook his head and went inside the office and sat in the dangerous chair, looking through the magazines. The men raised and lowered the hood and raised and lowered the Rambler and time stopped and this was Butch's eternity, at the entrance of a mechanic's bay watching the Rambler rise and lower while a distant radio did Top 40.

He looked at the evening star. Want to go there. Want to go.

# CHAPTER 32

They slept in a motel next to the station. In the morning, dad gave the mechanics some money and gassed up and drove away, handing Butch a C-Ration chocolate as they cleared the ramp. If he weren't starving, Butch would have tossed it out of the window. They did not speak.

The sun was on Butch's left, so they were going... south. Florida? That would be cool, beaches and bikinis and Cape Kennedy. Mexico? That would be weird. He didn't speak Spanish and besides, the food was too hot. He knew that from a *Madcap* cartoon. A fat lady in a shawl served dinner to a guy in a sombrero and white clothes while the narrator said, "Mexicans like their food spicy." Sombrero took one bite and screamed as flames shot out of his stomach. "My wife," he grinned, burned black, white teeth showing, "eees juan good cook!"

No thanks.

But Florida. Play all day in the ocean, er, Gulf, if he remembered his geography right. Maybe he'd learn to surf. He'd go fishing on one of those big boats, catch a giant marlin, stand proudly next to it while a naked Marianne stroked his weewee. Frank looked down from the captain's chair and said, "This is how it's s'posed to be."

"Know where we are?" Dad asked.

Butch jerked awake. He swore Marianne's hands were still on him and he risked a quick look but didn't see anything. "Where?"

"Selma," dad said.

Butch blinked. He'd heard of that town. "Isn't that in

211

Alabama?"

"Yep."

"We're in Alabama?"

"Yeah, we're in Alabama. Where'd you think we were?"

Butch looked down at his dingdong. "Florida."

Dad laughed. "No, we ain't in Florida, that's for sure." He paused. "So you remember what happened here?"

Butch peered out the window. "Was it in the Civil War?"

"No, well, maybe, but that ain't what I mean. Remember the spear chuckers marching and fighting with the police? This is where that happened."

Oh yeah, that.

Butch looked. It was a damp morning, drizzly gray. No one was on the street. The houses were everything he expected from the South: big, white, colonnaded, sitting back aways. Interspersed were auto shops and Mom and Pops...

Hey, that rhymes.

...an odd mixture.

"See this bridge we're on?" Dad asked.

Well, yeah, they were on it. "Okay," Butch said.

"This is where the chuckers started their big march to Montgomery," he said.

Butch remembered that, too from only a few months ago. It had been on TV. The police, big guys with clubs and funny helmets, chased blacks and hit them and there had been lots of tear gas. A couple of people got killed. Mrs. Wilson had talked about it the next day during social studies, but not a lot. Henry, one of the black kids in Butch's class, said nothing as they played tag during recess.

Butch looked back at the town. An air of slight stun hung over the place, as if no one could believe what happened. From now on, whenever anyone said "Selma," everyone would think of the police beating blacks. Who would want that? If someone said "Butch" and everyone pictured a nasty little boy wearing a French Tickler and trying to put it inside Marianne, he'd have to change his name.

Alabama. Jeez, how in the world did he end up here?

Until now, it was just some far, scary place where they burned crosses and drove old, patched-up trucks and lynched blacks. All the old men were Death Eye. All the kids were Carl and Pigface. It was Big Salt writ large. Butch sank down in the seat to make a smaller target.

They turned off a small country road and headed what Butch figured was southeast. It was very green here—lush, that was the word—with skinny pine trees marching up the berm. Red soil exposed in the fields and ditches made Butch wonder why the trees weren't red. The road dipped across little hillocks topped with houses that were mostly shacks. They crested one hill and a much bigger shack faced them, unpainted, with a raised concrete porch across the front. Lots of blacks sat on the porch or went in and out of the shack, which had "Lee's Place" painted sloppily across the door. Smaller words underneath said something about music on Saturday night. Vehicles, parked haphazardly around the side of the building, included a cart and burro. That was cool.

The blacks sat easy, shirts open to the flirty sun, talking and laughing and eyeing the girls who wore tight cotton dresses. Butch was nervous. He and dad were intruders. The blacks watched the Rambler pass and Butch just stared, not sure whether to wave or not. With the way dad's jaw was set, better not.

It was like that the whole road. Most of the shacks were overrun with kids, some of them naked, which was a bit shocking. Black women, wearing basically a torn bag for a dress and a scarf tied around their heads, stood in dirt yards holding a naked child on their hips, watching the Rambler drive by. Old black men, dressed in plaid shirts and overalls and big straw hats, led mules through long, long rows of cotton. They all looked like pictures of slaves before the Civil War.

Butch had seen cotton fields in Texas, but not like this. They were everywhere. Some of the fields were just stalks, others were springing into white bolls, others were full bloomed, snowfall in June...

Hey, that rhymes, too. I'm a poet and don't know it.

...Still others had been stripped, a field of wounded cotton, the survivors drifting here and there. There were lines of black people down the rows, the men in overalls and big shirts, the women in those bag dresses with the same scarves about their heads, the kids in T-shirts. All of them dragged long, long burlap bags secured over the head and shoulders. They pulled the white clumps off the bolls and shoved them down the bags.

Man. How long did it take to fill them?

A continuous panorama of slave shacks and slaves working. Butch wondered if this was an *Outer Limits* episode circling through a dreary landscape of stooped men and bent women and naked children, an accusation. Look what you did to us, white boy! Butch shivered. He didn't do this. He didn't think blacks were bad. It's not his fault.

They passed a field and all of the blacks whirled, cotton bags flying, ran to the side of the road and lined up, staring at Butch. They said things with their eyes. See our life, white boy? We make our houses out of what we find. We don't have bathrooms, just trenches next to streams. We ride mules, not white Rambler station wagons. Our kids don't even wear diapers. We eat what we kill and a big, sweaty white man in a nice felt hat weighs our bags at the end of the day and gives us a dollar. Watcha thinka that, white boy?

Frank stood at the end of the line. He shook his head as Butch passed. "Dead is better than this."

Butch opened his eyes and blinked hard and there was no file of accusing blacks and no Frank, either. He shuddered. "Dad?" he asked.

"Hmm?"

"How come they live like this?"

"'Cause they're stupid," dad said, absently.

"But, I mean." Butch wasn't quite sure how to ask it. "Can't they get nicer houses?"

"Nope, they're dirty and stupid. That's how they like to live."

Butch stared at a weathered gray shack, red dust patch where the lawn should be, the porch sagging, an old black woman sitting there in a flowered bag dress. He couldn't fathom it. "But, why?"

"'Cause that's the way they are. They're pigs." Dad had a satisfied look on his face.

Henry wasn't a pig. The black kids who swam at the Ft. Sill pool certainly weren't, although he'd never been to their houses. Maybe somewhere in Lawton were rows of clapboard shacks with mean dogs scratching in the dirt yards and washing machines rusting on porches. But Henry wore normal clothes and was clean and funny. Didn't make sense.

"But don't they want to live better?"

"No, they like this. This is great for them. All they want is a warm shirt, loose shoes, and a tight pussy." Dad chortled that last

214

into his black man imitation, which wasn't too different from his black woman one.

Butch squirmed. He didn't know what "pussy" meant and didn't like the way it sounded. It was sex talk and dad was leering and ugly and Butch wondered if it was dad's face under the felt hat paying out a dollar for the cotton bags, staring at the scarved women, evil in his eyes. Like now.

"Doesn't seem right," Butch muttered.

"It ain't," dad said, "They shouldn't even be here, should all go back to Africa where they belong. Can throw spears at each other all they want then. Tell ya," dad pointed a hand at him, "that's what all the marchin' and hollerin's about. They want to take your house and this car and all your clothes and toys for themselves. Just want the government to give it to 'em. And that commie Johnson is lettin' them."

"What?" Butch was alarmed. "Can they do that?"

"They sure can." Dad, smug. "The government is sending in the National Guard to throw you out of your house and give it to some monkey. How ya like that?"

Seemed academic, since dad had already taken him out of the house, but still, it was his house so, no, he didn't like it, not one bit. "That's not right," he said.

"You're damn straight it ain't right." Dad tapped the wheel for emphasis. "But they're doing it. Turn our house into that," he pointed at a place overrun with dogs, "if we let 'em. But we ain't lettin' 'em. We got fine men standing in the way, like that George Wallace. You know he's governor of this state, right? He doesn't take any crap from them. Not even from that Martin Luther King," dad sneered.

Butch remembered King speaking at the Lincoln Memorial. Seemed like a nice guy.

Why would he want to take Butch's house?

He looked at the dog shack. Can you blame them? If Butch lived there, he'd want a different place, too. "Can they really take our house?"

"They sure can."

Butch stared at the fields and the blacks stooped there with the long bags. Uh-uh, no way. You're not getting my house.

They drove on. The green woods and white cotton contrasted with each pitch of the hills, while the shacks did not. They were all the same. The blacks habituating them were, too. Butch felt them diminish in his mind. You've had it rough, Butch conceded to a group of them walking along the road, but that doesn't mean you get to take what I've got. Get your own.

The road gradually widened out and formed shoulders and this was a better place. The shacks disappeared and brick homes like his...

his, you hear me, Johnson?

...set in the middle of large lots with well-kept barns and sheds and well-trimmed green lawns, white men in jeans and shirts on riding mowers assuring that, replaced them. Kids ran around the riding mowers in the universal game of tag. Cars, clean and modern, passed from the other direction and the drivers tipped their fingers off the steering wheels, a greeting. Dad tipped back.

"Why do they wave?" Butch asked.

"They're just friendly here."

Hmm. Butch waved a tentative hand at the pickups and station wagons going by, catching glimpses of jowly men or crew cut teenagers or pointy-glasses women waving back. Cool.

They turned a few times and were on a main highway now. Farms interspersed with small towns, men in overalls leaning on gas pumps talking to each other, women with piled-up hair coming out of grocery stores. They crossed a long bridge with a brown river moving fast below, cars parked down there and men and kids and women dipping cane poles at the water. They made a turn at the bridge and over some hills until the road smoothed into a town. "Phacia, Alabama. Pop: 1278," a sign read. Butch knew that stood for 'population.' Was that a lot of people? He wasn't sure.

Certainly not as many as Lawton.

The houses were all brick, appointed with pines and evergreens and flowers, no fences to be seen, a cluster of neighborliness. Dad slowed almost to a crawl and Butch looked at him. What was he doing?

"There it is," he said with some satisfaction and put on the blinker and pulled into a driveway with a Studebaker parked under the carport. It was a nice house, single story brick with a big picture window flanked by green shutters, a gray-shingled roof and a gray slate porch with three steps up to a red door, which opened. A woman stepped out. She had neck-length brown hair and blue pointy glasses, was kinda chunky but very pleasant. "Owen!" she called out.

Dad smiled, his eyes down to a leer. Butch stared at him. Now he knew what dad was doing.

# CHAPTER 33

As they got out, the woman gave dad a big hug. "So good to see you," she said.

"You too, you too." Dad ran his hands over her back. "Been way too long." They stared at each other, holding arms. Butch was disgusted. So, dad had sex with this one, too.

"You must be Butch," the woman beamed.

Déjà vu. He looked at her suspiciously. Just how many strange women across America knew about him? "Yes," he said.

"I'm Beatrice," she said and held out a hand and Butch shook it and didn't want to be there.

"Well, come on in, both of you, I've got ice tea ready." She held open the screen door. Brown and green was Butch's first impression. Big cabinets, all pale warm wood, sat lined up next to each other around the living room, resting on top of emerald wall-to-wall pile carpet. A random painting broke things up, but the impression was a continuous cabinet holding tons of stuff: figurines of poodles, girls with long dresses, Hummels...

Hummels? Butch blinked. Just like Mom's. "Hey!" Butch said, pointing at the Goose Girl, "We have that!"

"Really?" Beatrice leaned over and smiled slightly. "Do you like them?" Her hand swept over the other Hummels.

"Yes, they're cute," he responded, noticing a lot of other familiar things, the painting that separated this cabinet from the others, f'rinstance. It was the same villa on a lake in Switzerland or Venice, whatever, as in the picture hanging next to dad's deer head back in Lawton. Swear this was Butch's living room.

"We'll look at them later." Beatrice ushered him away. Butch glanced at dad. He had an odd expression, like he'd been caught or something.

"Vonda! Company!" Beatrice called as she breezed through an arch into a kitchen. A girl at the stove turned and Butch stopped dead. Angels, the ones that heralded GI Joe, sounded again.

She was tall, at least a head and a half over Butch. Seventeen, eighteen years old, something like that. Her shoulder-length blonde hair swirled yellow…

No, gold.

…silk, imbued with life. Blue, blue ocean-drop eyes, sparkling gems filled with motion, set in wonderfully translucent, wonderfully glowing skin. Delicate features, immortalized by Greeks in marble, perfect. So perfect. Butch completely forgot Marianne. Completely forgot to breathe.

She smiled. Dazzling. "Hi," her voice, a lute on the wind. "Would you like some tea?"

"Uh," was all Butch could manage.

"We both would." Dad pushed Butch forward. He moved in a dream, slow, soft, melted into a chair.

"My, Vonda," dad said, "You sure have grown."

She regarded him coolly. "Yes. People do after seven years."

Dad turned his head and set his jaw. Butch recognized that expression. Someone had scored a rare point on dad. Butch savored it.

"So how old are you?" Vonda leaned over Butch while placing a tumbler, a strand of her hair brushed his brow.

He thrilled. "Just turned ten."

"Oh my," she smiled, "I could have sworn you were fourteen."

That was it. Marianne who?

They drank the syrup wrongly called tea. Butch liked a sweet drink as much as the next man, but Holy Hannah!

Beatrice and dad lit cigarettes and talked of people Butch didn't know, Vonda threw in a comment or two. One thing was very clear: dad had known Beatrice and Vonda a long time. How was that? Butch thought hard. Dad had been mobilized for the Cuban crisis and was gone for a while, but wasn't that in Florida? He'd also gone to Ft. Eustis for some school about a year ago, but that was in… oh, Virginia. That explains Dorey.

Jeez! Did dad have a girlfriend in every single state?

"So the boys started teasing that old bull and, wouldn't you know, he came crashing right through the gate!" Beatrice chortled about some cousins or friends or somebody, and dad shook his head.

"Wouldn't have to worry about that one." He pointed at Butch. "He's inside all the time, got his nose in a book." Usual tone of contempt. Butch's face burned.

Vonda looked at him, not with insult or contempt, but a raised eyebrow of interest. "You like to read?"

Cautiously, Butch nodded.

She stood. "Come with me," and waved a hand as she left the kitchen.

Didn't have to be told twice.

She led down the hall past some bedrooms to a room with a closed door. "I think you'll like this," she said and opened it.

A library, an honest-to-God library.

Dust-laden sunlight streamed in from a window opposite, illuminating ceiling-high shelves lining all the walls, taking a break only at the window. Tightly packed books lined all the shelves, a lot of them with that telltale blue cover usually gracing a series of some kind. A card table and chair sat in the middle with a small lamp. Butch swept the room, speechless. More books here than at the Boys Club, he bet.

Vonda nodded in satisfaction at his reaction. "They're all mine."

Butch looked at her, astonished. "Every one of these?"

"Every single one."

"Have you read them all?"

"Every single one."

Butch wanted to fall at her feet in worship. He took a careful step toward the nearest shelf, his hands locked to his sides. It seemed almost sacrilegious to touch anything in here. He peered at the titles. *Nancy Drew*.

"Ever read her?" Vonda asked and lovingly, gently pulled a volume out of its place.

Butch watched with approval. "No. *Hardy Boys*, though."

"Same thing. Just from a girl's perspective. You don't mind reading about girls, do you?"

"Well, no," and he didn't. A story was a story. There were lots of girls in the *Happy Hollisters* and he loved those books. Hey, wait a minute..."Does that mean you'll let me read these?"

"Of course," she smiled. "Come in anytime you want, even if I'm in here. Just be very quiet. All I ask is remember where you got the book from and to put it back, and take care of it. No eating in here, okay?"

"Okay, And thanks. Thanks so much."

She looked at him warmly and dropped an even warmer hand on his shoulder. "Anything for a fellow traveler," she said. He didn't know what that meant but loved her hand and her smile and her perfect, perfect skin. He could have stood like that for eternity, except something rubbed his ankles. He looked down, startled. An orange tabby cat with green eyes arched against him, looking up expectantly.

"Oh!" Vonda, pleased, cradled the cat. Its purring notched up forty ticks, until it sounded like a motor idling. "This is Thomasina."

"Like the Disney movie?"

"You've seen it?" The cat rubbed its head against her hand. Butch envied it.

"Um-hm. It was real good, very sad."

"It was."

Butch stroked the cat's chin. It looked at him approvingly. Vonda laughed. "She likes you," she said, "and she doesn't like anybody."

"I get along with animals." Butch scratched the cat's neck.

"Do you have any?"

"I have a dog. Cha Cha. She's funny, black and white, loves to play tag." Butch frowned. "I really miss her."

Vonda gently handed over Thomasina, who draped across Butch's arms and presented her neck for more scratching. "Maybe she'll do until you get back."

Butch looked into Vonda's sapphire eyes. There was a gift in them, a compassionate welling for others. "Thank you," he said and found the spot on Thomasina's neck that needed the most attention.

"There you are!" Beatrice exclaimed from the hall. "I figured you'd be in the library," said with a forced tone of amusement, half exasperation, half contempt.

So, Vonda got as much crap about reading as he did, huh?

"Yes, mother," Vonda said coldly.

Beatrice missed it; Butch didn't. Vonda didn't take the crap, huh?

Excellent.

"Oh, you've met Thomasina." Beatrice gave the cat a quick pat on the head, which it tried to avoid. "She's a good one. Well! Y'all feel like fishing?"

Huh? Butch stared at her.

"Nana's down at the krick. Let's go!" and she bustled back up the hall.

He looked at Vonda. "That's my grandmother." She shook her head slightly. "You'll like her. Trust me." She took the cat out of his hands and shooed it away, "C'mon."

# CHAPTER 34

They piled into the Studebaker, Butch squirming to avoid hooks as Beatrice shoved cane poles into the back seat. They whipped around the Rambler and drove to the bridge over the fast river, plunging down a too-steep trail right off the highway. "Pigeon Creek," she announced. The trail widened into a flat area of haphazardly parked cars disgorging kids and adults. People fished along both banks. Butch guessed an identical too-steep trail was on the other side of the bridge.

"What are they catching?" he asked Vonda as they got out.

"Catfish." She pulled out two poles and gave him one. "You come with me."

"Don't get in anyone's way," dad growled as Beatrice and he tended their own poles.

No problem, chief.

Butch fell in, still thrilled, as they headed upstream along a muddy trail. Vonda waved and called to a couple of boys on the far bank. Instant jealousy. And instant concern as he glanced at the bordering pine scrub next to him. Bears and snakes. Vonda didn't seem bothered so he swallowed his fear and trudged on.

They came upon an old woman dressed in men's overalls, plaid shirt, a pith helmet, and big rubber boots. She wore small round glasses and smoked a corncob pipe.

Butch was astonished. Mammy Yokum.

"'Bout time," the old lady groused.

"Sorry, Nan." Vonda smiled. "Visitors."

The old lady peered down. "You must be Butch."

223

Jeez! Another stranger knows his name! "Yes, ma'am."

"You don't look like a Butch."

Amazing she picked up on that. Butch considered himself the most un-Butch-like Butch who ever lived. "It's just a nickname."

"So what's your name?"

"Owen."

"Hmm." Nan considered. "Stick with Butch."

Vonda chuckled and gave Butch a carton of worms as Nan cast her orange bobber sploink! into the current. Butch dug out a fat worm and hooked it carefully. He cast his bobber not too far from Nan's line.

"You like to fish?" Nan asked, a long draw from the pipe wreathing her face.

Butch shrugged. "It's all right."

"All right? You know how to fish, you're never hungry. Your dad likes to fish."

"Yes," Butch said, "all day and all night." He looked at Nan curiously. "How do you know that?"

She snorted. "I got eyes, don't I?" and tended to her bobber. Butch turned. Farther down the bank, Beatrice and dad were both intent on their lines, dad's face pointed and singular, a big game hunt.

Butch stole a look at Vonda. The sunset gilded her hair to blazing, a sun in its own right, waving and wild and free. Her eyes picked up the light and right there, the entire sky, blue and eternal.

God.

She looked at him and smiled so clearly, so deeply. His heart stopped.

"So if you don't like fishing," Nan's voice broke the spell, "what do you like?"

"He's a reader," Vonda offered and her smile broadened and Butch soared.

"Is that right?" Nan spat out some loose tobacco. Butch nodded. "Speak, boy, don't nod, that's rude," Nan ordered.

Butch gulped. "Yes, ma'am, I like reading."

"Good, good." Nan relit her pipe. "Stick with that."

Hmm. Nan was a... fellow traveler. "You like to read?" he asked.

"Where do you think she learned?" she thumbed at Vonda, who dimpled and said, "Nan taught me."

"Really?" Not unprecedented. Didn't all those pioneer women teach their kids school stuff? "What did you use?"

"*The Elephant's Dilemma, Little Wooden Shoes, Merry Murphy*, the usual."

Butch looked at her blankly and she snorted. "You never heard of those?"

"They're old," Vonda helped.

"Old," Nan shook her head. "I suppose you learned on Dr. Seuss."

"I do not like green eggs and ham," Butch sang.

"I do not like them, Sam-I-am," Vonda responded and they both giggled.

Nan grumped, "Thought so," but smiled a little and recast her line and Butch warmed and Vonda glowed and this was just perfect.

"Hey, Vonda girl!" a voice from across the creek. Butch looked. An old black man wearing a white work shirt with rolled-up sleeves and a beat-up blue fedora stood with a cane pole and tackle box gathered in one hand. Two grinning black boys about Butch's age stood on either side of him.

"Hey, Alexander!" she called back, cheerful and sweet.

"Who's that stray?" Alexander gestured at Butch with his encumbered hand.

"This is Butch," she answered and Butch waved, hesitantly.

"Well, that boy looks like a fisherman. Don't you be catching all my fish now," and he waved a mocking finger.

Butch grinned. "I won't!"

Alexander took a formal pose and tipped his hat gravely at Nan. "Miss Forney." "Mr. Simmons," she answered just as formally with a slight curtsey that seemed hilarious. Butch suspected a long and satisfying friendship between them.

The two black boys smiled and waved and suddenly there were four or five black men and women towing several other children up and down the bank on either side of Mr. Simmons. Ice coolers emerged and fires lit and one old man started playing guitar and lines were cast and fish hauled in.

It all came together in about two minutes. Amazed, Butch looked down the bank and saw dad frown at the sudden festival and Beatrice talked to him with some earnestness but dad's expression didn't change. Butch looked further, expecting to see similar reactions down the white side, but only two or three others looked mad.

"I thought everybody in Alabama hated black people," he said to Vonda.

"Phw," Nan snorted, "Don't you believe everything you see on TV."

"There's some ignorant people here," Vonda conceded, eyeing the twitch of her bobber, sign of catfish. "But there's some good ones, too."

"Dad hates 'em." Butch made a furtive gesture to where dad stood glaring across the bank.

"That man's a bag of hate," Nan snorted again.

"Nan!" Vonda was sharp and Butch looked at the old woman. How'd she know that, too? "Do you hate black people?" Vonda asked him.

He shrugged, "No. Not really. I don't want them to take my house."

"What?"

So Butch explained. Vonda and Nan exchanged glances and Nan muttered, "Foolish talk," then went back to her pipe.

Vonda pointed across the creek. "Do they look like they want to take your house?"

Butch examined. It was fun and relaxed over there, a lot of fake slapping and chasing and calling out to each other. They looked pretty happy. Why give this up and move to Oklahoma?

Evening and smoke from the cook fires settled on the creek. The air stilled and changed into something a bit more comfortable and the mayflies dotted the creek like rain from clear skies. Butch caught sunfish but threw them back. The wood smell was perfume and the people calling, music, and Vonda graced the bank, Helen of Creek. Butch felt, unreasonably, safe. "This is nice," he said.

Vonda nodded but said nothing and Nan puffed a perfect cloud of contentment. Butch wondered if God, as a favor to them all, would just keep it going for a while.

# CHAPTER 35

"This is Joel," Beatrice said.

Butch looked up from *Bullwinkle*. Beatrice stood next to the couch. Beside her was a boy, maybe eleven or twelve, dressed in a plaid shirt and jeans. Dark tanned with brown eyes and short hair, all smoke and wind, and Butch was immediately uncomfortable. "Hey," Joel said. "Hi," Butch responded.

"Well, I got peas to shell," Beatrice said, "If you boys want something, come ask first," and she bustled out.

Joel regarded Butch a moment then turned to Rocky and Boris. "You like cartoons?" he asked. A tone of judgment.

"Yeah," Butch apologized. "Especially *Jonny Quest*." Joel frowned at that, but Butch pressed on anyway. "Does it come on around here?" Please?

"Dunno." Joel shrugged. "I don't watch cartoons."

Butch flamed. Okay, yeah, he was a baby.

"Let's go outside," Joel said and turned, no discussion, for the door.

Well, great. Beatrice had tried to get Butch off the couch and out of the house all week, and had now resorted to subterfuge. Butch sat for about a half second, disappointed because Fractured Fairy Tales was about to start, but, when in Rome... he followed Joel out.

It was a hot day, the main reason Butch had chosen the couch, but a breeze wafted and Joel faced it, eyes closed, smiling. Butch swore the kid grew an inch while standing there. Joel opened his eyes. "Let's go hunting," he said and jumped off the porch, trotting down the driveway.

Hunting? Butch's eyes widened but he leaped off the porch and matched Joel's stride. The boy grinned at him and sped up and they broke into a run. Butch paced Joel, who could easily outstrip him, but apparently wasn't in it for the win. They dodged through backyards and streets and Butch was hopelessly lost when they beelined through one yard and up to the sliding door of another brick house identical to Beatrice's. Joel stopped, caught a big breath, and slapped Butch a little too hard on the back. "That was good." He slid open the door and stepped in. "Mom!" he called, "We're going hunting!"

"Be careful!" a woman ordered from somewhere in the house, probably the kitchen. Joel led him through an overstuffed living room to a gun cabinet. "Here," he said, handing Butch a single-shot Remington .22. "You know how to shoot?"

"Of course," Butch snorted. Did he look stupid or something?

Joel handed him a box of Federals and pulled out a .410, dropping about ten shells into a pocket. "Let's go." They headed out of the backyard and up a bordering high ridge. It was steep and, after the run, Butch panted when they reached the top.

They were on the edge of a bowl, a fairly decent one that started out a cotton field and then became random patched woods gathering at the far end into a thin forest with skinny pines and brush lacing it, some of the trees dead.

"You grow cotton?" Butch asked.

"Nah, not our field." Joel surveyed the area.

"What are we hunting?"

"Whatever moves." He tromped down the hill. Butch followed. At the bottom, Joel opened the shotgun and loaded a shell. Butch checked the rifle's safety—on—worked the action, dug out the box and loaded a bullet. He checked the safety again. Always. It stayed on until the moment of fire. And, oh yeah, the barrel was straight up or down until brought on target. The rifle was a little too long for down, so he placed it against his shoulder.

Joel watched all this with approval. "You know what you're doing," he said.

"My dad taught me." Proud he could say that.

They headed to one of the wood patches, Joel taking point, moving carefully and examining the trees. There were lots of thorns and brake and Butch was surprised how tough the going got. He took the giant steps dad taught him, gathering brake under his shoes and padding it down so he could move gently, quietly. Joel nodded at him. Another proud moment.

The patch ended and they were in a clear spot filled with ankle-high grass of a strange bluish color, almost alien. Butch stared at it. "That's wiregrass," Joel said.

"Why's it called that?"

"Look at it."

Butch pulled up a couple of blades. It was thin and tough and could probably weave together very tightly. "I get it," he said.

They skirted the edge of the cotton and entered another patch of woods. It was cooler and darker and Butch missed a big drop-off right at the tree line, losing his footing and making noise. Joel frowned but, hey, this was new territory. A huge tree leaned precariously across the bottom of the decline, covered with pine needles and long gray strings of something. The same long gray strings hung down from adjoining trees, big clumps of it reaching the ground. It looked like hair, maybe of some wood witch. Butch glanced back nervously. If he had to run, he wanted a clear path. "What is that?" he asked, pointing at the clumps.

Joel grinned. "Spanish moss. Grows everywhere. Pretty creepy, huh?"

"I'll say." Butch watched the moss suspiciously. If it moved, he was out of here.

They stood quietly among the bearded trees and then, cautiously, moved through them. Butch reached up and rubbed a tendril. It felt brittle but that was all, not cold, not evil. 'Course it might change character at night, develop a cemetery glow, stir the trees and move them about. He shuddered. If he left his scent, the trees would sniff him out so he snapped the tendril to put in his pocket but, hey, it might come looking for its missing finger so he hastily threw it to the ground and stomped on it.

Try and find me now.

Joel watched, intrigued, but said nothing.

They moved deeper into the depression, careful for snakes, spongy and wet there. "Swamp," Joel said. Quicksands, big bugs, disappearing without a trace—all possibilities and Butch grew even more nervous. Joel took a game trail winding along the banks. A few minutes later, they were on the other edge of the bowl, among normal woods. Butch looked back at the mossy place. He hoped Joel took them home by a different path.

As they cleared the lip, they heard a shuffle and snap of undergrowth and a quick movement to their left. Joel brought up the shotgun, traced a line, and fired. Butch jumped at the louder-than-expected report. "Dang it," Joel said, "Missed." He popped open the shotgun and dug around for another shell. Butch looked in the direction of his shot. A rabbit sat about fifteen yards away, petrified, barely discernible in its summer pelt. Butch brought the rifle to bear, lined the sights, held his breath, clicked the safety off, and squeezed. The round spat and the rabbit spun in the air, falling heavily.

"Wow!" Joel was enthusiastic, "Good shot!"

"My dad taught me." Mantra by now and Butch said it like it was nothing, but he was quite thrilled. He'd shot at squirrels and birds before, but this was his first real hit.

See, dad? I don't always screw up a hunt by making too much noise and asking stupid questions and scaring all the deer away.

Although he did get lost once. Dad'd taken Tommy and Art and Butch to a deer camp around Mt. Scott, dropped them by a tree in the pre-dawn, told them to stay put until he whistled them up, and then tromped off. They sat there looking around, not sure for what, as the sun rose and, after a few minutes, Butch swore, swore, he heard dad whistle. So he called out and Tommy argued it was a bird and Butch said no and they started blundering around the black, impenetrable forest screaming, "Whistle again!" all of them scared, Art crying until dad finally stepped out from around a tree. He hadn't whistled and Butch had never lived that down. Until now.

Joel and he walked up the hill and stood over the rabbit. It was bleeding a little from the side of its head, eyes open and dull. Joel prodded it with the end of his shotgun. "Dead, all right." He turned the rabbit over. There was a sudden woodland smell of hot brush and dirt and old weeds and Butch frowned. The rabbit's soul was spreading around them. He glanced back at the swamp to see if the trees stirred in sympathy.

"You know how to clean it?" Joel asked.

"Uh..." he did, had seen dad clean a lot of squirrels, but had never done so himself. Revolting prospect, but of greater concern was doing it wrong in front of Joel and dashing the goodwill his good shot had created. Joel looked at him a moment then whipped out a knife and, expertly, cut the rabbit at the center of the back, stripping the hide in both directions until it draped over the rabbit's ears and feet like a bully doing the sweater prank.

"Uh-oh," Joel said.

"What?" Butch stepped closer.

"Nodules," Joel pointed at yellow growths clinging to the red, wet skin. "Can't eat this one," and he carelessly tossed the rabbit into the brush. Butch took his word for it. The growths looked unappetizing.

They potshotted squirrels for an hour or so, Joel bringing one down that he also left. "I don't eat squirrels," he grimaced and Butch didn't mention that dad considered them a staple. They eventually circled back around to Joel's house. He broke out kits and they cleaned the weapons on Joel's patio, Butch savoring the odor of solvent.

"Are you staying for supper?" Joel's mom, a sweet woman with dark hair and a unibrow, asked as she brought out Kool-Aid.

"No, ma'am." He wasn't sure what dad had in mind.

All right, then," she said, just as sweetly, but Butch detected relief. Which he shared. He was contacting too many strangers this summer. "Joel," she said, "Don't forget the trash," and left.

Joel nodded, concentrating on pushing the rod through the shotgun. Butch wiped oil from the .22's bolt and they finished up and put everything away.

"C'mon," Joel said and Butch followed him through the house as he gathered baskets of waste, magazines, cans and old food, pouring them all into paper bags. They relayed the bags into a wagon under the carport until it was overflowing. Joel grabbed a can of kerosene and trundled the wagon around the back. Butch followed, curious.

Joel stopped beside a barbecue pit with a tall wire basket standing in it, filled a quarter-way up with ash. "Help me," he said and started tossing in the paper bags.

Butch heaved a few. "What are we doing?" he asked.

"The trash," Joel said simply and Butch figured this was some local ritual. He threw the last one on top and watched as Joel poured the kerosene along the sides of the bags. Joel turned to the sun dipping below the hill. He waited, silent, and Butch squirmed, certain what was about to happen but still somewhat mystified.

"You burn your trash?" he asked.

"Sure," Joel said, his eyes still on the setting sun, "What do you do?"

"The trashmen get it."

Joel snorted, "That's city," and Butch felt the insult. But, uh, Joel, burning trash in the backyard? A little backward. Butch kept that to himself.

"Okay," Joel said as dusk enveloped them. He struck a match on his belt, one of those rough boy moves, anticipation on his face. He pitched it and the trash *whooshed* in fire and sparks, the bloom of light and heat driving them back. "Yeehaw!" Joel bellowed a primal, ancient call.

Dogs and other kids somewhere past the hills answered Joel. Butch felt the stir of it, but as observer. This wasn't his world. Just wasn't.

# CHAPTER 36

"You're not going out?" Beatrice, incredulous.

"No," Butch, unmoved. He fully intended to sit right here watching *George of the Jungle*. And whatever else followed.

"Did you and Joel have a fight?"

"No." Not in the sense she implied: yelling and fists thrown, which he'd have lost in about a half second. Butch had simply decided to return to his own world. He'd grown tired of Joel's, populated by rough boys enamored of fishing and wrestling and tree climbing. Some of it was cool but there were too many sneers at Butch's limited prowess, too many put-downs, and too many near-actual fights with Butch's heart pounding and his body trembling as he turned away, cowardice confirmed. He'd spent the Fourth of July with the rough boys throwing Ladyfingers and cherry bombs at the neighborhood cats. They considered it great sport; he thought it cruel. Shooting off the pop-bottle rockets and Roman candles that dad, in some incredible burst of generosity, bought by the bagful, didn't charm either, because the rough boys turned it into a contest over who could hold a firework the longest and naturally, Butch's Black Cat short-fused, hurting his fingers, and he cried so dad called him a baby in front of everyone. Vonda took care of him and the rough boys seized on it, repeating the "baby" label.

They also called him city boy and Yankee, both grossly incorrect, but he didn't have the vocabulary or patience to explain why, so he pulled back. In the middle of something, say an impromptu baseball game, he'd just leave, the rough boys silently watching him go, no effort to keep him. Do that enough times and he could spend hot afternoons on the couch watching TV; a sin in Joel's world, but Butch was a heretic, anyway.

Beatrice eyed him skeptically, but he didn't care what she thought. He didn't care about her at all. She was just dad's current girlfriend and didn't get it, wouldn't get it, because her whole life was a series of checklists. Sunny day? Check. Kid should be outside? Check. Is kid outside? Check 'no.' Refer to sub-paragraph A—Something Must Be Wrong. It wasn't; things were now, actually, right. But her checklist had no sub-paragraph for that.

He ignored her, focused on George. Watch out for that tree! Splat! Butch giggled.

Beatrice shook her head, "All right, then. When your dad gets home, he's gonna want the lawn cut," and she walked out.

Butch blinked at her retreating back. And just where was dad, huh, Beatrice?

Stupid question.

Butch had already read this book, seen this movie. Dad arrives at girlfriend's house all lovey-dovey then, a few weeks later, disappears for hours at a time, dumping the Unnecessary Kid on girlfriend. Silences built between girlfriend and dad and frowns increasingly directed at Unnecessary Kid. Butch stayed out of it, not asking dad where he went off to because, well, he could guess, and, more importantly, didn't want his head snapped off. He kept a watchful eye, though, noting the steam venting from the side of the volcano and wondering when Vesuvius would blow.

Safety lay in TV. And Vonda.

He'd made strenuous and rather silly efforts to be with her, sometimes with success. She occasionally took him to Nan's house, a wood-contrapted ranch built with no central concept, rooms appearing out of nowhere. "I'd get lost in here," he'd told Nan.

"Tie some string on a doorknob," she suggested and that struck Butch as hilarious; after a week, the house would be spider-webbed.

"Four generations lived here," Nan boasted, "going back to the Creek Wars. You know about those, boy?"

Well, no.

She told him about Davy Crockett and Andrew Jackson and half-breed Creek Indians fighting nearby at some place called

Horseshoe Bend. Nan's forefathers were there and at every other event in American history, it seemed, and each grandpap added a distinctive wing to the house as a mark of his passing. Depending on your view, the house was either a monument or schizophrenic.

Nan didn't have a TV but she made up for that. They played Scrabble, Butch learning new words he half-suspected didn't exist.

"Zygote!" Nan said triumphantly as she laid down the tiles and Butch eyed her. Now what was that, some kind of obscure mountain animal? But he'd learned not to challenge. A couple of times, sitting on the meandering front porch, shielded from mosquito assault by citronella candles, she read to them from an old book called *The Little Shepherd of Kingdom Come*, a title to make one retch, but turned out a very exciting and sad story about an orphan and the Civil War. Butch squirmed down in the overstuffed rattan chair and listened, throwing covert looks at Vonda, off in the shadows of the porch, a beautiful, moon-pale ghost.

But Nan-visits were more novelty than escape, and Vonda had her own world, too, leaving most nights in pickup trucks stuffed with teenagers, a backward scornful glance at dad whenever he tried to intervene. Butch watched her go, traitorously hoping the intervention would succeed, that she would turn from her friends and the dangers of the night and sit with him and hold him and, maybe—did he dare think it?—have sex with him, the right way. But, no, off she went, and, though disappointed, he was also proud.

Good for you, getting away from these jerks.

To avoid the inevitable carping that followed, Butch escaped to the next best thing than Vonda herself: her library. He shut the door as the words from the living room sharpened and bittered in an ever-increasing cycle, like some runaway power plant. Click of a knob then silence, a gift of inadvertent soundproofing.

Vonda had girls' books mostly, the Nancy Drews, several by someone named Monica Edwards about some place called Punchbowl Farm, *Island of the Blue Dolphins*, which he started then put away because the isolation was a bit too familiar, a very cool *Alfred Hitchcock Ghostly Gallery*, *The Secret Garden*, stuff like that. He stayed mostly with the Nancy Drews because he knew the formula: smart and resourceful Nancy, her goofy but reliable friends, George and Bess, boyfriend Nick, Togo the dog...

as Vonda'd said, female Hardy Boys. The covers all showed blonde and slim Nancy in a position of vulnerability: hiding behind a couch while a man opened a wall safe; chasing a guy from a burning house; catching a frightened glimpse of a white-robed figure in the distance. They always started with a supernatural event that turned out to be mundane. Predictable, but the reveal was fun.

Vonda's scent permeated the place, and he could hold one of her books and take in a deep breath and pretend she was behind him, saying, "Go mow the lawn."

Huh?

Butch shook himself. While daydreaming of Vonda sex in the library, *George* had segued into *Droopy Dog* and *Tom and Jerry* and then, simultaneously with dad's entrance, the evening news with Walter Cronkite.

"Go mow the lawn, I said."

Butch examined him as he stood in the door. Some pressure around the upper cone, internally generated redness of the face. Watch out. Dad glared. "Are you deaf or something?"

Okay, okay.

Beatrice had a wheezy Montgomery Ward that cornered pretty well so Butch didn't mind this. The sun had dipped enough to throw the front yard into shade, lowering the temperature to a survivable level. Overall, a pleasant way to avoid the two creeps inside, who were probably arguing about why Butch didn't play like a normal boy. Or where dad had been.

Vonda should be getting back from her job at Woolworth's any time now and the arguing would send her flying to the library so this could turn out to be a fairly decent evening, if he played his cards right. They'd start reading together and, on some pretense …

What? A board game? Monopoly or Wahoo. Possible, possible

…he'd get Vonda back to her bedroom and she would look at him as the night settled and breathe, "Oh, Butch, I think it's time you and I had sex." He went into a lust trance and, naturally, missed some spots, but when you're all on Vonda's nakedness, straight lines are impossible. He looked furtively around to see if anyone noticed and spotted two rough boys sauntering down the street and ducked his head so they wouldn't notice him noticing them…

"Supper's ready!" Beatrice, from the front porch.

Excellent. Butch played off the last row, counting on evening to cover errors, and dashed inside. He cleaned up and was at the table in mere seconds. Fried chicken, green beans, and mashed potatoes—had to give Beatrice proper due, she could cook. He placed his nose up like a bloodhound, savoring the perfume of dinner. Dad did the same.

Hmm, a lull in seismic activity, maybe a quiet evening.

Beatrice said the blessing and filled plates while Butch ministered his ice tea in small sips to avoid diabetes.

"Wadjew do today?" dad asked around a mouthful of potatoes.

Could ask you the same question. For half a second, Butch entertained the suicidal thought, but wisdom prevailed. "Nothin'."

Dad and Beatrice exchanged significant looks. "Watched TV all day, huh?"

Ah, so, Butch had indeed been the topic of earlier scathing talk. Great. A quake rumbled through dad's lower slope and began winding to the top. Had to relieve the pressure.

"When's Vonda coming home?" Butch deflected. He felt a little guilty about using her like that but it wasn't treason if she was absent.

"She's staying overnight at a friend's," Beatrice said absently as she rearranged disturbed green beans. Butch inwardly sighed as he watched the lust dream dissolve.

Oh well.

Dad was immediately on Beatrice. "What? I didn't know that!"

Wow, did he sound mad.

Beatrice was as surprised as Butch. "She called after you left."

The earthquake rumbled and lava spewed, the only saving grace its targeting of a different village. "That damn girl spends far too much time out!"

Butch was now more surprised than Beatrice. C'mon, dad, it's not like she's ten years old. "Well, she is seventeen." Beatrice made Butch's point for him.

"That's no excuse. There's things to be done around this house, lots of things. She could be helping you or watching this one," spear-point hand flung at Butch, "or studying or something!"

"But it's summer!" Beatrice raised another critical point; Butch silently approved. She looked bewildered because dad's tone was at odds with his words, like Vonda's absence wasn't so much dereliction, as denial of anticipated pleasure.

Anticipated pleasure...

Jeez! Dad wanted Vonda as a girlfriend! He truly, actually, absolutely wanted her!

Well, no! No way! She's mine!

Butch felt his own volcano rising.

Man, who do you think you are, just who do you think you are? You've already got about three thousand girlfriends all over the US, one right in front of you, and you want another? Mine? You want mine?

For. Get. It.

Butch threw down the gauntlet. "Yeah, it's summer! We're not supposed to work. We're supposed to play."

Of course he was dead, but he fought for his woman so it would be a noble death. Dad turned on him. "Play! That's about all you damn kids know how to do, ain't it?"

Well, yeah, they were kids! C'mon! It isn't like we have to haul ice blocks for a sack of potatoes, is it?

"It's summer!" Butch stressed the point, the fight now expanding to the rights of kids everywhere.

"Summer," dad said it like a cuss word. "I didn't have any summers. I had to work, not go out and play like some diaper baby!"

And then it all came clear. Butch cocked his head and thrust forward, the sheer unfairness of it pouring over him. "So that means we can't?" Dad didn't get summer, so no one does?

That's not right. Not right at all.

And the logic of it must have stroked dad a good one because he blinked and turned scarlet and Butch braced for the snapping of his neck but dad made no homicidal moves, merely sat there staring at him. His face worked, the mad lights flashed, all the signs of impending murder, but he didn't actually murder; seemed paralyzed, in fact. And it occurred to Butch that he'd just done something he'd never thought possible. Heck, in the face of the odds against him, which consisted mostly of personal wimpiness and weakness, was *im*possible—he had stood his ground.

All for the love of his woman.

Trumpets sounded. His chest swelled. He pushed back his chair and stood as tall as ten years old permitted and let dad see the triumph. Dad did, still staring, still paralyzed. Butch stepped away from the table.

"But you haven't had dessert!" Beatrice was mortified. The checklists.

Butch reached for his tea and took three or four great swallows. Now he had. Without a word, he spun and marched off to Vonda's library, flower girls sprinkling petals before him.

# CHAPTER 37

Butch sat at Vonda's little table. The flower girls had long since dissipated, leaving consequences in their wake. First, he had given dad the necessary ammunition for a good ole-fashioned neck-snapping. No court would convict him: "Your honor, my son embarrassed me in front of one of my girlfriends!" "What? He did that? Case dismissed!" Second, precedent had been established. Once you stand, you must always stand. And Butch wasn't made of standing stuff. That wimpiness and weakness, doncha know.

"Another fine mess you've gotten me into," Butch whispered to himself in a passable Oliver Hardy. Thomasina, curled up in the corner, mewed in agreement and went back to sleep. Yep, a pickle, a fine stew...

Hmm, need to change metaphors because he didn't quite finish dinner, all that taking a stand and stuff, and he was getting hungry.

A rock and a hard place. There, that better conveyed his situation. If he couldn't find a way out of this, then dad would break his head with a rock.

Okay, need a strategy, one that ensured surviving the night—heck, the next six years—until he could lie about his age and join the Army. "You don't *look* eighteen, son." "Just young for my age, Sergeant." "Well, that's all right, we need good American boys to take a stand against the Chicoms. Can you take a stand, boy?" "If pushed, Sergeant."

He giggled.

Okay, so, what do you do until then? Easy- lay back, stay

hidden, avoid further situations requiring life-threatening stands. If said situation arise anyway, seek a covering witness, such as Beatrice, to prevent neck-snapping, then allow time and distance to ameliorate.

Pretty much what he'd been doing for the past ten years, an MO his recent action had mooted.

What to do, what to do.

He glanced down at *The Secret of the Old Clock*, which he'd snagged on entry. Now that Nancy, she's a stand-taker. Butch studied the cover, Nancy hidden behind a couch looking rather entranced while the bad guy pulled out Crowley's will. Little slip of a girl taking on bad guys, well, in a book, anyway. How would she fare in a real encounter? Probably not so well. Be a one-book series.

He put Nancy away and rummaged through his comics, which Vonda let him keep here. She read them, too, the touch of a goddess on his pages, and he could use some residual magic so he pulled out Hulk, her favorite. Of course. A misunderstood misfit hunted by the world, bellowing defiance from mountaintops, an inspiration to them both. "I don't get Bruce Banner," she said.

"Yeah!" Butch nodded enthusiastically, "I'd kill to be the Hulk!"

"Me, too," she laughed…

A female Hulk? Possible, possible.

…"Look at Bruce here." she pointed at a panel. "All filled with angst and a heightened sense of adult propriety. It's more affectation than real."

"Yeah!" Butch didn't understand a word she said and didn't care one whit. "He can crush tanks!"

He read through the first Hulk, the gray one. Green was more Hulkish and he pulled out a couple of *Avengers* to see that. He wished Hulk had stayed with the team because his instability was a good plot point, but it was a bit much having Hulk and Thor together. He flipped through the last *Avengers*, where Hawkeye, Scarlet Witch, and Pietro joined. Weird having old X-Men enemies as good guys, but Hawkeye was cool, a real smart aleck, outsider by choice and skill. Hawkeye could take any stand he wanted.

But what if you were an uncool outsider, dipped in geekiness, how do you take stands?

Well, obviously, no longer be a geek.

How? Well, become a superhero. A better superhero, that is. His invisibility was too unreliable, but acquiring reliable and stronger powers was a bit problematic; radioactive spiders didn't just fall from the sky. Superhero without powers then, like Batman? Not one of Butch's favorites: Robin was more trouble than he was worth, but Batman did take pretty effective stands using mere strength, coordination and speed, and really cool inventions, all of which could be developed.

Butch thumbed to a Joe Weider ad. Hmm, gain a pound a day. In a year, he'd be huge. Butch flexed his arm, watching the bare ripple of skin where a bicep should be, and frowned. Might take two years. He flipped to a Jiu-Jitsu ad. Hmm, again. Throw rough boys against lockers and walk away with the cheerleader. But where would they send the instruction book? Lawton? That's no good. Here? Where exactly was here?

He shook his head. Too much time and distance and money involved; he needed a solution right now and the only thing immediately available was... lay low, stay hidden, avoid further situations requiring life-threatening stands.

That's it. That's all you got.

Butch let out a very long, disappointed breath. Thomasina stretched and strolled over and jumped into his lap and went to sleep again. Absently, he stroked her head. Face it, stand-taking was not part of his makeup. If he did what movies and TV required and stood up to bullies, he'd have ended up face down in the mud with his pants hoisted up a flagpole. The only way he'd lived through the last ten years was... staying low, staying hidden and avoiding situations that required life-threatening stands. That made him a miserable little dweeb, but a *breathing* miserable little dweeb. Best leave stand-taking to those built for it.

You miserable little dweeb.

He scratched Thomasina's neck. I yam what I yam, even though he didn't like what he yam. Miserable little dweebs didn't get the Vondas of this world. They didn't get much of anything. Lose their lunch money, repeatedly flee in terror, take sanctuary in comics and reading and safe spots held by brother dweebs while lions roamed the streets. The Vondas go off with the lions and the Mariannes do, too, and you are alone, bereft.

Invisible.

242

Had *that*, at least. Worked rather well in Newport News. Haven't tried it here.

Shall we?

Gently he lifted Thomasina to her sleep corner and opened the door a crack to listen. Voices. Dad and Beatrice in the living room, a consistent tone, devoid of anger.

Okay.

Butch turned invisible and silently crept down the hall to the dining room archway. Inside on the left was a china cabinet wider than him. Between that and his invisibility, dad and Beatrice couldn't see him standing beside it.

Perfect.

Butch slid into position, feeling like a spy, and had to bite his tongue to keep from giggling.

"It's just a part of growing up," Beatrice said.

Butch's ears perked. Hello? Being discussed, was he? He wriggled in anticipation.

"That ain't a part of growing up," dad growled.

"Yes, it is," Beatrice moved restlessly on the couch and Butch half-feared she would head to the kitchen, making him break cover and invisibility. But she settled and Butch gave a silent 'thank God.' "It's what kids do. It's how they find their way, find out what they want to be." Well, well, Beatrice was defending Butch's stand-taking. That raised her stock a bit.

"No call for that." Now dad shuffled and Butch's heart leaped then calmed as dad also settled. "She needs to get married."

Oh. Vonda, not him. Okay, well, can still gather intelligence, Secret Agent Man. He wriggled in pleasure.

"She's too young for that. She's going to college, first."

"Learn how to be a smart-mouth. Like Dale. Two of a kind."

Butch grinned. Good for you, Dale.

"No, she wants to be a teacher. She'll do all right."

"Still a smart-mouth. I see how she treats you. You should have taken more belts to her."

Dad's solution to everything, of course: beat the kids until they shut up.

"Wouldn't have helped," Beatrice said, "She needed her father."

Silence. "I was busy." Dad, sullen. "You know my circumstances."

Wait...

What?

What???

Oh. My. God. Dad is Vonda's dad.

Shockwave.

Butch almost gasped out loud, undoing the invisibility. The world spun a little and Butch desperately clung to the wall, barely hearing Beatrice consoling dad over his circumstances.

Vonda was his sister.

Oh. My. God.

Dizzy, unstable, the invisibility long gone, Butch held his breath and crept out, terrified he'd be heard and then killed but somehow remained silent and undiscovered all the way back to the library, the closed door proof against them. He sat heavily, stunned.

Vonda was his sister. The goddess, the beauty, object of unresolved fantasies, his sister. He'd lusted after her, plotted against her, daydreamed myriad sexual encounters with her. His sister, his own sister.

He was condemned.

God was stirred to Rage and Horror and His Almighty Finger pointed in accusation straight at Butch's heart. Immaterial that he didn't know; some things were so evil that ignorance could not save you.

He was going to hell.

Nothing could prevent that, even if he became a minister and led thousands of souls to the Lord. He'd stand at the Pearly Gates in his minister's collar, surrounded by his thousand converts, and St. Peter thanks him, snaps his fingers, and two demons jump up, seizing Butch's arms. "Why?" he shrieks.

"Because you thought of your sister That Way!" St Peter gestures and the demons drag Butch down, fanging his skull while friends and family turn away in revulsion.

Thomasina hissed and growled at him and ran to the door, scratching to get out. Animals sense evil and he opened the door and she ran like her tail was on fire and it was, scorched by the hellfire in his soul, and he closed the door and slid to his knees, trembling. "God," he said, "Jesus, I didn't know, I didn't know..." Maybe if he said it often enough and sincerely enough, God's Constant Anger would abate, and he'd at least get on the Porch of

Heaven. That's all he could expect. But, after what seemed like an hour he felt no better, so he stopped.

It wasn't going to do any good.

Butch sat in the chair, miserable. It was unfair, just completely unfair. Dad does this and Butch has to bear the consequences?

"Now you know how I feel," Frank said.

Butch looked up. Frank was sitting across from him, dead as ever. "So what did God say?" Butch asked.

"He won't talk to me." Frank collapsed, sobbing.

Butch recoiled and sat up, drool stretching from his forearm to his lips and he wiped it with his shirt, disgusted. It was late. He got up stiffly and went to the door, opened it a crack. Dark, silent. More curious than cautious, he stepped out. Nothing, no TV, no talking, but there was a slight glow from the kitchen. He crept along, feeling his way past the guest room where he slept and past Beatrice and dad's room, where they had sex he supposed, and entered the kitchen without mishap, but it was the stove light.

Had everybody left him?

He looked wildly about. Oh no! The neighborhood rough boys would break in, arms and legs draped over windows, eyes red, teeth elongating. "We've been waiting for you, Butchie boy!" Or the police come, big fat men in uniforms like that Bull Connor and bash him with their nightsticks. "Wadja do to the family, boy? Werdja bury 'em?" hitting and hitting.

There was another glow outside the kitchen door. Butch caught his breath: rough boys! The light seemed a bit small for a Vampiric Gang, though, and he peered out of the window. Vonda sat in a rocking chair on the screened-in porch, a couple of lit candles on the table.

Butch opened the door. She gazed at him. "Couldn't sleep?"

"No." Butch took the rattan couch at right angles to her. "I thought you were staying some other place tonight."

"Got bored."

"Oh. Where is everyone?"

"In bed."

"What time is it?"

"After midnight."

"Have you been out here the whole time?"

"No. I checked on you, but you were out like a light." She

smiled. "You talk in your sleep, you know. Who's Frank?"

"A friend of mine. So, what are you doing out here?"

"Enjoying the peace."

"Are you my sister?"

She was silent for a long time, rocking, watching the night. "I told them they should tell you."

"Why didn't you?"

"Because," her voice was gentle, "we should be friends before we're siblings."

"But we *are* friends," he protested, not liking the word because it was diminishing, a real let-down from his previous hopes... Butch chilled as God's Angry Face turned toward him.

"Yes," she agreed, "But we wouldn't have been if, right off, you knew I was your unknown sister." She looked at him sadly, "You'd have been too resentful, and we'd never have been friends. Don't you see?"

He did. "Would you have ever told me?"

"In a few years."

Huh? Did she think he was going to hang around here until she was some old lady or something? C'mon!

She must have read that. "There's too much going on with you right now, way too much. These are your last years of innocence, and they're being stolen from you." She shook her head. "I didn't want to be part of that."

"Yes, but..." and he couldn't help it, the tears flowed.

She got up, sat down on the couch and took him in. He folded into her arms, and sobbed against her soft linen blouse, the warmth of her wrapping him. He'd dreamed of this moment, but it wasn't the warmth of lovers.

It was consolation.

"It isn't going to be all right," she said, at odds with the comforting, "It never will. You'll always have holes in your heart. Something will always be missing. You'll be off balance." There was a catch in her voice and Butch's misery expanded to include her. "You can't fix it. There's nothing you can do. But, you have to know something, you have to remember it." She pushed his chin up, making him look through tear-blurred eyes right at her.

"It is not your fault."

His sobs freshened, louder and tearing. He felt the fabric of the universe rip and his life spin away, Jesus's frantic Hand reaching for him, but missing.

"It will never be your fault."

He collapsed into her and she held him and soon he was asleep. He had a long conversation with Frank.

# CHAPTER 38

"Get up."

"Hmph?" Butch and Frank were wrestling in some dark, tarry swamp while the Oz trees cursed them.

"I said, 'get up!'"

Dad.

Butch threw Frank into a green, nasty pool, dodged an apple, and sat up. He was in bed. In his underwear. So Vonda had seen him naked. Great. "What's going on?"

"Get dressed." Dad flicked a hand at Butch's suitcase. "And pack. We're leaving."

"Right now?"

Dad turned, murder on his face. "Yes, right now!" Murder in his voice. "So get up, pack up, and let's go!" Dad grabbed Butch's suitcase off the floor and hurled it, clipping Butch's flailing hand.

"Ow!" That stung.

Dad stormed out and Butch rubbed the wound, terrified. What's this? Who knew, but he'd better get moving or he was murdered.

In record time he dragged the suitcase down the hallway, sure he had forgotten an *X-Men* or two back in Vonda's library. Badly dressed and uncombed and hungry and he needed to pee, but a moment's delay could be fatal. He stopped and listened. He heard normal movement in the kitchen and an occasional voice and it seemed calm enough that he could risk a quick bathroom run.

Raised voices when he came out proved his margin of safety had evaporated. Cautiously, he slid the suitcase toward the kitchen and peeked around the corner. Beatrice studied the range top while Vonda sat at the table contemplating her empty breakfast plate. Dad, arms crossed, examined the frame of the kitchen door, standing so close to it Butch thought he jammed a toe. The earlier words had dissipated, like the smoke of a battle, and here were the casualties.

He stepped in, two-handing the suitcase. "Let's go," dad said, yanking the porch door open and slamming out. Butch wondered if he should go back down the hall and lock himself in the bedroom, but then dad would kill them all so, no, had to save Beatrice and Vonda. He bumped the suitcase to the door and stopped to look back at them.

Beatrice had not moved. Vonda turned those wonderful, blue eyes directly on him. "Not your fault," she mouthed.

"C'mon!" from outside froze his sudden urge to run into her arms and he drag-dropped the suitcase out of the screened porch. Dad heaved it into the back of the Rambler and pointed at the passenger door. Butch scrambled inside, convinced he'd soon join Frank. Dad got in, started the car, and they left.

They went west, past the turnoff to Pigeon Creek and Butch looked hard for Nan, but she wasn't there. Come to think of it, wasn't she Butch's Nan, too? Maybe that's why she'd been nice to him; gruff, but nice. He blinked. Lost opportunity.

Dad was pushed forward, rage bulging his face, and Butch turned invisible. About an hour later, they reached a town named Troy and Butch reappeared because any town so mythically named required attention. Butch strained for signs of Greek temples, but it was just a regular town.

They turned off on a bigger road labeled '231' and then dad immediately hit a side road and made a couple of switches and Butch was lost. Maybe they were going south, not sure, but best not to shoot north and call undue attention. About two hours later, they were in a neighborhood. Dad pulled up the driveway of a brown clapboard house set among other varicolored clapboard houses. "We're here," he said, stopping the engine.

"Here?"

"Our new place." Dad fumbled with keys.

Butch braced, expecting the door to open and another wife, trilling "Owen!" to emerge with a whole new brood of brothers and sisters in tow. The brothers would be Carl and Pigface and they'd treat him the same way he treated Art, slapping him around and pulling cruel pranks. The sisters hate him and make him sleep in the crawlspace, wear burlap bags, and eat gruel.

Dad went up the porch and opened the door and then came back, opening the tailgate. No one came out of the house. "Just us?" Butch asked.

"Yes, just us," dad snapped, "Now how 'bout you get your ass in gear and help me?"

With great relief, Butch grabbed his suitcase and slapped up the concrete steps.

Not bad.

White walls with brown floorboards and cornices, two or three odd hallways, a central bathroom, open kitchen and a big living room with, glory hallelujah, a 12-inch Philco on top of a chest against the picture window. He pulled the knob and held his breath. The little white dot appeared.

Glory, glory! He stood, patient, waiting for dot expansion. Please be three channels, please.

"Mighta known," dad said behind him and Butch hastily turned it off. "Pick a bedroom," dad ordered and Butch followed him down an odd hall, stopping in the first doorway. Cozy: chest of drawers and single bed flanking a big window overlooking a decent backyard open to the backs of identical yards across from it. "This one," he said and heaved his suitcase on the bed.

He put his clothes in the drawers and his comics on a shelf in the small closet. He dressed Joe for combat and messed up the sheets to look like a snowfield. Winter assault.

"Let's eat," dad called and Butch jumped up.

Okay!

Dad had put a C-Ration case on a metal-legged table and stirred a pot on a real skinny stove. Smelled good and Butch sat down, impatient. Dad pulled some dishes out of the overhead cabinet and spooned C-Ration stew, "Here." Butch fell to and dad joined him.

"Where are we?" Butch asked between bites.

"Ozark."

"Where Pappy Yokum and Lil Abner live?"

"No, dummy," dad said, "They live in Dogpatch."

"I know that." Butch was miffed. "But that's in the Ozarks."

"Yeah, but that's *Ozarks*, not Ozark."

"Oh," Butch immediately saw the difference. "Is this place like the Ozarks?"

"No." Dad wiped his mouth. "This is a town."

"Are we going to live here?"

"Probably."

Hope soared. "So this is going to be our house?"

"What'd I say?"

It would take a little more exploration before definite conclusions could be reached, but this looked like a good place. One giant deciding factor would be the filling of some major holes. "Can Mom and Cindy and Art visit us here?"

Dad went still and Butch braced for a slap. "We'll see," dad said.

He didn't say 'no!' Hope soared again. So, Mom drives up and Cindy and Art spill out and Cindy and he are racing up and down the streets dragging along a bevy of new, funny friends and Mom and dad are all lovey-dovey and the divorce is cancelled and even Cha Cha comes to stay. But there was another giant deciding factor. "What about Beatrice and Vonda?"

Dad stared at him. "What about them?"

Well, the Hitchcockian potential for Mom and Cindy and Art running into a nearby Beatrice and Vonda required coordination of stories, dad. "She's my sister," he said, pretty sure that conveyed it.

Dad frowned, deep and ugly. "Someone's got a big mouth. Who told you?"

Butch suppressed the impulse to blurt, "You did," because follow-on explanations of invisibility and unauthorized eavesdropping would lead to an immediate and rather painful dismemberment. "Dunno, just heard it."

Amazingly, dad bought it, even identified a suspect. "Nan," he snarled and sat back. Butch left it. "Yes, she's your sister, but you won't be seeing her anymore."

"Why?" Seriously, why? If dad dragged him all over Texas to visit the evil cousins, why not a sister? She had a better claim.

"Because, you won't." Finality of tone and Butch drew back.

You mean, dad, you can go through the rest of your life without ever seeing your daughter again? Well, when that daughter constituted nearby evidence of several crimes, dad couldn't very well risk discovery, could he? And Vonda *did* say it'd been seven years.

Precedent.

"Do the dishes," dad said and headed to the back. Dismissal. Vonda and Beatrice gone, just like that. In the expanse of one night and a car ride, lost a sister, a better version of Dale.

Pretty much the story of the last two months: Butch meeting, and leaving, people.

Like a zombie, Butch got up from the table and stacked the bowls in the big sink, which reached to his chest. There was a bottle of Joy and a green rag near the faucets and Butch squeezed a stream of soap into the flow. White mountains of foam swirled into being and he reached to knock them down. The water was hot, real hot, and he jerked his hand back.

And whistled.

Surprised, Butch pursed his lips and whistled again. And again. He experimented as he washed the dishes. He lost the tone then found it until he was fairly consistent. It wasn't loud, like dad's spine-shattering fingers-in-the-mouth tweet, but respectable. By the time he finished drying, he was doing a rather decent "If You Wanna Be Happy for the Rest of Your Life."

"I can whistle now," he said as dad walked in.

"I heard." Dad, amused. "How'd you learn?"

Butch pointed at the sink. "Hot water."

"That'll do it. I'm going to get some groceries. Stay here and watch TV." And he left.

Didn't have to be told twice. Butch threw the towel in the sink and beelined for the living room, whistling "My Boyfriend's Back" as he pulled the TV switch. The little dot blinked its colors and Butch watched as it suddenly bloomed to half screen, rolling vertical and then straightening out.

Okay.

Butch maneuvered the rabbit ears to sharpen the image and did a quick dial spin.

Oh boy! Three channels! Odds that *Jonny* came on here dramatically increased. He stopped at the last channel and made some adjustments. It was the end of a car commercial and the CBS eye stared at him for a moment before switching to some craggy-faced guy sitting behind a desk. "Welcome back to the Noon Farm Report. I'm Gene Ragan."

Noon Farm Report?

Butch watched, fascinated. Ragan gave, in the manner of

Walter Cronkite, a long, incomprehensible story about cotton and peanut prices. There followed a segment with Ragan and a farmer, both wearing big straw hats, standing in a field fingering the leaves of something called soybeans. The last report was live: Ragan in a barn with some overalls-and-ball-cap hick who spat tobacco juice all over the hay-strewn floor. It was a demonstration of goat milking and the goats walked around poking their muzzles into everything, including Ragan's dingdong. Butch giggled.

"Yer gotta grab da tit," the hick said, pointing a brown, withered arm under the goat Ragan was sitting beside.

Butch was blown across the room. Did that man just say 'tit?' On television?

Ragan looked uncomfortable and the hick said "tit" again.

Yes! Butch fell back laughing.

"What's so funny?" dad said, carrying a bag.

Butch pointed helplessly at the television as Ragan summed up the advantages of goat milk while trying to keep a straight face. "It's a farm show!" Butch convulsed.

Dad watched for a moment and then frowned at Butch. "Farming's pretty important around here." He took the bag into the kitchen.

Butch sobered as Ragan segued into *Guiding Light*. A farm show.

He was now living on Mars.

# CHAPTER 39

Morning, about seven.

"Aaaalways after me Lucky Charms. They're magically delicious!" Butch sang in his best leprechaun as he finished off a second bowl, smiling at Lucky smiling at him. Quite the treat, this. He wondered what prompted dad to buy it.

Answered when dad walked in wearing a bright orange flight suit, not the usual OD, and poured himself a bowl. Butch stared. "You're wearing a flight suit."

"Yep." Dad crunched a yellow moon.

"But it's a different color."

"Yep."

"What's it for?"

"Flying."

Butch blinked. "So, are you flying today?"

"Looks like it." Crunch.

"Are you back in the Army?"

"Nope."

Butch didn't know what to ask next.

Dad eyed him. "I'm testing helicopters for the Army now. As a civilian."

"You got a job?"

"Yep."

Oh, man! "A real job?"

"What'd I say?"

Relief washed over him. Dad was now made of money, and Butch now had permanence. "So, we're living here?"

"Maybe not exactly here, but the area. I want to buy a house."

"I thought you bought this one."

Dad snorted, "This piece of crap? Rented. I want a place in the country."

The country. Butch had visions of hayfields and brooks and walking creekside with rolled-up dungarees. "Cool," he said.

"Cool?" Dad blinked. "No, it ain't. Gonna be damned near 100 today."

Butch almost laughed but caught it because dad was in such a great mood. The prospect of flying, no doubt. "Can I go with you?"

"No."

Butch was disappointed. Dad read it. "I'm still setting up. Got lots of papers to fill out, test flights and certifications, that stuff. It's a long process. Maybe after."

Butch thrilled. Oh, man!

"So," dad continued as he spooned marshmallow remnants, "I got long days ahead of me. I need you to stay in the house while I'm gone."

"Why?"

"We don't know anybody here. Until we do, you just stay in."

"But..." objections teetered on Butch's lips. Summer. No school. Kids flocked in parks and woods and swimming pools and there were GI Joes to share. C'mon, dad, how many times do I have to make this point... but the look in dad's eyes stopped him. "Okay."

Dad nodded and finished and ordered Butch to clean the dishes, which he did, even though leftover milk in dad's bowl made him squeamish.

"Remember," dad said, "stay in the house," and he left.

Butch tidied up a bit then grabbed Joe and turned him into a helicopter frogman who swam in the oceansink and guided his invisible Huey with radio and thought commands. After blowing up the Chicom fleet, Butch went into the living room and turned on the television.

*The Today Show* broadcast pictures from the Mariner mission and Butch ran up to the screen so he could examine them closely. Craters, lots of craters, and the commentator said Mars was like the moon.

Jeez. No Martians.

He switched to *Captain Kangaroo*. Oh no, here come the ping-pong balls!

A shadow moved across the front of the house and Butch went to the window. A kid, dirty blond hair, kinda chunky, almost girlish eyes and brows and very smooth pasty skin was on the front lawn holding a bag and looking at him. Butch opened the door. "Hi," he said.

"Hi," the boy replied, "Can you come out?"

"I'm not supposed to."

"Oh," the boy looked disappointed. "But, it's just around here."

Butch considered. He wouldn't get lost and he'd be back inside long before dad returned, which was probably about sunset. "Okay." He walked down the steps. "I'm Butch."

The boy half smiled and stuck out a hand. "Name's Joel."

Butch blinked as they shook. "Really? Is that a pretty common name down here?"

"Guess so. Why?"

"'Cause there was a kid named Joel where we just came from."

"Where was that?"

Butch thought. "I don't know."

Joel snorted. "You don't know where you just came from?"

Butch shrugged. "It was nearby."

"Hmm," Joel stared at him. "You got any fireworks?"

"No."

"I do." He shook the bag. "There's anthills in the back. Let's go blow them up."

Way too cool.

Butch followed him around the house. The backyard was a yellow-grassed red-clayed field stretching the entire neighborhood. No fences. Some gaily colored swings sat here and there, with an occasional plastic pool in tandem. No one else was outside. Could be the merciless sun frying them alive.

Joel stuck a Ladyfinger inside the hole of a large mound, lit it and ran past Butch, who stood watching. *Bam*! Dirt flew everywhere, peppering him. He brushed at his face and felt something crawling. And then stinging. "Ow!" he yelped, slapping at his face, and then his hair and neck. Ants were all over him, bent on eating him alive. He danced and spun, shaking them off until just a few meandered up and down his shorts, biting from time to time.

Joel watched all of this solemnly. "Those are fire ants," he said.

"Why do they call them that?"

"Because, when they bite, it feels like fire."

"No kidding," Butch picked off a couple more. "Let's not do that anymore."

"Okay." They blew up piles of rocks instead, ducking the shrapnel. Joel ran home and grabbed some soldiers and Butch got his and they set up two opposing armies. Joel divided his firecrackers and they bombarded each other's forces until Butch conceded. They then sat on the back porch with a couple of ice waters Butch made from the fridge.

"Where's your mom?" Joel asked.

"Oklahoma."

Joel looked at him curiously. "Are your parents divorced?"

"I'm not sure. They said they were getting divorced and me and dad left and I've only spoken to her once since then..." and that didn't go very well.

A weight moved around his chest.

"Why'd they get divorced?"

Butch thought about Dorey and Beatrice. "I don't know."

"I wish my parents would get divorced."

Butch was startled. "Why?"

"They're so mean to me."

Butch felt immediate sympathy. "I know what that's like."

"Do you?" Joel frowned at him. "Do you really? Just because your parents got divorced, you think you know what mean parents are?"

Surprised, Butch looked at him. Joel's eyes were narrow and his face red. He suddenly stood up and threw the glass savagely across the yard, landing behind another house. Butch, stunned, braced for some adult charging out with belt in hand to deliver justice, but nothing. "What'd I do?"

"Nothing! You didn't do nothing!" and Joel scrambled around, grabbed his soldiers and the leftover firecrackers. By the time he'd stuffed them back into the paper bag, he was crying. Butch was sure Joel was going to beat him up, but the kid suddenly turned and ran, screaming inarticulately.

"Joel!" Butch scrambled up but the other boy had already cleared the front and was pell-mell down the street, heat waves from the asphalt making him shimmer. He was in full-throated agony as he reached a house way down at the end and flew inside the front door with hardly a break in stride.

Butch was sure Joel's mean parents would fly back out, boards in hand, and come after him, screaming "You bully!"

Bully? Him?

Butch stood breathless for at least a minute, too stupefied to move. Nothing happened. No doors opened anywhere. No cars passed. There was a dot of a helicopter moving through the distant white air and Butch wondered if dad was spying on him.

"Weird," he said and went inside.

# CHAPTER 40

Re-run the next morning: dad in his orange flight suit, bowls of Lucky Charms, *Captain Kangaroo*. Dad left without renewing orders to stay inside, which technically meant Butch could leave the house. Technically. Sitting in front of the fan watching Moose drop ping pong balls seemed the better option, though. Man, was it hot.

There was a knock on the door. Butch opened it.

Joel. "Can I come in?"

Butch hesitated. Joel carried a substantial paper bag, though, and potential treasure outweighed any concerns. "Okay." Wise choice; not only did Joel bring soldiers, but a whole fleet of plastic ships. They set up the Japanese and US Navies on the wooden floor. Epic sea battles interspersed with TV watching.

"Did you get in trouble?" Butch asked.

"Hmm?" Joel was distracted by Mr. Green Jeans. "For what?"

"Yesterday."

"What about yesterday?"

"You know..." Butch made a helpless gesture.

Joel stared at him a moment, then frowned. "No," he said.

Puzzling. Mean parents should have stapled Joel to a wall and then skinned him alive. Or smacked him with a baseball bat. Right, Frank? "You didn't?"

Joel was annoyed. "No."

"But..."

Joel jumped up with the same look that preceded yesterday's

running and screaming. "You wanna see? You wanna know? C'mon!" he shouted, fiercely scooping up ships and soldiers and then marching out the front door, bag clutched to his chest. Butch sat for a moment, as surprised as yesterday, then went after him.

He caught up halfway down the block as Joel slammed along, face set. It was already a furnace out here and Butch prayed for a cool breeze, but no luck. A couple of boys stood in a yard about three houses down. One of them waved a girl hand. "Yoo hoo, Jooooeeeel!"

"Who's your boyfriend?" the other one asked and both laughed nastily.

Butch stared, speechless. Joel ignored them.

They came to the far house and Joel walked straight in, Butch hesitantly followed but the moment he cleared the door..."Ah!"

Air conditioning! *Real* air conditioning, not swamp cooler. And that smell... baked bread!

"Mom!" Joel called.

"In here," a pleasant voice from the back and Joel marched in that direction. Butch noted the overstuffed couch and two chairs with doilies and the plush green-pile carpet and console TV-radio combination and the flower paintings on all but one wall, which contained about three thousand photos of smiling people, a lot of them Joel at various ages.

Wow. Nice place.

They entered a dazzling kitchen, white linoleum floors and yellow Amana stove and refrigerator and everything set against corn-on-the-cob wallpaper, sunlight beaming through French doors overlooking a swing-setted backyard. A man and a woman sat at a stainless steel kitchen table covered with a plastic daffodil tablecloth, steaming coffee cups and plates, evidence of breakfast, scattered across it.

"Hello," the woman said pleasantly. She was short and dark with a haircut suspiciously like Dorey's. Did every woman want to be Twiggy? She had huge black eyes, the same ones Joel sported. "You must be Butch. Would you like some breakfast?"

"Yes, he would!" the man, a brown-suited David Jansen in *The Fugitive* look-alike, gestured at a chair. "Sit yourself down there, young man!"

Butch looked at Joel who frowned, and wordless, sat. Butch

did, too. "I'll just be a minute," the woman fluttered about the stove and returned with several gigantic biscuits. "Help yourself," she pointed at the jam and butter, got her husband a coffee refill, and then sat down.

Hmm. Might be a setup.

Eyeing the adults, Butch filled the biscuit with butter and Welch's. "Oh, wow," he said around a mouthful.

Joel's mom beamed and Joel's dad chuckled and Butch glanced at Joel, who was busy with his own biscuit.

When did the meanness start?

"Well!" Mr, Joel suddenly placed the cup and Butch braced. This was it!

"Customers to meet, contracts to sign." He and his wife stood and he gave her an affectionate kiss on the cheek and a racy slap on the butt. She playfully pushed him with an "oh!" They were both smiling as the man ruffled Joel's hair. "Be good," he said. "Nice to meet you, Butch," grabbed a briefcase and went out. Butch heard the front door close. Joel didn't react.

"Do you boys want to go to the pool?" Mrs. Joel asked. Butch's heart leaped. Would he!

"Sure," Joel was noncommittal.

Butch's expression was answer enough and she smiled at him. "You can borrow one of Joel's swimsuits."

He changed in the bathroom, leaving his clothes there as instructed. Joel frowned at him when he stepped out. "Don't tear it," he said, pointing at the suit, "It's one of my favorites." Joel handed him a towel and a Frisbee and they piled into a Polara station wagon and drove off.

Oh, man, going to the pool! Butch wriggled in excitement, and then sudden concern. "What time will we be back?" he asked.

"Around dinner," Mrs. Joel said.

Fear leaped through him. "What?" That would be long after dad got home, which meant his death, technical arguments notwithstanding.

She smiled in the rearview mirror. "You aren't from around here, are you? 'Dinner' means 'lunch.' We'll be back around lunch." Her brows suddenly creased. "Do you want to tell your father first?"

"No, no," Butch said hastily, "It's okay."

"I don't want to get you into trouble."

"I won't be," he assured her. Especially if he was in the house before dad got back.

"All right, then," and she settled on the road.

Butch glanced at Joel. So when does the meanness start?

They pulled into Ft. Rucker and the MP at the gate saluted the Polara, Joel's mom returning it crisply. Butch was impressed and turned to Joel, who was staring out the window. "Your dad's in the Army?"

"No." Joel pointed at his mom. "She was."

Butch was astonished. "You're a WAC?"

"I was." She nodded vigorously. "A lieutenant."

"You're not anymore?"

"No. I was in London during the war and got hurt in an air raid. I was medically discharged."

Butch's eyes rounded. "You were hit by a bomb?"

"I sure was."

"Wow!" Butch couldn't believe it. Joel's mom was cool! "So, what did it do to you?"

"It broke both her legs and messed up her back," Joel sounded bored.

"Wow!" Butch said again. "My dad was in the war, too. He drove a jeep with a .50 machine gun, but he never got hurt."

"Well, he was lucky," Joel's mom said, "A lot of people didn't make it back. I'm grateful I did, even though it still hurts."

"Really?"

"Yes, I still have shrapnel in my knee."

Absolutely the coolest mom in America.

They got to the pool and Mrs. Joel signed them in and Joel and he ran, screaming, through the cold showers at the entrance. They stepped to the edge and Butch closed his eyes and lifted his face to the sun, savoring the waves of fire. Kids yelled and called and slapped running feet, even though you're not supposed to, and the lifeguard whistled and the air smelled of Coppertone and chlorine and resonated with "Marco!" and its "Polo!" response. Perfect, just perfect. Butch held his breath and jumped, cool blue washing over him and smothering the fire…

*Wham*! A pair of feet smashed onto his shoulders, driving him to the bottom. He yelped, a big mistake because that blew out all his air. Instantly, he struggled against the great lump of Joel-flesh holding him under. His lungs flattened, screamed for air. He pushed Joel off and clawed to the surface, gasping, and seized the drain gutter.

"That was fun!" Joel said, pulling up next to Butch.

"You almost drowned me!" Butch spluttered and would have said more but Joel splashed him hard, driving water down his throat and causing him to gag.

"Joel!" Mrs. Joel called sharply from a lounge chair where she had retreated with a big plastic bag of magazines, pointy dark sunglasses pulled down to see. Joel frowned at her, muttered something, and swam away. "Are you all right?" she asked Butch.

"Yes," he coughed. She wore a black one-piece with sequins, her legs pulled up to prop a magazine. Butch stared. There, that white line on her knee. Has to be the bomb scar. And look at those legs. Something stirred. Uh-oh. The Wicked Thing.

He pushed his hips against the plaster wall, liking the way it rubbed. He kicked frantically, keeping himself against the wall as he stared at Joel's mom. He wished Marianne was here.

"Go swim, Butch," she said and he started, face flaming. Did she know what he was thinking? She half smiled and went back to her magazine so, maybe not. The Wicked Thing beat at him, crying, but he fended it off and pulled himself along the wall to the deep end.

"Look at me! Look at me!"

Butch squinted. Joel was on the edge of the diving board, bouncing it a bit, his stomach draped over the top of his suit. He stared straight at Butch, a huge, dumb grin on his face. Rough boys in line behind him laughed and pointed at Joel. Some girls in the same line, arms folded crossly, stared at Joel with *twa* faces. Butch focused on the girls, their suits all clingy and wet. He knew what was underneath. The Wicked Thing lurched in his stomach.

"I said look at ME!" Joel shrieked. Startled, Butch blinked at him. Joel grinned wide, bounced once, and jumped into the water. No dive, just jumped, making a big splash. The rough boys gaped in astonishment and then broke into gales of derisive laughter, joined by the girls. Even the lifeguard chuckled.

Joel's head burst up. "I touched bottom! I touched bottom!" he screamed triumphant, bobbed in the water and pointed at Butch. The rough boys and the girls followed the point and Butch cringed. "Did you see? Did you see?" Joel swam desperately up to him, like a drowning puppy. "I touched bottom, I touched bottom!" Butch wished he could touch bottom right now.

He spent the rest of the morning doing his best to turn invisible, but it didn't work, not with Joel hanging on him. "Is that your brother? Is he retarded?" the rough boys asked Butch a hundred times. The girls moved away as if he had a force field herding them along. It didn't work on Joel, though.

"You boys ready to go?" Joel's mom asked.

"No!" Joel cried.

"Yes," Butch said, relieved. For a moment, he detected a spark of sympathy in her eyes. Parents were generally oblivious, but she had to know what Joel was like. Maybe she was thinking about taking a baseball bat into his room.

"Don't say that," Frank whispered in his ear.

They left. Joel cried as though hauled off to prison. Butch sat as far away from him as possible, and stared in disbelief.

"How 'bout some ice cream?" Mrs. Joel asked.

Joel shut up immediately and they pulled into Dairy Queen. They got soft cones. "Thank you," Butch said to Mrs. Joel, not sure if it was the ice cream or Joel's silence he appreciated more.

They went back to Joel's house. Butch changed into his own clothes; he paused a moment to look at his wiener. No signs of damage from the side of the pool.

Joel stood right outside the bathroom, and Butch wondered if he'd seen the wiener inspection. "You staying for dinner?" Joel was eager.

"Well..."

"Cheese sandwiches and tomato soup."

Oh, man, real honest-to-God mom food... but he'd have to spend more time with Joel. Ambivalence.

"Dinner's ready!" Mrs. Joel called and Butch surrendered, following Weirdo to the kitchen. It was all Joel promised and more. Piles of Lay's Potato Chips, Pepsi served over ice, Oreos on a paper plate. Heaven.

Butch ate while Joel fussed over bread crust and other mortal crises, from how hot the soup was to the number of chips on his plate. Mrs. Joel gently dealt with each. Butch watched, curious. She never raised her voice, never belted Joel away from the table or threw scalding water on him like any normal parent would. She worked with him. Butch was impressed.

"You miss your mom, don't you?" she asked while getting a

breath.

"Yes." He swallowed his crust. "But we might be going back." He said it offhand, so not to look pitiful.

"What?" Joel stopped mid-tantrum about the lack of Fig Newtons and cried, "You're leaving?"

The stricken look on Joel's face surprised Butch. "Well, maybe... I don't really know."

"No!" Joel shrieked and leaped from the table, knocking the chair backward. A plate of Lays fell upside down on the floor. Wailing, Joel stumbled out the kitchen and down the hall toward his bedroom, but not before giving Butch a hateful look.

Butch watched him go, dismayed. Mrs. Joel stood up quietly and gathered the chips from the floor. Butch shook himself and helped her, both of them silent. "Maybe it's best you went home now," she said, when they'd finished.

"Yes." He headed toward the door, Joel's muffled cries in the back. "Thank you. For the pool and lunch."

"You're welcome." She knelt on the floor and her face was sweet, beatific, and in the depth of her eyes was a well-guarded sadness. Butch was, more and more, familiar with that look.

He went home.

# CHAPTER 41

"Bing bing BIIIING! Ricoshaaaaay Rabbit!" Butch sang along as Ricochet bounded around the sheriff's office like a maniac. He giggled. Saturday morning line-up. *Mighty Mouse* had given way to *Magilla Gorilla*, and *Underdog* was next. He squeezed his legs together in pure pleasure.

"What are you doing?" Dad growled from somewhere down the hall.

"Nothing." Commercial. "Buuuuuuuy Beech Nut. Buy gum!" Butch sang with the Zebras.

"That's right, you're doin' nothin'!" Dad stormed.

Butch turned, instinctively hitting a defensive crouch because dad's tone had 'get-ready-for-a-beating all through it. Dad was at the hallway entrance in a white T-shirt and unbuttoned boxers, the inside of the fly dark and hairy. Butch gasped, tore his eyes away. Dad didn't notice. "You ain't gonna sit there all morning watching stupid TV! Go outside!"

"But..." He hadn't had breakfast yet. The Cheerios Kid was on the screen flexing an 'O' bicep. Go Power! Didn't he need that first?

Dad's eyes went all black and death. He pointed Clawhand at the front door. "Go. Out. Side," each word punctuated with a stab of Clawfinger as something in dad's shorts flopped in unison. Butch flew out the door.

And immediately sat down on the porch, ready to cry.

Jeez, dad, it's Saturday morning! Kids go outside after cartoons, not before! How utterly, completely unfair.

"No kidding," Frank said.

Butch pressed his lips together. Okay, fine, there were worse things. But, dang it! Simon Bar Sinister was brewing dastardly plans! "No need to fear, Underdog is here!" he toned.

"Do you wanna play?"

Oh, no.

Joel stood hunched on the sidewalk. Butch had managed to avoid him all week by doing full-blown reconnaissance before hitting the backyard to play soldiers or read comics in the porch shadow. Joel had knocked on the front door a few times, calling "Butch! Butch! I know you're in there!" and he'd hidden behind the couch until, ten or fifteen minutes later, Joel went away.

But now, trapped.

"Well?"

"No," Butch said.

"Why not?" Joel was stricken.

"I just don't."

"Why not?"

"Because I just don't!" Kid Tone of Petulance.

Joel glowered at him. "You don't like me anymore."

"Yes, I do."

"No, you don't."

"Do."

Butch didn't, of course, but he wasn't a hateful, sneering, mean rough boy who liked to hurt people. Being the object of a lot of rough-boy attention, he knew how that felt.

Joel sat down next to him. "Well, then, let's play."

"I don't want to."

"Why not?"

This was going nowhere. "Joel," he said, "you're driving me crazy."

"What? Why? I'm not doing anything!"

"Yes, you are. I told you I don't want to play, so I just don't want to play, okay?"

"You just don't want to play with me."

"Augh!" Butch borrowed from Charlie Brown. "I don't want to play with anybody. I want!" Butch stressed the word. "To watch cartoons!"

"Oh." Joel shrugged. "All right."

"You'll watch cartoons?"

"Yeah." He stood up and headed for the door.

Butch shook his head vigorously. "Not in there. My dad's in a bad mood."

"Oh," Joel stood back. "Then let's go to my house."

An immediate and quite elegant solution. Joel had a real nice TV and a real nice living room and a real nice mom. Butch could watch Underdog in comfort, like he used to do with Tommy. Except Joel was no Tommy. Joel was Joel.

But if it meant cartoons… Butch stood. "All right."

Delight and relief flooded Joel's face like a sunburst on a muddy bank. He giggled, running down the porch like a spastic baby. Butch watched in amazement. This kid.

"I gotta tell my dad," Butch called.

Joel fidgeted on the sidewalk. "Okay, hurry, hurry!" he said and waved a frantic arm.

Butch cracked the front door, cautiously peering inside. He expected a couch to sail past his head, but dad wasn't there. With a surge of hope he looked but the TV was off. Dang, no sneak-watching. Could risk turning it back on, but why? He had a safer alternative. "Dad? I'm going to Joel's."

"Who's Joel?" Dad called suspiciously from the bathroom, around a toothbrush.

"A…" Butch almost said 'friend' "…kid I know."

"Where's he live?"

"Up the street."

"All right."

Butch slipped out of the house before dad changed his mind. "We're gonna have fun!" Joel danced as they walked. Butch glanced around to see if any rough boys were about but, no, of course not. They, like every other kid in America, were inside watching cartoons, dad.

"Hello, Butch!" Mrs. Joel smiled at him from the kitchen. He smiled back. Mr. Joel came out from a side hall. "Hey, soldier!"

Butch grinned. Soldier, ha!

They plopped on the rug in front of the TV and Joel switched channels. Butch blinked. "*Casper*?" What's this?

"Yeah!" Joel was enthralled. Little Audrey was on the screen laughing hysterically, as usual.

"Where's *Underdog*?"

"*Underdog*?" Joel snorted. "I don't like Underdog."

"How can you not like Underdog?"

"He's stupid. A dog as a shoeshine boy?"

"It's not stupid. It's cool. Casper is stupid. It's for babies." Butch liked Casper, but not in competition with Underdog.

Joel's look darkened. "It's not for babies," he growled and turned back to the screen.

Butch let out an exasperated breath. This was no better than sitting on the porch; worse, because he had to put up with Weirdo Joel-o and the indignity of *Casper*. Might as well have stayed home... hmm. With a sly look, Butch pushed to his knees. "All right. See ya," he said.

"What?" Joel whirled. "You're leaving?"

"I'm gonna go home and watch Underdog." Butch made leaving motions.

"Thought your dad wouldn't let you."

"He will now."

"Joel," Mom called, "You have a guest. Play nice."

"All RIGHT!" Joel's face flamed and he savagely spun the dial. Sweet Polly Purebred was singing "...where, oh where, has my Underdog gone?"

Butch grinned. Perfect.

That's how it went for the rest of the morning. Joel wanted something lame, like *Astro Boy*, and Butch successfully employed the threat of going home for something cool, like *Bullwinkle*. By noon, Butch was exhausted. Joel was livid.

"Dinner!" Mrs. Joel called them in, defusing the situation. She had sandwiches stacked neatly in a pyramid with Campbell's Vegetable Soup in big cups nearby. Butch crumbled Premium crackers into the soup and reached for a sandwich, but stopped and stared. "What's that?" he asked.

Mrs. Joel smiled. "Peanut butter and banana." She pointed at the one Joel had just grabbed. "And that's mayonnaise and banana."

Butch was, to put it mildly, taken aback.

"Quite the southern delicacy, these," Mr. Joel, who was sitting at the table reading a book, toned. Mrs. Joel giggled.

Butch figured the peanut butter combination was the safer alternative and took an exploratory bite. Not bad, but he used the soup to ameliorate. Joel went for all the mayonnaise ones, which was fine. Butch wasn't ready for that.

He glanced at Mr. Joel's book cover: *The Keepers of the House*, Shirley Ann Grau. "What's that about?"

"A Southern family," Mr. Joel said, "A rather tragic one." He looked up. "You like to read?"

Butch nodded enthusiastically around his sandwich. "Yes, I do."

Joel made a face as Mr. Joel leaned forward. "What do you read?"

"Comics mostly," he said, then added hastily, "And books, too."

"What kind of comics?"

"*Marvel*."

"Oh, yeah," Mr. Joel nodded, "Me, too."

No way. Unable to keep incredulity out of his voice, Butch asked, "You like comics?"

Mr. Joel grinned. "Daredevil is my hero."

Butch couldn't believe his ears. Other than Stan Lee, no adult should know who Daredevil was. "And Doctor Doom." Mrs. Joel added from the sink.

Butch recovered from his astonishment. "Doctor Doom isn't a hero!" he scorned.

"True." Mr. Joel nodded. "But there's something about him. I think he wants to be a hero, but his vanity won't let him."

And they were off, Butch amazed that two adults could actually hold an intelligent conversation about Victor von Doom, the Inhumans, and the return of Captain America. Oblivious, Joel shoveled sandwiches down his throat. Butch realized why Mrs. Joel made so many.

"So you read more than comic books," Mr. Joel said.

"Yes!" Butch was still enthused from the prior conversation. "I've read *Tom Sawyer*. And the *Happy Hollisters*. And I just got done reading a bunch of Tom Swift's and..." Butch almost said Nancy Drew but that might be too girlish..."the *We Were There* books."

"*Tom Swift and his Nuclear Apple Peeler*," Mr. Joel winked and Butch felt warm and accepted. An adult who reads, and a real adult at that, not just an older kid. And an adult who likes kids who read.

Would wonders never cease?

"This is boring," Joel pouted and threw down the last bits of a sandwich too many. "Let's go outside." He pushed away and Butch saw it, just briefly, in Mr. Joel's eyes—disappointment.

Butch was already familiar with that look. Incompatibility of father and son generated it, but if Joel and he switched dads... Butch considered. He'd definitely get the better deal. And Joel, after about, oh say, ten minutes, would definitely get the baseball bat.

"I said, don't say that," Frank whispered in his ear.

With a commiserating glance back at Mr. Joel, which he didn't seem to catch, Butch followed Joel out the back door. It was hot, take-your-breath-away hot, and Butch gasped.

"I've got a Slip and Slide," Joel said.

Butch mouthed a silent prayer of thanks and helped unroll and hook it up. Chattering with anticipation, they ran back inside, Butch forgetting Joel wasn't his friend. They changed into available suits and spent hours rushing down the wet plastic in complete defiance of physics and common sense—backward, standing up, somersaulting, whatever. They took frequent breaks and rested under the shade of a magnolia tree as Mrs. Joel, in timed intervals, plied them with soda and potato chips and Oreos. Mr. Joel came out in a bathing suit and was just hilarious, flinging them, shrieking, down the slide at one hundred miles per hour. He left after a while and Butch watched him go, impressed. "Your parents aren't mean," he said.

He might as well have thrown a bucket of ice water on Joel. "What?"

Something warned Butch he was treading dangerous ground, but Joel had no clue what mean parents actually were. Right, Frank? "They're not."

Joel paled. "How can you say that?"

"Well, Jeez! They're just not!"

"But you've seen how they treat me!"

"I think they treat you pretty good."

"How can you say that?"

Butch let out a loud, exasperated breath. "Joel, your parents are real cool. Maybe you're the problem."

Joel, aghast, as Butch waved a hand over the backyard. "You've got a great swing set and a Slip and Slide and a big dirt pile over there," Butch pointed, "but no one's here. No one wants to play with you. I'm about the only one." And only *because* of those things, Joel. He kept that to himself.

Joel stamped his foot. "My parents ARE mean!"

"No, they're not."

"They are!" Joel was about to cry.

"Joel, I'm telling you, they're not. At all. It's you. You're weird."

Another bucket of ice water. "No, I'm not!" Stricken.

"You are!" Gawd, this kid. "You act weird. You jumped on me at the pool, and then you acted like you were retarded. And you run off and cry over nothing. It's weird."

Joel went grim. "It's not my fault," he toned.

Butch gave him a "c'mon" look.

"It's not," Joel insisted and marched to the back door, motioning Butch to follow.

The Joels were sitting in the kitchen, coffee and magazines between them. "Mom." Joel walked up to her, solemn. "I do weird things."

"Everyone does, Joel."

"But it's because of what happened, when the baby died in your stomach."

Mrs. Joel let out the kind of startled chuckle elicited by something absolutely bizarre. Mr. Joel simply dropped a jaw. Butch mirrored him.

"See," Joel continued, "it did something to me. I'm not sure what, but something." He turned to include Butch in the explanation. Butch didn't want to be.

"Joel," Mrs. Joel half smiled, "you're okay."

"I'm not."

"Joel, you're okay."

There was a knock at the door. Everyone turned to it with relief, especially Butch, who was convinced he had just entered another dimension of time and space. Mrs. Joel called out, "Come in!"

Dad.

Butch's guard went up. What was he doing here? "Hello," dad said, "I'm Butch's dad."

"Oh! Hello!" Mrs. Joel smoothed her hair and dress. Dad looked at her in a way that Butch didn't like. Apparently Mr. Joel didn't, either, because he hurriedly interposed, holding out a hand. "Hello, good to meet you. We enjoy having Butch over."

Dad eyed Butch. "He's not being any trouble?"

Yes, he is, Mr. Joel would say, your son said our son is weird and our son now thinks a dead baby is the cause and it's all Butch's fault! And dad yanks Butch's pants off right here and spanks him with barbed wire as the Joels applaud. He held his breath.

"Oh no, he's quite good."

Whew.

"Why are you all wet?" Dad asked.

"Slip and Slide," Butch said.

"Oh, all right. Well, you need to come home now."

That wondrous ambivalence: escape, but no more Slip 'n Slide. "Okay," he said in a disappointed tone to show Joel a reluctance he didn't really feel.

On cue, Joel wailed, "Do you have to go?" like an abandoned child. Butch inwardly rolled his eyes. Yes, he sure did.

"'Fraid so, son," dad in his 'I'm-a-normal-dad' voice, the one he used with strangers, "I gotta go somewhere."

"Well, then, Butch can stay here!" Mrs. Joel piped.

Butch could have strangled her.

"Yes!" Mr. Joel remained in intercept as dad eyed Mrs. Joel again. "That's no problem. We're happy to have him!"

Butch looked at the Joels and saw well-meaning expressions and sincerity and was genuinely grateful for it. But then he saw Joel's baby face, and wasn't. He turned to dad, desperation in his eyes. Be in character, dad, cruelly deny me the pleasure of these good people's company. Please.

And he was in character, but not the way Butch wanted. A gleam deep in dad's eyes, the spark of some black engine igniting as he said, "I dunno, I could be gone for a while."

Butch's eyes widened and he took in a breath, all ready to burst out with, "I better come home, then," take dad's hand and leave before whatever plan the Wicked Thing incubated in dad's mind broke the shell.

But, then, Joel sandbagged him.

"Can Butch sleep over?"

Mr. and Mrs. Joel squealed in simultaneous delight, Mrs. Joel actually clapping her hands, which stifled the "No!" rising in Butch's throat. The Wicked Thing hatched, stood full in the remnants of its gangrenous egg and crowed as dad, the leer wide and Satanic and swallowing them all, turned full on Butch and, in his Lucifer voice, said, "Well, sure!"

Joel danced and Butch immediately understood he was a rare overnight guest.

Gee, can't imagine why.

He saw dad eyeing Mrs. Joel's bent-over form while the Wicked Thing screamed with joy. Mr. Joel talked about an all-night comic convention, but Butch couldn't muster the enthusiasm. His feet spasmed, seeking an escape that wasn't there.

So this is what a sense of impending doom felt like.

# CHAPTER 42

Back in the swamp. Butch was waist-deep in muck. Nervous, he looked around for snakes. Frank sat on a nearby log, head in hands, fog and methane drifting by. A leprous moon silhouetted him. "What's wrong?" Butch asked.

Frank shook his head miserably, but did not look up. "I'm so cold. So cold and far away."

Butch struggled, but the muck held him. Vapors thickened, leaving only a hint of Frank. Something moved against his legs and Butch shrank but it settled on his calves. It was warm, a hand...

Butch woke. Dark, except for a weak nightlight. Sad clown pictures, alongside a wall-shelf of dinosaur models, stared down at him. Unfamiliar sheets and blankets tangled. Everything was wrong, and there was a hand on his calf.

"It's me," Joel whispered.

Butch forced his head out of an entrapping sheet. Joel stood right beside him, an arm slipped under the covers. "You going to the bathroom?" Butch asked. He suspected Joel was a bedwetter, so encouraged it.

"No."

"Then, what are you doing?"

Joel said nothing. Butch inwardly groaned. The weirdness did not end, even in sleep. As predicted, the evening had seesawed between Joel's delightful parents and the not-so-delightful Joel. They played *The Game of Life* and Joel got mad when he ended up in the Poor Farm so they stopped. Mrs. Joel made chocolate-chip popcorn balls but Joel didn't like them and threw his on the floor, prompting banishment to the bedroom where he wailed and screamed and promised to do better.

Mrs. Joel then did card tricks—card tricks!—easily picking out Butch's queen and showing how she did it. Absolutely fascinating and Butch was prepared to learn several more tricks but Joel pronounced it boring. "Time for bed," Mr. Joel decided. Butch was actually relieved, even though he had to share the bed and endure Joel's yammering until the idiot finally dropped off.

And now Weirdo had hold of his leg. "What are you doing, Joel?"

"Let's spank each other," Joel said.

"What?"

Joel spun, dropping his PJs and underwear, the giant moon of his butt half-lit in the nightlight. "Go ahead, spank me first," and he bent over.

"Are you crazy?" Butch yelped. He stared at Joel's offered cheeks, the wiener a little sack crunched between his legs. The Wicked Thing leaped in his stomach and Butch thought of Marianne, even though her smooth, round body looked so much better than this pasty, shapeless thing.

"Do you want to go first, then? Okay." Joel turned, stepping out of his clothes and jumped on top of Butch. "Oof!"

Joel tugged at Butch's way-too-big borrowed PJs, Butch yanking the waistband to counteract. They struggled but Joel used his weight to keep Butch down. His hands snaked inside the bottoms and grabbed for Butch's wiener.

Butch froze. What the heck? For a second, it was Marianne grasping at him. The sensation overwhelmed, took his breath away…

But it wasn't Marianne. It was fat, stupid, Weirdo Joel doing something really weird to him.

Frantic, Butch pulled his knees up. With a surge, he pushed hard and elevated Joel, then launched him off the bed. Joel crashed heavily onto the floor, taking a small nightstand with him. "Oooww!" he shrieked.

Butch spun out and scrambled along the wall, desperate. He bumped against the dresser, his hands closing on a baseball bat. He grabbed it and turned, heart pounding. "What are you doing?" he yelled at Joel.

Joel blubbered, flopped his uncoordinated limbs about, seeking purchase. It reminded Butch of a stupid movie he saw on *Lights Out*, some guy in a rubber frog suit creeping along the floor to eat some helpless woman. Joel moved exactly like that, eyes bugged, croaking at Butch and snapping his hands. Butch panicked, measuring the distance to the door. "Stay away from me!" he screamed and hefted...

   ...*a bat*
   *And gave him a whack*
   *And broke his head to the booone...*

"What on earth?!?" The light came on and Mrs. Joel stood there in a plush velour bathrobe with a gigantic collar, Mr. Joel hovered behind in PJ bottoms only. They looked at Butch, bat ready, PJs askew, fear on his face and murder in his stance, and at their half-naked, flopping son. "What's going on?" she cried.

Butch pointed the bat at Joel. "He wanted me to spank him! He grabbed my wiener!" Butch was as shocked saying it as they looked hearing it, and he braced. "Not MY son!" she'd shriek, hate and loathing on her face, "MY son would never do *anything* like that!" and she'd be a skull, blood flowing from her mouth as she pointed a claw at him. "It was you! It was you!" Fires burned in her eye sockets and Mr. Joel shot up ten feet and grew knee-length hair and big fangs and roared in, tearing Butch apart...

But that didn't happen. Mrs. Joel looked at Butch for a moment and then went to her frog-flopping son. "Oh, Joel," she said, the carefree-mom mask falling cleanly away. She gathered Joel, her wails matching his, but of defeat, not pain. Mr. Joel stood paralyzed, looking like someone had punched him in the stomach.

Butch readied the bat in case she became a bloody skull. The wails of mother and son grew louder, the mourning of the pack. Mr. Joel looked helpless, his hands flopping almost as much as Joel's, not sure who to console.

Butch's hold tightened. Look at them, all three of them, cool card-trick-playing shrapneled mom, bathing suit comic-reading dad, and Joel, Slip and Slide and lots of soldiers and toys, beset now by disaster, all their efforts to forestall it worthless. Liars. Fakes. In the grip of the Wicked Thing.

Just like dad.

"Butch, give me the bat."

Butch focused. Mr. Joel reached over the wailers, palm out,

fingers doing the "hand it over" twitch. He looked firm, authoritative, brooking no nonsense here.

"No," Frank whispered.

"No," Butch said.

Mr. Joel's eyebrows rose. "Butch, give me the bat. Please."

"Don't do it," Frank said.

"I won't do it." Butch gripped the bat tighter.

Mr. Joel actually smiled. "I know you're scared, but no one's going to hurt you," and he reached insistently.

"Let's get out of here," Frank whispered.

Butch nodded. Yes, let's go, before Mr. Joel takes the bat and breaks Butch's head to the bone.

He marched straight for the door, waving the bat menacingly. Mr. Joel flattened against the jamb. "Please, Butch."

"Leave me alone!" Butch screamed. Mr. Joel, for a second, moved like he wanted to grab the bat and probably could, but then his hands fell to his side. Butch dropped the bat with a clatter in the hallway and ran out of the front door.

It was very late, probably midnight, a bit of drizzle but still a bazillion degrees. Felt like the bathroom just after dad finished a shower. Stars manfully broke through the gauze while a crescent moon peeked over a cloud here and there, but it was still too dark, the only marker one feeble street lamp off in a direction Butch knew was wrong. He spun, disoriented, looking like a frenzied top to the vampires and werewolves creeping up on him from the sides of the tomb-dark houses. Panic fluttered in his ribs.

He stared fearfully at the Joel house. They were recovering by now, getting under control, and would want this kept secret. All three grinning evilly and sharpening long knives and, in moments, burst out of the door and chase him down. They stab and stab and stab and Joel cuts off his wiener and eats it and they bury him under the sand pile. Dad comes by in a week. "Oh, he left," they say and grin evilly and dad shrugs and goes off with Dorey or Beatrice or whoever.

Butch gasped. "Run," Frank urged.

He did, blindly, uncaring of direction, just needing distance. He was barefoot and the sidewalk was uneven and gravel-strewn and he stepped on a sharp pebble, stumbled, and cried out. On his knees, he looked wildly about for the descending werewolves and Joels but he was clear, for the moment. A dog barked, then another and lights would come on next, driving off the werewolves but putting adults in the yards. "Who is that? Some kid? What's he doing out here?" They shoot at him and get axes and chase him down the street screaming, "Thief! Thief!" and dad joins them, swinging the bullwhip and yelling, "He's not even mine!"

"Run!" Frank screamed in his ear.

In full panic, Butch did, up and down the sidewalk, spending more time picking himself up than anything, crying now but quietly, not wanting to make the vampires' jobs easier.

"Go home!" Frank ordered, "You have to go home!" and that was true. If Butch could get to dad before the mob got to him then he'd convince dad that the mob was wrong, that Butch was innocent, that he fled in the night to escape the Wicked Thing fluttering in Joel's stomach, not to avoid the punishment due a thief and, yes, maybe he wasn't dad's real son but dad, you are the only father I have, even if you're just an approximation. Protect me. Don't be Joel's dad, or Frank's mom. Don't kill me.

"Don't kill me," he wailed softly as he ran, bent and craven, up the sidewalk the wrong way on the wrong side of the road and he beelined across, a momentary cooling of grass on his feet, and then he was back on the torturous cement. Another dog picked up the calls, telling the werewolves Butch's position, and he ran faster and somehow found the house and spun through the yard and zipped in between the trashcans next to the back porch and huddled there, trembling. He held his breath and listened for the sound of slavering jaws approaching but, other than the dogs, it was quiet. After a moment, even they stopped.

It was still dangerous because wolves crept silently. Any second, their glowing eyes would rise over the trashcans, giving him just enough time to scream before they tore out his throat. He trembled and waited. But no red eyes, no snuffling, no triumphant growls.

Nothing.

He was full-tilt bawling now, sobs under-toned just in case, his breath a hot coal in his chest. He felt battered and helpless. And fooled. Big time fooled. When you do a sleepover, even with a truly weird kid like Joel, it's not supposed to turn into sex. And boys aren't supposed to have sex with boys. You only have sex with girls. The Joels had acted cool and clever and fun and had made Butch actually wish they'd trade sons with dad. But not anymore. They were just fooling.

All the adults in the world were fooling. Mom pretended to care for her adopted son. Dorey acted like she wanted Butch around and Beatrice fooled the neighbors with her checklists. And dad.

Dad fooled everyone.

A dad was supposed to teach you baseball and take you to Disneyland and be strong and stalwart and encouraging, not carry you about as witness to his sins, mere baggage, a smokescreen for all the people watching.

And Butch had fooled himself.

He'd gone with dad out of a grand sense of nobility. And what happened? He'd been dragged across the South, abandoned in strange places, scrutinized by low people, teased and ignored as the Wicked Thing crawled from its grave, seized Butch in scaly claws, forced its way down his throat and now hung, dripping, from his ribs. He knew things he wasn't supposed to—the smooth skin of a naked girl, how a French Tickler fit, that dad was husband to many wives and father to unknown siblings. The Wicked Thing beat triumphant wings and crowed its joy.

And all across the land its cousins crowed back, symbiotes up and down the street and around the world turning parents into raging, screaming beasts of vengeance and kids into cruel, taunting bullies. The Wicked Thing sat on their heads and grinned, blood dripping from its teeth, eyes glowing while urging girls to take off their clothes and have sex with boys, and even some of the boys to take off their clothes and have sex with other boys. It was the Wicked Thing's world. God stood above and shook His head in disgust.

Butch wasn't feeling very noble anymore. He was, instead, feeling very tired.

"Let's go home," Frank said.

Not home of the moment, this safe spot behind trashcans, but home. Real home, where a real summer awaited: the screaming joy of a bike ride across a dirt mound and runs through the backyard with Cha Cha; scooping tadpoles out of the storm drain near the sewer pipes and trying to catch crawdads in the dribbling little creek meandering through the park without getting pinched; the smell of a new comic book while hunched next to Tommy reading, reading, reading. Cartoons on Saturday morning—*his* cartoons, not someone else's—and KOMA, *his* radio, although that WBAM in Montgomery was pretty good, a lot like KOMA but he couldn't listen to it like he could at home; sitting on the couch and bouncing his head against the back of the cushions in time with the beat because they didn't really have a couch here, did they? And they didn't have *Jonny Quest*, either, and he hadn't seen a comic book in weeks and he had no idea what was happening to the X-Men.

I want to go home.

Butch stood and walked out of the trashcans, clanking them a bit and starting the dogs off again but he didn't care. The heck with the werewolves. He clomped up the stairs and twisted open the back door. It was dark but he knew the layout and went down the hallway and pushed dad's door hard enough that it bounced off the back wall.

A startled shuffling greeted that and there was enough dim light that Butch could see motion in dad's bed. Too much motion, and when dad snapped on the table light going, "What the hell?" Butch saw he wasn't alone. A black woman sat up and blinked, sheets clutched to her throat. She was, obviously, naked, as was dad, the sheets pulled down across his hips revealed the obscenity. "Boy! What the hell are you doing?" dad roared.

There were so many things wrong here that Butch could have picked a random spot and started screaming: dad and all his talk about black people; dad and his earlier pronouncement that he had to go somewhere and Butch had to come home, but, well, maybe not, maybe not, you can stay with strangers who turned out monsters. The plan in your head, dad, this was it? Willing to have Butch splayed on the altar of Joel's weirdness while you had sex, huh? The Wicked Thing stood on the head of the bed, smirked, and spread diseased bat wings.

More reasons to be so very tired of it all.

"I want to go home."

"Well, where do you think you are?" Dad, still sleep-confused, stared at Butch. The black girl shrank under the covers. Apparently, she was better tuned than dad to Butch's mood.

"I want to go home!" Butch emphasized every word.

"Boy, you get your ass to bed." Dad was angry now. He wasn't embarrassed that Butch had caught him having sex with a black girl, oh no. He was incensed that Adopto-Boy challenged his prerogative, his authority. His.

The heck with him.

"I want to go HOME!" and Butch leaned forward, arms pushed back to give great emphasis and length to the last word.

Dad's face became inhuman, demonic. He threw back the covers, almost taking them off the other side except the black girl clutched them to her, a shield. Butch understood that. Blankets repelled evil. Case in point, dad was out of the bed, feet slamming against the floor as he descended on Butch, his nakedness swinging in time.

Usually, at this point, Butch fled, bouncing off doorjambs and tripping over shoes in an ultimately futile effort to get away from the oncoming beast. Not now. He stood his ground, just like at Beatrice's. "HOME!" Butch screamed full in dad's face, "HOME! HOME! HOOOOOOME!"

*Wham!* Dad's forty-pound slap crashed into the side of Butch's head, spun him around and launched stars. He bounced off the door, which, unfortunately, knocked him back into position. *Wham!* The follow-up slap spun him the other way but there was no door to keep him up and he hit the floor. Dad was on him, fists raised, the fury in full possession. Butch looked at Frank, leaning against the jamb, watching quietly. "So this is how it happened," he said.

"Yep," Frank nodded.

Butch prepared himself. In just a bit, Frank, we'll have a real game of catch.

Dad stopped, actually stopped. He reached over and flipped on the overhead light, blinking away the sudden dazzle. "Who are you talking to?" he asked, then an immediate "Shut up!" at the black girl weeping in the bed. Wisely, she did. If the white man could do that to his own son, what would he do to her?

"Frank," Butch said from the floor, hoping the black spots he saw were just from the sudden rush of light.

"Frank who?" Dad looked around suspiciously, probably thinking Butch had brought someone as witness. Well, he did, but not in the usual way.

"Frank Vaughn, sheesh!" What other Frank was there? Butch's feet, of their own accord, sought traction on the slippery, sweat—or blood—covered floor.

"Frank V—" Dad never got past the first consonant. His eyes

widened as he suddenly recognized the name and its implications and took a step back, his face transformed from demon to mere subhuman. He looked about wildly. Butch stood, wobbly, the nerves in his head where dad had slapped him tingling but didn't feel like cuts so, yeah, only sweat. Dad's hands fell to his side, inner terror on his face. Not of Frank; dad couldn't see Frank. But he could see Frank's mom.

The black girl took advantage of the confusion to gather her clothes and quietly slip out of the back door. Butch nodded approval: smart. Dad looked down at his hands, an unreadable expression on his face. Butch hoped it was sorrow and guilt, but he doubted it.

Butch couldn't resist one last gibe of "Home!" and then wheeled about and went to his room and crawled under the bed. "Home," he whispered and fell asleep.

# CHAPTER 43

"Where we going?" Butch asked.

"To see a house." Dad tapped ash out the wing.

Great. Third one in as many days. Apparently, dad's idea of "home" was a little different from Butch's.

Fine.

All of dad's actions just bounced off him now, like bullets hitting Sue Storm's shield. Dad had tiptoed around him for about a week after the Night of Frank—his version of an apology. He'd retrieved Butch's stuff from the Joel's, telling Butch that Joel had been sent off. No discussion, ever, of black girls and near murder. Even the bruises on both sides of Butch's head were about gone. It never happened.

Fine.

Butch sat back and watched a town go by. "What's the name of this place?" he asked.

"Enterprise," dad said as they stopped at a red light with a big fountain smack underneath it, a statue of some Greek goddess in a long flowing robe standing in the spray and lofting what looked like a tick. Butch stared. Nice, but weird.

"Know what that is?" Dad asked.

"No."

"The Boll Weevil Monument." Dad said it as though he'd pointed out the Brooklyn Bridge.

Butch looked for signs of leg-pulling but dad sported his smirk of satisfaction, usually formed when he knew something you didn't and generally evidence against leg-pulling.

"Huh?"

"See, they all used to grow cotton around here, but the boll weevil kept wiping out their crops so they decided to try peanuts. Well, they got rich, so they all said to each other, 'If it weren't for that boll weevil, we'd still be trying to grow cotton.'" Dad gestured at the statue.

Butch was scornful. "No way."

"It's true." Dad raised a finger in emphasis. "What do you think she's holding?"

"I thought it was a tick."

Dad chuckled. "Does sort of look like one." He hummed, then burst into, the boll weevil song, "Jus' lookin' for a hoooome, gotta find a hooome." Strangely appropriate, given everything. The light changed and Butch watched the monument slide past. Maybe the locals sacrificed children in front of it to ensure a good harvest. He giggled.

Dad misread that as enjoyment of his bellowing so he redoubled efforts. Butch groaned in mock pain and clamped hands to ears. Dad laughed and pinched Butch just above the knee, a major tickle spot, and he shrieked and kicked away. They both laughed at that and Butch, shocked, felt Sue's shield waver and evaporate. Was it that easy?

Yeah, pretty much.

"So where we going?" he asked.

"I told you, to see a house."

"Like the other two?"

"What, you didn't like those?"

No, he didn't. The first one was set back in what Butch swore was a swamp. While dad and the realtor talked in one room, Butch watched a line of ants crawl down a window and disappear into a wall. He didn't want to live in a house that bugs traversed with impunity. The other was real nice but across the street from a two-story shack housing about 496 black people, all on the porch staring at him. Embarrassing to live in such a nice house while the neighbors had such a bad one. Besides, there were a lot of young girls over there and Butch didn't want to find one in dad's bed. The Wicked Thing fluttered a bit and Butch tamped it down. "Not really."

They turned at Piggly Wiggly, a name that never failed to amuse, passed some large peanut silos and went under a railroad bridge. In minutes they were in country, nice brick homes on large lots interspersed on both sides of a road that dipped between high red-clay banks. Pine trees clung precariously to the banks' edges, looking much like Stooges about to tumble off something. They came to a huge hill that bottomed over a fairly big creek. Great bike run. He'd be doing a hundred miles an hour when he hit the bridge.

They stopped at a T marked 'Damascus Road.' Sounded Biblical and, sure enough, there was a little white building in the distance with a cross painted on its side, all alone in the middle of a giant field covered with low-growth plants. Butch pointed at them. "What are those?"

"Peanuts."

Well, of course. They came to another intersection with a small building perched next to it. 'Bark's Store,' the sign read, and Butch glimpsed a big black chow dog panting in the shade of the store's overhang. Must be where the name came from. Another steep descent but dad slowed about three-quarters down and turned up a driveway. "Here we are," he said.

It was a thickly wooded lot, pine trees every four feet or so all the way to the edge. A row of junipers grew together on the left side of the driveway and blocked the view; a garage faced them. Dad drove to the end of the junipers and the house appeared.

Not bad, all brick with some green siding here and there. A patio immediately next to the driveway had an iron well-pump. Butch wondered if it worked. Attached to the side of the house was a screened-in porch. As Butch watched, the screen door opened and a man and woman stepped out, smiling. "Keep quiet," dad warned and ground his cigarette on the gravel as he got out. Butch followed.

Hot. Oh man, hot. Butch looked yearningly at the pump,

"Mr. Winters?" Dad walked up to the man. "I'm Deats. Called you yesterday?"

"Yes, yes." The man shook dad's hand vigorously. "Good to meet ya." He flourished his free hand around. "Well, this is it. Care to come inside?"

Dad followed them up the porch, Butch trailing. "Is this your boy?" Mrs. Winters smiled down at him.

"That's Butch," dad acknowledged and Butch nodded at the dark-haired woman. "Well, it's a real pleasure to meet yewwww," she drew out the last word.

They tended to hang on to syllables around here, didn't they? "Nice to meet you, too." Butch shook her proffered hand, cutting his words properly.

"Oh, you are some Yankees, ain't you?" she gushed and Butch frowned.

"Maybe he is, I ain't," dad growled and that got all three of them laughing.

"I'm not a Yankee. I'm from Oklahoma!" Butch was indignant. Jeez, what's with these Alabama people? But all that did was get them laughing harder. Apparently, this Yankee/Reb labeling was funny stuff.

They went through the screened-in porch into a kitchen. Hot in there, too, but a breeze flowed through the house. "Attic fan," Mr. Winters explained, "Keeps the air going. Gets downright cold in here after dark."

Not now, though, and Butch gravitated to an open window so he wouldn't burst into flames.

The kitchen flanked a big den, then two bedrooms at the end of the house separated by a bathroom. A living and dining room were on the left side of the house with a picture window in both overlooking a big front lawn, the road, and a huge fenced-in pasture climbing up a pine-clogged hill.

Overall not bad, but it still wasn't home. Couldn't dad see that?

They trooped out to the screened-in porch. Mr. Winters and dad took the two rocking chairs while the missus sat on a wicker stool. Butch jumped-sat on a freezer backed against the wall. Mr. Winters clicked on a ceiling fan before settling.

Ah. Butch leaned into the sudden breeze; now that was comfortable.

"Do you want some iced tea?" Mrs. Winter asked and Butch nodded gratefully. She left and came back with a tray of sweating, very tall tea-and-ice-filled red plastic glasses and everybody took one. Butch sipped and almost choked. Jeez, worse than Beatrice's! He sat the glass down hastily.

She caught it and smiled. "We like our tea real sugary here."

No kidding, lady.

Mr. Winter flipped a hand at the yard. "It's one and a half acres, mostly pine, some hickory. They's woods all around and, over there," he pointed vaguely toward the left, "is a creek," said as 'crick.' "That there." He pointed at a weathered gray shed against the back of the lot. "Is where we keep the tools."

"How's your water?" dad asked and he and Mr. Winters went into some kind of technical discussion.

Butch stared at the distant shed and all the trees beyond. No doubt, Comanche lurked in the thick, brambly woods. He scrutinized the border, expecting to see a hostile red face peer at him from the poison-colored undergrowth. Spanish moss shrouded the trees, thicker than the stuff near Joel One's house. These definitely walked around at night.

Mr. Winters gestured past a distant tree so moss-covered it was barely recognizable. "They's a peanut field about a mile straight back. Makes good dove hunting." Dad's eyebrows rose and he and Mr. Winters got into another technical discussion.

"Are there any kids around here?" Butch asked Mrs. Winters.

"We don't have any children." The sweet smile again but Butch detected a bit of a tremor. Why not? he almost asked but the tremor stayed him.

"No, I mean, other kids, like neighbors."

She frowned. "Well, no, not really. The old couple 'cross the street, the McDonald's, have some grandkids over from time to time. I see 'em in the pasture every once in a while but you be careful because there's an old well out there and Mr. McDonald has a bad tempered bull, too."

Really? "Old McDonald had a farm" suddenly ran through his head.

She continued, "Mr. McDonald's nephew lives in the trailer over at the end of the pasture. Did you see that? No? Well, he and his wife just had a little baby but I'm guessin' that wouldn't do you much good." She looked at him with sympathy. "Other than the little school over in Yoman," she made a vague outward pointy finger, "I'm afraid there isn't anyone for you to play with. We're pretty isolated out here."

No kidding, lady. Butch wondered, again, why no children. Didn't she want company? With her husband gone all day plowing peanut fields or weaving cotton, whatever he did, who did she talk to? A woman this sweet needed someone to be sweet to, and there was only so much of that a husband could take. "Aren't you lonely?" he asked.

288

"Oh, heaven's no," she laughed, flitting a palm to her heart. "I'm always at the church and we go to bingo and we have some good friends in Opp. And there's always the party line."

Party line? Butch had a sudden vision of people dancing the conga up and down the road, all wearing silly hats and blowing streamers. She must have seen his confusion. "That's the telephone," she explained, "You can pick it up at any time and there's six or seven gals gabbing away on it. If you want to call somebody, you ask if they're on the line or not. If they ain't, you ask everyone to hang up so you can call but you can be sure they'll all be back on listening when you connect through."

The phones here were walkie-talkies? Amazing. "Guess you have to be careful about what you say," Butch observed.

"Oh indeed, indeed," she laughed and got up for more tea.

"Can I go outside?" Butch asked dad, who lit a cigarette and offered one to Mr. Winters, who waved it off. "Don't smoke."

An adult who didn't smoke? What was wrong with him?

"Smart," dad said, "These things'll kill you."

"Can I?"

Dad shrugged noncommittally and Mr. Winters said, "There's a goldfish pond over on the side of the house," and pointed that way.

Butch jumped up and out, wanting to avoid another glass of iced syrup, giving the pump handle an affectionate pat as he went around. He'd probably have to get buckets of water from it.

That would be cool.

The sun ravaged and he moved close to the house, grabbing what bits of shade it offered. The front yard was treeless and bigger than Butch and Tommy's front and back yards combined. Could field an entire baseball team here, play a great game of freeze tag. He smiled at a sudden vision of Cindy and Art and him shrieking all over this yard trying to catch each other. He evaluated the porch, a tall brick edifice, for hide-and-seek potential. It'd do, but the openness of the yard made it pretty obvious.

Trees bunched on the side put Butch immediately in shade and coolness. He sighed in relief. The ground was a carpet of brown pine needles so thick it gave under his weight and might cushion any fall from a tree limb. That had possibilities. The pond was under the trees and had that stupid boy-peeing statue right in the middle of it, water flowing in a tight, tough stream from his wiener. Butch was embarrassed. Statue boy, though, seemed proud, maybe because of the arc and distance. Butch looked at the statue's wiener and felt uncomfortable. He bet Joel II would love it.

A goldfish surfaced, a big one, and popped its mouth. Two more showed up, one of them black and white, weird colors for a goldfish. Fascinated, Butch extended his hand and the zebra broke surface, caressing his finger a bit. He giggled and searched around for something to feed them but all he could find were pine needles. The goldfish followed him around the pond as he searched for something else and he threw in some bits of green moss, but they rejected that.

"Sorry, guys," he said and splayed his hands, but they remained expectant. Persistent little buggers.

He followed the tree line, ward against sun, down to the road and stopped at a rather steep ditch. It ran the entire length of the front yard to a big sewer pipe sticking out from under the driveway, and then picked up on the other side all the way back up to Bark's Store. There were big rocks scattered all through it and Butch clambered down to get a better look.

Wow! The rocks had shell fossils and lots of embedded crystals! Butch was examining them when he heard a car coming. A pickup truck, leaning a bit to the right, descended the hill, its bed closed by a homemade wooden fence. The sun glared off the windshield and Butch shaded his eyes to get a better look. The truck came opposite and slowed. Three teenagers wearing dusty straw hats and work shirts with the sleeves rolled up leaned forward and stared at Butch with pure malevolence. Exactly like he'd imagined back in Selma.

They frowned at Butch and looked at each other and laughed. Butch's face flamed as the truck lurched, picking up speed. Butch stepped out of the ditch so he could watch them go. As the fence on the bed cleared his vision, he saw all three of them against the back windshield still staring at him and grinning. Butch looked down at his jeans and golf shirt and Keds. Did he look that weird?

He heard cows mooing and located them across the road. Three or four brown ones walked single file down a trail on the top part of a pine-covered hill. Bringing up the rear was a gigantic black bull with heavy horns drooping from both sides of its head.

Wow, big.

The bull was pushing at one of the last cows, which hurried away. Butch shook his head. The Wicked Thing lived in cows, too.

The parade crossed a rise that bridged a rather steep gully running across the base of the pine hill in both directions. The bull herded his wives into the middle of the pasture and then walked right up to the fence. It snorted a couple of times, which signaled a bad temper, and gazed down the road as if it wanted to head that way. It probably could because the fence was just three thin pieces of wire running through some kind of ceramic holders hammered into weathered posts.

Flimsy.

Butch nervously watched the bull, which could snap those wires with a simple horn toss and trample Butch into hamburger.

He heard a puppy yapping happily and squinted to find it. Ah, there, at a yellow trailer about a football field-and-a-half away surrounded by a white picket fence, probably to keep the bull out. It had a nicely trimmed yard with flowers growing in various beds. Sheets hung from a clothesline beside the trailer and Butch spotted the puppy jumping and snapping at them as they flapped in the slight breeze. Butch laughed. The puppy was having a real good time.

The trailer door opened and a man stepped out. He had a crew cut and wore a short sleeve shirt and dark slacks; some kind of salesman, Butch supposed. The man stared at the puppy.

Uh, oh, you're in trouble now, gonna get a whippin'. Butch felt sorry but had to grin. Puppies were funny.

The man raised his arm and pointed it at the puppy. Butch blinked. Hey, wait, was that a gun?

Smoke filled the man's hand a split second before *Bam*! smacked into Butch's ears. The puppy jerked a split second before its yelp reached him. *Bam*! Yelp! *Bam*! Yelp! *Bam*! until the puppy lay still. The man looked at it for a second and then walked back inside.

Butch couldn't breathe. If a puppy playing with sheets invoked the death penalty around here, then surely a kid standing in a ditch deserved worse. He fully expected the man to reemerge, locate him, and start shooting, then drag his corpse into the pasture where the bull would stomp and stomp until all that remained of Butch was a bloody patch of ground. Maybe that's why the three kids in the truck had grinned—they knew he was about to die.

Shaking, Butch backed up the ditch slope, trying to blend in so the man, peering out the window to see who else needed chastisement, wouldn't see him. He reached the tree line and ran straight for the house absolutely certain a gun was zeroing between his shoulder blades. In terror, he reached the patio and threw himself onto the porch.

"Boy, what are you doing? And what were those shots?" Dad asked, more menace than concern in his voice.

"The man across the street," Butch gasped between breaths, "the man in the trailer, he shot a puppy!"

Mrs. Winters put a hand to her heart. "My Lord!" she said, extending the last syllable, "What on earth for?"

"Because it was tearing some sheets off the clothesline!"

The two men grunted and looked at each other. "Deserved it, then," dad concluded and they went back to talking business. Butch stared at them and then at the woman, who shrugged, picked up the glasses, and went inside.

He stayed on the patio after that, within easy reach of the porch should the murderous salesman appear around the corner. Not that he expected rescue from the porch dwellers; apparently, they approved of puppy shooting. They might approve the shooting of children, too, if the salesman had a convincing enough complaint.

"Your boy was in the ditch!" and dad would say, "Let him have it!" Bam! pistol emptied into Butch's stomach. The porchers might do it themselves for some other perceived breach, such as Butch squeaking the pump handle, so he played quietly with random pebbles.

About fifteen hours later, dad got up, shook hands with the man and woman, and came out to the patio. "Let's go," he said.

Butch scrambled to the car, barely attending to his goodbyes and thank yous, intent on escaping the salesman. He didn't resume breathing until they had pulled far from Bark's Store with no indication they were followed.

"Nice place," dad said.

Butch said nothing. Dad had already rendered his verdict so it was pointless to express concerns. Besides, yes, it was a nice place; that is, if you ignored the bull, the puppy murderer, and the wilderness.

"Hope you liked it because I bought it."

Might as well have hit him with a bat. "Stop," Frank whispered.

"And I've got other good news." Dad paused for dramatic effect while Butch attempted to find the first good news. "Your mom, Cindy, and Art are coming to live with us here."

"What?" From sheer terror to soaring joy in one second. How does the heart cope?

"Yep." Dad sounded pleased. "I talked to your mom last night and she agreed."

About a million questions raced through Butch's mind, the primary being 'hey, dad, why didn't you let me talk to Mom, too?' but he summarized it with, "So you're not getting a divorce?"

"No."

"But..." and Butch froze because dad had turned murder-eye his way. Expressing a conviction that dad's behavior over the past two months was eminently divorceable would, no doubt, get a pistol emptied into his stomach. Change subject. Now.

"So when are they coming?"

"They're not. We're going back to get them. Tomorrow."

Tomorrow. Oh my God, home, actual home, tomorrow. Mt. Scott in the distance and horny toads running around the driveway, Tommy and he stalking each other like Krauts and GIs in the field in front of Carl's and Carl's, itself, with the latest *X-Men*—please don't be sold out, please—and Cha Cha running around the fence trying to grab his ankles and Cindy and he playing hopscotch on the sidewalk and sitting on the storm cellar watching the sunset, oh man. He was getting his summer back. He was getting his life back. "Good," he said, the word not really conveying his immense satisfaction.

All's right with the world.

Sort of. "But then we're coming back here?"

"Yep." Dad made the turn for the Boll Weevil monument.

"But why?" Butch couldn't help sounding desperate.

Dad was suddenly irritated. "You like eating, right?"

Well, yeah, hamburgers and milkshakes, especially. What's that got to do with the price of tea in China? "Huh?"

"My job is here. You know, the job that pays for your food?" and he poked Butch hard in the stomach.

Butch squirmed away and looked at dad. So the last two

months was about getting a job? That's it? Dorey and Marianne and Beatrice and Vonda, merely part of an employment search, ha ha, no big deal, hope you had a good time, boy, I sure did.

No, dad, I didn't.

Butch had corpse wings beating against his chest every minute of the day now. All those nights spent alone in a dark apartment or house with boogeymen crawling around outside while you were off doing whatever...

Sex, Butch, he was having sex with Dorey and Beatrice and the black girl and who knows who else.

...had kicked the supports out from under him, dissolved his surety, and taught him this life was an uncertain, precarious, unsafe thing.

But, according to you, it wasn't that at all, it was just a leisurely search for employment while, incidentally, stopping off at various wives.

Something inside Butch wadded up and blew away, landing somewhere behind the car. Butch turned and caught a glimpse of it waving frantically in the heat shimmer.

He looked at the fields running in the distance, red and dusty and beaten by the sun. Dad, this place. So empty. So flat.

So not home.

But, Butch, you're getting your family back. Mom. Art. Cindy, his Cindy. There were necessary reckonings, explanations demanded, wounds to be sutured, but oh, God, he was getting them back. A bull in the front yard and a puppy murderer across the street suddenly didn't seem so bad. They'd somehow protect each other, put up shields, the Avengers flying shotgun overhead. They'd keep the bull out of their yard, the salesman placated with sacrificial puppies, the three grinning teenagers on the road. They could walk through this wilderness unscathed, restore what was lost, make things like they used to be, all of them together...

Hey, wait a minute. "What about Dale?"

"What about her?"

"You didn't mention her."

Dad shrugged. "She left."

"Left?"

"Yes, left. She went to California with Carol to be a damn beatnik."

That had been Dale's plan but the divorce upended it, or so it seemed from the little information she conveyed during the phone call. Now that there was no divorce, off she goes. Without even a goodbye. "So she's not coming with us."

"Now how can she do that if she's in California?" Dad snapped.

"But..." his voice trailed. Rift. Disruption. Things would never be right again, would they?

"They never are," Frank whispered.

# CHAPTER 44

They left so early it was still night, Butch sleepy and wandering around the house and driveway bumping his suitcase along. "Can I help you with that?" Frank reached for the handle.

"Wake up," dad snarled and Frank, rather hastily, fled. Butch tilted the suitcase into the back and flopped on the passenger seat, sighing with relief, instantly unconscious.

It was a hot, grueling drive. Butch slowly came to. Dad bent over the steering wheel with mad purpose and Butch thought it wise to go invisible and stayed out of view except when they stopped for frantic gas and frantic C-Rations, no words, other than functional ones, spoken. Butch perked up at Vicksburg. "What's all that?" he asked.

"Monuments to the battle here."

"Why so many?"

"It was a pretty long battle. The townspeople ate rats to stay alive."

Butch's stomach flipped and he peered among the cement columns of sword-lofting generals to see if rats were memorialized like boll weevils. No.

They crossed the Mississippi and Butch looked hard but Tom and Huck still weren't there. Arkansas was a green monotony. The sun went down. Butch fought sleep, but driving for 972 straight hours, stopping only for gas and potty, was too much.

Frank sat on the edge of the wrestling swamp, white miasma drifting about. "You're going to leave me," he moaned.

Butch pulled out of the muck and sat next to him. "I'll never leave you." A consoling hand on the shoulder.

"You'll have your family back."

"Won't matter." Butch picked up a pebble and threw it in a pool. It made an oily splash.

"It's still very dangerous," Frank said, his face somber.

Butch woke. Art stood next to him. "Who's Frank?" he asked.

Butch sat up. He was undressed and in his bed, his own, real bed. "Friend of mine," he said, "How'd I get here?"

"Mommy put you in last night when you guys came back. You were asleep. Are we really going to Alabama?"

"Yes."

"What's it like?"

"Lots of trees," he said, "and there's a murder bull living across the street."

Art's eyes widened and Butch, satisfied, pushed him out of the way, dressed and peed and walked into Dale's room. The closet was empty. All the albums were gone. When you get to California, Dale, play them real loud so I can hear.

He walked through to the kitchen. Mom was taking something out of the oven. "Mom," he said.

"Oh, Butch," she put down the hot thing and folded him into her and he was crushed, unable to breathe, but it was okay. He felt waves of relief and true welcome coming off her, not a hint of the usual indifference. He smiled. She pulled back and kissed him on the cheeks. "Are you all right?" she asked.

"Yes."

"Did he hurt you?"

How to answer that? The usual slapping around, Mom. And, oh yes, I've acquired the Wicked Thing. "No," he replied.

"So where did you go?"

"Pawpaw's first. I didn't like that. Then we crossed the Mississippi and we went to Newport News and we were there for a while and then we went to Alabama." Glossing over a few things on the way, Mom.

"Who else did you meet?"

Warning. Minefield. Butch shifted uncomfortably. "Joel. And another boy named Joel. He was weird."

"Anybody else?" She bore into him, mouth trembling.

So, the interrogation begins. Ve haff vays to make you talk, old man. Butch hesitated, looking for escape. You know, buddy, you could just tell her—yes, Mom, you already know of Dorey but there were other wives and he was having sex with them. I never saw them having sex but there was strong evidence, especially during the Night of Frank: a black girl, Mom, and the way dad talks about black people. And, oh yes, I have another sister, a goddess. And I was left alone many nights by myself, also strong evidence of sex taking place in other locations between dad and other women. Yes, Mom I know what sex is. I had it, you know. "Just Dorey," he said.

Her hands tightened on his arms, hurting. "Are you sure?"

Ow.

Her eyes blazed with mad lights, reaching down and pulling The Truth up to his mouth, but he said nothing. He had this sudden urge to protect dad. It was perverse. It was wrong. But you did not go on this trip, Mom, and all that happened is forbidden you.

"No!" he said with the kids' Tone of Avoidance and yanked free, stepping back and hearing something rip. He checked his sleeve and then realized it wasn't something tangible—it was the tear between Mom and him, grown permanent.

She must have felt it, too, because she looked utterly helpless, as though she could see him drift away, the ice floe hazy in the distance. Her face was down, the lines gathered at the top of her throat and Butch thought she would cry. Maybe he would, too, but why? They'd been on separate ice floes their whole lives.

"Where's Cindy?" he asked.

"She went outside to play. Are you hungry?" Just like that, Mom mode, the widening gulf pointedly ignored.

Butch accepted a doughnut and went out the back. He stood in the full morning light and breathed. Ah, the honeysuckle, the gathering heat...

Without the humidity, thank you very much, Alabama,

...the storm cellar a baby mountain in the middle of the yard, grape arbor already buzzing with bees and locusts, the storage shed against the fence bordering the alley. He smiled. Home. He looked over into Tommy's yard eagerly but no one was there.

A black-and-white furball walked out from behind the shed. "Cha Cha!" Butch called. Startled, the dog went to his one-foot raised position, which always made Butch laugh, and then bounded toward him at about 175 mph. Butch met him at the base of the stairs, the dog spinning and jumping and rolling and barking. Cha Cha had not forgotten him and was so joyful, so happy.

He hugged the dog, which licked his face and tried to do the Cha Cha on his leg but Butch pushed him away. "I know what that is now," he told him.

They played for a while, wrestled and chased each other around the yard, Cha Cha grabbing sticks for tugs of war. The sun rose higher and so did Butch's heart. He gave the dog a pat and walked out the gate to the front of the house. The catalpa trees swayed and puffy clouds went by, turning into tanks and Indian scouts and spaceships. He smiled. Home.

He knocked on Tommy's door, who answered. "Hey, squirt."

"Hey, beanpole."

"So, what'd you do?"

Butch shrugged. "Drove around. A lot."

"Sounds reeeel exciting. Did you hear what happened to the Thing?"

"No."

"He joined the Frightful Four."

Butch was shocked. "Get out of here."

Tommy was grim. "No, true. It's a good issue. And I got the Annual, too, with the wedding."

Butch licked his lips. "Can we read them?"

"Not right now. I gotta go shoe shopping with my mom," and he rolled his eyes as he rolled the last word, kids' Tone of Exasperation. Butch grinned, despite his disappointment. Tommy punched him in the shoulder. "Good to have you back, squirt."

"Good to be back, beanpole. You seen my sister?"

"Saw her walking up to the field. Did you see all the sewer pipe they put in there?"

"No. I was asleep when we got here."

"Go look. It's neat. Come back after lunch and we'll catch up with everyone." Everyone, of course, being the Marvel Universe.

"Cool," Butch said and noted Tommy's appreciation of the word. "'Nuff said."

"See ya, true believer," and closed the door.

The sun was building and Butch squinted through the heat waves, the kind that warmed the soul, not sapped the strength, Alabama. He strolled toward the fields, center of kid social life on

Lincoln Avenue. He cleared the last house and stopped, amazed. In the smaller field on the right, the one that fronted Sheridan Road, were about 3000 big concrete pipes. Most were laid end to end, creating an endless series of tunnels, the rest perpendicular. Cindy was on top of them in the middle of the field.

"Hey!" he called.

She turned. "Butch!" she cried and waved frantically. "Come up!"

The mechanics of cement-pipe climbing took a bit to master, but Butch caught on and wriggled his way to a standing position. It took longer to figure the off-balances required to jump from pipe to pipe and must have been amusing to watch because Cindy was giggling by the time he got to her. She hugged him. "I thought you were going to fall off."

"I thought I was, too," Butch said, and then gazed at the undulating sea of pipe tops. "What are they doing?"

"They're putting in some kind of sewer all up and down Sheridan, but for now, it's pretty cool." She reached down and patted the top of the pipe affectionately.

"You like that word, too, huh?" Butch helped her pat the pipe.

"Yeah." She gazed at him and his heart flopped. His Cindy. "Have you heard the word 'fuck'?" she asked.

Butch frowned. "No. What's that?" It sounded vaguely sinister.

"That's when a boy and girl are in the hallway and she backs into him while he's leaning against the locker."

Butch nodded. He'd seen that before. "It sounds like sex," he said.

Her eyes narrowed. "How do you know about sex?"

"I had sex." He told her about dad's instructions and his experience with Marianne.

She was open-mouthed. "So, well, how was it?" she asked.

He shrugged. "I don't really know," he confessed.

"Dale was worried about sex," she said.

"Hmm?"

"Before she left." Cindy absently traced something with her foot. "She said she had to go before all the sex started again."

"What does that mean?"

Cindy shrugged. "I don't know. She was on the phone. I think it had something to do with dad."

"What?"

Another shrug.

Butch considered. "He was having a lot of sex while we were riding around."

"Who with?"

"All these women. Do you know we have a sister?"

"What?" So Butch told her about Vonda and Beatrice and Dorey, but he left out the black girl. And he didn't tell her about Joel II, either. Both seemed a bit too embarrassing.

"Don't tell Mom," he said.

"Huh?"

"About Vonda or everything else dad was doing," he clarified, "Don't tell Art, either."

She snorted. "What, you think I'm stupid?"

He grinned. "Yeah. And ugly, too."

She socked him and they were off, chasing around the top and then jumped down and went inside the cement caverns, screaming to hear their echoes, and had a long-running hide-and-seek through the tunnels. They played Pirate Queen and Moon Queen and Lost Under the Earth. After a while, they were back on top, basking in the sun.

"So what's Alabama like?" she asked.

"Hot. Worse than this."

"Is it fun?"

He shrugged. "I don't really know. It's way out there. There's a lot of animals. The guy across the street is mean. And crazy."

"Mom didn't want dad to come back, you know."

He sat up. "Really? Did she want me to stay away, too?"

She puckered a brow. "I don't know. She was talking to Lynn's mom and I couldn't hear everything. Lynn has a boyfriend now," she said that last slyly.

"Huh?" Great. "Who?"

"Chucky."

"No way."

"Uhm hmm!" Kids' Tone of Confirmation. "She even kissed him."

"Humph!" Butch was stung. "Why does she like Chucky?"

She shrugged. "He's funny, I guess. Why? Do you like Lynn?" The slyness heightened.

"Noooooo."

"Yes, you do!" She was in triumph. "You always have. Butchie loves Lynn, Butchie loves Lynn!" in the hated sing-song.

"Man!" he squawked, trying to hide the truth of it, "Stop!"

She did and they lapsed into sun coma, savoring the heat and sizzling and eternity of summer. "So, did she?" Butch asked again.

"What?"

"Mom. Did she want me to come back or not?"

"Well, yeah, but…"

A warning tone sounded in Butch's head. "But? But what?"

She was silent and Butch went on an elbow, staring at her. "What?"

"I'm not supposed to say."

"Huh?" Butch didn't know whether to be scared or baffled at this suddenly odd conversation. He chose the easier stance. "What are you talking about?"

She let out a long exasperated breath and crooked her arm over her eyes so Butch couldn't see them. "Mom and I were talking about what we were going to do and I said we had to get you back from dad"—he warmed, and not from the sun. Good ole Cindy—"and she said that may not be legal because he's your dad."

Complete and utter bafflement now. "Who's my dad?"

"Dad."

"Dad."

"Right."

"What are you talking about?"

"Dad is your dad."

He blinked. "Well, yeah, I know that."

"No, you don't. You're really my brother."

"Well, yeah. Jeez, why you being silly?"

"No, no." She shook her head savagely. "You're not getting it. You're not adopted. Well, you are, but dad is your dad."

It took a moment, but then an iceberg flowed up from the ground and encased his heart. "What?"

She nodded, solemn. "It's true. Mom said dad got their housemaid in Germany pregnant and made Mom adopt you."

"What? What?" The iceberg squeezed his heart to a frozen atom, a trip hammer slammed his chest, and he could not breathe. No. No.

"So you're really my brother, you really, really are." She engulfed him, sobbing, hugged him to her with great love and relief and all Butch could think was No! It can't be true. I cannot have the Beast within. And then the word formed, black, ugly, dripping with blood...

Bastard.

He'd sort of misapplied it, hadn't he?

The earth whirled, sickening and broken, nothing on which to stand, assumptions and protections gone. The scaly beast spread its wicked wings and crowed, just crowed, its claws shredded Butch's stomach and kidneys and threw them in the air and gulped them down with glee, its eyes saying, "One of mine, you are!" He'd thought dad had merely awakened the corruption, but it was far worse than that:

Dad had implanted it.

She released him. "I'm glad you're my brother. I really am."

"But..." and what could he say? Yes, God, Cindy, you beauty, you wonder, I am your real brother, not just a reasonable facsimile, and we are, now, true bond and kith forever. We stand against the dark winds and monsters of this world, hand in hand, shoulder to shoulder, sword and spear leveled at the wolves.

But, Cindy, I am evil spawn.

"You okay?"

So many things suddenly became crystal. Mom. Her stares from darkened doorways, the way she turned from him, threw an extra insult or slap...

Oh God. Of course. He was the demon in her closet, the creature peeking from under her bed grinning and slavering, the Wicked Thing perched on her bed board crowing and calling and slashed her every single time Butch walked by or sassed or cried. No wonder she kept him at arm's length. He was a leper.

He turned his leper head and stared into Cindy's sea-green eyes and saw worry and sadness and acceptance. Acceptance. Of the leper. The shield grew longer, the spear sharper, and he was the leper king. He slipped his hand into hers and they both laid back shoulder to shoulder, sword and spear leveled at the wolves, to watch clouds build and float by. She pointed at one. "That's a fat gramom with a bag of groceries,"

"I see it. That one's a dog wagging its tail."

"Yeah!" she laughed, "it is. There's a sad kid looking for his mom."

Goosebumps. "It's Frank Vaughn."

"What?" She sat up and peered at the formation. "Why would he look for his mom? He should be scared of her."

"He is. But he's also lonely."

"How do you know?"

"We talk."

She went pop-eyed at him and then at the cloud. It covered the sun and the sudden breeze, distinctly cooler, made Butch smile: Frank saying hello.

"Your sister's cute," Frank said.

"I know," Butch acknowledged.

"She's going to have lots of boyfriends." Frank dug into the pool at the edge of the swamp.

"Probably." Butch felt the stirrings of jealousy.

"It's not going to be good," Frank concluded.

"Hey!"

Butch, startled, opened his eyes. Cindy had stood up, waving frantically. "There it is!" she called and pointed at the road.

Butch followed her point. A green Mayflower van trundled down Lincoln, picking its way through parked cars. "What's that?" Butch asked.

"Our moving truck," she answered, watching its progress.

"What?"

"Yeah. We're leaving tomorrow." She looked at him. "Didn't you know that?"

Gasping, Butch slid off the pipe and frantically weaved his way out to the road, Cindy calling, "Wait up!" In the distance, he watched the van pull to a stop in front of the house and then back up on the wrong side of the street until it was partly in the driveway. Lots of people came out of their houses to look. One came out of Butch's house and shook hands with the driver. That was dad.

"No," Butch breathed.

"Yep." Cindy caught up, standing solemnly beside him. "They're supposed to finish tonight."

"It's too soon."

She shrugged. "We gotta go."

"It's too soon." Way too soon. He figured he had at least a week, maybe two, even a year before this happened. Enough time to catch up on Peter Parker and Reed Richards and Professor X, play ten or twenty more games of army and Civil War, try to learn chess, try to have sex with Lynn, ride around the block at night chasing bats. But, not anymore. No time anymore, to say goodbye.

The leper king half ran, half walked down the block. "Where you goin'?" Cindy called, but he ignored her, pulling out of range.

He stood at the open back of the van, staring inside. It was a cave, the front partially lit by the morning sun, the rest stretched to a dim infinity. It could swallow a person's entire life, chew on it for a while, then throw it up in some strange place. Once that happened, everything would be wrong.

"Hey, kid!" A jovial man in gray overalls emerged from the back murk pulling several straps behind him. Probably used to bind kids inside, hot, dying of thirst, mourning the world most recently abandoned while the van swayed and screeched across the country. Butch took a wary step back.

"You wanna help?" the man, big, gray-haired, amused eyes, asked him. "We can always use another strong back."

"He couldn't lift a feather," dad snorted behind Butch. "Won't do anything like real work. Now if you have a book you want read..." and dad chuckled.

Butch turned and stared at him. The mirth was real. The gray man laughed, too, but uneasily.

"Comin' through," a voice called and a teenager with longish blond hair and Marlboro Man features came up hefting the deer head, forcing Butch and dad to the side. The gray man eyed the teenager. "If you drop that," he observed, "you'd best take off running."

Dad and the gray man laughed and the teenager grinned and took the head into the murky back and emerged, seconds later, empty-handed. Butch was undone. If the deer head moved, then they all did.

"We're leaving now?" Butch asked dad.

"Yep."

"You never said anything like that."

"Like what?" Dad's voice took on the danger tone.

Butch didn't care. "That we were just packing up and leaving."

"And what'd you think we were going to do?"

"Well," Butch blustered because, really, what had he

thought? "That we were going to, well." He made a futile gesture. "You know, stay for a bit."

"And how can we do that?" Dad using the 'stupid kid' tone. The gray man wisely moved to the back. "I got a job waitin'. We gotta get settled. You kids gotta get ready for school."

All logical answers. So what? "But we're home now."

"No, we ain't." Dad was obviously irritated. "We'll be 'home,'" dad emphasized the word, "tomorrow."

Butch shook his head. "That isn't home."

"It is now."

"No, it isn't. This is." And Butch's gesture took in Lincoln Avenue.

Dad moved toward him threateningly. "Boy, I'm getting a little tired of your sass." The teenager wisely followed the gray man.

Butch quailed, anticipating a blow, but did not move. He stared at the reddening dad. Dad. His Dad. His son, imbued with the dad essence of wickedness and sex and hate. He was not safe. He was not immune. He could not be different, Dorey, not anymore; he would not think of others because he must carry on his dark father's work for he was the leper king, inheritor of wickedness and red-eyed leers, world without end, amen. He was hate. He was rage. Act the part. "You just can't wait to get back there, can you?" he sneered.

Dad's jaw actually dropped. "What?"

"Can't wait to see Beatrice again, huh? Or maybe someone else?" Butch at least didn't mention the black girl, which would guarantee his murder. As it was, he braced for a good slapping.

"Boy!" Dad hissed, "You better watch your mouth!"

Butch noted the panic his words induced and warmed to the subject. "What's your hurry? Got a date?"

It wasn't exactly a slap, more a push. He'd had worse. Butch bounced off the side of the van, which hurt more, but that may have been incidental. He rubbed his elbow and watched as dad stalked away. This was usually the part where dad went in to grab the bullwhip or a gun or club then returned to finish the job, but the set of dad's shoulders conveyed retreat, not war. He wanted to get away from Butch's mouth, not break Butch's mouth, which was a far more subdued reaction than expected.

Struck a nerve, had he?

The Wicked Thing grinning at Butch from between dad's shoulder blades confirmed it. Underneath dad's seeming concern for the logistics of moving, the bat wings fluttered, whispered of Beatrices and black girls and a whole new territory of Doreys to conquer. Dad could lay waste to the countryside while keeping Butch, who knew his secrets, who was his secret, and a befuddled Mom and Art prisoner in Alabama woods that dripped pestilence and heat and depravity. Dale would never find them. And Cindy, his Cindy… the creeping rot would invade her, turning her insides green. Because bat wings beat in dad's chest. And now beat in the leper king's.

The Wicked Thing ruled. God had no power against it.

Butch gasped, shaken by the blasphemy. God warded innocent children with His Strong Safe Arms, frowning at the bullies and teasers. But God could not protect you from the bigger crimes, like murder and the moms who committed it, nor from the Wicked Thing. It was stronger, turning dads into slavering beasts who stalked the Beatrices and Doreys and German housemaids and conceived Vondas and Butchs. Vonda, in her time, would yield to the groping, slobbering embraces of boys impelled by their own wicked things and Butch, when his hour came round at last, would be one of those boys, sacrifice to Moloch.

It was the way of the world, the way of all flesh, and the embryo bat wings in Butch's own chest, the ones that had tasted sex and wanted more, the ones dad had injected, would grow and overwhelm and he would join dad in his nightly hunts, father and son together at last, while other sons came for Cindy, the Wicked Thing standing above it all and nodding its red-eyed approval. Dale was already their victim. And Butch was next.

God would not save him.

Butch was hellspawn, damned, assured of God's wrath and an eternity in the Lake of Fire next to the fibbers and cheats and dad.

He couldn't breathe. How unfair, how completely unfair of God to allow a beast with more power than Scripture to reside in his heart. It was a long life, in theory, and one momentary succumbing assured your damnation. The streets of Heaven, then, were reserved for those of iron will and golden purity but it must be a sparse population made up mostly of those who died long before the Wicked Thing spurred them toward a naked Marianne, fumbling at her parts.

But Frank dwelt in a swamp and walked alone and mourned in mist and mud, and he had not succumbed. At least, as far as Butch knew. Maybe he'd merely thought the Wicked Thing for a second or two, and that was enough to earn separation from God. At least it's not the Lake of Fire, Frank.

"You all right, kid?"

Butch looked up. The gray man stood above him, the teenager hovering behind, genuine concern on the man's face, but it was pointless. He could not help. Butch shrugged, pushed off the curb, and walked down the street. At the corner, he turned toward the school.

He approached Lynn's house and paused, wondering if he should knock. Lynn's mom had never been very welcoming...

and now you know why, demonspawn

...so, no. Besides, he didn't want to find Lynn and Chuckie playing kissy-face in the living room.

Head towards Joseph and Maria's? Joseph was always good for a laugh, even if he was like a girl...

Hmm. He and Joel II might make good friends.

...but Butch didn't want to see Maria in her Catholic schoolgirl uniform and ever-present cross while the Wicked Thing fluttered in his chest. It would mean consignment to an even lower level of hell, if that were possible.

He passed the park and considered going in but it was uncool to enter from the street. Kids got here by walking through the underground sewer pipes accessed at various strategically placed openings, mostly in alleys, and converging at the big culvert running the park's length. A scramble up the side and, presto, swings and merry-go-rounds and baseball fields galore. A game was going on right now, and Butch squinted at the players. He didn't recognize them and didn't want to tempt any bullying, at least not without Tommy here for protection, so he moved on.

He ended up on a swing in the strangely empty schoolyard, the sun turning slides and seesaws and merry-go-rounds into molten metal. An odd air of abandonment hung over the place. The yard breathed sorrow, yearning for the tramp of feet and screams of recess. Things were best in context and schoolyards thrived when the kids were prisoners of the education system, released in short bursts to vent enthusiasms contained by frowning teachers. It was a mutually supporting relationship; one without the other was a half shell.

Butch spun the swing a little, scuffing his toes and watching little dust clouds gather then whirlwind away. Two months ago he'd had a life, but it was gone now, flushed down the toilet, gone all gone, just like the toe whirlwinds. Dad had stolen it from him. Pursuing the call of the Wicked Thing, he had kidnapped Butch out of this world, imprisoned him with trolls, and taught him the dark arts. He had animated Butch's own Wicked Thing, one he had personally implanted one dark, rutting night in some German bedroom, chip off the old block now, ha ha! Lightning bolts playing across Frankenstein's monster, it's alive, it's alive! and every day the Wickedness grew stronger, crushing the child within.

Tainted. Unclean. The leper king.

So damned unfair.

"Tell me about it," Frank snorted from the swing next to him.

Butch looked over. Frank seemed more robust, with a little gleam of life in his eyes. "What do I do?" he asked.

"What can you do?" Frank scuffed out toe whirlwinds to match Butch's. "We're at the mercy of our parents." For a brief second, he grinned, and Butch watched as his face cracked open and half his cheekbone fell out. "Sorry," Frank said and pushed it back in.

"Does it hurt?"

"All the time."

"Is dad going to do that to me?"

Frank stared off to what Butch knew was the future. "No, not that," he said, "but he will destroy you."

"I don't want that to happen."

Frank shrugged. "Nothing you can do. Just try not to hurt other people."

"Will I?"

Frank looked again. "Yes." Pause. "Badly."

"I don't want to."

Frank said nothing.

They matched toe scuffs for a while then Butch asked, "Are you coming with me?"

Frank shook his head. "No. I'm going to stay here." He pointed at the monkey bars. "Right there. I always liked those."

Butch's sense of loss went nuclear. "You'll be lonely," he sobbed.

Frank patted him on the shoulder. "So will you."

Butch jerked awake and almost fell out of the swing. The sun descended and shadows reached out from the school coaxing him inside. He refused and stood and dusted himself and walked down the hill, heading... home.

# CHAPTER 45

Early.

In a flurry of bumped suitcases and sharp talk and the occasional slap, they ordered themselves into the Rambler. "Just one suitcase each," dad had barked, which wasn't that much of a problem for Butch because his most precious comics and the even more precious Joe, which he guarded from Art, were still packed from the first time. Cindy went through agonies trying to choose between Barbies and clothes while Art... well, Mom did his. Everything else went in the moving van.

Dad had set up the backward-facing seat and Butch and Cindy claimed it, triggering a wail from Art that earned the little brat a place between them. Butch vowed a thousand miles of elbow jabs and Wet Willies. Cindy was in charge of Indian burns, so the trip promised some diversion.

Cha Cha was settled next to a window in the middle seats and already had his head out, tongue lolling, dog joy. Dad and Mom had platformed the suitcases in an interesting way, allowing the placement of armies or precariously balanced board games or books and crayons to keep them occupied. Butch was examining the possibilities when dad and Mom got in. They were in mid-discussion of the route.

"We'll sleep in Big Salt tonight," dad said.

Butch groaned inwardly. Great, just great, Death Eye and Ricky and Carl, and a Belinda who'd been spoiled in a manner he now understood. The Wicked Thing pecked at his heart.

"Oh, boy," Cindy whispered excitedly in his ear, "We're

going to Mawmaw's!"

Butch stared at her. Yes, Mawmaw's your favorite, isn't she? But it's a honey-baited trap, Cin. The leper king must protect you, keep you away from the shed and Ricky and Carl. Keep the Wicked Thing at bay for as long as possible. Somehow.

Dawn was red and pink and Butch squinted at the clouds forming around the bowl of the earth. Mt. Scott was silhouetted against them, subdued blue in fire, and there was something final in it. His breath caught.

Someone tapped on the side window: Tommy, making roll down motions with his hand. Butch leaned over and did so.

"Hello, Tommy," Mom said to him, "come to say goodbye?" Dad, as usual, said nothing.

"Yes, ma'am," he answered, ever polite, and turned toward Butch. "Hey, squirt, thought you might like these." He reached through and gave Butch a stack of comics.

Butch leafed through them. New ones. *Strange Tales* #135, Nick Fury was back? *Magnus* #11, Beasts of Steel. *Tales to Astonish*, #135, the new Sub-Mariner series, and an *Avengers* with the Swordsman as the villain. At any other time, he'd be in paroxysm of joy, but this was consolation prize.

"Wow," Butch said, lackluster and toneless.

Tommy frowned at him. "You all right?"

No, Tommy, I'm not. My life has ended. I am losing you and my home and my surety and everything I thought I was. I am taint. I am... bastard. But there was boy code, and if he explained how his life had ended, how the joys of new comic books and bike rides and summer days had given way to a pestilence in his chest and a dad-enforced exile into shadowlands, then he would cry, an egregious code violation. His boyhood was already suspect and he didn't need relegation to Joseph or Joel Two status, even though this was an eminently cryable moment because, Tommy, my only and best friend, this is pretty much the last time we'll see each other for ever and ever... unless...

Unless all of this *was* just a lesson and Mom and dad were waiting until the moment right before Butch burst into tears and both would laugh and point and go, "Ha ha! Fooled ya!" and so would Art and Cindy, and punch his shoulders, "Ha! Ha!" and Dale would pop out of a nearby car and run up laughing and there he'd be, looking stupid—again—because it was just a lesson, that's all, about taking things for granted. You love this house? You love this neighborhood and the kids and school and Oklahoma and winter blizzards and grasshoppers and dust storms, do you, do you? How'd you feel if you lost it all?

Lost it all.

But the moving truck had already taken 95% of them away and Dale had already gone and the car was gassed up and packed and he'd learned nothing. Except how to survive.

Butch put on his best face. "Yeah, I'm good." He waved the stack of comics. "Thanks for these."

Tommy looked at him guardedly and backed from the car, looking gone, too. Something shriveled in his chest.

The car started, a hammer blow, and Butch gasped. They moved, slow at first, dad picking out the road through the morning glare but gaining speed and there they were, too soon, around the curve toward Sheridan, Tommy now just a far figure on the sidewalk, quickly lost to sight.

"I'm excited," Cindy whispered in his ear, the tremor in her voice underscoring that. Butch looked at her. Don't be, he thought. They turned at the corner and there it was, Mt. Scott framed in the back windshield. Butch couldn't help it; he started to cry.

Silently, unobserved by Art who was already asleep and by dad and Mom who were intent on where they were going, not what they were leaving behind. Cindy saw, of course, and put silent arms around him.

Goodbye, Frank, have fun on the monkey bars. Come visit some time.

The mountain flared in red and gold and, this time, Butch got to watch it disappear.

# ABOUT THE AUTHOR

D. Krauss currently resides in the Shenandoah Valley. He's been a cottonpicker, a sod buster, a surgical orderly, the guy who paints the little white line down the middle of the road, a weatherman, a gun-totin' door-kickin' lawman, a layabout, and a bus driver, in that order.

Website:
http://www.dustyskull.com

Goodreads:
https://www.goodreads.com/author/show/6563354.D_Krauss

YouTube: Old Guy Reviews Books.
https://www.youtube.com/channel/UCwKqtFLjKdHhvQxs3Q3TJCg

Clouthub:
@DKrauss

Gab:
@Dkrauss

Sayscape:
@Dkrauss

Email:
dokrauss@gmail.com

# OTHER BOOKS BY D. KRAUSS

**The Frank Vaughn Trilogy**
Frank Vaughn, Killed by His Mom
Southern Gothic
Looking for Don

**The Partholon Trilogy**
Partholon
Tu'An
Col'm

**The Ship Trilogy**
The Ship to Look for Good
The Ship Looking for God
The Ship Finding God

**Story Collections**
The Moonlight in Genevieve's Eyes
*and other Strange Stories*
The Last Man in the World Explains All
*and other strange tales*